I0831874

The characters and events portrayed in this book are fictitious. Any similarity to real persons, living or dead, is coincidental and not intended by the author.

ISBN-13: 9798992918281

Cover design by: Magdalena Pietrzak
(barn-swallow.carrd.co)
Library of Congress Control Number: 2018675309
Printed in the United States of America

Wretchedly Royal

Kayla Robinson

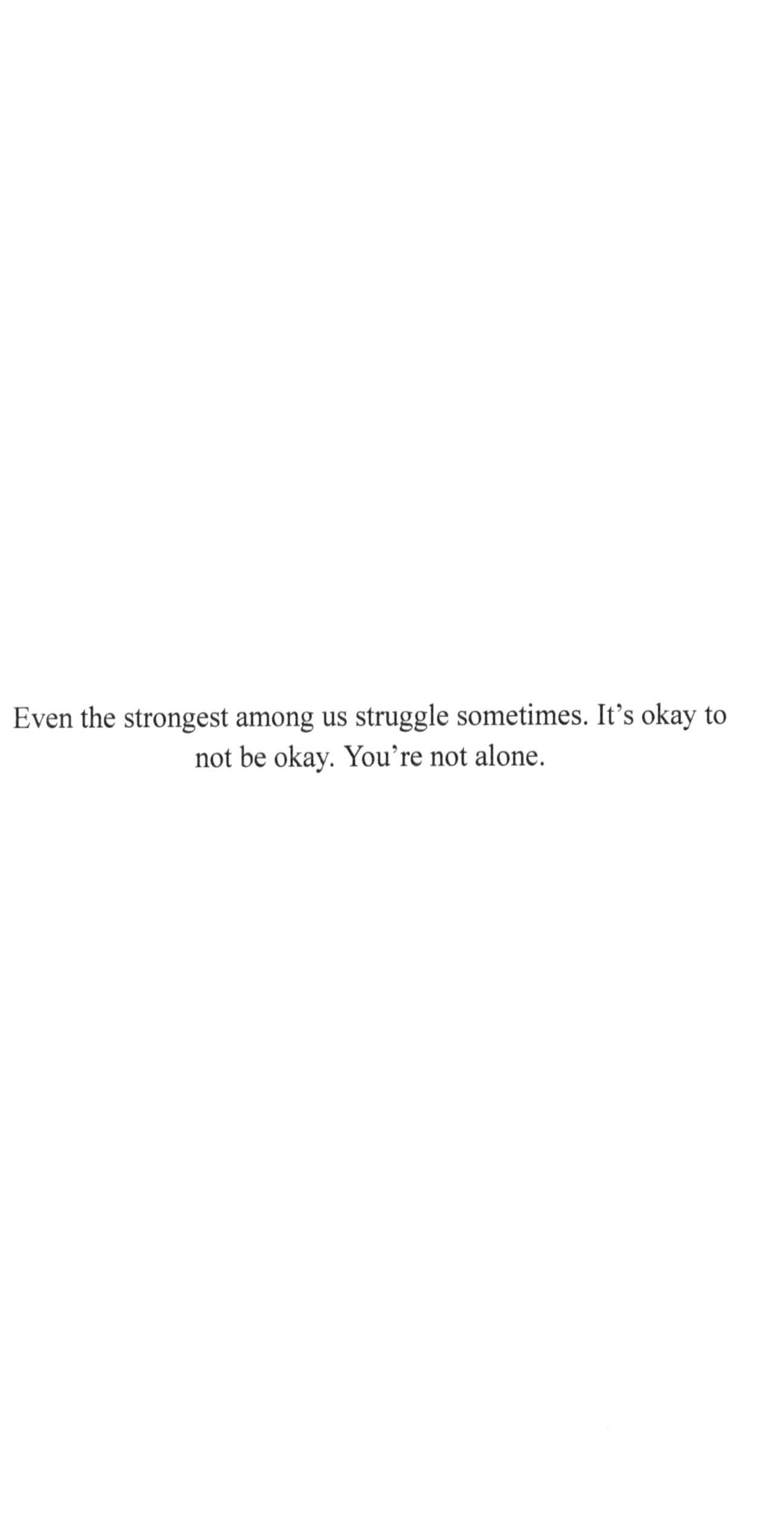

Even the strongest among us struggle sometimes. It's okay to not be okay. You're not alone.

Pronunciation Guide:

Eimear - ee-mur
Oíche - ee-ha
Aris - air-iss
Aodhan - ay-dawn
Gaisgeach - gays-gee-ach
Fiadh - fee-ah-d
Mira - m-ear-ah
Deiric - derek
Malachy - mal-ah-kai

Chapter 1

Mira

In the couple of months that followed the treaty's creation, I'd been involved in so many meetings everything started to flow together. I thought perhaps I'd get the chance to just enjoy the fact that all that fighting and hiding was finally over, but I found myself thrust into the thick of acting as an archmage at our manor, while simultaneously playing the role of 'Elder Mage'. I started to regret suggesting the title. Perhaps being a magister would've been a much easier role. It was too late now though.

With the help of Devlon and Garrick, we created a beautiful temple for the Morrigan. She seemed to approve based on the energy I felt each time I visited. I had also set aside a small area in the manor as an altar to her. It seemed only fitting.

Now I was sitting at the end of a table with Deiric on my left and Xander on my right. Despite that at this point I was certain we could trust Devlon and everyone else within the higher rankings of Solas, I still had to bring them along. Lazarus absolutely demanded it. I was distracted, thinking of what I needed to work on with the young mages at home.

"Mira." Devlon's voice was a bit annoyed and jolted me back to the present.

I locked eyes with him. He looked annoyed and frustrated, but that was not unusual in these meetings. I had a feeling he was just as tired of them as I was.

"Were you listening?"

I sighed and sat up straighter. "Sorry, I was stuck on a different thought. What were you saying?"

"Clearly."

I rolled my eyes.

"We're still working on figuring out who hired the assassins. At this point, we think it was either a rogue mage that hired them, or someone who is working with a rogue mage. A large number of those who supported attacking Oíche all those years ago have left the coven and gone off on their own. The ones that stayed never supported the attacks, but went along with it and fought against us because they feared for their lives otherwise."

I don't know how I missed him bringing up this subject. "Do you know how many, specifically?"

"Unfortunately, no." He grumbled. "We're still working on getting organized with all of our new leadership, as I'm sure you know."

I nodded. At each meeting for Solas lately it wasn't uncommon to hear about how disorganized things had become. They were getting better but many of them didn't understand the responsibilities that came with being a magister for a certain region. It was chaotic at best.

"Things on our side aren't a whole lot better." Garrick commented. "We had a handful of our magisters still in power after the attacks, but the newer ones are… challenging."

Devlon chuckled. "That's putting it mildly."

"You can't expect perfection." I shrugged. "It isn't like any of them truly understood everything that would be expected of them when they accepted the positions."

"Still." Garrick continued, barely sparing me a glance. "We need to get things in order before we lose control entirely."

"The assassins were an issue but at this point we haven't had any other incidents. Perhaps they gave up?"

"You don't seriously think that whoever did that has given up, do you?" Devlon asked, shooting me a doubtful look.

I crossed my arms and arched a brow. "It's not entirely out of the question to assume they may have given up. It was so soon after we set up the treaty, perhaps they realized that it was a lost cause?"

Neither of them seemed convinced.

"I'm not saying to stop investigating if you feel strongly that you can find answers. I'm just saying that so far we've been safe. If they are still out there something will come to light eventually and we'll sort it out when it happens."

"You seem oddly optimistic." Garrick commented, raising a brow. He was leaning back casually in his chair, resting his elbow on the arm of it with his head on his hand.

Devlon also leaned back casually in his chair, facing slightly toward me. These meetings had gotten far less formal the more often we had them. Something I was immensely thankful for. Politics were truly exhausting.

"I wouldn't call it optimism," I said after a few moments. "It's more that I just don't see it as a worthwhile use of our resources if we don't have any leads. Our time would be better spent in training the new magisters or continuing to focus on training our newest prospects."

"How is that going, by the way?" Garrick asked. Caught off guard by the question, I looked at him with a hint of surprise. This was more of a topic to discuss at the Oíche meetings rather than in front of Devlon, but the lines got blurred sometimes.

"So far it is going well. They're all learning at different rates, but most of them are only training with their magic."

"Only with their magic?" I shifted my attention to Devlon and he looked immensely confused.

I immediately regretted finishing that statement. Solas, much like Oíche before we went underground, only trained mages how to use their magic. They didn't train them to fight hand to hand, or with weapons of any kind. If they chose to learn, it was on their own.

"We'll be training them to use their magic *and* some hand to hand combat."

Devlon raised a brow. "Do you really think that's necessary?"

"I don't think it is a bad idea to learn both. If there's ever a situation where one can't use magic it is always good to be able to defend in another way."

Devlon looked at me incredulously, like he couldn't understand when that *would* be necessary.

"If I can speak freely?" I asked.

"You always do." Devlon said with an amused smile.

"I know I can trust you, and the new magisters of Solas, but I'm sure you can understand my hesitation not to teach them other methods of defense given your–" I quickly corrected myself. "Our coven's propensity to use magic blocking weaponry?" I raised a brow now and leaned forward a bit in my chair. "As you said, there are many who simply left the coven that still despise us. What's to stop them from organizing on their own?" It was still odd to me to say 'our' coven when speaking to Devlon. It just didn't feel right.

His lips pursed and a muscle in his jaw tensed. "I guess you have a point."

I held his gaze for a few moments. "It probably wouldn't be a bad idea for you to teach your mages the same way. There are more rogue mages out there now than there have ever been."

"I'll take that into consideration." His slightly dismissive tone irked me a little.

"Do we have anything else to discuss between the covens?" I asked when the ensuing silence lasted longer than I liked.

Their continued silence gave me the answer I hoped for.

"Fantastic. Until next time then."

Devlon nodded, and shifted away.

Garrick looked at me. "Do you need another mage to help out when you're occupied with these sorts of things?"

I shook my head. “I think we’re alright. We’re almost running out of open rooms at this point and these meetings don’t take up that much time.”

“We could always add on to the manor if we need to.” He offered.

I shook my head again. “Honestly, I think we’re alright. Between Liala, Eimear, and myself we have it covered. When I’m away they step in and teach other lower level spells, herbalism, and healing.”

He nodded. “If that changes, just let me know.” Then he shifted away also.

I sighed and sank back in my chair, rubbing my forehead.

“He offered to send someone to help.” Deiric said softly from beside me.

“It’s not the training that is exhausting. It's these damned meetings.” I mumbled.

Xander chuckled. “All that power a little too much for you?”

I looked over and scowled at him. “Would you like to be their go between?”

The little bit of amusement quickly faded from his face. “No, not really.”

“I didn’t think so.”

Aris wandered into the room now. “You look thrilled.” He half smiled, locking eyes with me for a moment.

“I don’t understand why I always wanted to be so involved in these meetings.”

He chuckled. “Well, back then it was because they were mostly about *you*. Now they’re about everything under the sun I’m sure.”

“That’s putting it mildly.”

"Still no luck figuring out who hired the assassins I take it?" He asked.

"I know you were eavesdropping." I half smiled at him. "You don't have to ask and pretend you weren't lurking in the hall like I used to do."

He smiled. "I'm surprised you noticed."

"You weren't exactly quiet about it."

He raised an eyebrow. "I was nearly silent."

I shrugged. "I guess my hearing is better than I thought."

"Will you be staying much longer, or do you need to get back?"

"We should get back. I need to check in on how things are going with Liala and the mages this afternoon."

Aris nodded. "See you at the next meeting then."

I nodded and smiled. We all stood, and I shifted us home.

Chapter 2

Mira

Deiric woke me the next morning with a few kisses on the back of my neck. I groaned and pressed myself back into him.

"Good morning, love." He said softly.

"Good morning." I mumbled. I wasn't ready to get up yet, despite that the sun's position in the sky told me it was far later than I would usually sleep.

His arm was around my waist, and his hand started to wander. I stopped him before he could go any further and gave him a sideways glance over my shoulder.

"You didn't get enough last night?" I asked coyly.

He chuckled and leaned over to kiss my cheek. "I can never get enough of you." He kissed down my neck and shoulder, nipping gently as he went.

I rolled so I was laying on my back and looking over at him. "You know, I wouldn't be so tired if you didn't keep me up so late."

He smiled. "Oh sure, because you didn't have any say in the matter." He leaned in and stole a kiss. "You drank from me last night, so you shouldn't still be that tired unless you didn't get enough." He looked just slightly concerned and ran his thumb gently over my cheek.

"I'm fine." I said softly. "I don't want to take too much from you."

He sighed. "I've told you countless times I won't let you." He studied me for a moment. "When we drink from each other around the same time it doesn't weaken me at all."

"I promise I–"

He stopped me with a kiss. "You are not fine, and I'm not taking no for an answer." He rolled onto his back and smiled, pulling me on top of him so I was straddling his hips.

"Deiric. I said I'm–"

"Would you just shut up and bite me?" He said as he sat up and leaned into me, tilting his neck to expose it for me.

I huffed a sigh, but slipped my hand into his hair while I kissed down his neck. His hands slid up my thighs to my hips. I nipped his neck without my fangs first.

"Mira." He breathed, his voice feigned annoyance. It was far too much fun to toy with him. I kissed his neck again before finally biting him and drinking.

He moaned and kissed my shoulder and neck while I drank. He wrapped his arms around my waist and pulled me into him. He let me drink until I thought he *should* stop me, and for once I didn't hold myself back. He slipped one hand into my hair and I felt his fangs graze my neck and shoulder. He kissed down the side of my neck before he bit me as well.

I gasped, and arched myself into him. The feeling was nothing short of pure bliss. I didn't know why we hadn't ever fed together before. Every single fiber of my being was on fire with a pleasure I didn't even believe was possible. Between the normal drunk with pleasure feeling that came from drinking from him, and the pleasure that came from his bite, I could hardly contain myself.

His hand slipped up under my nightgown. I forgot all about everything I needed to do today, and all I could think about was how much I wanted *him* instead. I rocked my hips against him and he moaned in response, pulling me into him like we might just melt together if he held me tight enough.

I could feel him smile against my shoulder after hearing me think of exactly how I'd rather spend my day. His hands continued their exploration under my nightgown, while mine did some exploring of their own.

A few more moments passed before I withdrew my fangs and kissed up his neck. He did the same less than a heartbeat later until our lips met and he pulled me down with him as he laid back down onto the pillows. He pulled away from me just long enough to yank my nightgown over my head and toss it away.

I started to kiss my way down his chest when there was a gentle knock on the door. Deiric let out a low growl and I sighed, stopping in my tracks and looking up at him.

"Yes?" I asked, projecting my voice beyond the permanent sound shield I'd put around our room.

"Just making sure you're up." Zane mocked through the door. I could hear the amusement in his voice since he probably knew precisely what he was interrupting. "Your mages are already lining up outside for their training this morning."

I groaned and rolled off of Deiric back to my side of the bed. "I'll be down in a few minutes." I called out again, projecting that through the shield.

Deiric chuckled. "You know, if you took Garrick up on his offer to send another mage here we wouldn't get interrupted during the day."

I gave him a small glare before I shuffled out of the bed to get dressed and get ready for the day.

"You're just lucky you don't have to do much of anything other than occasionally teach someone compulsion and mind reading when they call on you for it." I shot back at him. "It wouldn't be right of me to ask for an archmage to be assigned here just so we could have limitless sex."

I locked eyes with him in the mirror while I fumbled with my corset. He smiled smugly at me. "Well, someone killed all the beasts around here, so I don't have anything else to do at the moment."

"Oh bite me." I snapped.

He was behind me in an instant with a sly smile on his face. "I mean, I'd love to bite you *again* but I think you have other things to do." His hands slid around my waist and he kissed up the back of my neck.

I shivered and squirmed out of his grasp. "Would you stop that?" I rubbed my neck. "I *do* have things to do and now I'm not going to be able to think straight."

He just smirked and walked over to rummage through his own drawers and get dressed. "As if what you're feeling from feeding just now isn't going to keep you distracted anyway."

I couldn't deny the fact that it took all the self control I had to pull myself off of him just now, and to squirm out of his grasp when he *did* come over to bite me again. It didn't seem to matter how often we came together, it didn't stop me from always wanting more. It didn't seem to stop *him* either.

*

Just as Zane said, they were all lined up outside. We had five mages here with various kinds of elemental magic among them. Stella was gifted with lightning, Aodh, true to his name, was gifted with fire, Zemora could manipulate and create plants, Gerald gifted with ice and snow, and Sorcha was also gifted with fire. Aodh and Gerald had some previous practice with their magic, but the girls were much further behind in their training.

They were able to summon their magic and do basic movements with it, but only Gerald and Aodh had gone through some of my combat training just yet.

"Good morning." I said when I approached them.

They returned the greeting in unison.

Zemora, Sorcha, and Stella all wore some variation of the same dress, very plain and practical. None of them wore corsets like I preferred to. It wasn't really necessary when they weren't attempting to strap weapons to themselves.

Zemora's long brown hair was braided behind her and hung halfway down her back. Sorcha's shorter golden hair was pulled up in a rather messy bun on the back of her head and Stella's auburn hair was tied in a plain ponytail at the base of her neck. Both Gerald and Aodh had tied their hair in a bun, just like Zane and Xander usually did.

Zane appeared behind me before I said anything else, just like I'd asked him to.

"Gerald and Aodh, you're going to train with Zane today."

Both of them looked confused. Zane stepped out from behind me holding two smaller and very dull training blades for them to use. Their faces lit up with excitement.

"I thought we had to master our magic first?" Gerald asked.

"You've been improving. We'll crosstrain today so that if I'm not around you have something else to work on while I'm away."

Zane motioned for them to follow him and they went to a different area out of the way of the rest of us.

"You all are going to practice your aim, summoning your magic and striking an enemy." I said with a smile.

"What are we going to try to strike as our enemy?" Stella asked.

"Me."

Their eyes went wide. "We've only ever tried to hit trees and the other targets you've set up for us." Sorcha said.

I shrugged. "They don't move." I smiled. "I can move."

Zemora looked more perplexed than the other two. "How am I supposed to practice aim?"

I understood her confusion. She manipulated vines and plants. She likely hadn't considered sending them out as an attack like one might send a blast of flame or ice. She thought of them as creeping objects, coming up from the ground.

"You can send a vine out through the air." I explained, and demonstrated by creating one, pulling it up from the ground, and then sending it out to yank on her braid.

She flinched and scowled. "That's not quite the same."

"It is in a way. You'll start off doing it one by one, and then I want the three of you to try to work as a team to see if you can actually hit me."

I motioned for them to follow me and we walked away from the manor, where Sorcha hopefully wouldn't accidentally catch anything important on fire.

"Stella, you try first."

She smirked, and almost immediately sent a ball of lightning flying for me. I leaned right and dodged it. She cursed under her breath.

"Try again." I said, mildly amused.

It had the same result.

"Sorcha?"

Sorcha threw a ball of fire at me, which I caught and sent flying back at her. She shrieked and just blocked her face with her arms.

I didn't let the fire hit her, but instead stopped it right in front of her arms. After a moment, she lowered her arms and looked around at me confused.

"You're now aiming for a target that can move or strike back." I said with a smile. "You'll have to block me or do like I just did and catch it to deflect it."

"But how did you do that?" She asked.

"I also have fire magic, in case you forgot. I can manipulate it just as you can."

She stared at me for a few moments and I extinguished the ball of flames with half a thought. "You would deflect fire the same way you would summon and throw it. Try again."

Again she created a ball of fire and sent it to me. I sent it back to her and she put up her hand to catch it. She didn't do it correctly though, and burned her fingers. She cursed under her breath.

"Heal it, and try again." I demanded.

She glared at me, but used her other hand to heal herself and then tried again. This time, she managed to catch it.

"Good." I turned to Zemora. "Your turn."

She sent a vine toward me and it got halfway before it fell to the ground. She frowned.

"You need to focus your energy a little differently when you're not using the ground or some other medium to lean on. Try again."

The vine made it further this time before it fell to the ground.

"How about you practice just that with the tree over there?" I motioned to the tree at the edge of the woods that we often used as a target for throwing our knives. "Once you can do it at a longer distance, we can revisit this exercise."

She sighed and walked over to the tree.

I turned to Stella and Sorcha. "Alright. You two should try to attack and work together." I smiled. "Do your worst."

Stella attacked first with a straight shot of lightning this time, followed quickly by Sorcha's fireball. While they weren't really *trying* to work together, they did manage to be so chaotic with their lack of teamwork that if I didn't have superhuman speed they certainly would've landed a few blows.

We worked through the afternoon, and eventually they got a little bit better at working more as a real team rather than just sending shots at random. The more they worked together, the closer they came to hitting me even with my speed and general agility.

That evening, as I did most nights now, I lit the candle on the Morrigan's altar. Things had been quiet since the battle aside from her approval of the temple, but I still made sure to honor her even outside of our original agreement.

Chapter 3

Mira

I sighed when I finally opened my eyes the next morning. I had been awake for a while, but didn't get out of bed. I'd just been laying with my eyes still closed for probably an hour or two before I finally gave up. The sun was just barely starting to rise over the horizon. I couldn't seem to quiet my mind enough to fall back asleep.

My sigh caused Deiric to stir next to me. He rolled over and slipped his arm around my waist to pull me back into him. "Good morning, love." He whispered into my ear.

"Good morning." I said, unable to keep the mild annoyance from my voice.

He lifted his head and looked down at me. "What's wrong?" His voice was quiet, still laden with sleep, but concerned.

"I've been awake for a while. I couldn't go back to sleep."

"Take the day off today." He said softly. "You've more than earned it, besides, it is Samhain afterall."

I sighed again. Samhain. That certainly explained it, I couldn't ever seem to sleep well on Samhain. I hadn't been paying attention to what day it was. I was so busy lately I barely even knew how much time had passed if it hadn't been for the changing of the seasons. The veil would be incredibly thin today. Years ago I would have celebrated this with everyone in the manor. They would have a feast, a "dumb supper" as they called it where we all ate in silence and welcomed anyone who had passed on to join us at the table.

For a half a breath, my heart ached, but I pushed that away. When I was on my own, I never celebrated even our most sacred holidays. I was supposed to be a mercenary then, not a sorceress and it was hardly worth the effort or risk of possibly revealing what I really was to celebrate.

My silence must've been concerning, or he heard my thoughts, I couldn't be sure, but he reached up and turned my head to face him, gently cupping my face with his hand. "You don't have to partake in any of the celebrations or rituals if you don't want to. You can hide in here all day if that would make you happy." He gave me a small smile that didn't reach his eyes, which still glimmered with a little bit of worry and concern.

I rolled to my back so I could look at him without having my neck at such an uncomfortable angle. "It's not that I don't want to partake, I just haven't celebrated *anything* in so long, and we haven't had a free moment to do anything for the other holidays. Are we actually doing something for Samhain?"

"I know Liala planned to." He mumbled, surveying my face for any reaction. "We certainly have enough mortal inhabitants now to merit a feast. If it were just us then we likely wouldn't do anything at all."

I let my gaze move from his eyes to the ceiling. "I doubt half of them have ever celebrated. They won't know what to do. Some of them will probably be freaked out by it."

Deiric chuckled. "Well, it's a good thing we have you, Eimear, and Liala here to help with all of that then."

I locked eyes with him again and the faint smile that was on his lips faded when he saw my frown.

"I told you you can stay in here all day if you want to, but I hope you'll at least come out for dinner." He brushed his thumb over my cheek before sliding his hand down my hip and putting his arm back around me.

"The idea of hiding in here for a day sounds nice." I said softly. "What are you going to do?"

"If you'd like some company, I'll do whatever *you* want to do today." He smiled, and this time it actually reached his eyes. There was something suspicious about his expression that I couldn't place.

I decided to ignore that and give him a sly smile of my own. "Well, I have a few ideas." I said as I leaned in to kiss him and slip my hand up around his neck into his hair.

"I thought you might."

*

Later that afternoon, we went out for a quiet ride through the woods surrounding the manor. I managed to track down Draga a little more than a month ago, but had yet to ride her. It was nice to finally be in a saddle again, despite that this was a part of my life that I really only did out of necessity not long ago. Draga had been a companion for years when I was otherwise alone. She seemed just as eager as me to get back out again. Perhaps a little too eager at first.

We set up a small pasture for them behind the manor, and built a three sided shelter for them, rather than stalls. While Deiric and the others didn't really see the *need* for the horses, given how fast we could travel on our own, I convinced them it would be a good idea to have horses just in case we needed to move around more discreetly. While things seemed to be going well with our treaty, I had trouble not having a backup plan just in case.

Deiric rode next to me on a slightly larger gray gelding we called Vellor. His coat was mostly white, having faded over time from the brilliant gray I'm sure it was long ago. I was surprised Deiric even knew *how* to ride, though I suppose I should've guessed he learned at some point. He was human once.

"Follow me." Deiric broke the silence of our otherwise quiet ride finally and kicked Vellor up to a trot before he veered left in front of us, up a rather steep incline toward the mountains.

I clucked at Draga to pick up the pace and follow him. I didn't know *where* we were going, but she wasn't eager to be left behind so we caught up quickly. By now, I thought I knew most of the woods around us, but we never went up into the mountains. We snaked up a narrow trail for several minutes before he finally stopped Vellor where there was enough space for both horses to stand side by side again.

Draga and I stopped beside him. I looked around. "We're stopping *here*?" There was hardly anything around us that seemed to give any reason for us to stop here.

"Just trust me." He smirked and swung his leg over to slip off of Vellor.

I swung myself off of Draga and walked around her head to where he stood in front of both of them. Draga and Vellor lowered their heads to graze in the small patch of grass and weeds that somehow managed to grow in the otherwise barren rock around us.

Deiric took my hand and pulled me along behind him to a tiny path barely wide enough for us to walk on. A path I certainly wouldn't have seen otherwise. After blindly following him for a few moments, we came out onto a plateau that stuck out of the side of one of the mountains. He gestured out in front of him.

I stepped up and looked beyond to where he motioned with his hand and gasped. It was incredible. It felt like I could see half the world from here. I don't think I realized how high up we'd come while trotting along that path. The view before me took my breath away. The trees beneath us were varying colors of orange, red, and yellow. The land spanned forever, with the hills rolling on for miles and miles. We could see the villages in the distance, and random farm houses scattered throughout some of the open plains. The gloom from the overcast sky did nothing but amplify the bright colors of the trees.

"I used to come up here to think sometimes." Deiric said softly. "It isn't nearly as beautiful under the moonlight as it is during the day."

I had forgotten that until these last few months he likely hadn't seen the sun in nearly 600 years. "I think I'd like to see it under the moonlight anyway." I breathed, unable to take my eyes off of the gorgeous view ahead of us.

He was quiet for a few moments, and then held his hand out to me. "That isn't the *only* surprise."

I reluctantly pulled my eyes away from the view to look at him. He had a small mischievous smile on his lips. I looked down to whatever he was holding out to me to discover a pretty little black box with a plain black ribbon on it. I raised a brow and looked up at him again.

"Did you think Aris *wouldn't* tell me when your birthday was?" His smile pulled up into an even larger and more wicked grin. "Or did you think he forgot?"

I huffed a laugh and couldn't stop the half smile that rose to my lips as I looked down at the box still sitting in his outstretched hand. "Honestly, I didn't even think about it at all actually." When my eyes met his again he had a small frown on his face.

"You forgot your own birthday?" He stepped a bit closer to me and brushed a small tendril of my hair out of my face.

"I haven't thought about my birthday in a *very* long time." I went to reach for the box, then stopped and smirked at him. "When is *your* birthday?"

He snorted. "That's not important right now." He gently handed me the box. "You're not going to avoid opening this. Or the next one either."

I raised a brow again and smirked at him. "Please tell me there aren't any more after that." I shifted uncomfortably on my feet as I pulled on the bow to untie it. It felt odd to receive a gift of any kind.

"There aren't any more after that."

"For some reason I'm not sure I believe that." I mumbled under my breath and pulled the lid off of the box. I looked down and inside the box was a beautiful blue goldstone pendant. The stone was carefully wrapped with small pieces of silver that attached it to the bottom of a thick piece of black satin.

I didn't own a single piece of jewelry. Even the bands around our ring fingers were tattoos, rather than silver which most couples would wear. Given that our connection went beyond just *marriage* we had decided on ink instead when we snuck off last month to officially bind ourselves to one another.

"It's beautiful." I breathed, lifting the stone out of the box with one hand so I could get a better look at it.

I looked up at him again and he smiled. "I know you're not usually interested in finery and jewels but I thought you might like something to wear when we have to drag ourselves to balls and parties." He said softly, walking around behind me to help me put it on. It felt far too formal for what I was currently wearing, but I didn't object.

"You act like we're going to go to hundreds of them." I pulled my hair out of the way for him.

"Well, we've got an eternity of attending parties so whether they're frequent or not I don't think *hundreds* is all that far off." I could hear the smirk on his lips. When he had finished fastening it he came back around in front of me and handed me another, much longer and larger box, wrapped the same as the first one. "I promise, this *is* the only other one. From me anyway."

I took the second box from him, pulled the bow free, and opened it to find a beautiful ornate silver dagger. The same stone I wore around my neck was also in the hilt. Beneath it was a black leather strap and sheath for it.

"I know how much you like keeping that dagger with you." He gestured to my right leg, which did have my old dagger on it under my skirt. "It only seemed fitting to get you one that matches the choker."

I laughed. "What, and the dagger I have doesn't match my evening gowns?" I made a face of distaste at him.

He shrugged. "If you don't like it, I can always return it."

I pulled the box in toward my chest, careful not to tilt it in a way that the dagger would fall out. "Oh no, I love it." I smiled. "Thank you."

His eyes sparkled a bit, and he kissed my cheek. "Happy Birthday, love."

Chapter 4

Mira

By the time we returned to the manor everyone was preparing for dinner later that evening. We would be doing the same sort of ritual I had been a part of many times with my parents. Several empty place settings would be set up to honor the dead, giving them a place to come sit with us while we ate in silence. All the vampires, myself included, would stand back from the table while those who actually *needed* to eat would take any seats that had not been left empty on purpose.

Eimear offered to have me lead it, but I declined. I had a million reasons, but the easiest one to explain was simply that it had been far too long since I had done the ritual and would rather someone else take care of it. She didn't pressure me or ask any questions after that.

As the sun began to set, everyone gathered in the dining room. Even the four new vampires we had living here now came down to join us, to my surprise. I imagined that they didn't usually do these rituals at the manor they came from. Lazarus had sent them here specifically so that they could alternate shifts on guard around the manor and grounds overnight. He was extra cautious, even with our wards. These four didn't have daylight rings, so they couldn't be out during the day even if they wanted to, and I didn't get the feeling that they *did.*

I walked over to pour myself a drink while Eimear got ready to begin the ritual. The mages would all help to set the table backwards, before she would invite in the spirits of our ancestors and begin the meal. Deiric appeared beside me to pour himself a glass as well.

I heard them beginning to set the table behind us and I grabbed another glass. We didn't *technically* have to be silent yet, but Deiric just gave me a confused look. The silence of the rest of the room was already overwhelming aside from the clanking of silverware and plates.

It's not for me. I thought when I met his gaze. His confused look didn't change much and for a moment I thought he hadn't heard me. After I finished pouring a very short glass, I walked over to the head of the table where most of the vampires had gathered. The side of the table for the spirits we invited.

Stella was about to put a place setting there and I waved her off. She looked at me with the same look of confusion that Deiric had given me, and I sat the glass of whiskey right where the plate would go.

Stella opened her mouth as though she was going to speak, but I raised my own glass, which was in my other hand, then I gestured to the vampires lingering in the shadows along the wall. I imagine that even after death, one of us would likely *not* go looking for the food on this table. On the off chance I was correct in my assumption, it seemed fitting to include a setting for one of us.

Stella simply moved around me and continued on her way around the table. Everyone else ignored that seat as they went through the process of finishing their place settings. I settled back into a spot along the wall between Deiric and Zane.

I'm not sure they've ever thought to include a place for us. Deiric thought.

I met his gaze for a moment and half smiled, though I know it didn't reach my eyes. *I don't think they remember that we* can *die.*

He raised a brow like he was surprised and then a look of understanding settled over his face. How could we expect them to think of us? It was rather rare for one of us to die, unless it was in battle. Deiric leaned back against the wall behind us and took a sip of his whiskey.

I listened as Eimear said the opening words to invite in the spirits of our ancestors to sit down to this meal with us. The moment that she finished I finally had a sip of my whiskey and they began to serve everyone, including the empty plates. Each got a small portion of each food they'd prepared for the evening.

Anytime I had been a part of this ritual, I rarely noticed anything different about the room. I was used to the shadows moving some, and I didn't have anyone myself that I had lost to invite to the table, or rather, that I *knew* I lost. My parents and everyone at that manor were the only family I had.

The heaviness that filled the room now was like nothing I had ever felt before. It made me a little uneasy, to say the least. I did not realize that I had let some of my shadows slip out of me until Deiric gently grabbed my elbow.

I glanced at him and he had a concerned look on his face. I glanced down around me and called them back, just slightly.

The shadows around the room, entirely out of my control, seemed to move more than I had ever seen them do before. I took another sip of my whiskey hoping that might calm my nerves about it.

I felt a hand on my shoulder, which I would have assumed was Deiric's if I hadn't looked over to him to see that he was now also watching the shifting shadows around the room, with the hand that had grabbed my elbow in his pocket and the other holding his drink.

I stiffened, realizing that Zane also had not moved. The hand moved off of my shoulder and I felt something cold brush against my cheek that sent shivers down my spine. Finally, I was met with a painfully familiar smell that almost broke me. The sweet aroma of patchouli and lavender filled the space around me, so overwhelmingly that for a moment I wasn't sure if I could breathe through it.

My mother's perfume. I could smell it like she was in the room and standing directly in front of me. I let out a short and shaky breath which caught Deiric and Zane's attention, but thankfully no one else. Tears welled in my eyes, despite my attempts to blink them away.

Without hesitation Deiric slipped his arm around my waist and pulled me closer to him.

Are you alright? He thought.

I barely shook my head, but didn't look at him. I was frozen, staring at the empty air in front of me like I might see her standing there.

I felt Deiric jump slightly and then stiffen next to me. I looked over at him and he was staring at his arm with an expression that resembled his 'What the fuck?!' face.

He looked at me like he'd seen a ghost, which probably wasn't far off from the truth. His nostrils flared slightly. I realized he must smell her too, or smell *something*.

That cold feeling appeared on my cheek again for just a moment before the smell of her slowly drifted away.

Deiric finished his whiskey and sat the glass on the serving table beside him. I finished mine as well, before he took it and sat the glass with his. He reached over and wiped the few tears that I couldn't hold back from my cheeks.

I was immensely thankful that only a few minutes later Eimear stood up to say the closing words for the ritual. Everyone stood at once, blew out the candles and made all kinds of ruckus, as they were instructed to do at the end of this ritual, to scare away any lingering spirits.

"What the fuck was that?" Deiric whispered into my ear, leaning all the way into me in the darkness that now filled the room. Everyone else was quieting down now.

"You smelled lavender and patchouli?" I whispered back.

He nodded.

"That was my mother's favorite perfume." My voice cracked just slightly when I explained.

He pulled me into him and gently traced his thumb across my cheek.

Suddenly, Sorcha lit up the space with a small ball of fire so they could all see what they were doing to clean things up.

Zane scoffed. "Getting a little frisky in the dark I see." He mocked quietly as he pushed past us. "There are *children* here." He hissed, though his tone made it obvious it was a joke.

"We are *not* children." Zemora snapped at him. She was right, they were all teenagers, certainly capable of seeing two adults in an embrace like this and not acting like children about it. Like *he* always did.

I glanced over at her. Her hair was braided and hung over her shoulder. She was in a plain and modest black gown this evening. Her hazel eyes glimmered in the light of the fire. She gave me a small smile and then continued cleaning up. I wondered how much she saw, or if she had any experiences like I did. I couldn't believe with the number of times I'd been through this I never noticed anything like that before.

Zane had grumbled and walked out of the room.

"I assume it was her that grabbed my arm then?" Deiric asked.

I nodded. "I would assume so."

"Have you ever had that happen at one of these rituals before? With other people who have passed?" His question was genuine, and I guessed based on his reaction this was a first for him also.

"No, but I also hadn't lost anyone I knew before *this* ritual." I said softly. "I always saw the shadows moving, but I never had any other experiences myself, and it never felt as heavy as it did today."

"Let's get another drink." Deiric smiled and turned away to grab our glasses. "We have other things to keep celebrating." He said as he walked over to get more whiskey. No doubt changing the subject because he didn't want me upset on my birthday.

Zemora walked over and stood next to me. I could see her out of the corner of my eye while I watched Deiric go to get us each a drink.

"Who was that?" She asked softly.

I shifted on my feet so I was facing her. "What?" I asked.

Her eyes sparkled with curiosity. "The woman that came to you tonight." She smiled slightly. "She seemed to be someone very close to you given how she reacted to seeing you, and how much she looked like you." She glanced over toward Deiric for a moment and then back to me. "She seemed to like Deiric, too."

I gaped at her. "You *saw* her?"

She chuckled. "Yes." She paused for a moment to look me over and then continued, "I've always seen spirits, but it is always a lot more interesting on days like today when we actually *invite* them and the veil is so thin. I could see them today like they were actually in the room."

I opened my mouth to speak, and at that moment Deiric appeared beside me. I glanced over at him, took my glass, then met Zemora's eyes again. "She was my mother, I think."

A look of sorrow or pity flashed across her face for a brief moment before it returned to its curious look again. "I'm sorry." She glanced at the ground, then back up at me. "Happy Birthday." She said gleefully before she turned and walked away.

I raised a brow and watched after her for just a moment before Deiric's chuckle brought my attention to him. He was smiling. "Did you tell *everyone* about my birthday?" I asked.

He shook his head. "I didn't tell anyone." He sipped his drink before finally saying, "it may have been Liala."

I huffed a slight laugh. "Of course." I shook my head. "I forgot Liala would know too. I'm surprised she remembered."

"Most people you're close with will never forget your birthday." Deiric pointed out with a slight smile.

I rolled my eyes. "You never told me when *your* birthday was."

"August 15th." He looked over toward the table as he said it.

I shoved him gently. "You let me miss *your* birthday, but you made sure you knew mine?" I feigned annoyance in my voice, but I was a little bit upset with myself for not noticing or asking him before now. I had genuinely not even thought of birthdays, and didn't even think they mattered when you were immortal.

He chuckled. "I don't really celebrate." He met my gaze again.

"And you think *I* do?"

He slipped his arm around my shoulders. "Well, you *will* now. And I guess *I* will too unless you forget between now and next year." He smirked, and pulled me along with him toward the foyer, and then the stairs. "Right now, we should *probably* get some rest though." He said softly. "We have to go to the temple tomorrow to give the Morrigan her offering, remember?"

"How could I forget?" I smiled. "I'm surprised Macha didn't jump in at all today to remind me."

I heard a caw moments after I said that, and when we got into our bedroom she was sitting on the windowsill.

You didn't give me the chance *to remind you. He said it first.* Her voice rang through my mind and I rolled my eyes at her.

Honestly Macha, I appreciate the reminders but I do pay attention to the moon at least. I may not remember what day it is, but I know what phase the moon is in! I replied.

She just ruffled her wings in response.

Chapter 5

Mira

The smell of stale blood filled my nose and I blinked my eyes open. Everything felt… weak and disorienting. It took me a few seconds to realize that I was not in bed. I was in a dark, dreary stone room that resembled a prison cell and I felt like I was starving.

Fear and horror overwhelmed me. I felt the shackles and chains on my wrists, and heard footsteps in the hallway outside of the cell I'd been thrown in. The place smelled damp and earthy, the floor of the cell was just dirt, and I heard pests scurrying around the place.

This didn't make sense. Surely no one could've gotten beyond the wards and abducted me in my sleep. And even if they had, I wouldn't wake *this* thirsty unless I'd been out for a very, very long time.

My head spun as I pushed myself up off of the floor and stared at the door, waiting for my captor to come into view.

There was the sound of a lock clicking, but no key and the door began to creak open. I reached for my magic, but there was nothing there. And for some reason, I was silent, not speaking a single word despite that I wanted to cry out. It was like my body wasn't my own.

A ball of light entered the cell, dimly illuminating the space as a male figure came into my view, but stayed far enough back that I was certain I couldn't reach him beyond my restraints.

"Have you reconsidered our request?" The man asked.

He was tall, wearing a long plain gray tunic and navy pants with simple black boots. The glint in his hazel eyes was anything but friendly, and his light brown hair was pulled neatly back into a ponytail. A wicked smile pulled at his lips when I remained silent.

"Very well then." He mumbled and sat a small cup down on the ground. Magic propelled it out to me.

That was the blood I smelled. My stomach turned just looking at it. I was thirsty as all hell but I did not want to drink it, and I didn't even understand why. Aside from the fact that it *smelled* stale, there was something telling me not to drink it.

"Oh come now. We can't have you withering away to nothing. Drink." He mocked me. "Then again, I'm not sure how much longer they're going to even give you the option to work with us." He went on, leaning down so he was eye level with me. "I have half a mind to simply put you out of your misery now."

He brought his hand out in front of him, which I hadn't even noticed he was hiding behind him to display a wooden stake.

Shit.

I was going to die here.

He smirked. "Don't worry. They decided to give you a little more time to think it over. For now. And I'm sure even if you refuse, you'll work well as a bargaining chip." They wanted me to *work* with them? What the hell? Had I missed something here? It didn't make sense.

He huffed a small laugh and stood up. "You'll drink it eventually." Then he turned on his heel, slammed the door shut behind him, and I heard the metal lock click into place again before his footsteps headed down the hall again. Leaving me alone to stare at the cup of blood every fiber of my being was telling me *not* to drink.

I jolted straight up in bed with a gasp, suddenly finally able to control my own body again and lashed out in front of me as though I could grab for that cup anyway.

Deiric startled awake with my sudden movement, but just lifted his head abruptly. "What? What's wrong?" He asked, his voice still weary with sleep.

I moved my wrists, touched them, and found myself checking all over to make sure I was in fact in our bed and not shackled in some dark dreary cell somewhere. I couldn't shake the feeling of how *real* that all felt despite that it was clearly a nightmare.

"Are you alright?" Deiric sat up and gently grabbed my arm to still me.

"I'm fine. I'm sorry I woke you." I mumbled and layed back down before pulling the blanket up over my chest.

He looked down at me, fully awake now. "Another nightmare?"

I was certainly no stranger to nightmares at this point, given that for the first few weeks after the battle I relived every moment of it, but it always ended differently. Sometimes I saw it exactly as it happened and others it didn't go our way. We didn't lose anyone *I* was close with that day, despite being mere moments from losing Deiric but still, it replayed in my head for weeks after.

Those nightmares drove me nuts. Hell, I hunted monsters for a living for nearly ten years and *that* never gave me nightmares. Nightmares only ever seemed to happen when I was at risk of losing someone I loved or when I *did*.

This was different though. This was new. I didn't ever recall being in a situation like that.

I finally nodded in response to Deiric's question.

"The battle again?" He asked. We'd been over every variation of that nightmare until I finally worked through it, and it had been almost three months since my last nightmare about that.

"No." I shook my head. "This was… new. Different." I didn't even know how to explain it to him. "This felt *real*."

"Your battle nightmares *didn't* feel real?"

I looked up at him. "I– Well, I guess not. This was…" I couldn't find the right words. "I could hear and smell everything like I do *now*. In the nightmares about the battle I didn't smell it all, didn't hear everything and it was hazy. This was clear as day."

He layed back down next to me and hooked his arm around my waist. "Walk me through it."

So I did. He listened intently while I described every single piece of the nightmare, and every smell, every sound, and each little minute detail.

When I finished he sighed and squeezed me a little tighter. “That is… oddly specific.” He said, thinking it over for a moment. “Maybe your subconscious is just overly active because of Samhain?”

“Maybe.” I looked up at the ceiling. “It makes me not want to go back to sleep if that’s the case.”

“Well, staying up all night isn’t really a good idea either.” He shifted me onto my side and pulled me into him so my back was against his chest. “If you really want to though, I’d be glad to keep you up all night with other, far more exciting activities.” He whispered into my ear and kissed down the back of my neck onto my shoulder.

I let out a soft sigh and leaned back into him. “As fun as that sounds, I probably *should* get some sleep.”

His hand started to trace lazy circles on my stomach and work its way further down. “Are you sure about that?” He breathed into my neck and sent shivers down my spine. “It would give you something better to dream about instead.” He nipped at the base of my neck where it met my shoulder.

I shrugged him off, despite that I could really use the distraction. His slight sigh of disappointment didn’t go unnoticed, but he snuggled in closer to me and laid his head down on the pillow behind me. After what felt like an eternity, I finally dozed off again.

Chapter 6

Mira

I was standing in the temple, after having just completed my offering and prayer to the Morrigan. It was quiet, with Deiric and Zane lingering by the door in silence waiting for me to stand up and turn to leave.

As I have now become accustomed to, her energy flowed through the space in acceptance of the offer, but this time there was more power behind it, and it lingered rather than passing me by and continuing on. I lookcd up to see her standing before me just like she had that evening at the manor many months ago. Her face was hidden beneath her dark cloak.

"There is another who requires your instruction." Her voice rang through the room as she spoke.

I raised a brow. "I have collected all the sorcerers and sorceresses that we are currently aware of to bring to the manors for training. There is another one we missed?"

She nodded. "Her magic has been hidden from everyone, even her own people."

Even her own people. Cryptic, and vastly unhelpful. I could think of a hundred people who might fit that description.

"She is the princess of Leinster." She said plainly, likely growing impatient with my lack of understanding, while I sat quietly picking through the people in my head that would fit that description.

"Why on earth wouldn't they have said something after the peace treaty went in place last year?" I probably was a bit too bold in my questioning with her, but I said the words before I could stop myself.

"Her magic was kept a secret because she is a shadow wielder, like you. She is also capable of Eldritch magic."

My face paled. "Eldritch magic?"

"Yes." She paused, surveying me. "There's no need to look so fearful." Despite the cloak masking her face, I could see an amused smile beneath it. "She is only able to conjure beasts from other realms."

"You speak like that is not an issue."

"If she is trained well, she will know better than to use those abilities unless they are necessary. If she is not trained at all, she could unleash beings unto this world that would *destroy it*. You must begin her training *soon.*" She paused again, just for a few moments. "She will drive herself mad with the shadow magic alone without instruction, but she will be queen one day, and she will need to have a handle on herself before then."

Then she was gone. Swept out of the room on the same swift wind that brought her into it. The force of it and change of energy knocked me off balance and I nearly fell to my knees.

Deiric was beside me in an instant, his hand on my back, steadying me. "Are you alright?"

"I'm fine." I looked back at him. "We need to request an audience with the King of Leinster."

His brows furrowed in confusion. "The king?"

"Yes. It seems that the princess is not only gifted with the ability to use shadow magic, but also has other… *abilities*." I hesitated to even say it out loud.

"What?" Zane stepped forward from his place by the door, and I turned to look back at him.

"We need to do it soon." I said as I turned around to face Zane and Deiric directly. "She's already been left without any help in understanding or using her powers for far too long."

"We probably shouldn't try to do this without Garrick and Devlon." Deiric said. "Obviously her magic puts her in *our* coven, but Devlon is likely on far better terms with the King than we would be."

I nodded. "Devlon will be able to talk sense into them and get them to let her come with us for training. I wouldn't want to try to train her there with the shadow magic, let alone with what else she can do."

"What other abilities does she have?" Zane finally asked.

"She has the ability to summon creatures from other realms. Old Eldritch magic." I cringed at the mention of it. Those kinds of abilities were incredibly rare, and usually drove the castor's that had them to insanity. In most cases, they were barred from using their magic at all if they couldn't control it.

"I've never even heard of that." Zane shrugged.

Deiric was rigid, standing like a statue next to me. "Be glad you haven't," was all he said before I shifted us home. I had to wonder *why* or *how* he knew what that was, but I didn't ask.

"I'll contact Devlon, Garrick, and Lazarus. I'll see how soon they can meet with us and then have Devlon send for the audience with the King." I said as I walked up the stairs to head into the manor.

"Do you actually think the King is going to be willing to let you train her?" Zane cut in.

"Honestly, he doesn't really have a choice. If she doesn't get a handle on her magic and," I lower my voice as we walk through the door and into the manor, "her other abilities, she'll drive herself mad."

"I didn't think it mattered that much." Zane commented and walked past me toward where I could hear Liala in the kitchen.

Deiric came up next to me and whispered, "Are you sure we want her *here*?"

I locked eyes with him and there was genuine concern in his gaze. "Do you have a better idea?" My voice was quiet and colder than I intended.

He looked away, considering it for a moment, then returned my gaze. "No, but I don't think anywhere is safe if she's reached this age without *any* training."

I shrugged. "We're the least likely to *die* if she does summon some undesirable creature from another realm. Can you imagine if she does that by accident in the palace?"

"Fair point." He mumbled and walked toward the stairs.

Macha?

Yes?

I need you to carry out a few messages for me. I thought. I could almost hear her sigh.

You could just send them with magic.

I smirked. *I'm sure I could, but it will be a little more* official *coming from you.*

Bring them to your bedroom window when they're ready. She sounded less than thrilled.

Thank you. I headed into the den to write the messages to them.

Chapter 7

Mira

After I sent messages and got responses from Garrick and Devlon that they could meet, with assurance from Garrick that he would clear it with Nedra, the archmage at Aris' manor, I shifted Deiric and I to Lazarus' manor to retrieve him for the meeting.

Arriving without warning to his manor was always an interesting experience. Half of the vampires there lately were all newly transitioned, or he had nightmages who would be transitioning in the near future. I never quite knew what to expect. Given that this manor consisted *only* of vampires, I didn't really need Deiric with me, but I brought him out of habit, more than necessity.

We arrived at dusk, but all the curtains and shutters were still closed, which made the inside gloomy and dark, lit only by a handful of candles. Some of his usual crew were just beginning their day, while others who had daylight rings were winding down. We got a few confused and wary glances, before Darragh approached us.

"I assume you're here for Lazarus?" He smiled. Other than Lazarus, he was who we tended to interact with the most. He was about the same height as Deiric, with short dark brown hair that was always a bit messy. His deep brown eyes looked black in the dim light of the room, which only added to his general brooding mood and look. The pleasantries and smiles never met his eyes. As usual, he was dressed in his fighting leathers, similar to what Deiric often wore hunting or sparring.

I nodded. "We needed to call an emergency meeting."

"So you need your guard dog." He smirked. For once I actually saw a glimmer of amusement in his eyes. "I'll be right back. Please make yourselves at home."

We didn't move, and instead just waited patiently in the dark foyer while they all milled about. Some gave us curious glances while others pretended we didn't exist. I could smell that there were a few mortals nearby, but I didn't look at any of them close enough to determine who might be what before Darragh came walking back out of the hallway with Lazarus in tow behind him.

"An emergency meeting at this hour?" Lazarus asked, his voice dripping with annoyance.

"We can certainly go without you if you prefer." I said with a small smile, which earned me a glare from him.

"You already know that I'm going to say no to that." He rolled his eyes. "What prompted this and why do you need me specifically?"

"We have another sorceress I need to retrieve and train."

Both Lazarus and Darragh finally came to a stop side by side in front of Deiric and I, with Lazarus in front of me. He frowned and crossed his arms over his chest.

"You collect sorceresses without me all the time, what makes this one so special?" He raised a brow.

"She's the princess." Deiric mumbled.

"What?" Both Lazarus and Darragh said in unison, their mouths gaping at us.

"See, it's complicated," I said with a small but devious smile. "Hence our last minute meeting so I can tell Devlon and ask him to request an audience with the king, which I'm sure you'll also want to attend."

Lazarus let out a hefty sigh before glancing at Darragh. "I'll take care of it." Darragh assured him. I had to wonder what Darragh is going to be taking care of on Lazarus' behalf, but I didn't feel it was in my best interest to delve too much into whatever it is they do here. Before I could consider asking, Lazarus turned to us.

"Well, what are you waiting for?" He asked.

I shifted us to Aris' manor. We arrived in their foyer in almost the same place we were in Lazarus' dark and dreary manor. The brightness of the space caused me to blink a few times until my eyes adjusted.

"There you are!" Aris said with a smile as he approached from the bottom of the stairs. Always the welcoming host these days. "Garrick and Devlon are already here."

"They certainly wasted no time." I mumbled as I walked over to him. "Good to see you again. Sorry to barge in at the last minute."

He shrugged. "It's not like we have a choice." He waved his arm toward the stairs. "I'll leave you to it." Then he walked off to whatever it was he had been planning to do at this point in the evening. Everyone always seemed busy since the treaty.

The three of us walked up the stairs in silence and then made our way into the meeting room at the top of them. Garrick and Devlon were already sitting down in the same chairs they always occupied when we gathered together for our monthly check in meetings.

"Want to explain why we had to urgently meet this evening?" Garrick was more than annoyed. Devlon didn't seem to care, but was dressed far more casually than I'd ever seen him. His black shirt was mostly unbuttoned revealing his entire chest, and his loose fitting pants suggested he had likely been getting ready to turn in for the evening.

"We need to request an audience with the King and I thought Devlon would be the best one to ask for it." I said, making my way to where I usually sat, though I doubted this would take long enough to merit sitting down.

"Why?" Devlon asked before I reached my chair.

I raised a brow at him as I walked the last few steps to my chair then sat down. Deiric sat to my right and Lazarus to my left. "Why what? Why do I think you should ask or why do we need the audience with him?" I paused for a half a second, but continued before he could reply. "You are the most logical person to request it, since Solas was very heavily involved with the King's court over the last several years. We need the audience because he has been hiding the fact that the princess is gifted with shadow magic, among other things."

I don't think I've ever seen Devlon truly stunned until today. His jaw practically hit the floor. Even when he'd found out who I was the night we met, he hadn't been *this* shocked.

"I'm sorry, you expect me to believe that the princess is a shadow wielder and he's just never told us?"

"That's exactly what I'm telling you." I said flatly. "But why would he tell you? Shadow magic is forbidden in Solas. And other than the last several months our coven was basically shut down. I would half expect the former leadership to just execute her."

A slight frown ghosted Devlon's lips for a moment before he looked at the table and leaned back casually in his chair, resting his elbow on the arm of the chair. "I suppose you're right, but why hasn't he brought it to our attention since the treaty?"

I shrugged. "Honestly, it doesn't make sense, but who am I to question?" I asked, glancing between him and Garrick who just looked perplexed and was now leaning forward with both elbows on the table. "The most important thing is that we convince him we need to train her, and we most certainly need to do it somewhere other than the palace if what I've been told about her other abilities is true."

"She's a castor?" Garrick blurted out, both brows raised.

"Yes."

"And how did you come to find out all of this?" Garrick asked.

"The Morrigan."

Garrick's jaw tensed. They all knew that I still gave the Morrigan regular offerings, but for some reason it seemed to bother them that she would occasionally speak to me during my visits to her temple.

"I'll put in a request with the king." Devlon said, not even questioning my sources. "It may take him a while to respond. What exactly should I tell him?"

I smirked. "Tell him we have information that is important to the safety of his kingdom, and that it is a matter of life and death, because in some ways it is." I glanced at Garrick before continuing my explanation. "Make sure he understands that we need this sooner than later. And don't include this part, but if what I know is true, she'll drive herself mad if we *don't* train her, so I don't even care if you have to lie, but say whatever you have to to get us in the door as soon as possible."

"You don't want me to give the true reason?" He asked.

"No." I shook my head. "If he knows the real reason for our visit I'm certain he'll just decline it."

Devlon nodded. "Was that all?"

"Yes. Unless Garrick has anything he'd like to add?"

"What exactly *are* her other abilities?" Garrick finally asked.

"I'll share that when I'm sure what I'm told is correct. I don't want to share that until I see it for myself."

"That sounds suspicious." Garrick commented, with a little bit of frustration in his tone.

"It is ancient magic. I don't doubt what I was told, but it is something I'd like to see for myself before I share it with anyone else. For all of our sake." I looked back and forth between them with an expression that said this wasn't up for discussion.

"Fine." Garrick said.

"I think this wins an award for the shortest meeting." Devlon smirked and then shifted away.

Garrick rolled his eyes before doing the same.

"They were quite pleasant." Lazarus mocked.

I chuckled. "I mean, I did interrupt *all* of our evenings with this. They have a right to be at least a little bit annoyed." I stood up. "We should probably at least let Aris know we're done before we leave."

Lazarus disappeared in the blink of an eye, and was back just inside the door of the room moments later. "All clear."

I looked over and raised an eyebrow. "You're way too eager to get out of here."

He leaned against the door frame with his arms crossed. "I was in the middle of something. Forgive me if I'd prefer get back and take care of things myself rather than have Darragh handle it."

I just rolled my eyes and shifted us back to his manor.

"That was fast." Darragh said from across the foyer.

Lazarus shot him a look that would make most people shut up or shy away.

"I'll send you a message when I know what time our audience with the king will be." I assured Lazarus.

He nodded, and then I shifted Deiric and I home. I wasn't sure how quickly the King would reply, or how soon we'd be able to get an audience with him, but I was eager to get things moving.

Chapter 8

Mira

The king agreed to an audience with us the following day, which was a lot sooner than I would have expected. Whatever Devlon had decided to share with him must have peaked his interest enough that he understood the importance of it.

I opted for a navy gown this time, which had thin straps that went up over my shoulders. Both the front and back had a deep v shape to the neckline, and the dress was very form fitting until it reached my hips, where it had a soft flow to it until it reached the ground. There was a very light shimmer to the fabric, but was subtle enough to not be noticed unless I stood in direct sunlight. I paired it with the choker Deiric had given me and put the dagger on my thigh despite the fact that this dress didn't have a slit to allow me easy access to grab it if I needed it. My hair was braided, as always.

Deiric and Lazarus both wore black tunics with a silver embroidery, like they'd planned to match. They had their swords sheathed at their hips, and wore black pants with tall black boots. Even in their finery, they looked like warriors prepared to head into battle.

Devlon and Garrick met us at Aris' manor and I shifted the five of us into the foyer of the palace, which jolted several guards to attention, but they relaxed shortly after realizing who we were. For a moment it occurred to me that the palace likely should be warded *against* anyone shifting in and out, but that was a problem, or rather, a discussion for another day. Today, we needed to focus on the princess.

A man in an emerald green tunic and a navy cape fastened to his shoulders approached us from one of the halls leading further into the palace. He had the king's seal embroidered on the chest of his tunic, and a simple sword sheathed at his hip. He wore plain black pants, with knee high boots fit for riding. His golden hair was partially pulled back into a braid atop his head while the rest hung loose to just below his shoulders.

"Good afternoon." He said, his voice carried through the room. "My name is Lorcan O'Byrne. I'm the captain of the King's Guard. Welcome." He smiled and gave us a slight nod in greeting.

I nodded my head in return. Garrick and Deiric stood on my left, while Devlon and Lazarus stood on my right.

"The king has been expecting you. This way." He gestured to the hall he'd come out of and began to walk that way while we quietly followed him. As we walked through the hall, guards filled in beside and behind us. Eight in total, trailing us all the way to where we were to meet the king.

We reached the end of the hall and walked into a large throne room. The king and queen sat on the dais at the end of the room. The prince sat slightly back to the right of the king, while the princess sat slightly back and to the left of the queen.

The prince had an emerald tunic very similar to that of the captain of the guard, with a plain white shirt visible beneath it. His dark brown hair was short, a bit scruffy, and his eyes were so brown they almost appeared black. He had a mildly disgusted look on his face as we approached, though he seemed to be trying to look pleasant and failing.

The king wore a white and gold tunic, with white pants and plain black boots. He had a fur lined cloak on, likely leopard fur, with a beautiful gold fabric on the outside. His brows were knit together resembling a look of concern, with a polite smile that did not reach his deep brown eyes. His dark hair was mostly hidden beneath his ornate white and gold crown.

The queen and the princess were both dressed in beautifully embroidered gowns, with gaudy and puffy sleeves. Their waists were pulled in tightly, likely aided by corsets underneath the gowns. The queen's gown was a brilliant sapphire, and the princess's gown was a seafoam green. Both had their hair done in some intricate updo that I imagined might've taken an hour to put in place.

The queen's hair was a soft golden brown, and the princess's hair was a striking contrast to all of them and was a bright white. They both looked just as concerned as the king with slight smiles plastered to their lips. The crown adorning the queen's head paled in comparison to the king's, but still glimmered. The princess and prince wore no crowns.

The air of the room was tense, and they did not seem very eager to hear what we had to say. When Lorcan stopped, we also stopped. When he bowed, low at his waist, we all followed suit.

"You may rise." The king bellowed.

"Your majesty, the magisters of the Oíche and Solas covens have arrived, along with a few others." Lorcan said, and motioned to us, before walking over to the edge of the dais closer to the king and standing guard.

"You said this was urgent." The king grumbled. "What could possibly be so urgent that you needed an audience this quickly?"

"Your majesty, I apologize for our insistence that we meet so quickly." I said in as kind of a voice as I could muster. We hadn't really discussed who would do the talking, but I took it upon myself. "We have recently been notified of another sorceress in need of training." I dared to meet his gaze, after bowing my head before I spoke. His eyes flickered with something I couldn't place for just a moment, but his face did not change.

"Am I supposed to guess who this might be?" I could tell he intended his voice to have more bite, but it was laced with a lingering concern.

"The princess, your majesty." I said rather matter of factly and held his gaze.

"She has no magic." The prince snapped, earning him a quick glare from the king before his eyes fell to me again.

"My sources say that she possesses shadow magic, which she should be trained to use sooner than later."

"She has no such magic." The prince said again.

I met his gaze now, and the hatred in his eyes was overwhelming. "My source of this information is all knowing, and she would not lie." I kept my voice even and emotionless. "I understand that her abilities were hidden due to the nature of her magic and that anyone using *dark* magic was hunted for years, but she *needs* to be trained, if for no reason other than to keep her safe and sane, *your highness*."

The prince snorted.

"Enough Ronan." The king roared. "Who exactly is your source?"

I met the king's gaze again. "The Morrigan, your majesty."

His brows raised, and the queen shifted in her seat. The princess remained unmoved.

"She claimed that the Morrigan came to her in her dreams. I thought she just had an overly active imagination." His face softened some, and he looked exhausted.

"The magic will truly drive her insane?" The Queen spoke up now, her voice soft, almost a whisper.

"Yes, your majesty." I replied, before anyone else could speak. I was surprised that Garrick and Devlon hadn't attempted to say anything at all yet. "She is nearly 14 years old now, is that right?"

The queen nodded, worry cascading across her face.

"She should have begun her training several years ago. We will have a *lot* of work to do, but the sooner we start the better." It didn't seem relevant to mention that the Eldritch abilities were far worse than shadow magic, but the shadow magic itself can be overwhelming.

The princess finally made a face other than her forced smile, and looked a bit insulted. Her eyes were a piercing golden color, nothing like her mother's hazel eyes or her father's deep brown eyes. She hadn't even really looked at us until I had made that comment. I watched as she carefully evaluated each of us, with her gaze finally settling on me.

There was a slight look of curiosity in her eyes now, while she examined the tattoos down my arms. Garrick's were hidden beneath his shirt. Come to think of it, I'd never even seen them.

There were a few more moments of uncomfortable silence when I looked back at the king again to see he was deep in thought.

"I suppose there is no hiding it if the Morrigan has already told you, and come to her in her dreams." He mumbled, but was looking at the floor while he continued to stroke his chin with his index finger, thinking. "Will you arrange to train her here?" He finally looked up and met my gaze.

I raised a brow, but otherwise didn't show the genuine shock I felt when I realized this was far easier than I'd thought it would be. "With all due respect, your majesty, it would be far safer for her to come with us and learn at one of our manors." I glanced at the princess for a heartbeat before looking back at the king. "And far safer for the rest of you as well."

He scowled. "You think I'm going to let her *leave* here with you?"

"I think it would be the best decision, your majesty." I said plainly. "She would be safe with us, not at risk of hurting or killing anyone by accident, and we could send regular updates, or bring her back here for you to see her as much as you'd like."

Rage flared in his eyes. This was more like what I expected. She was a royal heir and his daughter. They were not brought up within the covens, so did not understand that it was easier and safer to send the mages out for training rather than try to do it at home.

"But we would not be welcome there?" He asked.

Movement from the prince, Ronan, caught my eye and the devious glimmer in his eyes with a smile to go with it made my skin crawl. I got nothing but ill intent from him, and when I focused enough I could hear him thinking, *This is my chance.* Reading thoughts didn't come natural to me yet, with the exception of reading Deiric, for some reason.

I met the king's gaze again. "No, your majesty. Our warded manors are kept hidden for our safety. No one outside of the coven is permitted to come to them."

"The princess is not a part of your coven." He insisted.

"No, but she will be if we train her." I replied before I could stop myself.

The queen grabbed the king's arm before he could snarl a response at me. "You are sure that this is necessary?" The queen asked softly.

I nodded. Something about the way the queen was looking at us was just… odd. I couldn't put my finger on it. She didn't seem worried about the princess being in our care, but I couldn't hear her thoughts to dissect what I was seeing in her face.

"Adriana." She looked at the princess. "Do you have any issues with going with them for your training?"

"No." Adriana replied without any hesitation. "But they are not all human." Her tone was rather flat, very matter of fact like.

"They are vampires." Ronan spat hatefully. *I'd gladly kill them if it wouldn't cause a scene.* He thought after he finished speaking. He broadcasted his thoughts, while the queen guarded hers. I found that interesting.

I didn't look at Ronan. "We're not *all* vampires." I gestured to Deiric and Lazarus. "They are, and I am, but Devlon and Garrick," I gestured to them now, "are just mages. Magisters to be more specific."

"I didn't think vampires possessed any magic." Adriana said.

"They don't." I smiled. "I'm one of a kind." For the sake of proving it, though I knew I didn't need to, I let some shadows fill the floor around me. Lazarus and Deiric didn't move or react, and stood like statues as the shadows surrounded them as well.

Adriana just looked more curious. "Will I be in a manor with other mages, or with vampires?" She raised a brow at me.

"Both. I would be training you, with help from a witch and another vampire."

Her face contorted in confusion. "I'll be trained by a vampire *without* magic?"

I nodded. "She was once a witch, and will help with some of the lesser magic and spellwork you'll learn while you're with us."

She looked away, deep in thought. What I could read from her suggested she was excited to be able to use her magic and learn, but in that moment I realized I couldn't actually sense her power at all, which seemed suspicious. Usually, I could at least *sense* the power of another mage if they were nearby. For example, I could sense both Garrick and Devlon beside me, even if I couldn't see they were there.

"How long will this training take?" The king asked.

I shifted my gaze back to him. "That entirely depends on her, your majesty." I said with a smile. "She could master it quickly and it would only take a few months, but it could take her much longer since she hasn't started any training yet and she's already fourteen."

"When did you start training?" Adriana asked.

I looked back over at her. "I started training very young, almost as soon as I could understand what magic *was*. I was a master by the time I was eight."

Mastered at eight, I didn't even think most sorceresses trained until age ten. Deiric thought. I hadn't ever shared any details about my past beyond what he'd asked about, and he didn't often ask me questions about things like this.

Both of her brows raised almost to her hairline.

"You'll go through accelerated training, since you're starting so late," I explain. "Generally, we will start training at ten years old, but shadow magic is… a little bit more complicated. So when we have someone with shadow magic their training usually starts as soon as they can handle it."

The king sighed. "Are you ready for her to come to train *now*?"

"Yes, we could take her to start her training today and begin at dawn tomorrow." I said quickly. "She would be welcome to bring one of her ladies maids with her, if she would like as well." I thought that might ease her mind.

She looked at me for a moment, and I couldn't read the emotion on her face.

"Lorcan, please advise her attendants to pack her things." The king didn't even consult his wife, though she still didn't seem at all concerned.

"So you're going to send her to a house full of vampires?" Ronan couldn't seem to keep his mouth shut.

The king was absolutely enraged, and for a moment looked like he might strike his son. I assumed this meant Ronan had a habit of speaking out of turn, and I certainly would've found it amusing to see him slapped given his thoughts about us.

"Ronan, if you cannot keep yourself composed you will be dismissed." He spat at him.

"She will be in a house with vampires, witches, sorcerers, and sorceresses alike." Garrick finally spoke up. "All of the vampires in the manor she will go to have been around for a *very* long time. New vampires are kept at manors without humans until they've adjusted completely and are capable of controlling themselves in *any* scenario. There is nothing you'll need to worry about."

I was still technically *new* for all intents and purposes, but now likely wasn't the time to bring that little snippet of information up. Garrick, wisely, refrained from mentioning it. Adriana was now looking at Deiric intently, like she knew he was the Elder in the manor she'd be going to.

The king looked to Lorcan again. "Please, go have them prepare her things now."

"She will have no need for fancy gowns." I caught myself speaking before I could stop the words from coming out again. Clearly, I was not used to speaking around literal *royalty* and needed to try to reign myself in so I didn't also get scolded for speaking out of turn. Lorcan had stopped mid turn and looked at me. Adriana also looked at me again.

"If she has plain shirts, pants, or even simple blouses, skirts, and corsets that would be more suitable for her to train in." I said softly. "If she has none of those things, we can arrange to have them supplied for her."

"They will pack accordingly." The king said.

Lorcan nodded and headed for the door.

"Would you like to stay for dinner?" The king asked.

I opened my mouth to speak but Devlon's voice cut me off. "We would be honored to, your majesty."

I raised a brow and glanced back at him. He merely smiled and shrugged.

The king stuttered a bit. "I, er–, I forgot that you don't *eat.*" He stammered, and my gaze fell to him again. "We have wine?" He offered. His sudden politeness struck me as odd, but I didn't question it.

I shrugged and offered him a small smile.

"The guards will show you to the dining room." He said and waved his hand to dismiss us.

We all bowed in unison and turned to follow the guards to the dining room.

Chapter 9

Mira

All of the seats at the table had place settings in front of them. It was clear that whoever set the table in the short time between when he'd offered for us to stay for dinner and we'd arrived in the dining room wasn't aware that Deiric, Lazarus, and I wouldn't eat. Not that we *couldn't* if we wanted to, but I knew enough to know that the food would taste like ash and offered us nothing. We all took our seats along the side of the table closest to us as we walked in the door. Devlon took his place next to the seat at the head of the table, which I assumed would be the king's place. Garrick sat down next to him, followed by Deiric, me, and then Lazarus.

Are you sure it is a good idea to bring her and *her ladies maid back to* our *manor?* Deiric thought.

I'm sure that it wouldn't matter which manor we chose, and it would be a hell of a lot easier for me to train her if she's with everyone else.

What do you think of the prince's thoughts during our meeting in there? Deiric asked.

The king arrived, followed by the queen, Ronan, and then Adriana. The king took his place at the head of the table just as I expected, with the captain of his guard taking the place at his right hand. The queen sat next to him, followed by the prince, and then the princess, setting her right across from me.

I'm not sure what to make of all of it, but he clearly has a distaste for vampires. We'll just have to see what we can find out. I thought.

The servants began to make their rounds, pouring wine for everyone. When they reached Deiric, he covered his goblet with his hand. The woman came around to me and I also covered mine.

"You don't drink either?" The king asked, his tone was surprisingly polite rather than offended.

The servant had moved to Lazarus, who also covered his goblet, following our lead.

"We prefer not to drink in mixed company, your majesty." I replied calmly. "We appreciate the offer though."

Ronan scoffed. "Afraid a little alcohol will cause you to lose control?" His annoyance was very clear from his voice.

"Contrary to what you might think of us, alcohol wouldn't impair us to the point where we would lose control and *bite* you if that is what you're insinuating." I snapped. "But if it bothers you so much." I waved my hand and a single glass appeared in front of each of us. "We prefer whiskey." Whiskey filled the glasses before a servant could try to fetch any.

Lazarus half laughed, before reaching for his glass and taking a sip.

Ronan just scowled.

"You'll have to forgive my son's attitude." The king said with a hint of irritation in his tone. "He has always had an issue with vampires."

I raised a brow and looked at the king.

"I'm hoping that we can shift his misguided hatred if we work together." The king added with a small smile in my direction. The king then shifted his focus to Devlon and Garrick and began discussing matters of the covens, their alliance, and who we might assign to his court from both sides. A discussion that I had little interest in being a part of. I was responsible for keeping the balance between the covens themselves, not the covens and the monarchies. I had no interest in being involved in the more intricate political details.

After a few moments of silence at our end of the table, with Ronan's steely gaze never leaving me, Adriana finally spoke again.

"You're married." She motioned to the ring finger on my left hand which held my glass of whiskey. I casually and quietly created an enchantment over Deiric to hide his tattoo.

"In a manner of speaking, yes."

"I didn't know vampires got married." She said softly. "Was it arranged?"

Lazarus chuckled. "We haven't usually turned women into vampires." He said softly. "We certainly don't arrange marriages."

"So you're the first female vampire?" She asked. So curious, this princess. I wondered if she knew anything about vampires or magic at all.

"I am not the first." I said softly. "I might be the second, I think."

She partially nodded. "Where is your husband?"

I glanced at Ronan, who now had a slight smile on his face. "You'll meet him eventually." I said softly and looked back at her. I wasn't giving him anything to use against me.

"How old are you?" She asked.

"I'm twenty seven."

"So you're new." She said it as a statement, not a question, but I nodded anyway.

"How old is your husband?"

I should have seen that question coming, but I didn't have an answer prepared. I realized for a moment that I didn't even know. I opened my mouth to say as much, but Deiric answered for me.

"He's six hundred and forty nine." Deiric said. I glanced at him and he had a slight smile on his face.

The princess' jaw practically hit the floor, and I smirked slightly before taking another sip of my drink.

"I– uh–" the princess stammered. "I know vampires are immortal, but I guess I never considered there were some who were already so old."

Lazarus leaned forward with a bemused look on his face. "Well you're in luck, princess, because now you've met one even older than that." He paused as she looked him over. "I've been around for nearly sixteen hundred years."

Her eyes widened, but she didn't reply.

"You'll meet plenty of others of varying ages." I said softly. "You'll also meet other teenagers that are a lot like you. We have five other mages learning to master their magic at our manor."

"Others that are like me?" She asked, with a glimmer of hope appearing on her face briefly.

I nodded. "You're the only one with shadow magic, but yes."

She smiled. "Is the vampire who used to be a witch your mother?"

I frowned slightly, despite my best efforts to hide how that hit me. "No, but she knew her."

Adriana must have read what I didn't say on my face. Her eyes darted over to Deiric and then down at the table in front of her. "I'm sorry."

"Death is a part of life, especially when you're immortal. While hers was certainly unexpected, you have no reason to apologize. You didn't know and it was an honest question."

Adriana nodded, but didn't look up and didn't ask any further questions. The rest of the meal we spent mostly in silence while the king, Devlon, and Garrick continued their discussions about politics, court assignments, and our plans for Adriana.

Shortly after we'd finished our meals, Adriana's ladies maid appeared in the door of the dining room along with two large trunks. We all stood after the king rose from his seat.

"Lorcan." The king said.

Lorcan walked over to Adriana and she raised her arm. He pulled a key from his pocket and unlocked what looked like a small bracelet on her wrist. The moment he pulled it away I realized what it was. They forced her to wear a small shackle, fashioned to look like a bracelet around her wrist that blocked her magic.

Deiric laid a hand on my arm, and it wasn't until he did that that I realized shadows had appeared at our feet again because I was furious. My control only seemed to slip when I was triggered by rage or fear.

"You keep magic blocking shackles around here?" Devlon asked cautiously, a hint of annoyance in his tone. It was so dainty I'd hardly call it a real shackle, but he made his point.

"It's a safety precaution." The king said dismissively. "You're welcome to take that one if you would rather we *didn't* have it. It's the only one we have, which Ronan retrieved discretely from your former leadership."

I glanced at Ronan, who smiled a little bit wickedly at me. I waved my hand and the bracelet came to me, then I handed it to Devlon.

Devlon nodded. "We'll take it back, if you don't mind."

The king waved his hand dismissively.

Deiric, Lazarus, and I walked over to the small brunette woman, her ladies maid, who had been designated to come with us. The smell of her fear was nearly overwhelming, but she stood tall despite it. We waited quietly while the princess said her goodbyes and then came over to us.

Devlon and Garrick waited until I shifted Deiric, Lazarus, Adriana, her maid, and her things out before I assumed they followed suit.

When we arrived at our manor, Adriana and her maid both looked like they might be sick.

I smiled. "You'll get used to that eventually." I waved my hand and their trunks disappeared. "I sent those to your rooms. Allow me to give you a tour of the manor?"

After a few deep breaths Adriana nodded. The maid still looked a bit green, but we walked into the manor and I showed them around. I made introductions as we went and ran into people. Deiric and Lazarus did not follow us for the tour. I showed them to their rooms and let them know that Liala would be handling making their breakfast in the morning, but the maid was welcome to help if she chose to.

"We will get started with your training tomorrow. For now, please make yourself at home." I said to Adriana. I turned to her maid before she wandered to her own room. "Please make sure she's dressed in something more suitable for training in the morning. A simple skirt, blouse, and corset will do. Or she is welcome to wear a tunic and pants."

The maid nodded. She seemed much more at ease now. "I packed as many of those as she had. Please let me know if they're not suitable and I can request more be made and sent here."

I shook my head. "No one can come to this manor without our invitation, and no one will be able to find it if they try. If what you've packed is not suitable we will send someone out for it."

She looked a bit shocked and concerned for just a moment, but then nodded. "Understood." She glanced around me at Adriana for a moment. "Will there be anything else you need this evening, your highness?"

"No. Thank you, Esme." She said softly. "Please take the rest of the evening off. I can take care of myself."

I turned to Adriana again. "My room is the first one on the right at the top of the stairs, which I suppose is actually the last one on the left from this angle." I paused and she glanced down the hallway. "If you need anything, please don't hesitate to come find me." I looked down the hall to see Deiric walking out of our room. "Please be sure to knock first though." I smiled.

We both looked back at one another again. "He's your husband?" She asked.

I nodded.

"I didn't see a ring on his hand." She said plainly.

"I put up an enchantment to hide it." I explained. "Your brother seems to hate vampires. If he knew who meant the most to me he could easily use that against me." I arched a brow at her, and added, "I trust you'll keep that to yourself?"

A look of horror and understanding swept over her face and she nodded. "I won't tell anyone."

"Thank you." I turned to walk away.

"I'm sorry that you have to hide those things, and that he hates you so much." She said and I stopped to look back at her. "I've never been around vampires, but you have shown me more kindness in the few hours since I've met you than anyone in that entire castle. I can't understand why anyone would hate you so much."

I frowned. "We are just as human as you in what we feel and how we act. The only differences are that we're immortal and survive on blood rather than normal food like you do." I turned back to look toward the stairs. "We are viewed as monsters, but I have yet to meet a vampire who is truly a monster. I've met humans and sorcerers who certainly *are* monsters."

"Maybe one day we can show them you're not monsters." She said quietly.

"Maybe." I said softly and started to walk away. "Have a good night princess."

"Please, call me Adriana." She said softly.

I glanced back and nodded. "Good night, Adriana."

"Good night."

Chapter 10

Mira

There was a shrill and horrified scream that yanked me from sleep. For a moment, I thought I dreamt it, but Deiric had jolted awake as well. We looked at one another in disbelief for a few seconds, and then another scream echoed through the manor.

"Shit." I flew from the bed and ran into the hallway faster than I had ever moved before. Deiric was less than a step behind me. In that moment, I was thanking the gods that both of us had actually donned any sleepwear this time.

Down the hall, by Adriana's bedroom was a thick cluster of shadows. Zane had entered the hallway now from his bedroom on the left and looked down at it just as we did.

"Stay back." I shouted, and sprinted into the shadows, letting my own out to choke out the magic spewing from

Adriana. I knew all too well how dangerous this magic could be when summoned before you truly knew what you were doing, especially in moments of fear or heightened emotions.

I burst through her bedroom door and she was laying on the bed, thrashing in a nightmare. Before I could reach her a horrifying creature that appeared to be made of darkness itself came flying for me. I blasted it back with a jolt of lightning and then pinned it down with shackles of shadow. It screeched, a horrifying noise that made my ears ring.

"Adriana!" I shouted. She continued to thrash. I launched myself at her, landing on top of her on the bed and shook her violently. "Adriana, wake up!"

Deiric came running into the room now that I had cleared the way and killed the creature with a swift stab to the chest. He decapitated it for good measure. I didn't even see him grab his sword.

I shook her once more. "Adriana! For fuck's sake wake up."

Another creature, just as horrifying as the first, dripping in darkness and screeching with rage came flying at me out of seemingly nowhere.

Zane was in the room now, though I hadn't seen or heard him enter, and slammed into it, blocking it from hitting me. He and Deiric began fighting it back while I focused on waking Adriana.

"What the fuck is going on?" Xander shouted from outside of the room, finally coming to investigate all the chaos.

I couldn't figure out why this wasn't working. Even the shadows I tried to summon to soothe her didn't wake her. I finally smacked her, hard enough that I was sure it would jolt her from sleep and likely leave a nice mark on her face.

Her eyes shot open and she blasted me back with a wall of shadow. I don't even think she understood she summoned it herself.

I slammed back into the wall of her bedroom, and collapsed to my hands and knees on the floor, gasping slightly after having the wind knocked out of me.

Xander was next to me in an instant and helped me to my feet. I had yet to figure out who had been screaming, and I wasn't entirely convinced it wasn't Adriana. I looked up to her and she was cowering on her bed, having scrambled all the way back to the headboard with her blankets wrapped around her. Deiric and Zane finally killed whatever the other creature was.

I summoned a ball of light to illuminate the room. The creatures were quite possibly the most grotesque I'd ever seen. Their blood was like ink, and their leathery skin was just as dark. They were truly the stuff of nightmares and she was summoning these creatures *in her sleep*.

"How in the hell did this not happen at the palace?" Deiric asked, looking from me to Adriana.

I stared at her, and she looked horrified. "Do you often have such awful nightmares?" I asked her.

She was looking at the creatures with nothing but terror on her face. "They started a few months ago." Her voice was barely a whisper. "After that they made me wear that bracelet all the time, even while I slept." Tears filled her eyes. "I'm so sorry."

"That would've been nice for them to mention before you brought her back here." Xander practically snarled.

I shot him a glare.

"Where did the creatures come from?" She asked softly.

I looked back at Adriana and very slowly approached her. "They came from another realm." I said softly. "You summoned them while you were dreaming."

I didn't think it was possible for her to look *more* terrified, but she did.

I sighed. "I'll be right back." I looked at Zane and Deiric, who each had the inky black blood from the creatures splattered on their bare chests. "Keep an eye on her and do *not* let her fall asleep until I get back." I doubted she would anyway, but it felt prudent to say it.

"Where are you going?" Deiric asked.

"To put something together to prevent more nightmares until she knows how to control this." I walked past Xander, but glanced at him before I turned to go down the hallway. "Check on Esme, would you? I don't know where the screaming was coming from."

He nodded, then I headed down the hall toward the stairs.

Zemora appeared beside me. "I overheard," she said quietly. "Can I help?"

I sighed. "Sure." I rubbed my face as I walked down the stairs. "We need lavender, ashwagandha, chamomile, thyme, and passionflower."

"Got it!" She ran off to go retrieve the herbs.

I wandered slowly behind her, going through the archives of my mind to come up with a satisfactory listing of herbs for a spell bag as well. When I finally reached the training room at the back of the manor she had gathered all of the herbs and placed them on the table.

"Can you also find me mint, sage, salt, and a piece of amethyst if we have that lying around?" I asked, examining what she had brought to the table.

"Sure!" She wandered off again to raid our supplies for the items I requested.

I went over to the storage cabinets and pulled a small satchel out of one of the drawers, grabbed a mortar and pestle, and a jar to put the herbal tea blend I was making into.

"Here we go." Zemora said with a smile as she put all the items I requested on the table.

"Thank you." I began to mix the lavender, ashwagandha, chamomile, thyme, and passionflower into the mortar in front of me to grind into smaller pieces for the tea.

"Aren't you going to explain what you're doing?" Zemora asked.

I looked up at her. "I'm making tea for her and a spell bag."

"Well, I can see that, but aren't you going to explain the ratio of how much of each herb you're using?" She was far too awake for this being the middle of the night and I was not interested in teaching at this very moment.

I frowned. "Perhaps you can remind me of this during the *day* and I can go over it in one of the training sessions." I said sternly. "I'm too tired to go over the details of each plant and the reasons why I'm using it right now."

She sighed, and sat down to just watch.

I poured the mixture into the jar and continued to grind them down until the jar was full. I grabbed the satchel, poured salt into it, added the amethyst, mint leaves, lavender, sage, and chamomile. I mumbled a simple incantation over it as I tied the knot on the top of the satchel, and then grabbed it and the tea blend to take it out to the kitchen.

I looked up at Zemora. "Would you prepare some water for tea?" I asked.

She frowned slightly, but nodded and darted off to the kitchen. By the time I caught up with her she had the tea kettle over the fire and was waiting patiently for me with a tea ball. I put some of the herbs into the ball and when the kettle began to scream I tossed the ball into it to let the tea steep.

"A tea and a spell bag?" She finally asked.

I nodded. "The spell bag will help, but it doesn't hurt to use both if she's having nightmares that are *that* awful. We need to get them under control or stop them entirely until she can control her magic at all times." I yawned. "Otherwise, we're all going to be exhausted if she wakes us up every night."

"Couldn't you just use that bracelet she mentioned?"

I didn't realize just how much of the situation she'd heard. "I won't willingly block someone's magic if I can avoid it. It is a helpless feeling that I wouldn't wish on anyone."

"You stole the magister's magic." She said very matter of factly.

"That was different." I snapped. "*They* often blocked the magic of anyone they didn't like or agree with and caused a lot of pain and suffering. I could have just killed them."

Zemora's eyes widened and she shrunk away from me just slightly. "I didn't think of it that way." Her voice was barely a whisper.

"Adriana is innocent and scared. She's gone far too long without learning to control her magic. I won't take it from her just because she doesn't know what to do with it." I poured a cup of tea for her.

"I don't understand." Zemora said when we both walked up to head back to Adriana's room. "Why does it matter that she is learning later, but not the rest of us?"

"Shadow magic is more powerful and darker than most of the magic the rest of you have been blessed with. Darkness is scary to some, and can drive you mad until you know how to control it, and understand that it *isn't* inherently bad and evil." I said softly. "Your magic is easy and fun to play with. If she summons the wrong kind of shadow magic she could kill someone without realizing it."

Zemora was wide eyed, and simply nodded.

"Go back to bed. Remind me in the morning and I'll explain everything I did tonight."

She scurried off to her room.

I walked back into Adriana's room to find Xander leaning against the wall, Deiric and Zane just awkwardly standing over the dead creatures, and Adriana still sitting up in her bed, leaning back against the headboard.

"Esme is frazzled, but fine." Xander mumbled as I walked by.

I nodded and walked around the bed to her and handed her the cup of tea. "Drink this."

She eyed it suspiciously and then looked at the satchel in my hand. "What is it?"

"It is just a tea to help prevent your nightmares and help you sleep more peacefully." I paused and lifted the satchel. "This is a spell bag to do the same thing."

She looked at the satchel again and then met my gaze. "It's not going to block my magic?"

I sighed and laid my hand on her shoulder, squeezing it gently. "I'm not going to block your magic unless we absolutely have to." I stuffed the spell bag into her pillow case. "Drink the tea and go back to sleep."

She nodded, and took a small sip. A smile found its way to her lips. "This is *really* good."

I smiled and waved my hand, removing the creatures from the room and shifting them outside so we could burn them later.

She settled a bit into her bed and continued to drink the tea silently. Deiric, Zane, and Xander all filed out of the room before me. I turned around one last time and smiled at her. "I'm going to put a shield around your room, just in case. Is that alright?" I asked her.

She nodded.

I raised my hand and put a very simple shield up to protect everyone from any magic she might summon if she was hit with another nightmare, then closed her door and walked back to my room.

Chapter 11

Mira

The next morning I walked downstairs to find Adriana sitting by herself at one end of the table while the rest of the group was sitting in the den and chatting amongst themselves over their morning tea. Adriana's maid, Esme, was working in the kitchen to put together some breakfast for the two of them.

"Did you *want* to sit by yourself, or are you just too afraid to go in and chat with them?" I asked Adriana as I leaned against the threshold and crossed my arms over my chest.

She was staring off into space, and apparently didn't notice my approach. She was startled when she heard me speak to her and then met my gaze.

"I'm not really sure what to say to them." She said softly.

I half laughed. "Well, you could start with 'good morning' and go from there." I gave her an encouraging half smile, but she didn't seem convinced.

"I don't often get to talk with anyone, or make *friends*. I've never been outside of the palace." She looked down at her tea. "It's odd not to have people telling me where to go and when to be there, not having everyone bow or curtsy when they see me." Her voice trailed off.

Zane walked in with Liala. They tried to play it off like they *didn't* come down together, but I could see right through it. I wondered how long they really thought they could keep their relationship a secret. I seemed to be the only one who noticed it, even though lately they were not nearly as closely guarded about hiding it as they were before the treaty was signed.

"Trouble adjusting to things, *princess*?" Zane smirked.

I elbowed him where he stopped next to me.

"Ouch. I was just trying to make conversation." He rubbed his side as though I'd actually hurt him.

"By mocking her?" Liala scoffed from across the kitchen where she'd poured herself a cup of tea.

"I wouldn't be me if I didn't mock her a little." Zane mumbled. Adriana just watched them both quietly, but didn't reply.

"What Zane is trying to say is we're not *formal* here. If our complete lack of formalities makes you uncomfortable, you just have to say so. But I can't promise that anyone will actually try to change to accommodate it, so you'll just have to get used to it." I smiled at her. "No one is going to tell you what to do or where to be aside from when we're training."

She nodded. Esme brought her breakfast over to her and then sat down with her.

Liala began to work on breakfast for the rest of them, who slowly filed back into the room and began to take seats around the table.

"Have you used your magic at all yet?" Sorcha asked Adriana excitedly. She sat right next to her, and had both hands around her mug while she leaned into the table.

Adriana studied her for a moment, finished the bite of eggs she was eating and finally softly said, "not on purpose."

Sorcha chuckled. "I know how that goes." She took a sip of her tea. "I accidentally set my mom's favorite dress on fire and I thought she'd kill me for it. Thankfully she had a bucket of water close by!"

Adriana's brows shot up practically to her hairline.

Aodh spoke up next. "I almost set my *house* on fire." He said with a smirk. He sat across from Sorcha. "At least you can't catch things on fire."

Her mouth opened like she might reply to him, but she shut it and didn't say anything.

"Relax. We're just trying to make you feel better about last night." Sorcha said and shifted in her seat. "You'll get the hang of it."

"Hopefully before she scares the shit out of Stella again." Zemora said with a smirk.

"You were just as scared!" Stella snapped.

Zemora scoffed.

Adriana's cheeks flushed. "I'm sorry."

"Are you kidding? It was funnier than hell." Zemora smiled.

"I put a shield around her room. It shouldn't be an issue again." I said, giving Adriana a reassuring smile.

"Are you still going to explain what you did last night?" Zemora looked at me now, with a hopeful smile on her face.

I nodded. "After you work with Liala, yes." I glanced over at Liala. "I would bet Liala could probably explain it to you too, but she's going to work with you on basic stances for hand to hand combat today."

"We actually get to fight?" Sorcha turned around and smiled.

"Eventually. Today will just focus on getting a solid stance and working through some movements on your own."

"That's not how you trained me." Liala raised a brow and walked over to sit down. "Breakfast is ready." She said to them.

No one got up to get the eggs or fruits she'd gotten out and prepared. They all just looked at me. "You had time to watch and learn without actually *trying* first. They haven't watched us spar for weeks like you did." I glanced around at each of them. "Besides, I'm sure they'd rather *not* get their asses kicked by me or you, so we'll start out small."

Stella scoffed. "What if we had training before this?"

"Did you?" I asked.

"I fought my older brother." She lifted her chin up and acted like she knew everything there was to know already.

"Oh well in that case you can jump right in with Aodh and just for fun we'll bring out the real swords." I smirked.

She sucked in a breath and stared at me like I'd grown three heads.

"Well, if you're *that* confident who needs training on stances first, right?" I raised a brow at her and crossed my arms over my chest.

"Okay we can just start with stances and movements on our own." She said in defeat and sunk down in her seat.

"That's what I thought." I smiled. "Adriana, when you're done with breakfast go outside and around to the left side of the manor. We're going to work on meditation first."

"Meditation?" She asked.

I nodded. "You need to learn how to ground before we can do any work with your magic." I pushed off the threshold and walked over to get myself a cup of tea. "I'll be out there waiting."

"You don't need…" she looked down at her plate and then over at Zane and Liala before she locked eyes with me when I turned around with my cup of tea. "Nevermind."

I smiled. "Like I said, you'll get used to things around here."

Chapter 12

Mira

Later that evening, we all went out to spar. Leo was out running "errands" for Deiric, so it was just Liala, Zane, Renwick, Xander, Deiric, and myself. We paired off, Deiric and Renwick, Zane and Xander, and Liala and myself.

Most of the mages had gone off to do their own thing, but Adriana and Zemora seemed to want to watch us. We had a small fire going, since it was already dusk, and we started off sparing with our swords.

Liala and I went blade for blade for a long while, starting off slow and increasing in speed as we went along. She had finally gotten to a point where she could not just keep up, but if I was out of practice she managed to deal a few solid blows against me.

She lunged for my left side, and I blocked the blow, knocking her off balance but not enough to truly break her stance. She spun around and kicked my sword out of my hand. It flew through the air and landed just two feet from where Adriana sat watching.

I saw her flinch backward, but couldn't take my eyes off of Liala long enough to see anything beyond that.

"You certainly aren't holding back tonight." I smiled and spun away from her next lunge with her sword.

"Are you?" She smirked, and then lunged at me again.

This time I ducked under the swipe of her blade just in time. "Well, no, but I didn't expect *this*."

I let her push me back a few steps before I had a plan, and I ducked under her sword again, but this time I went for the side she left wide open with that advance and elbowed her in the ribs.

She stumbled sideways with a grunt, and then I kicked her sword out of her hands. "Fuck sake Mira." She gasped.

I smirked. "Well, if we're not holding back at all."

She unsheathed two knives and prepared to advance again.

"Go on, I'll wait" I smirked and put my hand on my hip in a gesture to completely mock her.

She growled and lunged at me, but I blocked both knives with my forearms and then knocked them loose from her grip. They stabbed into the ground next to us.

"You're a little rusty with the knives it seems." I smiled wickedly at her.

She sighed in frustration and then we went entirely to hand to hand combat. She threw punches and I dodged or blocked them. I returned her advances with a few swings of my own.

Finally, she managed to land a blow right to my cheek which knocked me back a few steps.

"What are we going full on tavern brawl tonight?" Zane commented from somewhere behind me.

I brushed my hand on my cheek and there was a little bit of blood there, but it had already healed. "You can do better than that." I said with another smirk. It was fun to taunt her.

She lunged at me again, but this time I caught her fist and spun her around to lock her arm behind her back.

In the blink of an eye she spun me around with her and knocked my feet out from under me so she was on top of me with her forearm pressed against my throat.

"Yield." She snarled.

I smiled again. "No." And I used a pressure point on her hand to force her to release her arm from my throat before I pulled a similar maneuver on her to spin her around but this time I put her face down and into a headlock with my knee in her back.

"That's enough." Zane snarled. He yanked me off of her and sent me flying into a nearby tree.

Deiric was next to him in a heartbeat and shoved him back against the side of the house. "Do. Not. Touch. Her." He growled at Zane.

Zane scowled at him, despite that Deiric had his arm against his throat and looked like he might simply rip it out instead. "She took it too far." He growled.

"We were *sparring*." Liala snapped. "Relax."

"Tell that to *him*." Zane snarled at Deiric, who only pressed him harder into the house and growled again, fangs bared in a scowl.

"I'm not going to call him off." I glared at Zane while I dusted myself off. "You interfered in an otherwise harmless sparring match. I'm fine but I have half a mind to hit you for it myself."

Deiric held him there for a few more moments before he finally released him.

I looked at Adriana now, who looked absolutely horrified. Zemora was just smirking, finding this little disagreement entertaining. Zemora glanced at Adriana and laughed.

"If you think this is bad you should see it when any of the guys spar with Mira and take it too far." She pointed at Deiric. "He almost loses his gourd everytime. Mira handles it herself though, most of the time."

"You just fight… for fun?" Adriana just looked perplexed. I wondered what *she* did for fun.

"Well, for fun and to train, yes." I said with a smile. I looked at Zemora. "Deiric might get bent out of shape about it but he knows better than to intervene." I turned to Zane. "Someone needs to learn a few lessons in self control from Deiric it seems."

"Bullshit." Zane spat.

"Dude, you just left your own sparring partner and manhandled Mira because she put your girlfriend in a headlock. Deiric *never* interferes when we're sparring with her, no matter how intense it gets." Xander smirked and crossed his arms over his chest. "So, yeah, some self control would be advised before Deiric kills you for being an idiot."

Zane's face turned bright red with rage and he scoffed.

I chuckled. "Did you think we didn't know?"

He scowled at me.

"You're not exactly secretive about it anymore." Renwick added, and the look Zane gave him had him regretting saying anything and retreating a few steps.

"Relax." I rolled my eyes and put a hand on my hip. "If Liala couldn't have handled it she would've tapped out. Right?" I looked over at Liala, gesturing to her with my hand.

"Right." She said, her lips pressed into a tight line and her eyes flaring in a combination of rage and disapproval at Zane.

"Maybe you two should spar?" I pointed between the two of them. "Sometimes the results can be quite exciting." I smirked and raised a brow.

Deiric finally smirked now, walked over to me and slipped his hand to the small of my back. *Maybe we should spar*. He thought to me.

Maybe we should. I smiled wickedly and looked up at him with so much heat behind my gaze that he sucked in a breath.

Oh don't look at me like that or we are *going upstairs right now.* He looked down at me with just as much burning hunger in those beautiful blue eyes.

What's stopping you?

He started to lean down to pull me into a kiss when we were rudely interrupted by Xander.

"I'm not sure what silent conversation the two of you are having but I'm *very* sure that I don't want to be around for it. So either you're going to break it up and we're going to get back to sparring or you two need to go find a room." He paused and I looked over to see him smirking. "Preferably your own."

"Silent conversation?" I heard Adriana whisper to Zemora.

"They can both read minds." Zemora explained without whispering back. "They communicate with each other in their thoughts a lot. It's just like when she communicates with her familiar. And don't bother whispering either. They can hear everything anyway."

"Her familiar?"

"Oh you haven't met Macha yet?" Zemora asked and smiled.

As if on cue, Macha cawed and flew down to land on my shoulder. *You know, you could've introduced me to your newest pupil when she* arrived *to avoid some of her inevitable confusion.*

Where's the fun in that? I asked her.

I swear I heard a scoff, even though she certainly couldn't make the noise out loud.

"This is Macha." I gestured to her on my shoulder. "And yes, she's my familiar. The Morrigan sent her to me." I scratched Macha's cheek gently. "She's always here, and we communicate sometimes without anyone even noticing, but she doesn't often jump in unless I ask her to or if she needs to for one reason or another."

"I didn't know that there was such a thing as a familiar. What does that mean?" Adriana asked. For a moment I felt awful for not explaining that, among many other things she probably had yet to understand. It is easy to forget what someone who grew up outside of a coven or magical background might not know. She was at such a disadvantage compared to any of the other mages.

"I could explain it all to you if you want." Zemora said with a smile. "I'm sure that Mira has… other things she'd like to do tonight, but I don't mind."

Adriana smiled and I think it was the first genuine smile I'd seen her have since she arrived here. "I'd like that."

"Come on." Zemora said as she stood up and offered her hand to Adriana. "Let's go to my room. I'm sure Stella will have something to say about some of it too."

Adriana took her hand and followed her to her room.

At least she's got a friend now. Deiric thought, still looking down at me like he had no interest in *real* sparring.

It's certainly good to see her happy and making friends. I replied, locking eyes with him again.

I don't need to be here for this. Macha said, and then flew back up to the roof. Her favorite place to perch.

I chuckled.

"So, sparring or… *sparring*?" Xander gave me a knowing look when I glanced over at him.

I snorted. "Sparring." I shifted my sword from where it lay on the ground back into my hand. *We can* spar *later.* I gave Deiric a suggestive smirk.

"We're going to change pairs." Deiric said, without taking his eyes off of me. "I'm with Mira. You all can figure out the rest of your pairs on your own."

I raised a brow at him. "Are you sure you want to spar with *me?"*

Is that even a question? He thought.

I rolled my eyes and spun my sword as I stepped back from him to take on a fighting stance. *I guess not.* I saw Xander shake his head out of the corner of my eye and square up with Renwick before Deiric collected his own sword and lunged forward to make his first move.

Chapter 13

Mira

We didn't get very far with *actual* sparring before I grabbed him by the collar, yanked him into a kiss, and shifted us into our bedroom.

Well alright then. He thought with a low laugh and dropped his sword before grabbing both of my hips and yanking me into him.

I dropped my sword and grabbed at his leathers, desperate to rip them off of him as he deepened the kiss. I kicked off my boots while I pushed him back toward the bed. He did the same, nearly stumbling back into the bed with how quickly I pushed him there.

I yanked off his shirt so forcefully that I nearly tore the leather, only breaking the kiss long enough to pull it over his head. He pulled my lower lip into his teeth and I let out a moan before he yanked my shirt off just as viciously as I'd done with his.

His hands slipped into my hair and he held my face an inch from his for a moment while a sultry smile rose to his lips. "You're a little extra viscous today." His lips grazed mine for only a heartbeat before he said, "I like it."

He yanked me back into him again, our lips clashing in a wild and passionate kiss before his hands slipped down my back, past my ass and gripped my thighs. He pulled my legs up around his waist and spun around before dropping us down to the bed.

He kissed and nipped his way down my neck, chest, and stomach until he reached my navel. He made quick work of the buttons on my leather pants before he pulled them off of me as well, leaving me in just my bra and underwear. He let out an approving growl, then proceeded to remove both with his teeth.

I rose from the bed, grabbed him, and spun us around too quickly for him to stop me before I threw him down on the bed this time and *I* was on top of *him.* He smiled up at me while I leaned down to kiss him, my hands entangling themselves in his hair.

His lips parted and I deepened the kiss. He groaned and gripped my hips again, rocking me against him. He flipped us over and threw me further up on the bed before lowering himself over me.

He slid his hands up my sides, then up my arms and pinned my hands above my head, lacing his fingers into mine. He stared down into my eyes and the heat behind his gaze set me on fire. He moved both of my hands to one of his, and kept them pinned above my head while he kissed down my neck.

His other hand lightly traced my side, tickling me as he moved it lower. I twitched away from him and he let out a low laugh into my neck. *Oh this is going to be fun*. He thought.

When his hand reached my hips he slipped it between my legs and he toyed with me, gently stroking just above my entrance and huffing a laugh at every buck of my hips or movement I made when he touched me. Each touch was torture. I wanted more. I *needed* more.

"Patience, love." He nipped at my neck. "Good things come to those who wait."

I groaned. *You're killing me*. I thought to him.

He pulled his hand away and lifted his head so he was looking down at me. I tried to fight against him and turn us over so I could get on top of him but he held firm this time.

A wicked smile found its way to his mouth. "I mean, I wasn't going to torture you for that long, but if you're going to fight against me…" His eyes danced from mine to my lips as his voice trailed off.

I stilled almost immediately and just stared up at him.

"Good girl." He growled.

My gods, this man. If I wasn't already, I was drenched now. The heat in my core only intensified at his words. I was entirely at his mercy.

He leaned down and kissed me gently, then kissed and nipped his way down my jawline, and my neck. His hand returned to me, *finally*, and he thrust one finger into me, using the palm of his hand to brush against my clit and set me on fire again.

Then he released my hands and kissed down my chest, stopping just for a moment at my breasts to nip and lick at my nipples before heading lower, while he toyed with me with his fingers. Thrusting two of them now into me so, torturously slowly.

I arched up into him, but his other hand slid down. He slipped it under my left thigh lifting it up over his shoulder, and then settled on my hip to hold me still.

He stopped kissing just before his lips grazed the top of my thighs, looked up at me and smirked. "You're mine." He growled, then lowered his head between my legs, removed his fingers and replaced them with his tongue.

He pushed my right thigh up over his shoulder and I gasped. Each stroke of his tongue and light brush of his teeth was pure bliss.

Gods, You taste so *good.* He thought.

He reached up and grabbed my breast with his free hand, teasing and pulling at my nipple with his fingers.

I couldn't breathe, couldn't think beyond the parts of me he touched, teased, and kissed. My fists curled around the sheets.

At the next stroke of his tongue I shattered, my entire body shuddering beyond my control as I climaxed with his name on my lips, but he didn't stop. Not until I was completely limp with pleasure and unable to breathe or form words.

Only then did he rise from between my legs. He slipped off the bed only long enough to remove his pants, then slowly crawled up to bring his lips to mine again. *My turn*. He thought, before he thrust himself into me.

I gasped into his lips.

He drove into me, harder and faster with each thrust. And somehow, I was brought right back to the edge again.

I clawed at his back, gasping and moaning as he thrust deeper each time. I couldn't think, couldn't breathe beyond the pleasure that washed over me.

He kissed down my neck and bit me *hard.* His fangs sank into me and I shattered into him again. Moments later, he reached his climax as well and shuddered into me.

When he finally retracted his fangs and pulled himself out of me I thought I might be able to breathe normally again.

"Holy fuck." I mumbled.

He flopped on his back next to me and huffed a laugh. "That good, huh?" He breathed.

I managed to force myself to roll over so I could rest my head on his chest. "Do you even have to ask?" I breathed. "You're… incredible."

He half laughed again. "I know."

I jabbed him in the ribs gently. "And insufferable."

Chapter 14

Mira

We were just wrapping up the following morning's training and instead of sparring I decided I would read. Leo had returned from wherever Deiric sent him, and it made the pairs even if I sat this one out. I was browsing the books in the den when Elias shifted into the foyer. He walked into the den behind me.

"Is Deiric around?" He asked. I assumed that meant he was here on behalf of Silas with a message for him.

I pulled a book off of the shelf and turned around to face him. He was dressed in a tunic as always, but also wore a cloak for a change. I assumed that meant this wasn't his only stop for the day.

"They are all outside sparring." I glanced down at the book in my hands for a moment. It looked interesting enough. I looked back up at him and he hadn't moved. "Is everything alright?"

He nodded. "Silas wants him to resume his training with Alaster, and has been told that there's another he'll be getting from Lazarus when he's ready that will also need training in reading minds and compulsion."

I raised a brow. "Is Alaric not capable of doing that?"

He cocked his head and raised a brow now. "You knew Alaric could do that?"

I crossed my arms across my chest and cocked a hip to the side, slightly annoyed that he thought I wouldn't have noticed. "Obviously, but that didn't answer my question."

Elias looked me over for a moment and a small smirk found its way to his lips before he finally replied. "I never thought to ask him. He always requests Deiric."

I rolled my eyes. "Of course he does."

Elias huffed a laugh and his smirk widened into a grin. "You're welcome to tell him to have Alaric do it instead, but I'm not delivering that message to him. I would rather not have him at my throat today."

As if Silas were really a threat to him. He glanced out the window where he could now probably see them sparring. "If I can trust you to deliver the message, and then deliver *him,* I'll leave you to it. Silas wants him there tonight at sundown."

I nodded. "I'll tell him."

Elias shifted away. As much as it annoyed me I didn't feel the need to get involved. If Deiric didn't want to deal with it he was certainly capable of telling Silas himself. Though, the thought of sending him out beyond the wards without me left me just slightly anxious. I shook my head to try to shake off that feeling before I shifted outside. I shifted right next to Adriana, who I didn't notice was sitting on the porch to watch them spar again and I scared the absolute shit out of the poor girl.

I glanced down at her with a slight smile. "You'll get used to *that* too." When I looked back up at the guys, Deiric had stopped his sparring with Leo and looked over at me. I figured he didn't expect to see me outside again, and was surprised that Leo didn't advance when Deiric turned away from him.

Silas wants you to come train Alaster, and said there will be another for you to train soon as well. I thought, and didn't hide my annoyance in the tone of it either.

The corner of his mouth tilted down just slightly in a frown for a fraction of a second before he rolled his eyes and went back to sparring with Leo. *Of course he does.*

Elias said we're welcome to tell him no, but he won't be delivering that message on our behalf.

Smart man. Silas has always been the kill the messenger type. Deiric didn't miss a beat with Leo, blocking each advance Leo made on him even while we held this conversation mentally.

He wants you there at sundown tonight.

Deiric didn't reply, but switched to the offensive with Leo and dealt a few blows with his sword before Leo retaliated.

I sat down next to Adriana and opened the book to read. It was a very old book about dragons, dragon riders, and tales of all their adventures together. It seemed the most interesting out of all of my options.

"You enjoy reading folklore?" Adriana asked as she took her focus off of the sparring and looked over my shoulder at the book.

"I enjoy reading all sorts of things." I said quietly. "Now that I have the time to, anyway." I was delighted to see this book included illustrations of the dragons too, which very closely resembled the tattoos Deiric had.

"I've always been fascinated by dragons." Adriana mumbled, still looking over my shoulder as I read. I would have been annoyed at the lack of silence to focus on the words in front of me, but I was just thankful she was opening up a little bit beyond her training.

"It's too bad they're just stories." Adriana continued. "Could you imagine how much fun it would be to ride a dragon?"

"If by fun, you mean mildly terrifying, then sure." I commented, reading further into the tale of the first dragon rider.

"I'm sure it is exhilarating." She said softly, and then leaned back against the house to watch the guys spar again.

Reading about dragons? Deiric's thought drew my attention away from the book and back up to him. I looked beyond where I had the book propped on my knees to watch him for a few moments.

Does that surprise you? I raised a brow, and our eyes met for a heartbeat while he swung at Leo.

Not really. He smirked, but still didn't miss a single block or jab in their sparring match. *They are quite fascinating. If you want other books when you finish that one I can recommend a few.*

I'd like that. I thought, and then went back to reading again.

*

Just before sundown, Deiric came down to the den, where I was sitting once again still reading the same book. He leaned over the back of the couch and kissed the back of my neck.

"Still reading the same book?" He whispered, and slipped his arms down around me.

"It's not exactly a *short* read." I smiled and looked up at him. He stole another kiss before I could say anything else.

"We should get going." He mumbled. "Wouldn't want to keep Silas waiting."

I sighed and sat the book down on the couch next to me. "We?" I said softly. "You know I can shift you there without actually going with you right?"

He raised a brow. "Actually, I didn't know that." He studied me for a few moments, I suppose to figure out if I was lying or not. "I didn't think anyone could do that."

I shrugged. "Most can't, but to be fair I don't think many people have actually tried it."

He stood back up and I turned to look at him. "Well, in that case, I guess *I* should get going."

"I guess there's no hope for you telling him to fuck off and train his own people is there?"

He shook his head. "It's not worth it. It won't take me that long to finish training Alaster, and I'm sure it will be at least a little while before I have to train whoever else Elias mentioned."

I sighed. "I guess I'll see you later then?"

He nodded, and before he could say anything else, I shifted him to Silas' manor.

I sat in the den reading until almost everyone else had gone to bed and the vampires that Lazarus assigned to us to keep watch on things at night had come down and started going about their evening. I finally went upstairs when two of them went out to take up their watch.

When I got into the bedroom, I found a small leatherbound book on the bed. It resembled more of a journal than a book like the one I had been reading downstairs. When I untied the binding on it to open it, my suspicion was confirmed. It was all handwritten and a little disorganized and messy, even compared to some of the grimoires.

I sat it on the bedside table and decided I'd read that next. Then I wandered into the bathing room, cleaned myself up, put my nightgown on and slipped into bed. Despite my best attempts to fall asleep, I lay awake for most of the night. I couldn't seem to stop my mind from racing. All I could think of is what *might* happen to Deiric if assassins showed up looking for me and only found him. Which was entirely illogical, and I knew that, but quieting anxious thoughts like that was an entirely new challenge I'd never run into before. I'd never feared for anyone other than *myself.*

Finally, in the very early hours of the morning I heard the bedroom door very quietly open, and Deiric came in. He moved around so quietly I was certain I wouldn't have heard him if I had actually been sleeping. I barely heard him making noise in the bathing room. Even when he slipped into bed, he did it slowly and quietly to avoid waking me. He still snuggled against me though, and put his arm around my waist. It was only then that he realized I wasn't actually sleeping. I don't know if my breathing just wasn't steady enough, or if he could sense that I wasn't entirely relaxed.

"You're awake." He propped his head on his elbow and looked down at me.

I turned my head so I was looking back at him. "I couldn't sleep."

He frowned. "Have you been up all night?"

I shrugged. "I might have gotten some sleep, but not much."

"You'll be exhausted tomorrow."

"I'll be fine." I mumbled and yawned.

He sighed and then laid his head back down and pulled me back into him. It didn't take him long to fall asleep, and after what felt like an eternity, I too *finally* drifted off to sleep.

Chapter 15

Mira

I woke up when the sun hit me in the face through the window. Even Deiric grumbled and rolled over so he faced away from it when I moved and no longer blocked him from it. He pulled a pillow over his face. I begrudgingly got up and closed the shutters on the windows, then pulled the curtains closed as well so he could sleep. I went about getting myself dressed for the day as quietly as I could.

By the time I made it downstairs to the kitchen to get myself a cup of tea everyone was already finished with their breakfast.

"It's unusual for you to sleep so late." Liala commented, walking up to stand next to me while I poured my tea.

I sighed. “I didn’t sleep much last night. I wouldn’t even be awake now if I hadn’t literally been smacked in the face by a ray of sunlight when it reached the window.”

“I’m surprised you’d struggle that much to sleep alone, when you did it for almost ten years in significantly more dangerous circumstances.” Liala said softly so no one at the table could hear her. Zane, I’m sure could, but I didn’t particularly care.

“It’s not being *alone* that kept me up.” I replied just as quietly.

“You don’t honestly think he’s in any danger when he’s out with them, do you?” She asked, still keeping her voice low, but turning to face the table and leaning back against the counter next to me.

“I don’t know.” I stared down into my tea. “They sent assassins after us at the party last year, and with how much it sounds like the prince hates us, I wouldn’t be surprised if there’s a lot more people out there with the same feelings.”

I turned to face the table as well and took a sip of my tea.

Liala shrugged. “I guess it’s possible. I am sure he can handle himself though.”

“I hope so.” I said softly. I know he can handle himself in a fight, and is faster than any mortal so it was probably a ridiculous notion to be worried, but in an ambush or taken by surprise we are *far* too easy to kill.

The tea didn’t do much to push away the general exhaustion I was feeling. Meditating with Adriana certainly wasn’t helping either, so instead I just sat back and watched her, guiding her through grounding and making sure she was truly calm and collected before we began working with shadows.

"Alright, now that you seem to be much quicker at grounding and staying grounded, let's try to summon any kind of shadow you can muster." I was sitting cross legged a few feet in front of her, with both of us sitting right next to the small stream that flowed by the manor. It was the best place to do this sort of work, where we needed to be calm, grounded, and relaxed.

"How on earth do I do that?" She opened her eyes and looked at me like I was completely insane and asked her to climb the nearest cliff.

"When you're grounded, can you *feel* your power?" I asked.

She closed her eyes again and took a few deep breaths, before finally giving me a subtle nod. "I think so."

"Good." I said softly. "Hold onto that feeling and pull a little bit of that power into yourself, then pretend you're going to let it leak out around you."

She nodded. After a moment or two, shadows flooded out of her and enveloped both of us in complete darkness. I put up a shield before they could go too far.

"Dial it back a little." I said quietly. "That was not a little bit."

I couldn't see her face through the shadows, but I could tell she was less than amused at my instructions when I heard her let out an exasperated sigh.

"That felt like it was just a little bit." Her voice had a slight edge of annoyance to it.

"Open your eyes."

She gasped.

"This is all you." I said softly. "If that was 'a little bit' then we need to think more along the lines of a single sliver of that power and cut it off before you try to use it." I paused for a moment as the shadows began to fade away slowly until I could see her again. "You are calm, so the shadows you summoned aren't harmful. They'd just give you some cover or camouflage when you're fighting. If you'd been angry and summoned something more dangerous I'd be in a world of hurt right now and would've been blasted into the forest behind me."

She chuckled. "That would've been sort of funny to watch."

I raised a brow at her. "It wouldn't be funny if it were one of the other mages. They could've been seriously hurt while I would heal almost instantly."

Her smile faded and she just nodded.

"It is all about control." I said flatly. "Try again."

It took her several tries to finally only summon a small amount of shadow around her. When I was satisfied with the results I let her have the rest of the day off.

Deiric came downstairs just in time for everyone to get ready to spar, and this time Aodh and Gerald joined in as well, but they stuck to sparring each other with our less sharp training blades rather than taking on one of us. Deiric insisted on pairing with me, and was clearly taking it easy on me because he knew I didn't sleep much.

At one moment I was too slow and he caught me by my braid, which I was too lazy to tie up beforehand, and then held his sword at my throat similarly to how we'd ended up the first time we ever sparred together. This time though I didn't have the chance to get my sword into a similarly damning position for him.

You should be sleeping instead of sparring. He lowered his sword but didn't release my braid or relax the grip he had on my shoulder and chest with the rest of his left arm.

I'm fine. I insisted and tried to pull away from him, but he held firm.

You're absolutely not fine. He finally let go of my braid and released me. I stumbled just slightly because I didn't expect him to do so that abruptly. *Case and point.*

I scoffed. *If I sleep now I won't sleep later.*

He rolled his eyes and waved his hand dismissively. *At least go read a book and rest that way.*

I sheathed my sword and crossed my arms over my chest. *Last I checked you don't decide what I do and when I do it.*

He sheathed his sword and then stepped closer to me until there was barely any space between us. I had to look up to hold his gaze, but I didn't back down. *Last I checked, you don't ever seem to know your own limits.* He thought. *Go. Rest. Now.*

I scowled at him, but turned on my heel and walked away.

"I'm not sure I've ever seen them actually *fight* before." I heard Zemora whisper to Adriana while they watched.

I shot her a glare as I walked by and she quickly looked away. I walked into the house, then into the den and went back to reading the book I started yesterday.

*

When Deiric came home this time I was laying in bed reading the journal he'd left for me with an orb of light I summoned floating above my head.

He frowned and closed the door behind him. "You know, I didn't give that to you so that you'd spend the evenings I was away staying up to read it." He started unbuckling his weapons and sitting them on the dresser, not bothering to be quiet. "I meant for you to read it when you finished the other book *during the day*."

"I finished the other book *during the day*." I grumbled, marking my place with part of the leather strap that held the book closed and sat it on the bedside table.

He started to undress on his way to the bathing room. "You know exactly what I meant."

I shrugged. "It's not my fault I can't sleep."

"You could always make tea."

"I'm a little bit insulted that you think I haven't tried that already."

He stopped in the doorway to the bathing room and glanced back at me only looking slightly less annoyed to see I was still awake. "A spell bag then?"

"I'm not stupid or desperate enough to use what little energy I have to cast a sleeping spell on or for myself." I gave him a small glare. He just sighed and continued into the bathing room without another word.

I finally settled myself down into bed to try to sleep again. I heard him turn the water on, and I could have sworn I heard him mumble that I could join him before I drifted off to sleep.

Chapter 16

Mira

I woke the following morning to Macha gently pecking my shoulder.

You should be awake already. She said when I finally stirred.

I sighed and pushed my face further into the pillow. *I'd rather just sleep through their training.* I replied. *Eimear can handle it today.*

Eimear cannot train Adriana in anything other than basic spellwork and healing. She needs you. Macha followed her points with a few pecks for good measure until I waved my arm at her to shoo her away. She flew back to the windowsill and watched me. *If I fly away are you going to get up? Or do I need to sit here and watch to be sure?*

Fine. I grumbled and drug myself out of bed. Deiric didn't stir at all next to me. I walked around the bed and got myself dressed quietly before going to the door to head downstairs. It wasn't until I opened the door that Macha finally flew off of the windowsill.

"You look like hell." Xander said when I walked into the dining room.

"Gee, thanks. That's what every woman wants to hear when they wake up in the morning." I snapped at him.

"I'm just pointing out the obvious." He followed me toward the kitchen where I went to grab some tea. "You sure you're up to training them today?"

"I'm fine." I snarled at him, and let my fangs slip out for just a moment before I got myself back under control again. It was unusual for my temper to slip that quickly, but I hadn't been this tired in a long time.

He raised a brow and took a step back. "I realize arguing is only going to piss you off more, but I definitely don't think you should be around them today if you're already lacking control over a minor insult."

I took a deep breath in through my nose and let out a sigh as I reached for a mug and then poured myself some tea. "I told you I'm fine."

"When was the last time you fed?" He walked over so he was standing right next to me at the counter and lowered his voice.

I realized then it had been a couple of days. I don't think I had gone more than a single day without feeding since I transitioned. That certainly explained why I was so exhausted. I have missed a lot of sleep before without ever getting this tired or this cranky.

"A few days ago." I mumbled, and then took a sip of my tea.

He leaned his hip against the counter and crossed his arms over his chest. "And you think you're alright to train them today?" It wasn't a question he intended for me to actually answer, but I turned to him before he could say anything else.

"I told you, I'm fine. I'll go hunting after I'm done with Adriana's training today."

His disapproving glare almost made me snap at him again, but he didn't say another word. He just watched me while I walked over to the table.

"Meet me outside when you're ready." I said to Adriana, who looked at me with a little bit of concern but nodded. I wondered if she somehow managed to hear our little chat.

Xander followed me outside and sat down close to where I was going to be training Adriana.

"I don't need a babysitter." I snapped at him and gave him another glare.

"We'll have to agree to disagree on that." He said with a slight frown. "I'm not taking my eye off of you until you've fed."

I just rolled my eyes. I might be new but I didn't transition *yesterday.* When Adriana came out we sat down and worked on grounding again and controlling the amount of shadow she summoned. She was already showing an improvement from yesterday, which told me that she would probably progress quicker than I originally thought. We were still nowhere near ready for her to summon anything other than just cloaking shadows, but progress was progress.

Around lunch time, she went in to eat with the others. I followed her and didn't get any further than the front door before Deiric caught me off guard, scooped me up into his arms, and sprinted us off into the woods. I didn't even know he'd woken up yet. He sat me down when he finally came to a stop and I was too stunned for a moment to react.

"What the hell was that about?" I snapped at him.

"You haven't fed in *days?*" He didn't even try to hide the frustration in his voice, and glared at me. I guess Xander filled him in, though I hadn't even realized Xander had time to slip off and do so.

"I've been a little bit preoccupied."

He crossed his arms over his chest and raised a brow. "You've had *plenty* of time to go hunting over the last couple of days, so don't even try to say that."

"Yeah, I've had time, but I *forgot.*" I crossed my arms over my chest as well and glared right back at him. I was in no mood to argue, but I also wasn't going to take his criticism either.

He sighed. "How do you *forget* to feed?" His shoulders sagged and he rubbed his face with both hands, completely flabbergasted that I could forget something like that. "Why didn't you even say anything to me?" He pinched the bridge of his nose in frustration. "Honestly, Mira, this is reckless, even for you."

"I'm *sorry.*" I almost shouted, my voice taking on a mildly sarcastic tone. "You threw a wrench into our schedule when you caved to Silas' ridiculous request to train his men, when you have your own men and manor to worry about and *he* has a second who is perfectly capable of training them instead. I just tried to keep myself on task with what *I* needed to worry about despite the fact that I can't get myself to sleep when you're out there galavanting around beyond the wards by yourself. Hunting was the *last* thing on my mind, especially considering half of the time we don't go out hunting because we feed on each other."

"I'm not *by myself*." He snarled back at me. "I have Alaster with me."

I growled. "Alaster *does not* count." I threw my hands up, rubbed my face in frustration, and then turned in a circle to try to calm myself before literally shouting at him. This wasn't like me. I am not normally this quick to rage and arguments. "He's not going to look out for you, and certainly not going to stop someone from *killing* you while you're too focused on training him."

"That's what this is about?" Deiric's voice softened a little bit, as did his tense posture. "You're worried that someone is going to kill me while I'm out training them?"

"Of course I'm worried about that." I waved my arm in frustration. I was still almost shouting but trying my damnedest to keep myself calm and still. "They sent assassins after me to that gods forsaken ball we attended, and the prince of this fucking kingdom wishes to end all vampires and you don't think I'm concerned when you're out there on your own?"

The last few words came out much louder and angrier than I intended. There was no controlling myself at this point. I'd simply snapped. Maybe it was exhaustion or the fact that I was basically starving myself, but all my self control had officially left me.

He grabbed my shoulders gently to hold me still, realizing that I was no longer able to do so myself. "You know damn well no one is going to beat me in a fight, especially a *human*."

"You can absolutely win in a fight but what if they take you by surprise? You're not going to be able to do anything if they ambush you. What if it's a rogue mage that attacks you?" I could feel the tears trying to break through now. Gods I hated this. My emotions have been so much harder to control since I transitioned, but for the most part I kept them in check. Exhaustion changed things, apparently. And this gods damned anxiety I was feeling was driving me a bit mad.

"Would you be able to sleep if *I* was out there on my own?" I tried to fight back the tears with more anger again.

He cupped my face in his hands and sighed. "No. I wouldn't." He said calmly. "But right now, you need to feed." He released one side of my face and pulled the collar of his shirt away from his neck.

"Do you–" I started, but he stopped my question by putting his finger to my lips.

"Bite me, Mira." He smirked. "I'll be fine. Unlike some people, I don't forget my most basic needs."

I bared my fangs and growled at him.

He just huffed a laugh and pulled his collar back again. "Go on, do your worst."

I grabbed his shirt and yanked him into me before I sank my fangs into his neck. He let out a soft gasp. There was nothing intimate about the bite at first, and despite that, he still slid one hand into my hair and his other arm around my waist.

After a few moments, the rage and frustration I felt melted away. I relaxed into him, sliding my left hand up his chest and neck, then into his hair. He made no move to stop me until I finally felt I'd had enough. I withdrew my fangs, kissed his neck gently and laid my head on his shoulder

"I'm sorry." I whispered into his neck.

"I'm always going to have to make sure you feed when you're stressed out aren't I?" He mumbled.

"Probably."

"I'm starting to wonder how you survived by yourself as a human if you forget to *eat* sometimes." He chuckled.

I pulled back just slightly and gently punched him in the ribs with the hand that had still been gripping his shirt. "I got by *just fine*." I looked up at him with a tight lipped smirk.

"Oh sure you did." He had a cocky grin on his face. "At least an angry and hungry human doesn't have to worry about accidentally killing someone when they get really starved."

I laughed. "I don't know about that, but no one ever pissed me off when I was hungry as a human so I never had to find out."

"Now that you're not going to rip my head off for criticizing you." He raised a brow and then smiled. "I'm guessing you're going to ask me to tell Silas to fuck off and train his own men now aren't you?"

"If you won't tell him to fuck off, I certainly don't have a problem with doing it." I smiled wickedly. "I've been waiting for a reason to do it just because he calls me 'little wicked one.'"

"He might take it better if it comes from you." Deiric rested his forehead against mine. "He'll just throw a fit if it comes from me."

"Then I'll come with you tonight." I locked eyes with him. "I could stand to learn how to compel people myself anyway."

"I was wondering when you'd ask me to teach you that."

I shrugged. "It didn't really seem relevant to learn when you're always with me and able to do it for me."

"And so long as there are assassins after you I'm pretty sure it's safe to say I'll *always* be there to do it for you, because I'm sure as shit not letting you out of my sight outside of the wards until we know there aren't any threats to your life." He turned back toward the manor and tugged me along with him. "We should get back. You have more training to do and I'm sure they're wondering why I ran off with you."

I rolled my eyes. "I'm sure that they have plenty of exciting theories as to why we ran off into the woods together."

"Surely they'd realize that if we were going to do *that* I would've just taken you to the bedroom." He pulled me along with him as he started to walk toward the manor. "And I know that at least Xander and Zane know precisely why we ran off out here. He sent Zane to come tell me about your… rather volatile mood and predicament." He glanced back at me with a smirk.

I scoffed. "Well, if he didn't *criticize* me, I doubt I would've been so volatile in the first place."

"You were even snippy with me last night, if you recall." Deiric said quietly. "Still, I was surprised you didn't join me in the bath until I looked out and found you sleeping so heavily that I don't even think the house falling apart would have woken you."

"I was tired." I said flatly.

"You were *exhausted.*" He clarified.

Chapter 17

Mira

I shifted us into the foyer of Silas' manor, and we were met immediately by Silas, Alaric, and a vampire I recognized almost instantly as the bastard who grabbed my elbow in the tavern with Deiric the night we met.

"You're late." Silas said, clearly annoyed. His arms were crossed over his chest, and he looked like he had a million things he'd rather be doing.

"I do have *other* things to do." Deiric replied, his tone just as icy and annoyed as Silas' was.

Silas' gaze shifted to me. "You don't usually accompany him when you shift him here. Surely you have better things to do this evening as well, little wicked one?"

I scowled and crossed my arms over my chest. "Of course I do, but you seem to enjoy ruining my plans, so I'll be tagging along this evening."

Silas smirked. "I'm sure I could offer far more exciting company for you tonight if you'd like."

Deiric was across the room in an instant, throwing Silas back against the wall just like he'd done the first time I met him, but this time was even more vicious. He had his hand at his throat, slowly but surely cutting off his windpipe. For a moment, I had to wonder if *he* needed to feed, given his propensity for violence right then.

"This is a little excessive don't you think." Silas managed to say despite Deiric's grip on him, and gripped his arm like his life depended on it. In some ways, it probably did. I made a mental note to demand that *Deiric* make sure he drank his fill from me when we were done this evening.

"I've had about enough of your suggestions and comments toward her." Deiric snarled.

"As fun as it would be to watch him rip you to shreds, Silas, I'm here to tag along *and* to let you know that he won't be coming back to do anymore training after tonight. So I don't need *more exciting company.*" I said calmly. "Let him go, Deiric. It's not worth the effort."

Deiric snarled and reluctantly released him, then slowly turned and walked back over to me. The vampire standing next to Silas just stared at me confused as hell to see me again, and I assumed his name was Alaster, since that's who Deiric was to be training. How I didn't encounter him any of the other times I'd come here I didn't know.

I guess I'm not the only one who might be a little cranky because they need to feed? I thought.

Deiric just shot me a quick glare, but turned around and stood facing Silas next to me again.

I smirked at Alaster. "Don't worry. I promise not to hold a knife to your throat tonight if you keep your hands to yourself."

He scowled in response, but didn't say anything.

Silas rubbed his throat and glared at me. He was about to open his mouth to speak, but I didn't give him the chance to.

"Before you open your mouth to say something that would probably indirectly insult Alaric, let me be very clear." I started and Silas raised a brow. "Alaric is perfectly capable of teaching them the same way that Deiric does. If you think I was stupid enough not to notice that he has the same abilities the last time I was here, you're sorely mistaken." I glanced at Alaric who merely smirked. "You only called on Deiric because he *used to be* on the same schedule as your lower ranking death dealers. He's not now. So after tonight, you're on your own."

"You don't get to tell me what I do with my men, and you certainly are not in charge of what Deiric does either." Silas snarled.

"Oh really? Don't I?" I let a wicked smile find its way to my lips. "Last I recall, I'm now an *Elder Mage*."

"You are *not* seriously pulling rank on me." Silas looked genuinely shocked, and I think for a moment he forgot I *was* actually higher ranked than he was.

"Do I need to?" I raised a brow at him and cocked my head.

He frowned. "Fine."

"Great. I'm glad that's settled."

Elias wandered through the foyer, undoubtedly on his way to go upstairs and retire for the evening. He smiled when he passed me. "I'm surprised you even let him come the first night." He mumbled, and continued on toward the stairs to the second floor. I guess he had been eavesdropping just off the main foyer.

"Alaric." I looked over at him. "Would you like to tag along so you can get a refresher for *how* Deiric trains, since Silas seems to think he's the best around?" I glanced back at Silas for a moment and rolled my eyes before fixing my gaze on Alaric once more.

"I suppose it wouldn't hurt." Alaric said with a flicker of amusement in his eyes.

"We should get going then." Deiric said flatly. He was still glaring at Silas. I reached over and slipped my elbow into his before I tugged him back toward the door as I turned to walk out of the manor. He finally relaxed some and turned to leave with me.

"Come on Alaster." I glanced over my shoulder at him. "I promise I won't bite," I said with a less than convincing smirk.

He grimaced and then begrudgingly followed us out the door, with Alaric in tow.

*

An hour later we were sitting in the corner of a local tavern, one I surprisingly hadn't been to before. I was sitting quietly, listening and observing while Deiric worked with Alaster. Alaric listened or gave some pointers as well. The tavern was practically filled beyond its limits, with almost each table occupied and very few open spaces by the bar.

I had my cloak tossed back over my shoulders, revealing the majority of my arms, which made me easily identifiable to anyone who knew the stories about me, but it was too hot with it being so busy in here to keep myself completely covered.

Alaster wandered to the bar to give compulsion a try on one of the women that seemed to be sitting alone. I couldn't tell whether or not he'd attempted to use it yet when I saw a large burly man walking up to them who looked *pissed.*

I shifted myself in his path before I could even think of what my plan was. I smiled up at him, and he jumped, clearly startled by my sudden appearance.

"Good evening." I said softly.

He scowled and went to move around me, but I stepped with him. He looked down and locked eyes with me. Now was as good a time as any, so I decided to give compulsion a try.

"Forgive me for the intrusion, but my friend really needs to practice some things. You're going to calm down and let him speak to that woman. He won't harm her." I *felt* it work, acting entirely off of instinct as I willed my intentions onto him.

His facial expression relaxed, as did his posture, and he nodded. I genuinely couldn't believe it actually worked, but I kept going.

"You will return to your seat now. If anyone asks, the man she's speaking to is just passing through and you decided she's fine to speak with him for as long as he'd like." I added.

He nodded and turned around to walk back to wherever it was he came from.

I turned around just in time to catch Alaster's surprised gaze fall on me. I smiled, then shifted back to the table with Deiric and Alaric.

"Did you just–?" Deiric started to ask.

"Yes." I smiled. "I think I did."

"That's mildly terrifying." Alaric said quietly. "Have you ever tried to compel *anyone* before?"

"Nope." I glanced over at him and my smile only widened.

"How?" He studied me for a moment and cocked his head to the side.

"I just acted on instinct, I guess." I shrugged. "I didn't really think about it too much and put all my energy into willing him to do what I was saying."

"Fascinating." Alaric mumbled with a faint glimmer of amusement drifting over his face, then looked back over to where Alaster was still *unsuccessfully* trying to compel the women.

"Is he usually this awful at it?" I asked.

Deiric chuckled. "Not everyone is so naturally *gifted* at it."

I glanced over at him, where he sat resting his chin on the back of his hands, with both elbows on the table. "Were you?"

He nodded. "For the most part, yes. Only took a few tries to get it right."

"For some reason that doesn't surprise me." I smirked and looked back at Alaster. It was sort of sad to watch him struggle. I was pretty certain even if compulsion *had* worked on me the first time I met him he would've failed miserably at it.

I heard tiny footsteps approaching from my right, and turned to see a child, no older than five or six approaching me. She was smiling, and giddy with excitement. Her long brown hair hung loose down her back, and she wore a very simple pink long sleeve shirt and thick brown pants. Her bright green eyes were wide as she approached.

I looked up beyond her to see her mother sitting at a table a few feet from us and casually watching. She was smiling, but her similar green eyes showed nothing but concern for the child. Like she had worn her down to allow her to walk over here, but she *really* didn't want her to.

Finally, the girl stopped less than a step away from where I was sitting. I heard Deiric shift beside me, and then felt his hand on the small of my back.

"You're Scáil." The little girl said with a smile.

I nodded. "I am."

"You're a sorceress!" She said excitedly and I nodded again. "Can you show me your magic?"

A small smile found its way to my lips. I was not a fan of children, generally, but something about how genuinely excited she was, and how innocent she seemed forced my hand. Before I could think the better of it, I had small wisps of shadow circling around her in various shapes, horses, stars, butterflies, and anything I could think of that a little girl might enjoy if she hadn't grown up being trained to be a fighter and a mage like I had. She giggled and spun around, looking at each shape like it was everything she'd ever dreamed of.

"There are so many songs and stories about you." She said when she finally stopped admiring the shadows and turned to face me again. "You're famous!"

I just chuckled. "So I've heard."

"You're not just a sorceress, though, right?"

I raised a brow. "Is there a song about that?"

She nodded excitedly. "You're a *vampire*!" Then she leaned in closer to me. "I don't see your fangs though. Is that song wrong?"

I blinked, and my smile faded. For a moment I was genuinely taken aback by her question. "It's not wrong." I said finally, after studying her for a few moments.

"Then where are your fangs?"

I glanced up at her mother for a moment, who was now just cautiously watching with not even a hint of a smile left on her face. I looked back down at the little girl in front of me. "I don't have them out all the time. If I show them to you, will you promise to go back to your mother and then *never* approach another sorceress or vampire again?"

She looked at me with nothing but confusion on her face, and cocked her head. "Why shouldn't I approach them?"

"They're not all as nice as me." I looked beyond her to her mother again, arching a brow and sending a slight disapproving frown in her direction, then back down to her. "And you need to tell your mother I said that too. Do you understand?"

She nodded.

"Is that a promise?"

"Promise!" She almost jumped with excitement and smiled.

I let my fangs out, and she jolted backwards as her eyes went wide. There wasn't any fear in her, just surprise. I relaxed and retracted my fangs. "Don't forget your promise."

She nodded and smiled. "It was nice to meet you." Then she turned and ran back to her mother.

I sat up and then leaned back against the back of my chair. Deiric's arm slipped around my shoulders. He leaned into me. "I didn't realize you were so good with children." He whispered in my ear.

"I'm really not." I said softly. "I tend to *avoid* children."

"So why did you do all of that for her then?"

"Would you rather I crush her spirit and tell her to fuck off?" I glanced over at him, nearly brushing noses with him because I didn't realize how close he was leaning into me.

"No." He smiled. "I just didn't expect you to humor all of her questions and requests."

I shrugged. "I was feeling generous today. And I've honestly never been approached like that before today so it caught me by surprise." I looked over at Alaric. "Are you alright to finish his training this evening? I'd like to get back to our manor and get a real night's sleep so I'm not as miserable tomorrow as I was this morning. My generosity in sharing my mate for your benefit is nearing its limit."

Alaric nearly spit out the sip of whiskey he had just taken and laughed. "Oh, certainly. I didn't even expect you to stay this long, to be completely honest."

"Great." I smiled. "Enjoy the rest of your evening." Then I shifted us to our bedroom, so we were sitting on the bed instead of the chairs we'd been sitting in at the tavern.

Before Deiric could move at all, I spun around, straddled him, and shoved him back on the bed. "Now." I smiled. "I'd like to get back to our *usual* routine and I think *you* need to feed before you're just as cranky as I was this morning."

A sultry smile made its way to his face. “In that case.” He pushed us up off of the bed and hooked my legs around his waist. “I think we should start in the bath.”

Chapter 18

Mira

Over the next several days, Adriana continued to improve in her individual training, and was coming close to where she might be able to do training with the others. Today, I had another idea in mind that would be equally as important for any of them.

We gathered outside of the manor. They all looked confused and frustrated that Liala, Eimear, and myself were waiting for them with a couple small sheets of paper in each of our hands.

“What exactly *are* we doing today?” Stella finally asked when she walked up and joined the group of them gathering in front of us.

"You're going to harvest herbs." Liala said with a smile.

"Harvest them?" Aodh asked. He looked a little more frustrated than the rest of them. His expression and general body language also suggested that he felt this sort of task might be beneath him.

"Yes." I smiled. "You know what the herbs are in the manor because they are all labeled. Now we're going to see if you can identify herbs in the woods and collect them for us."

"So this is a test?" Zemora asked.

"Yes." Eimear said and handed her a paper. "You're each going to get a list of herbs that you need to find and identify from memory. If you can't figure it out, after an hour, you can work together to find them."

"I don't understand why we'd need this sort of skill. We won't need to do simple spells like this." Sorcha protested and I handed her one of the sheets of paper I had.

"If you recall, I had to make a spell bag for Adriana to help with her nightmares, so you *will* actually have use cases for spell bags and lesser magics at some point in your life." I handed another paper to Adriana. "And this is also important because if you're ever out in the woods by yourself and something goes wrong, you need to know what's safe to eat, what's poisonous, what can help doctor wounds, and so on. It is an important life skill."

"Exactly." Liala said, and handed her papers to Stella and Gerald.

"Oh, and there's one more twist." I said with a smile, as the guys finally filed out of the house dressed in their fighting leathers and carrying all of their weapons.

"Oh gods." Stella mumbled.

"They are going to be out there hunting *you.*" I gestured toward them. "So you need to find and collect these herbs without getting caught too."

"What the fuck?" Gerald said. "They can literally *smell* us and probably hear us wherever we go. How is that fair?"

"*You* have magic, remember?" I asked. "You'll just have to get creative with how you use it to camouflage and hide yourselves."

"Don't worry, if we catch one of you we're just ordered to bring you back here to admit your failure and then you'll go out again and be off limits for the rest of us." Leo said with a wicked smile on his face. "It'll be fun."

"This doesn't sound fun at all." Stella mumbled.

"I like a challenge." Adriana said with a hesitant smile.

I glanced at her and couldn't hide the surprise on my face. "Good." I smiled. "We're giving you a ten minute head start. Best of luck."

Adriana ran off immediately without hesitation, and the others spent some time studying their lists first before they each slowly wandered into the woods.

"Are we *actually* giving them a 10 minute head start?" Renwick asked.

I nodded. "And, they're right. You are at a significant advantage so you're each going to carry one of these." I waved my hand and a spell bag hovered in the air in front of each of them. They all stared at them like they were poison.

"What exactly are those?" Zane pointed at it and looked both disgusted and intrigued.

"Spell bags to level the playing field a little bit." I walked over and plucked one out of the air. "You won't be able to track them by their scent while carrying these, and your hearing will be closer to that of a human."

"So you made spell bags that will weaken us?" Xander scowled.

"Not exactly." I tossed the one in my hand in the air and caught it. "Do you really think I'd *weaken* you?"

"Not being able to track them by their scent and hear as much as we can normally is a bit weakening if you ask me." Xander retorted and stepped away from the bag hovering in front of him.

"All you have to do is drop it and it loses its effect. It only works if you have it on you somehow, and it is only temporary."

"Fine." He said and grabbed the one intended for him.

I handed the one that I was holding to Leo. "Once you take yours you can go and hunt them."

Leo and Xander ran off into the woods in the blink of an eye. Zane, Renwick, and Deiric grabbed theirs and ran off after them.

"Who wants to have a drink?" I asked, and motioned back to the house.

Eimear and Liala smiled. "I'd love one. They'll be out there for hours." Eimear said.

"Give them a little credit." I smiled. "I say at least one of them comes back within an hour and has all the herbs. I'd put an entire bottle of whiskey on it."

"Betting Deiric's whiskey is a bold move." Liala chuckled. "I'll bet that only one of them finds their entire list, gets them all correct, and gets back before dark."

"Oh shit." Eimear laughed. "I guess we should've specified they need to come back by dusk."

I shrugged. "They'll give up if it takes them that long. What are you wagering, Liala?"

"Two bottles of mead." She started to walk toward the house. "What about you Eimear?"

"Just to spice things up, I will bet that two of the guys come back with one mage each before noon, but I don't think any of them will find the whole list." We walked together toward the front door. "I'll bet two bottles of whiskey."

*

We were all sitting on the front steps and at least one glass of whiskey deep by the time Adriana walked up to us, and to Eimear and Liala's surprise, she *just* made the hour mark of my bet.

"Impressive." Eimear smiled. "Let's see the list."

Adriana handed over her list, and her basket of herbs. She was supposed to locate purple dead nettle, yarrow, nightshade, mint, and mullein. Liala validated that all of the herbs were there.

"How did you evade the guys?" I asked, leaning back against the pillar holding up the porch roof and sipping on my second glass of whiskey.

"I put up a shield so that no one could hear me, and then I used the shadows of the trees along with my own to keep me hidden." She smiled. "Deiric almost found me, but I sent him the wrong way when I used a shadow to rustle some leaves."

I couldn't help but laugh. "I'm never going to let him live that down. Nice work."

"Did you bump into anyone else while you were out there?" Eimear asked, passing the basket up to me so I could sit it on the porch behind me.

"I saw Zemora and Stella, but no one else. They didn't say anything to me, but they aren't nearly as quiet going through the trees as I was. I wouldn't be surprised if you see them with one of the guys any minute now." She came over and hopped up onto the porch next to me, letting her legs dangle where there weren't any steps. "Now what?"

"Now, we wait and see if anyone else loses their bets." I smiled.

"You were betting on us?" Adriana's brows raised and she looked a little offended.

"Of course we were." Eimear chuckled. "I'm going to grab some mead. I don't think I should have any more of this whiskey."

"That's probably a good call." Liala laughed. "I am not sure you'll even need the mead though."

Eimear stood to go retrieve the mead and swayed. "Woah." She put her arms out to balance herself. "Okay, maybe I'll wait on the mead."

"Could I have some mead?" Adriana asked. "I was allowed to have some during parties at thc palace."

I shrugged. "Sure."

Eimear sat back down. "Just go ahead and grab it. It's in the cabinet in the den, to the right of the book shelves."

Adriana nodded, jumped up, and headed in the house to get the mead and a glass for herself.

About twenty minutes after she came back outside Deiric came back dragging Zemora along with him.

"Let me guess. This little game was a ploy to get the house to yourselves so you could do some day drinking?" He asked and rolled his eyes, finally releasing Zemora's basket so she could return to her search.

Zemora looked at us and scowled. "This is bullshit."

I narrowed my eyes at her and leaned forward. "This isn't bullshit. This is a genuine test. I didn't expect to see *you* get caught. Go find your herbs. I'll let the rest of them know you've already lost and that they don't need to drag you back here."

She scoffed and wandered back into the woods. I sent word mentally to the guys that she was off limits, but to still report to me if they saw her again.

Deiric chucked the spell bag at me. "You didn't answer the question."

"Technically, I *did* answer your question. It was a real test. Day drinking by ourselves was the perk. Adriana finished the list in an hour." I sat the spell bag on the floor behind me. "You're welcome to sit down and drink with us, since you've already done your part."

He walked up the steps and sat down next to me before snagging my almost empty glass and finishing it for me. "Since you're drinking *my* whiskey, it only seems appropriate that I join you."

"I think you mean *our* whiskey." I bumped him with my shoulder.

"And I think someone is cut off from *our* whiskey." He teased. "You're already buzzed."

"Only a little bit." I scoffed.

"Sure." He smiled and leaned into me, while he poured himself a glass.

Leo wandered out of the woods now, with Stella and Sorcha in tow. "These two were fighting over who knew what the herbs were." He rolled his eyes. "Stealthy apparently went out the window the moment the first hour was up."

"Congratulations Eimear." I smiled. "You bet correctly too. Well, partially anyway."

"What the hell?" Stella and Sorcha said in unison.

I shrugged. "Go find the rest of your herbs and come back when you either have them all or the sun is setting."

Leo chucked the spell bag he had at me. "Is this our reward for participating in this ridiculous challenge? Drinking?"

"If you want it to be." Deiric said with a smile. "Just don't drink it all, please."

Leo walked up the stairs and sat against the pillar opposite of Deiric and I after he poured himself a glass. "I'll never turn down a drink." He said with a smile.

Liala ended up being the only one who lost her bet completely. To her surprise, both Aodh and Gerald returned with all of their herbs without getting caught before dusk. Sorcha, Stella, and Zemora came back with some of their herbs, but not all of them. It was sort of sad, to me, that my newest understudy had outdone all of them, but at least she was making quick progress.

Chapter 19

Deiric

I waited in the foyer for Mira to come down so we could go to do an offering for the Morrigan. Renwick agreed to go with us this time. He walked down the stairs now and came to stand next to me.

"Is it really necessary for two of us to accompany her everywhere?" He grumbled. This was the first trip out he'd decided to come on, excluding all the monster hunting excursions before she transitioned. It wouldn't have mattered what my opinion of this was, but I did agree with Lazarus. This rule came directly from him and while I was technically his equal by rank there was no way in hell I would question him.

Renwick didn't know this came from Lazarus though, he thought it came from me, and I could hear him thinking I was an overprotective ass for forcing them to always tag along with Mira and I when we went out.

"Yes." I replied. I tried to keep the annoyance I felt from hearing his thoughts from my tone. They all knew I *could* hear what they were thinking but tended to forget, and I wasn't keen on reminding them lately either.

"And she doesn't mind having us follow her *everywhere?*" He asked, he wasn't going to drop it. "She doesn't find it a little overbearing or controlling?" I doubt he actually cared about what she thought. Though it seemed odd to volunteer himself this time only to complain.

"She hasn't ever complained about it." I said flatly. "Even if she did, I didn't make this decision."

"You're telling me the most powerful mage and mercenary *asked* for escorts?"

"No. I said she hasn't complained about it, and I didn't make the decision. Lazarus gave the order, she didn't protest, and I am *not* fighting him on it." I snapped at him, glancing in his direction with a glare that I was sure would shut him up.

"Oh." He said quietly with a hint of surprise on his face. I could hear the questions building up in his mind now. "Why?"

I turned to face him now. "She may be the most powerful mage and a formidable fighter but all it takes is one well placed stake." I said gravely. "We go along with her so we can keep an eye on *everything* around her while she does whatever it is she needs to do."

His brows rose slightly, like he forgot that's all it takes for any of us. The difference being, there were a lot of people who would want *her* dead specifically. The rest of us were meaningless to most people. After a few moments of his mind racing he finally just nodded and dropped it.

I turned and looked up the stairs when I caught her scent and heard her light footsteps in the hall. She glided down the stairs almost silently. She almost reached the bottom when a thunderous set of footsteps began to follow her. She paused and turned to look back up the stairs.

Adriana stopped at the top and stared down at her. "I'd like to go with you."

Mira let out an almost undetectable sigh and stared up at her for a few breaths. "It is probably better if you stay here."

I looked up at Adriana again, and she frowned. "Why?" She came down a few steps closer to Mira. "I would like to give the Morrigan an offering too."

Mira shifted on her feet, and her cloak fluttered like she was moving to cross her arms over her chest. "Do you even know what offerings I usually *give* to the Morrigan?" Her tone was curt and dismissive.

Adriana arched a brow and considered for a moment. "No, but I still want to go along."

I swear I could *feel* the aggravation that came with Mira's inevitable eye roll. "Fine." She finally mumbled under her breath, and then turned to walk down the remaining steps.

"Thank you!" Adriana said excitedly. "I'll go get my–"

Mira smirked and Adriana's cloak appeared on her shoulders. "Let's go." She said as she reached where Renwick and I were standing. Adriana ran down the remaining steps and stopped right next to Mira.

Mira tried to hold back a smile as she glanced at me, but failed miserably, then she shifted us to the temple.

"Wow." Adriana said softly as she looked around and took in the space. It was quite breathtaking. The covens spared no expense in building it. The marble statue of the goddess was beautiful, and all of the decorations and carvings on the walls of the large circular space were equally as impressive.

Mira turned away from us without another word and walked up to the large stone bowl that was placed in front of the statue of the Morrigan at the back of the space. The torches were lit and constantly burning with magic, but the candles around the altar did not remain lit at all times.

Mira pulled her hands out of her cloak and with a flick of both wrists fire flickered to life on each wick. Adriana walked over to stand at her side just a step or two behind her and watch.

Renwick and I stood in the doorway, blocking it entirely, shoulder to shoulder. He faced outside and I watched Mira and Adriana.

Mira drew her sword from the sheath under her cloak and I could feel the anxiety from Adriana. Mira switched her sword to her left hand, to cut her right palm. A change she'd made after that first offering where she ended up with the tattoo on her left hand.

She held her hand over the bowl and carefully cut open her palm, letting blood drop into the stone bowl. As she did so, Adriana started to take a step back, but then thought the better of it and stepped next to Mira instead.

Mira removed the blade from her hand and let it heal, before looking down at Adriana.

The princess didn't hesitate, and held her right hand out. Mira just quietly shook her head, and then handed the blade to Adriana. "If you're going to give her an offering, you're cutting your own hand."

I could visibly see Adriana wince, but she took the sword from Mira and stepped just slightly in front of her when she stepped back to make room. She lifted her left hand now, and very carefully sliced her palm over the bowl. She let out a small hiss of pain, but otherwise was silent.

I had to admit I didn't think she'd have it in her to do this sort of offering. I thought she'd pass out at the sight of the blood from Mira. I never thought she'd willingly slice her own palm. She didn't seem to stop surprising any of us with her curiosity and general resilience.

A few quiet moments passed before Mira reached up to grab Adriana's left wrist. "That's enough." She waved her right hand over Adriana's palm and the cut healed with a flash of white light. Then Mira took her sword back and sheathed it at her side. Adriana stepped back so she was once again one step behind Mira.

Mira mumbled the prayers she always said to the Morrigan quietly, and then bowed low at her waist. Adriana followed suit. As always, with these offerings, a phantom wind swept through the space and blew out the candles, taking the offering with it like the goddess flew through the space to collect it.

Mira and Adriana rose together, and then she turned to walk back to us.

"That's it?" Adriana asked, turning with her and following as she walked over to us.

"That's it." Mira smirked. "Sometimes she comes and speaks to me, but I guess she doesn't have anything to say today."

When they reached us, Mira shifted us back without another word.

"Thank you for letting me come." Adriana said with a small smile and then ran back upstairs.

"She's interesting." Renwick mumbled.

Mira barely glanced at him. "She was raised by people who know nothing of magic. She's figuring it out." She turned and looked up the stairs to where Adriana had run off to. "I'm surprised she didn't pass out."

I chuckled. "I was sure she was going to the moment you sliced your hand."

She looked back at me and smiled. "I guess neither of us gives her enough credit. She barely flinched when she cut her palm."

Renwick shrugged and walked up the stairs, leaving just the two of us alone in the foyer. Everyone else had already gone to bed and Lazarus' men were quietly chatting in the dining room before two of them would head out to their posts for the evening.

"Have you finished the journal yet?" I asked her. I hadn't seen her reading it since that evening when I came home so late, and she hadn't mentioned it since.

"Almost." She smiled, stepped closer to me, and slipped her arms up around my neck. "Why?"

"What did you think of it so far?" I smiled down at her and slipped my arms under her cloak and around her waist.

"I think that it is an interesting first person account of interactions with dragons and riding one. Where did you get it?"

I shrugged, slightly avoiding the question. "I have had it for a while."

She arched a brow. “I didn’t see it among all the others in the den. Where was it all this time?”

I gave her a confused look, that I hoped she didn’t see through. “It’s been in the den. You must’ve just missed it.”

The look in her eye said she didn’t believe a word I’d said, but she didn’t press me for more details. “Are there other books I… missed?” She asked, arching a brow again and staring up at me with a little more suspicion.

I shrugged again. “I’ll look again when you finish this one and see if I can find another you might like.” I said with a smile.

She stood on her toes and pulled me down into a kiss. “You are an awful liar.” She mumbled. “I guess it's a good thing that I find some secrets more alluring than annoying.”

I smiled and pulled her into me, pressing another more passionate kiss to her lips. She let out a soft moan and shifted us to our bedroom.

Chapter 20

Mira

A few more days passed where we did different variations of training in the mornings and sparring in the afternoons. As the mages figured out their magic they started to learn hand to hand combat, and then they were allowed to partake in the sparring when they were ready.

Adriana's training was coming along well. She was able to summon different forms of shadow, and make it move in the way she wanted it to. Zemora's aim began to improve with her vines, and she could keep them up and moving off the ground for much farther than she could when she first started practicing.

Aodh and Gerald were nearing a point where they were becoming masters with their magic. In a few more days, I planned to give them both their respective tattoos, marking their magic and mastery of it. They were probably the quickest studies, but they had been working on their magic discretely before they came to us too, so that came as no surprise.

We were all sparring when Garrick shifted in front of the steps leading up to the manor. Deiric and I stopped almost immediately when I saw him and he walked over to us.

"I just thought I'd check in on how Adriana's training was going, and I also received this today." He handed a scroll over to me. I opened it. It was a summons from the king. "He wants her to come to the palace tomorrow so he can see for himself how well her training has been going."

"It's only been a couple of weeks since we brought her here." Deiric said, reading the summons over my shoulder. "He already wants to call her back to the palace to check on her?"

I looked up at Garrick and he shrugged. "They don't know how all of this works, so I guess they're just worried." He paused, and took the scroll back after I rolled it up. "Either way, we can't decline a request from the king. Would you like me to accompany you, or do you feel comfortable taking her there on your own?"

"I think we can go on our own. I feel like bringing a full entourage with us everytime will become more of a problem than it's worth." I glanced over to where Adriana sat watching Zane and Xander spar. "Unless you feel otherwise?" I met his gaze again.

"I think you're probably right." He looked at Deiric, then back at me. "Do you all need anything? Are the other mage's coming along well?"

"We don't need anything that I know of." Deiric said.

"The other mages' training is coming along well." I smiled. "Gerald and Aodh are close to mastering their magic already. The others are moving along a little slower, but they'll get there."

He nodded. "I'll let you know if we find out about any others in need of training. In the meantime, let me know if you need any help with anything. Our next meeting is next week. We'll meet at Aris' manor, as always."

I nodded. "I'll make sure I'm there."

He shifted away.

Adriana came running over almost immediately. "What was that about?" She must have seen the scroll and recognized it as having come from the palace.

"We've been summoned to the palace tomorrow at noon." Deiric explained. "They want to check on the status of your training."

She frowned. "I guess that means I have to go with you."

"I think it would be a bad idea for us to go without you even if you weren't explicitly mentioned on the request." I said softly. "Surely it can't be *that* awful to go back just so they can see how you're doing?"

She shrugged. "I'd rather just stay here, but I'll let Esme know. She'll probably dress me up in a more formal gown just to appease them. They wouldn't like seeing me in this." She gestured down to the blouse, corset, and skirt she was wearing.

"I guess that means *I* should probably find something nicer too." I smiled.

"Knowing them, I would say you should." She said flatly, and then turned and walked back over to sit with Zemora and watch Zane and Xander spar.

“She really doesn’t seem to want to be at the palace at all.” Deiric said quietly. “I wonder what sort of hell it must be living with someone as miserable as Ronan.”

“I get the feeling it isn’t just Ronan that is the problem.” I watched her for a few moments before I turned and looked at him. “I am guessing that life as a royal isn’t all it's cracked up to be. Especially for her.” I took a few steps back and lowered into a fighting stance again. “We can worry about that later.” I raised my sword and motioned for him to come for me. “Let’s get back to sparring.” I said with a smile.

Deiric also took a step back and lowered into a fighting stance before lunging at me with his sword again.

*

I sent Macha with a note for Lazarus after we finished sparring yesterday stating that we’d need him to come along for an audience with the king today. I offered to shift him here, but he arrived first thing in the morning on his own without having sent any response at all other than shooing Macha off and saying he’d be here.

I put on a simple sleeveless black gown with a slit up the right side, the choker Deiric had gifted me, and the dagger on my thigh. Deiric and Lazarus wore their formal tunic and pants, and Adriana wore an absurdly formal silk and chiffon navy gown with similar puffy sleeves to the one she’d worn when she came back here with us weeks ago. When we were all ready, I shifted us to the palace foyer.

Chapter 21

Deiric

We arrived in the foyer and the shadows that usually appeared around us when she shifted us had barely dissipated when the sound of the soft clunk from the firing of crossbows filled the air around us, followed by a strangled cry from Mira. None of us even had the chance to get our bearings before they fired at us, though Mira sounded like she was the only one of us who got hit.

Adriana screamed as Mira stumbled backward. I could just barely make out the prince standing a few feet in front of Mira with a murderous smile on his face and three men standing behind him holding crossbows.

I growled, but before I could even step forward and catch her, she began to shift us away. Then, like her magic simply gave out mid-shift we practically dropped from the sky and landed in the woods. Mira collapsed back between

Lazarus and I, and Adriana, who had dropped to her knees when we fell, was reaching for her.

Lazarus and I knelt down next to her and I couldn't quite believe what I was seeing. A combination of rage and panic welled up in me so quickly I could barely think straight. It was clear they didn't intend to kill her. Each stake narrowly missed her heart, but they were right around it. One above and two on either side of her heart.

She was weakly reaching for the stakes in her chest, trying to pull them out and not succeeding while she struggled to breathe beyond the stake above her heart. Gods only knew what else it had severed or what damage it had done. The pain and panic in her eyes when she met my gaze almost broke me. She was getting weaker with each second we wasted staring at her, trying to determine what to do. She grabbed my tunic with her left hand, but her grip faltered and her hand fell almost as soon as she grasped it. She seemed like she blacked out.

Lazarus growled and cursed, each word that left his mouth was worse than the last. I looked up and looked around us. We were in the woods, but we didn't get far from the palace or the city surrounding it.

I grabbed the stake at the top of her chest and ripped it out, hoping that would help her breathe and regain consciousness, but when I did she *didn't* heal. Blood poured out of her chest and she nearly choked on the blood coming out of her mouth even while seemingly unconscious.

"Why isn't she healing?" Adriana asked, panic rising with her voice. She'd learned enough in her time with us that Mira should've healed nearly instantly.

I turned her on her side, toward me, so she wouldn't choke and tried to put pressure on the gaping hole in her chest to stop the bleeding.

Lazarus reached over and pulled a dart from her neck, which had been hidden by her hair. He sniffed it.

"Dead man's blood." He snarled. "Fuck."

"She needs a healer." I looked at Adriana. "She showed you how to heal didn't she?"

She just stared at Mira in silence. I hadn't watched much of their training, but I thought that was usually one of their first lessons.

"Adriana!" I shouted desperately trying to get her to break out of the shock I was sure she was slipping into. "Tell me she taught you how to heal. She can't heal with dead man's blood in her system and if we don't do something soon she's going to bleed out."

Her eyes finally met mine and she shook her head. "I– She was going to teach me that soon, but we hadn't gotten to it yet. Is she going to die?" I knew they hadn't even begun practicing or learning shifting yet, so we were stuck here, or stuck with trying to run Mira somewhere.

"Stand up." Lazarus demanded, looking at Adriana now with the same amount of rage that I felt, but there was no panic in his face.

"What?" She asked.

"Stand. The fuck. Up." Lazarus snarled, and then practically yanked her up to her feet without even giving her a moment to obey. In a movement so swift I was sure she didn't even register it, he sliced most of her skirts off with his sword and returned to a kneeling position next to Mira.

"We'll use this to stop the bleeding as much as we can until we can get her somewhere safe." He said with deadly calm. He nearly ripped her from my arms and wrapped the fabric around her chest. "We need to take the other two stakes out. We can't risk moving her at speed when they're so close to her heart and we sure as shit can't stay here much longer."

He looked up and looked around us. "My manor is the closest one to this godforsaken city. Elias and Silas should be arriving any minute now with nightmages they've gathered up for me. Do you remember how to get there?"

I just nodded.

"Good. As soon as I pull the other stakes out, I'm going to wrap the rest of this around her and you're going to take her and run like *hell* to get there. Do you understand me?"

Again, all I could do was nod. I'd seen her near death before, but nothing quite like this. Nothing when I couldn't just give her my blood and heal her. With the gaping hole in her chest, she couldn't even *drink* from me to heal herself.

He looked at Adriana. "If she bleeds out she won't die but she'll be comatose until we can get her to feed, which she won't be able to do if she can't heal because of where they've staked her." He looked at me again and I'd forgotten she even *asked* if Mira was dying. "I'll carry Adriana and be right behind you. Ready?"

I nodded, rolled her onto her back between us, and he yanked both remaining stakes out, then wrapped the remaining shreds of fabric around her to stop as much of the bleeding as he could. It barely seemed to make a difference, but I scooped her up into my arms and took off, without looking back to see if he had Adriana and was moving behind me.

Every second that passed while I ran with her felt like an eternity. By the time I reached his manor and passed through their wards she had bled through the makeshift bandages and her blood had soaked both of us. I smashed through the front doors of his manor without thinking or caring about anyone inside who might not have daylight rings. I ran into the dining room and laid her on the table.

The vampires that were in there at that moment all jumped up from the table, swords drawn for a half a second before they realized who I was, then relaxed. I rolled her on her side, hoping that would at least prevent her from drowning in her own blood, though at this point I figured that was the least of our concerns.

"What the fuck is going on?" Darragh shouted as he appeared beside me less than a second later. As if on cue, Lazarus arrived behind us and sat Adriana down.

"What the hell happened?" Darragh demanded, spinning around to face Lazarus.

"We were ambushed." Lazarus snarled. "Have Elias and Silas arrived with the newest set of nightmages?"

"No." Darragh said. "Not yet."

More of Lazarus' men gathered in the dining room now and I could see the shock and confusion on their faces. Despite that I assumed several of them were still new, they didn't seem to react at all to the blood, though I don't think any of us would go particularly crazy over the blood of our *own*.

"She's already bled through what we tried to bandage her with. We need to slow the bleeding until we can get a healer." I said, more of an order than a statement. Darragh and another vampire rushed out of the room.

"Yarrow." Adriana said. "We need Yarrow." I locked eyes with her for a moment, only willing to take my gaze off of Mira for a second, but I saw her turn to Lazarus. "Do you have any?"

I didn't hear him respond, but she stormed out of the house as she spoke. "I will find some." It seemed she'd snapped out of her shock long enough to think straight again.

Darragh and the other vampire returned with towels and bandages. They ripped off the shards of fabric we had placed on her and began to wipe away what they could before wrapping and bandaging her. I helped by putting pressure on the wounds while they diligently and quickly wrapped her tightly with whatever supplies they had. By this point, there was blood *everywhere*. I began to wonder if she had lost too much already.

A few agonizing minutes passed before Adriana returned to the room with her hands full of the plant she asked Lazarus for. I watched her walk past us and into the kitchen where she dug through the cabinets until she found whatever she was looking for and began to grind the plants down before she came back to the table.

"This will help slow the bleeding more until they get here." She explained, and motioned toward Mira. "Can you help me put this under the bandages?"

I nodded, and lifted each compress we'd put on. She placed a handful of the herb on each of her wounds, being careful to make sure we kept her on her side.

Her breathing was so shallow and erratic, and so slow I almost questioned it a few times. Lazarus sent one of his men to get Elias and Silas sooner, but I didn't know if they'd actually make it there before Elias and Silas arrived on their own.

After what felt like an eternity of just watching her to make sure she was still breathing Elias and Silas finally showed up with the nightmages they had been planning to bring today. The moment they arrived Silas ran to this room and cursed.

"What the hell happened?" He asked me, his face was paler than I'd ever seen it.

"We were ambushed."

"Elias!" Silas shouted, and the archmage walked into the room.

"Fuck's sake. Is she *alive*?" Elias asked, rushing over to her.

"Barely." Lazarus' voice was barely a whisper from where he stood behind me again. "She's lost way too much blood."

At some point he had stepped away to show Adriana to a room where she could clean herself up and I hadn't even heard him return. Adriana had been drenched in Mira's blood and covered in dirt from searching through the woods for the plant.

"I can see that." Silas mumbled under his breath.

Without hesitation, Elias came to stand at the head of the table and began to work on healing her. The nightmages wandered into the room slowly and some of them looked like they might simply keel over at the sight. There was still blood everywhere. I was soaked in it, and so were her clothes, all of her really.

"How did they do this to her?" Silas breathed, watching carefully as Elias worked on her.

"Vervain soaked stakes and dead man's blood." My voice was cold, harsher than I think Silas had ever heard it. He stiffened where he stood.

"How did they even know to *use* that?" He snarled.

"I'm not sure, but I intend to find out." Lazarus cut in before I had the chance to. His voice was like ice. "They shot at her as soon as we arrived, before the shadows from her shifting us there had the chance to fully clear. None of us saw it coming. Suffice to say the king's summons for Adriana was a trap, it actually came from the prince."

There were a few moments of silence among us, aside from the shuffling of fabric as Elias worked to heal her.

"They didn't shoot to kill." I finally said. "They missed her heart on purpose, three stakes, right around it with deadly precision." I reached out and gently held her hand. Her breathing was a bit steadier, but still too shallow. Elias had one more wound to heal. "The dart of deadman's blood must have hit her the moment she tried to shift us out. We didn't make it very far before her magic gave out."

There was a lot of chaotic tapping on the window to my left, and I looked over to see Macha frantically battering against it. I motioned to it, and Silas walked over to open the window.

The raven flew in and landed by her head, impatiently prancing around and examining her. She eyed me for a moment, and then settled down next to Mira, resting herself against Mira's shoulder and neck. The sight of her must've startled and unnerved some of the vampires in the room, because they all shuffled backward and some left.

"I've healed her wounds, but I can't do anything about the vervain or dead man's blood." Elias explained. "That will have to work its way out on its own at this point." He looked around the room for just a moment. "Perhaps it wouldn't be a bad idea to have a sorcerer at these manors, so there's a healer available in case one is needed?" He suggested, looking up over me at Lazarus.

"We rarely need one, but if they're using shit like this I think it might be wise to have one now." Lazarus replied. "We'd just need to make sure that the fledgelings couldn't get to whoever is assigned here."

"We should get her back to your manor Deiric." Elias said. "The further from that gods forsaken prince we can get her, the better. I can shift you."

I stood and nodded. Adriana appeared in the doorway.

"Is she alright?" She asked softly.

"She will be." Elias gave her a half smile that didn't meet his eyes. "Shall we?"

"I'll be coming along." Lazarus walked up behind me. "I just want to make sure she wakes up and recovers alright."

I reached out and scooped her into my arms. Lazarus mumbled something to Darragh, and then Elias shifted us all back to my manor.

I swore for a moment when we arrived at the manor her eyes fluttered open up at me, but she didn't move otherwise. When we walked in the front door we were surrounded almost immediately by Zane, Xander, Leo, and Renwick smelling her blood and asking what happened.

I ignored them all and walked her up to our bedroom. Liala caught up with me while the rest of them stayed with Lazarus, Silas, Elias, and Adriana slinging question after question that I didn't care to answer.

"Let me help you." Liala said softly. "You *both* need to get cleaned up."

I kept walking, and the moment I tried to open the door to the room she grabbed my arm.

"Deiric." Her voice was stern.

I looked at her. "I've got her. Just give me a few minutes."

She frowned and opened the door for me, let me walk in with her, and then shut it behind us. I carried her into the bathing room and laid her gently on the floor so I could wash the blood off of my arms. Then I knelt down next to her, bit my wrist and held it to her mouth to try to get her to feed, hoping that might bring her back sooner and negate the effects of the dead man's blood and vervain.

A few moments passed by and nothing happened, but then finally she stirred and bit my wrist herself. My shoulders sagged with relief and I leaned my forehead against hers. "Thank the gods." I mumbled.

When she finally stopped drinking and opened her eyes she threw her arms around me. I dropped back so I was sitting on the floor and wrapped both arms around her before pulling her into my lap. I rested my chin on her head.

"Are you alright?" I asked softly.

She squeezed me a little bit harder, but didn't reply. It was a ridiculous question. She was obviously physically okay, but the gods only knew what that experience did to her mentally and emotionally.

"We should get you cleaned up." I whispered after a few minutes.

Lazarus walked into our room, without knocking, and walked over to where I sat leaning back against the wall with her.

"Is she alright?" He asked.

"No." She said into my chest. "I'm not alright."

"Physically. Are you alright, physically?" He knelt down next to us. His voice was softer than I think I'd ever heard it. Like he was worried he would break her.

I looked over at him and I don't think I've ever seen him actually, genuinely, look concerned before, not like that. I didn't even think he was capable of caring for another being in any way anymore. He always seemed so indifferent.

She shifted her head against me so she could look at him. "Physically, I think I am okay."

"Good." He said quietly. "Get yourself cleaned up. Adriana is a mess and demanding to see you."

"I don't want to see *anyone* right now." She mumbled, and turned her face back into my chest.

Lazarus sighed. "I'll relay the message, but I don't know if she'll listen." He stood back up and then walked back out of the room, closing our bedroom door behind him.

"I can go out and stop her from coming in, if you want me to." I offered.

"You are not going anywhere." Her voice was muffled by my shirt, but I could hear her breaking.

"Mira." I said softly, and kissed her head. "At least let me get you cleaned up."

She sighed, and pulled back enough that she could look at me. Tears streamed down her face, and I'd never seen her so broken. "I'm going to kill them all." Her voice wavered, but behind the wariness, there was murder in her eyes.

"I think you'll have to get in line." I tried to offer her a half smile, but that only made that look in her eyes more intent.

"They are *mine*." She growled. "You and Lazarus can get in line behind *me*."

I just nodded. I could give her that, if she needed it. "Will you let me help you get you cleaned up now?"

She nodded.

I shifted her so she was sitting on the floor just long enough for me to get my feet under me and then lift her up. I sat her in the tub, unstrapped the dagger from her thigh, cut off her dress, and then carefully removed the choker I'd given her, which somehow managed to make it through this whole ordeal without getting a single drop of blood on it.

I walked over and locked our bedroom door, filled up the tub, stripped off my own blood soaked clothes, and got in with her before gently cleaning all of the blood off of her and helping her wash it all out of her hair. Thankfully, Adriana respected her wishes and *didn't* disturb us.

Chapter 22

Mira

I woke up later than usual with my arm across Deiric's waist and my head on his chest. He was already awake and gently running his fingers through my hair.

"Good morning, love." He said softly and leaned down to kiss my head.

I sighed and squeezed him gently with my right arm. "Good morning." I mumbled.

"We don't have to get up now, but at somc point we're going to need to get out of bed so you can prove to Adriana that you're okay."

I shifted my head so I was resting my chin on his chest and could look at him. "Does she really *need* reassurance?"

He smiled, but it didn't reach his eyes. "She spent half the night sitting outside of the locked door worrying about you, so yes." He paused and studied me for a few breaths. "I could hear her thoughts racing. I doubt she got any sleep last night."

I groaned and laid my head back down on his chest. "She's probably traumatized."

"You lost a lot of blood, Mira." He whispered. "What she saw would have seriously messed up even some of *us*, let alone a princess who likely has never seen any real injuries in her life."

"That will make the king happy." I said sarcastically. "I traumatized his poor daughter."

"You didn't traumatize her. Ronan and whoever he had there to incapacitate you did." He said sternly. "None of that was your fault."

"Why didn't they just kill me?" I couldn't help but ask. It didn't make sense. And just killing me would've been a hell of a lot more merciful and less painful I was sure.

"I have no idea." His voice was barely a whisper and he sighed. "I'm glad they didn't though."

"I don't know if I share the same thoughts on that."

He moved so he was laying next to me and held my face so he could look me right in the eye. "Do not *ever* think that way." His eyes were wide with worry and steely determination.

"I was helpless." Tears welled in my eyes. "That whole time, I was awake but completely unable to move." I tried to blink away the tears and look away from him but he held my face so I couldn't. "Death." I said softly. "Death would've been more merciful than that hell."

He frowned, and he looked like I'd just ripped out his heart. "I'm so sorry, Mira." He kissed my forehead. "I can't imagine what that was like for you, but I will not let *anyone* do that to you, ever again. I'd rather die than lose you. You are… everything to me. If I could've taken those stakes myself I would have, rather than watch you go through that."

I put my hands over his. "I'm sorry. I just…" My voice trailed off. I didn't even know how to explain what I felt at the moment. If anything like that was ever done to him I would rip them to shreds without a second thought.

"I love you, Mira."

"I love you too."

"I don't know what they wanted to do with you, or what their plan was for any of us after that, but we'll figure it out. And I can promise you that I'll *never* let that happen again. No matter what I have to do."

I nodded.

"Now let's get up and go show Adriana you're alright before she takes up her post outside of our bedroom door again." He half smiled, but it didn't reach his eyes, which still glimmered with concern.

"Alright." I said softly and started to get out of bed.

*

When we walked downstairs Adriana jumped up from the table and ran over to me the moment she saw me. She threw her arms around me in a hug and breathed a sigh of relief. It took all the self control I had not to flinch, and I certainly didn't return the gesture. There were few people I allowed *this* close to me.

"Thank the gods you're alright." She said excitedly. "When you didn't come out of your room last night I was so worried."

"I heard."

"Are you alright? Like, fully healed and okay?" She said quickly, releasing me and standing back to look at me like she could see through my clothes and see whatever injuries I might still have.

"Yes, I'm fully healed." I offered a small smile, but I know it didn't reach my eyes.

Her face dropped. "You're not really alright, are you?"

"I'll be fine." I assured her, with a tightlipped smile. "I promise."

She frowned. "Don't make a promise that you don't even look like you're going to keep." She studied me for a few moments. "You're *not* fine." She said, her tone laced with a small amount of concern.

"Your brother will *not* be fine if I get my hands on him." I thought maybe if I changed the subject she'd drop it. I wasn't fine, and I couldn't wait for the day I got to get my revenge on him for this, but I didn't want to talk about it more than I had to.

She didn't even bat an eye. "He'll deserve whatever comes to him." She said coldly. "He *pretends* to care about me in front of the king, but truthfully he would probably have killed *me* too."

She called him the *king*, not her father. That was a snippet of information I would save to dig more into later. "You don't care for him at all?" I asked.

She shook her head. "He is a bastard. Quite honestly, after what he did to you, I'd like to kill him myself."

I studied her for a moment. “Are you alright?” I finally asked. This didn’t seem like the same naive and innocent teenager I’d been working with before the ambush.

“We’re not talking about how I am.” She said very matter of factly. “We’re talking about how *you* are.”

“I’d rather not talk about that experience anymore than I already have.”

“Do you remember any of it?” She asked.

“I remember *all* of it.” I looked past her to where Lazarus now stood behind her in the foyer. “I was awake for all of it. I just couldn’t move.”

Lazarus frowned. “I was afraid of that.” He glanced behind me at Deiric for a half a second before looking back at me. “I honestly hoped you lost so much blood that you actually blacked out.”

“I wasn’t that lucky.” I said coldly. I looked down at Adriana again and she was as pale as a ghost. “Good thinking with the Yarrow.” I said with another half smile. “I don’t know if it made much difference, but it’s good to know you remembered something from everything we’ve taught you so far.”

“You–” she started.

“Yes.” I replied before she could finish her sentence. “Now, if you don’t mind, I’d rather not have to relive it again, so can we move on please?”

Her jaw dropped open like she might speak, but then she closed it. She opened her mouth again, but thought the better of it and closed it.

I gave her one more moment of staring at me before I stepped around her and walked toward the kitchen to get some tea. “Shouldn’t you be training with the others?” I asked her over my shoulder as I walked away.

"Yes, but–"

"No buts." I said flatly. "Go train with Liala."

She gave me an exasperated sigh and stormed off to the back room of the manor to join the rest of them for training. If I let her, I imagined she'd sit by me for the rest of the day just to make sure I was actually okay. And I certainly didn't need someone fussing over me anymore than Deiric likely already had been or would be.

I poured myself a cup of tea and turned around to go sit at the table. When I sat down, Lazarus sat down across from me and Deiric took the seat next to me.

"I'm staying here." Lazarus said. "Darragh can handle things in my absence."

I looked up at him and started to open my mouth to protest when Deiric cut me off.

"Not that you need my permission," he started, "but you can stay as long as you want." Lazarus nodded. "We'll find a room for you. I'm sure since Zane and Liala seem to spend more time in Zane's room, we could give you Liala's at least temporarily."

Lazarus nodded and then locked eyes with me. "You are not shifting *anywhere* but our manors unless someone else arrives first or you're shifting to someplace in the middle of nowhere and no one is expecting you." The look on his face said that this wasn't up for debate. This was a rule he was setting here and now and I didn't have any say in the matter.

I just nodded.

He raised a brow. "That was easier than I thought."

"I'd rather not shift anywhere after that. You're not going to get an argument from me." I took a sip of my tea. "I wouldn't wish that experience on my worst enemy. Although, actually, if I'm being honest, I'd want to do worse to him. So I take that back. That is *exactly* what I would wish on my worst enemy if I wanted to break them to their core."

He just frowned. "We will need to figure out why they didn't just kill you." He looked over at Deiric. "I don't even have a guess as to what that was about. Didn't you say he seemed to just want to exterminate all of us?"

Deiric nodded. "They must need her for something, I just don't know what. He's clearly not working alone, so maybe whoever he's working with wanted her for something."

"Three stakes was a bit of overkill, don't you think?" Leo walked in and sat down next to Lazarus.

"I'm sure that was the prince's idea." I said flatly. "If he had to incapacitate me or capture me for someone, why not do it with the most torture and pain possible?"

"Still, that's… a little excessive." Leo said, his nose wrinkled with disgust.

I huffed a laugh. "No, that was a very clear message to show how much he hates us and how easy it would be to kill us. And let me tell you, message-fucking-recieved. Loud and clear." They all sank a little bit in their seats, and frowned. I sighed, put my elbows on thc table, rubbed my face for a few moments with both hands, and then just rested my face in my hands.

Deiric gently put his hand on my back. "We're not going to let that happen again."

"That's not going to fix the fact that they did it in the first place." I said coldly, my voice slightly muffled by my hands. "And you know damn well that the king *will* summon us himself at some point. We can't avoid it forever."

"We could just send Adriana with Devlon and Garrick." Leo offered.

"No." I shook my head and lifted it from my hands. "She doesn't go anywhere without us. Not until we figure out why he wanted to incapacitate me instead of kill me, and what he planned to do to her after that." I stared into my tea.

"Fine." Lazarus said. "We'll figure it out. For now, just use today to rest."

I looked up at him and he glanced over at Deiric.

"You make sure she actually uses today for *rest*." He said to Deiric.

"I'm–"

"No. I don't care if you're fine. I don't care if you're stronger than you've ever felt." Lazarus locked eyes with me and it felt like he was staring straight into my soul. "You need to take some time and relax, process what just happened, and collect yourself. You don't just go through something like that and pretend it didn't happen."

I just nodded. Nothing I could say would change his mind and I certainly wasn't in the mood to really argue.

Chapter 23

Mira

I was outside with Adriana the next morning reviewing what she had learned so far. I could hear Deiric and Lazarus discussing what their spymasters had uncovered about Ronan.

I sent word to Devlon and Garrick this morning, notifying them of what happened two days ago and letting them know that we would *not* be accepting any summons from the king from this point forward unless we could be absolutely certain it was truly from the king.

I did leave out a lot of important details though, like *how* they nearly killed me. And I specifically made sure to mention that we were not going to go to the king with Ronan's involvement just yet. We needed to gather more information and proof. I was certain the King wouldn't just accept that his son had attacked his daughter's magic tutor without any real evidence.

Zemora finally made her way outside to continue working on seeing how far she could stretch the limits of her magic. How long she could stretch out a vine through the air before it dropped and she lost control of it.

"Nice work." I said to Adriana. "Keep practicing summoning the different types of shadow. I'll be back in a few minutes to work on shifting."

She gave me a half smile, which I could see through the shadows that surrounded her now, then she nodded.

I turned and walked over to Zemora, moving so quietly she didn't hear me approach.

"Late start this morning?" I asked when I stopped behind her. I had most of them practicing independently when I worked with Adriana, and that allowed them to choose their own schedule to some extent.

She jumped and the vines she'd been playing with fell to the ground. She spun around to look at me.

I chuckled. "You need to be a *little* bit more aware of your surroundings."

"How do you do that?" She all but shouted in frustration.

"Do what?" I asked coyly and crossed my arms over my chest.

Her posture straightened and her lips formed a tight line. She looked at me for a moment disapprovingly. "How do you move so *silently*?" She seethed.

"I'm a vampire. I'm *supposed* to move silently." I smirked rather smugly and shifted my weight, cocking a hip out. "*You* should be more aware of your surroundings for any being. What would you have done if an enemy came up behind you just as silently?" I asked, leaning slightly forward toward her. "Jumped and abandoned your magic?"

She snorted and her brows furrowed in further frustration while her stance shifted to mimic mine. "I'm not training for *battle*."

I heard Deiric chuckle from where he and Lazarus were still standing in the shade of the manor.

"Not *yet*." I replied. "But you will be learning proper self defense, which is not far off from training for *battle*." I snapped back at her. I tried to keep my tone more mocking than truly annoyed, but my patience was thin today.

She scoffed. "I may be forced to learn how to wield a blade and partake in the savagery that passes for entertainment among you all, but I have no interest in ever fighting anyone." She uncrossed her arms and waved like she could shrug it off.

Savagery. The word stung a little more than I should've let it. I think on any normal day it wouldn't have even bothered me, but today *wasn't* normal despite how much I tried to make it so. She rarely complained, so I assumed this stemmed from simply being upset that I'd embarrassed her or perhaps it was hormone related, but that was no excuse.

I kept my face entirely devoid of emotion as I turned her own magic against her. Thick dark green vines as sturdy as tree roots shot up from the ground, encircling her wrists and pulling her down to the ground until she was on her knees despite her attempts to fight against it. Then even thicker and denser vines filled in around her until she couldn't move at all. This was her element, and yet she was completely defenseless, because she let her fear and shock take over. She just stared up at me, gaping as though she couldn't understand what just happened.

"Your powers are as much of a weapon as a blade would be." I explained, walking a circle around her through the shadows that snaked about the ground. "A blade is only savagery to you because you prefer to play with pretty little flowers. Flowers or plants of any kind could be used just as savagely as a sword."

I stopped in front of her again so she could look me in the eye as I leaned down toward her. When my face was inches from hers, I smiled. "Tell me, how would your pretty little flowers save you in this situation?"

I could *feel* the vine that was creeping up behind me, aiming for my throat. I could also feel Adriana's eyes on me, as well as the rest of the mages who had now gathered behind us to start to practice on their own. It was sad really, that she didn't even realize she could just fight back against what I had wrapped around her if she had the mind to. This was a lesson she would only learn the hard way.

I let her vine almost touch me before I raised my hand. A shadow slid from my fingers up to the vine and just touched it, making it whither and crumble to dust as it died.

She gasped as though I'd physically hurt her.

"I'll give you an A for effort I suppose." I stood up straight again and released her, the vines disintegrating into nothing but dust. "You'll need to be far faster and more aggressive than that if you were going to survive something like that with a *real* enemy. It's a pity really, you could've just manipulated the vines I held you with, if you'd thought of it. But you have no fighting or survival instincts."

Instincts I had to learn the hard way, even with the vigorous training I had to go through when I was a *child*.

They didn’t even understand how much better off they'd have it with the training we were doing for them. A modified version of the training I got, which was a little less vicious but still had the same effect.

She scowled and in the blink of an eye she had vines wrapped around my wrists trying to pull me to the ground just like I’d done to her. I didn’t budge. Vines wrapped around me entirely now, pulling, squeezing and writhing around me. Still, I held firm. These were still flowery and pretty vines, nothing like the thick and sturdy near tree-like vines I created. If I moved, they’d just snap.

She grumbled in frustration.

“You’re not strong enough to move me yet.” Shadows blasted out from me and the vines again withered and died, turning into the finest dust as they dispersed into the air. “Keep practicing. Perhaps one day you’ll find it a bit less *savage* when you can actually use them more aggressively and land a more significant blow. Or, when you find yourself in a situation where you’ve got no choice to *savagely* protect yourself.”

“You’re an awful teacher.” She spat.

I smiled. “Correction.” I spun around to walk back to Adriana. “I’m an effective and irritating teacher that pushes you to be the best you can be.” I glanced over my shoulder as I walked away. “You just want to be coddled and play with magic.”

I heard her mumble a few curses under her breath. I turned to look at the mages who gathered behind us. Aodh and Gerald didn’t seem to be even remotely shocked or concerned with what I did. Stella and Sorcha looked shocked and maybe a little horrified by Zemora’s little lesson. Aside from the test where we had them collecting the herbs and had the guys out 'hunting' them, they hadn't ever had to learn how to be aware of their surroundings. Nor did they learn how vulnerable they were when they didn't have full control over their magic just yet and an enemy overpowered them like I just did to Zemora.

It seemed that I needed to be a little bit more harsh with their training as well. I decided I'd think of a few other ways to challenge them to be aware of their surroundings *and* set up ways to fight them where they'd truly understand the art of self defense. We'd need to do one on one battles for that rather than group lessons. Today though, I had other priorities.

"Pair up and practice attacking and blocking with one another." I said to them before I turned back to Adriana who was looking at me in awe.

"How do you do that?" She asked. I assumed she meant how I sensed the vine Zemora tried to use to attack with, without seeing it, but any of what I just did wasn't important now. Shifting was something that would be more useful for her sooner than later. Healing too, but at least shifting would get her to someone who could heal more quickly. I know it sure as shit would've saved us from some of that misery the other day.

I forced a smile to my face. "We'll get to that." I looked her over for a moment. "For now, let's practice shifting. Tomorrow, you'll work with Eimear on some healing."

She nodded.

"When you need to shift somewhere, you have to be able to either clearly picture *where* you want to go, or know *who* you want to shift to. For example, pretend you want to shift from where you're standing now, to that tree over there." I gestured to the tree closest to us along the tree line. "Then, you focus all of your energy on snapping yourself there. Or, perhaps a better way of thinking of it, would be taking a step from *here* to *there* without actually physically moving your legs."

"So, I just picture where I want to go and imagine myself *stepping* there without moving." She asked and her brows furrowed while she considered it.

"Yes." I smiled, genuinely this time. "Magic in most cases, is simply wanting something, and then letting yourself have it." I gestured toward the tree again. "So, focus your power, and *decide* to appear there."

She looked over at the tree, closed her eyes and after a few seconds, she disappeared from in front of me and reappeared next to the tree. A huge smile spread across her lips. "I did it!" She exclaimed excitedly.

For a moment, I relaxed a bit and breathed a sigh of relief that she didn't ask me to demonstrate, because I wasn't sure I wanted to shift again. Not yet. She looked over at me and noticed my lack of excitement, and I smiled the moment I saw her excitement fading. "You did it." I looked her over for a moment. "Now shift back here."

She closed her eyes again to focus, and then appeared in front of me, albeit a little closer than she was when she shifted away the first time, but that didn't matter much.

"Good." I said with a smile and she opened her eyes again. "Though you do want to be able to do it *without* closing your eyes. For… somewhat obvious reasons." I said a little too quietly.

A slight frown found its way to her lips.

"Keep practicing." I said flatly. "Shift different places around the manor or around here."

She nodded, and I watched as she continued to decide on new places for her to shift. She started with just short distances around the clearing and even slightly into the woods a few times.

Zemora had always been very strong willed, despite her lack of desire to partake in anything that required any form of real violence. It came as no surprise that not even thirty minutes later she was trying to redeem her failure at fighting back against me by striking me while I wasn't looking. It was foolish on her part, but she I'm sure didn't see it that way.

I heard her and Stella discussing how they would attack while I wasn't paying attention. It took all my self control to hide the smile from my face when I sensed Zemora's vines finally making their approach. I let them get within inches of me. Adriana shifted in front of me again, noticing the vines Zemora was sending my way.

"Great work Adriana." I said before she could speak to warn me about them. "Our next lesson will be shifting an object to yourself, like this." I summoned my sword to my hand, spun around, and shredded the vines that were stretching out both across the ground and through the air toward me.

An exasperated noise came from Zemora, something between a grunt and a growl. Stella laughed. Adriana even chuckled behind me.

I glanced back at her. "Summon something from your room. I don't care what it is. Picture it, and call it to you." Then I looked at Zemora again. "It is going to take a hell of a lot more than that to actually land a blow on me. Especially when you stood there discussing it for several minutes before you tried it. You know I can hear everything you're saying right?"

She scowled. "Clearly it doesn't take *that* much to best you. You almost died two days ago at the hands of a handful of *humans*." As soon as the words left her lips, her face filled with instant regret, and her hands clamped over her mouth. "Shit." She started. "I'm sorry, I–" She backed away a step.

A searing and seething rage built up within me and I did my best to choke it down, but the tension now filling the air was so thick I wasn't even sure a knife could cut through it. She was right. I had failed so miserably that day to see what was waiting for us there and was bested by a few blood thirsty humans who had it out for vampires.

I took a breath, as though that would help keep my feelings from boiling over, before I spoke. "Using someone else's failure in order to feel less bad about your own shortcomings is hardly commendable." I seethed. "These lessons will not save you from shifting into a trap, but they *will* save you from certain death when you take the time to take in your surroundings during any *normal* circumstance."

I took a few steps toward her, slowly. "For example, I don't have to look to my left to know that Lazarus and Deiric are now standing at attention, watching and waiting to see if they will need to intervene because I'm still *new* and my emotions can get a little out of hand sometimes. Which is only amplified by the absolute *hell* that I went through two days ago that will scar me for the rest of my *eternal* life. As you've so astutely decided to point out.

"Nor do I need to look around us at everyone else to see that some of them are trembling in fear because they can *feel* my rage right now. I also don't need to turn around to see that Adriana failed to follow my instructions and summon anything because she is too focused on seeing what happens to mages who decide to challenge and then *insult* me because they're insecure about their fighting ability." I stopped just two steps from her, glaring down at her with all the rage I bottled up over the last two days.

"Luckily for you, I'm not in the habit of actually causing *real* harm when I teach you, and I'm willing to let your little insult slide because even you realized the mistake you made as soon as you said it out loud." I bared my teeth in a scowl at her, my fangs slipping for a few heartbeats before I composed myself and turned back to walk toward Adriana. "I hope that for your sake, you never have to use *any* of the skills I am teaching you. But you're going to learn them regardless of whether you will need them or not, because one day they might just save your life."

I took a long, deep, steadying breath as I reached Adriana and I looked over my shoulder at Zemora. "You have been blessed with an element that will allow you to blend in if our coven ever has to go underground again. *You* should count yourself very lucky for that, but it isn't going to earn you special treatment. If you would rather *not* learn skills that will help you survive any situation, you are more than welcome to ask to be transferred to a manor where the archmage will give you a gold star simply for having any magic at all."

My sword disappeared in a puff of shadow when I shifted it back to its sheath in my bedroom. I looked at Adriana now, whose face was rather grim. "Summon something, and then I'll let you have the rest of the day off." I offered a small smile, that I was sure didn't reach my eyes.

She held out her hands and summoned a small tiara she brought with her when she came here.

"Excellent." I smiled. "You may have the afternoon off while everyone else continues to practice if you'd like. Or, you can practice with them."

She smiled up at me and the tiara disappeared. "I'll take the afternoon off if that is okay. I'd like to review some of the grimoires."

I nodded and she excitedly wandered into the house. "Back to practicing with one another. Switch to a different partner and work on attacking and defending." I said to the other mages, without looking at them, then I walked up past Deiric and Lazarus into the house. They both glanced at me, their faces unreadable, but they didn't say a word.

I walked through the foyer and into the dining room, where I could watch them practice from the side window. I poured myself a glass of whiskey, and quietly kept an eye on each pair.

"It's a bit early for a drink isn't it?" Lazarus mumbled when I heard both him and Deiric walk into the dining room with me. Deiric I could have identified by scent alone, but the sound of his footsteps also gave him away. Gods, I really was far more over vigilant now. I'd always been pretty observant, but never to this level of watchful.

I didn't take my eyes off of the training outside when I replied. "Don't act like you've never had a drink this early in the day." I also didn't even try to remove the bite from my tone.

He scoffed. "Of course I have, but that doesn't negate what I said." He stopped and leaned against the buffet table where the decanter of whiskey was sitting. He paused for a moment, and I heard Deiric take a seat at the table behind me. "Drinking isn't going to change what happened." He added softly.

"No, but it sure as hell will take the edge off of my feelings about it at the moment." I mumbled and took a sip of the whiskey.

"You didn't *fail* you know." Deiric said softly. "It was an ambush. We *all* would have met the same fate."

I let out a heavy sigh. "I'm growing tired of ambushes. They ambushed us years ago, ambushed me in the woods when I made the daylight rings, and ambushed us *again* two days ago. It's getting a little old."

"Ambushes are the only way they *can* get to you." Lazarus half laughed, but there was no real humor in it. "That in itself should be all the reassurance you need that you *didn't* fail. No one can touch you unless they catch you by surprise."

I spun around now and faced them. They both visibly flinched at the look on my face. "Yes, no one can come close to me unless they take me by surprise. Which, as we've already established, means shifting anywhere that we don't have warded and protected is now probably entirely out of the question *forever*." I snarled. "And I had to thank the gods just now that Adriana didn't *ask* me to demonstrate it while I was teaching her because I'm not even sure I can fathom doing so *here*."

The moment I said that out loud, I wished I hadn't, but it was the truth. I just didn't really want them to know it. Something told me Deiric read my thoughts and already knew. His lack of reaction when I said it told me enough. I continued speaking before I could think too much about that confession.

"We need to figure out who he's working with. Something tells me it goes back to the magisters and everyone who supported them. I should've just killed all of those bastards that day. They knew *all* of our weaknesses. Now the fucking prince knows how to exploit them and we're going to have to constantly look over our shoulders and be mindful of anyone who supported destroying our coven."

"Killing them probably would've resolved *some* of this, but it hardly would've harbored the peace between the covens that we *needed*." Deiric reminded me. "Besides, you're not a killer. Not unless you have to be."

I glared at him for a moment. He stared back at me with a look that said he knew exactly how broken I was, and also recognized my tendency for violence when it came to revenge and protecting those I loved. I hardly considered revenge 'unless I have to be', but that's neither here nor there.

"He's right." Lazarus spoke up again, pulling my gaze from Deiric over to him. "As much as I hate to admit it, you did make the right call. You're not a cold hearted killer. You used more power than you should have to heal all of them that day. If anything, they should be glad that you *didn't* kill them."

"They should be, but they'll never admit that." I turned my back to them so I could watch the mages training again.

"Your training methods are… interesting." Lazarus chuckled, noting that it was time for a change in subject.

I smirked even though he couldn't see it. "They're effective." Zemora seemed to have shifted from summoning cute and flowery vines to summoning real threatening plants now, *finally*.

"You clearly got your methods from your father in that regard. I'm certain your mother wouldn't have been so cold about it." Lazarus mumbled.

I glanced over my shoulder at him. "My mother didn't quite know what to do with me." I looked back out the window again. "I was trained more by Aris than my father. He wasn't allowed to train me once the coven found out about me." I finished off my drink and sat the glass on the window sill. "Aris and I trained at night, when everyone else was sleeping."

Lazarus laughed now, a little actual humor coming through in it, unlike the half hearted chuckle he did when he changed the subject. "Do you *really* think your father slept through that?"

"If he didn't, he never said a word." I watched Stella make some decent blows against Sorcha, nearly requiring her to have to heal herself if she hadn't stopped them at the last possible moment. "We made sure we were far enough away though that no one should've heard us." I paused for a moment, glancing down at my empty glass and then over at Lazarus while I considered whether I'd have another drink.

"Aris was ruthless with his training. It certainly kept me alive all those years that I was by myself. I just hope that I can do the same for these kids." I looked back out at them again. "They have *no idea* how lucky they were to have escaped all of that and stayed hidden from it for so long. And likely have no idea just how thin this little alliance between our covens is right now."

"We have the treaty signed by everyone." Deiric said. "It's hardly a *thin* arrangement."

I turned around and faced them both again. “That piece of paper won’t hold up if everyone I spared decides to spark an uprising. So it is *thin* at best. We’ll be dancing on thin ice for a long time.”

“That’s a very pessimistic way of viewing things.” Lazarus said with a look of mild distaste.

“One day, I hope we’ll be on more solid ground, but it is a little bit hard to be optimistic when there’s not much evidence to suggest our conflicts are entirely *over*.” I grumbled. I grabbed my glass from the windowsill and placed it in the sink before I made my way back out to where they were all training.

Chapter 24

Deiric

I rolled over, half awake to reach for Mira, but the bed next to me was empty. I rubbed my face and sat up to look around the room. She was nowhere to be found. I sighed. She'd had trouble sleeping lately, but this was the first time she actually got out of bed. I laid back down and just listened for a few moments to see if I could hear her, but there was nothing other than the occasional sound similar to someone turning a page of a book. I guessed that had to be her.

I drug myself out of bed, headed out of our bedroom and down the stairs. The first level was dimly lit from the light of the fires in each hearth and a handful of candles. There were no mage lights at this hour. All of them were sleeping soundly, except Mira, it seemed. I followed the sound of pages turning to the dining room, where instead of finding Mira, I found Lazarus.

He looked up from the book he was reading briefly, took a sip from the glass sitting next to him, and then looked back at the book. Aside from that, he didn't really acknowledge me.

"It's the middle of the night. Shouldn't you be sleeping?" I mumbled and leaned against the doorway.

He sighed. "I would say the same thing to you but I imagine you're down here because Mira is too." He slipped a small piece of parchment into the book to mark his place before closing it and looking up at me again with a raised brow.

I frowned slightly and crossed my arms over my chest, but nodded.

"She's outside. She asked not to be disturbed."

I raised a brow. "Why is she outside?" The weather was still mild, even for autumn, but I certainly wouldn't want to be outside at this hour if I didn't otherwise need to be. While the cold didn't bother us as much as it did mortals, it was still mildly annoying.

He shrugged. "I'm not sure *what* she's doing if I'm completely honest, but she said she couldn't sleep. Looks like she's sleeping out there to me, but I'm not going to go out and investigate." He motioned to the window behind him. "See for yourself."

I walked around the table and him to glance out the window. She was laying on the ground flat on her back, and appeared to be sleeping with one arm behind her head. She had her cloak wrapped around her.

"How long has she been out there like that?" I knew Lazarus' men were out somewhere in the woods keeping an eye on the edges of the wards, but it was still a little worrisome for her to be laying outside like that by herself. She survived ten years probably doing that more often than not though so I had no room to complain or judge her for it.

"Probably about an hour." Lazarus replied as he got up from the table and walked over to where I stood by the window. He leaned against the wall beside me, also looking out at her. "She's been through more in the last twelve years than any of us have been through in centuries." I looked over at him, and he met my gaze. "I'm honestly surprised she seems to be taking it all so well." He said finally.

"I wouldn't consider laying on the ground outside in the middle of the night when she's got a perfectly comfortable bed upstairs, *handling it well*." I frowned.

He shrugged. "She could've just flipped the switch, turned off her humanity, and actually *become* a monster, but she hasn't. Maybe she doesn't know she can, but either way she's handling it well all things considered." He walked back over to the table. "She might've just needed some time alone. At least she's not like me and drowning in depression to the point where she's considered taking her own life."

I jolted at that statement and turned to look at him. "What?"

He sighed and took another sip from his glass as he sat down. "When Aodhan was killed I lost it entirely." He paused, his fingers tapping the side of the glass for a few moments. "When I finally came back to my senses, I just wanted to end it all. I couldn't face Gwen after that. I spent years drinking and wallowing in self pity before I finally got past it. Why do you think Killian was around so much back then? I could've trained all of you myself if I hadn't been such a mess."

I don't think I ever questioned why Killian had been the one to oversee our training rather than Lazarus. I just thought he'd grown bored of dealing with new recruits. I guess looking back he did seem more melancholy than usual after that meeting. Though he never seemed *drunk*, which made me wonder just how much he had to drink to actually appear inebriated at all.

"You've never talked about Aodhan. I barely knew him. Why *did* his death affect you so much?"

"I prefer to leave the past in the past." He said flatly, then he pushed off the wall and walked back over to the table again. He sat down and picked up the book he'd been reading. "The two of them couldn't be more different. I hated her before I even met her, because I assumed she'd be just as reckless and careless with her magic as he had been, but I didn't realize how wrong I was." He looked up finally.

"She's not reckless or careless. She's everything he wasn't. Careful, calculating, and clever. A literal godsend that's pulling us all back together and balancing things out again. A reminder that even though we come from darkness and dark magic, we're not inherently evil. It is just unfortunate that not everyone can see that yet."

"One day they will." I half smiled. While I had a feeling one day would be *much* farther away than I hoped, I knew that somehow, at some point, she'd convince everyone we weren't inherently evil.

He returned the half smile and looked back down at his book. "Hopefully. One day."

I turned and walked back upstairs to grab my cloak before going outside to Mira. She may have asked not to be disturbed but it seemed absurd to leave her laying in the grass all night. Especially if she *had* actually fallen asleep. I approached quietly, so quiet that she shouldn't have heard me coming, and yet, just before I reached her she spoke.

"I asked not to be disturbed." Her voice was quiet, but stern, and I didn't notice until I was practically standing beside her that her eyes were actually open and she was watching the moon and stars.

"You're awake." I said softly, and sat down next to her.

She lifted her head and looked at me. "Yes, I've been awake the entire time." She didn't seem annoyed or bothered by my presence, despite her pointing out that she'd requested no one bother her. She just seemed a little surprised to see me out there with her.

"I can go back inside if you prefer to be alone." I said softly, hoping the answer was no.

She frowned just slightly, then laid her head down and shifted her gaze back up to the moon. "You can stay."

I laid down next to her and stared up at the moon with her. "You'd rather lay out here than in bed?"

She let out a long and low sigh. "When I was younger, I would lay out and just stare at the stars and the moon. It was so peaceful. Sometimes I would even dance under the full moon and stars." Her voice was barely a whisper.

I rolled on my side and propped myself up on my elbow so I could look at her while she spoke.

"When I was out on my own all those years, a lot of the time I found myself doing just this, laying and staring up at the moon and stars like I did when I was a child. Except instead of staring up in wonder and peace, I was staring up and hoping, praying that one day I could lay here again and just dream and be at peace."

Her eyes were glistening in the light of the full moon. I could tell that at the moment she still didn't entirely feel at peace.

"Within the wards and shields, I can lay here without a care in the world, but the moment I leave any of these manors I'm at the risk of dying by the hand of whoever has decided that they hate me or hate what I am this week. I like to think one day we'll reach a point where they realize that we're not evil, or maybe one day they'll just forget about us, but I hate to think how long that will take." She paused for a moment, and looked over at me. "I didn't even think I'd get this far, so while I might seem like a depressed and pessimistic shell of myself these days, there is still a little hope in there. I'm just not sure how much more of this bullshit I can take."

I found myself at a loss for words. I don't think there was anything I could say that would make it better or ease her mind, because I genuinely had no idea that we'd face this after we finally signed that treaty. And yet, here we were.

We had a handful of months of quiet before we were thrust back into the chaos of whatever this shit storm was. I suppose those quiet months were only thanks to the fact that we rarely left the manors. No one could get her here, but she wasn't the type to hide. Part of me wished she would though. A small selfish part of me that never wanted to see any harm come to her. A part that would stand by and watch the world burn just to make sure she was safe and happy.

She rolled onto her side and propped herself on an elbow so she was nearly at eye level with me. Those beautiful violet eyes searched my face for something, though I didn't know what and her thoughts gave away nothing. She finally leaned in and pressed a light and gentle kiss to my lips. "Thank you for coming out here." She whispered, resting her forehead against mine. "I would have stayed out here all night just staring at the stars."

"Is that what you *need* right now?" I asked softly, locking eyes with her and holding her gaze.

"I don't know what I need right now." She admitted, looking down, but then meeting my gaze again. "But it is nice not to have to get through all of this alone."

I reached up and cupped her cheek in my hand. "If I have anything to say about it, you'll never have to go through *any* of this alone again." She leaned into my hand and let out a soft sigh.

"I don't know what I did to deserve you, but whatever that was, I'm glad I did it." A soft smile found its way to her lips.

I pressed a kiss to her forehead. "I wonder that myself, about you, every single day." I whispered and then let my forehead rest against hers again. "I love you."

"I love you too." She said quietly.

"May I take you back inside?" I said with a smile.

She met my gaze again and a hint of playfulness appeared in her eyes. "Take me back inside?" She asked.

I scooped her up into my arms, hooking one arm under her knees and the other around her shoulders before she had the chance to react. She just chuckled and nodded.

I walked into the manor, through the foyer and up the stairs. The doors opened on a phantom wind, provided by her I assumed, and closed behind us. I set her down, on her feet, next to the bed and unclasped her cloak. I pulled it off of her shoulders and then did the same with mine before draping them over the edge of my dresser.

When I turned around to walk back to the bed she'd already started to climb under the blanket. I moved and was next to her in the blink of an eye. She snuggled in next to me and laid her head on my chest while I put my arm around her shoulders. I kissed her head. "Get some sleep, love." I said softly. She didn't reply, but it didn't seem like it took her long to fall asleep.

Chapter 25

Mira

The following morning I was sparring with Zane while Deiric, Lazarus, and Leo chatted a few feet away. The mages were in a lesson with Liala today, learning more lower level spells and herbs that would be helpful to them in a myriad of situations. She offered to train them when I caught her and Eimear before breakfast and asked that they take over today. I just wasn't feeling up to it. To my surprise, they didn't even question it.

I was casually listening in on what Leo was telling Deiric. We still didn't know who the prince was working with, and he was guarded enough about his interactions that I wondered if we'd ever figure it out without just interrogating him ourselves. I'd asked Macha to send some ravens to keep an eye on things as well, but I hadn't heard anything from her since I'd asked for that.

Devlon and Garrick had still not replied to the messages I sent to them, which was growing more and more frustrating by the day. They sometimes waited a day or two to reply, but never this long.

Zane swung at my left side and I was swinging to block him when my vision shifted. It knocked me off balance and caused me to stumble and drop to a knee. Zane somehow caught himself and stopped mid swing when he realized that I faltered, thank the gods, or I would've taken the blow to the face. I blinked and shook my head.

"Mira?" Deiric was next to me in a heartbeat, but then I was seeing through someone else's eyes.

"Where is Adriana?" The king demanded.

The eyes I was seeing through were high up in the palace wall, through a window. A raven's eyes, I guessed, which was wild given the vibrancy of the color of everything. It was like nothing I'd ever seen. Devlon and a handful of the Solas magisters were clustered in front of the king's dais. The king, queen, and the prince sat on their thrones with the captain of the guard standing at the base of the dais.

"She is safe, your majesty." Devlon said simply. "She is still at the manor with Alesmira, still training." It drove me a little crazy that they used my full name. No onc cvcr called me that, but I suppose when we're dealing with royalty they *should.*

"I asked for her to be brought *here*." The king's tone was angry, but steady.

"I understand, your majesty." Devlon replied. "Unfortunately, a falsified summons was sent to them, and they came here days ago only to be ambushed and attacked. Alesmira has informed me that they do not intend to reply to any further summons until we can sort out the matter of who brought them here or find a way to ensure their safety."

"I did *not* send a summons days ago. I sent it yesterday. There should be no way for something like that to be *falsified*. Did it not have the royal seal?" The king spat.

"I was able to see the summons myself and I confirmed it did have the royal seal on it, so whoever falsified it went to great lengths to make it look legitimate, your majesty." Devlon's voice was eerily calm. How he managed to entirely avoid hinting at the prince's involvement was beyond me. However, he wasn't there, and we didn't have any proof.

"If you must see the princess, we will have to find a way to confirm it is *safe* for them to come here. The princess could have been harmed, or worse, in that ambush." He paused, studying the king's face. "I can assure you she is acting as much on behalf of the princess's safety as she is her own, your majesty."

"We would like to see the princess to confirm she is still safe. Have *you* seen the princess?" The king's voice edged on rage.

"I have not, your majesty." Devlon admitted.

"You have seven days to bring her here." The king snarled. "Or there *will* be consequences."

"Understood, your majesty." Devlon's voice was still level and calm. "We will make arrangements."

The vision ended as abruptly as it started and I had to blink and rub my eyes to confirm that what I was seeing now was in fact the grass in front of me at our manor and not the palace.

"Mira?" Deiric had his hand on my shoulder and sounded more than a little concerned. "Are you alright?"

Macha appeared in front of me and beyond her I could see Zane standing and looking both confused and concerned for me.

You will need to find a way to get her there, or you'll risk the king declaring war on both covens. Macha's head twitched as she looked up at me.

"Mira." Deiric's voice was a little more stern now. "Are you alright?"

Panic overwhelmed me as the gravity of the situation hit me all at once. How in the hell could I even consider shifting there? How could I take *her* there at all? Any of them really. I couldn't imagine going back there myself and taking them with me would be as dangerous for them as it was for me. The thought of just waltzing back into the palace after what happened made my skin crawl.

Breathe. I had to breathe.

I couldn't.

It was like someone dropped a massive weight on my chest. My hands were trembling, and I couldn't think. Deiric was saying something, he was trying to snap me out of it but I couldn't hear him beyond the thoughts whirling around in my head. I had to get away and think. I couldn't be near any of them right now.

One moment, I was kneeling where I'd been sparring with Zane, gripping the grass to stop the trembling in my hands, and the next I was sprinting, running away from all of them and everything as it seemed to cave in on me all at once.

I ended up in the shelter we'd built for the horses, still struggling to breathe beyond the heaviness in my chest. I sat down in the corner where I was certain no one would see me and pulled my knees into my chest.

I didn't know what they wanted with me. I didn't know why they hadn't just killed me. I didn't want to run into them again to find out. I didn't know how I'd get out of that situation alive. Gods. I've never felt this kind of panic and fear before. This isn't me.

Deiric appeared beside me less than a minute after I found my way over here. He knelt next to me and put a hand on my shoulder. "Mira. I don't know how to help you if I don't know what's going on." He said softly. "You're shaking. Are you alright?"

I managed to shake my head. "I can't–" I started to say, but stopped short. "I–" I wasn't breathing, or if I was it was hardly at all.

"It's okay." He spoke like he was trying to calm a wild animal. "Just breathe."

"It's NOT okay." I said and locked eyes with him. He looked startled, and I was sure my face conveyed all of the fear, panic, and general anguish I was feeling.

"Okay." He said just as quietly, without breaking eye contact. "It's not okay." He squeezed my shoulder. "But you need to breathe."

Draga startled me when she appeared in front of me, sniffing and nuzzling at my legs. I didn't even hear her approach us. I was still too stuck in my head. Deiric moved so he was sitting down beside me with his arm around my shoulders. Draga stepped closer and shoved her nose between my knees and my chest until her face was pressing into mine.

She snorted and then nudged my chest with her nose hard enough to toss me backward into the wall behind me. The movement shocked me and forced me to take a real breath. The first real breath I felt like I'd had in several minutes. She continued to sniff and nudge at me until I felt like my mind stopped racing and my breathing came a little bit more regular. I reached up to gently pet her cheek.

Deiric chuckled softly beside me. “If I’d have known I could snap you out of it by whacking you in the chest to force you to breathe I’d have tried that before you even ran off.”

I looked around her and over at him. He had a smile on his face that didn’t reach his eyes, which were filled with nothing but concern. “I’m sorry.” My voice was barely a whisper.

“You don’t need to apologize.” He brushed a piece of hair out of my face with his other hand. “What happened?” He studied my face for a few moments. When I didn’t immediately respond he continued.

“You stumbled and fell to your knees, then it was like you weren’t here at all for a few moments. When you seemed to be aware of your surroundings again, Macha appeared, but then you panicked. I couldn’t even read your thoughts.”

I continued mindlessly petting Draga and looked up at her again. She lingered for a few more minutes before she turned and walked back over to graze with Vellor. I let my hand fall to my knee and leaned into Deiric.

“I had a vision.” I said quietly. “I saw through the eyes of a raven that was sitting on a windowsill in the throne room of the castle, while the king demanded that we bring Adriana to him. Apparently, Devlon received another summons after we were attacked. He responded to it himself, without even reaching out to us, and the king was furious.”

“And I’m guessing there were threats involved, and we have to go there as soon as possible?” Deiric whispered, resting his chin on my head.

I nodded.

"And you panicked because you're not ready to shift again, let alone go *there* again?"

I nodded again.

Deiric sighed softly. He pulled me further into him and idly traced circles on my back with his fingers while he held me. I felt so pathetic and sad. Sitting here while he held onto me because I was terrified of merely *shifting*, let alone going to the godforsaken palace.

"You are *not* pathetic." He said sternly.

"I just had a meltdown, ran off, and now I'm sitting here just letting you hold me while incapable of thinking of a way out of this or a way to do it without one of us being seriously hurt." I mumbled. "That's pretty pathetic."

"You don't have to have all the answers, Mira." He kissed my head and then rested his chin on it again. "You're allowed to have a meltdown and panic when you've been through a traumatic experience like that. It doesn't make you pathetic, and before you can think of it it doesn't make you weak either." He paused and we just sat in silence for a few moments.

"What you felt and are feeling makes you *human* and you shouldn't be ashamed of that." He lifted his head off of mine, hooked a finger under my chin and lifted my head so I was looking at him. "We will figure out how to get her there, and make sure that *no one* has the chance to hurt you like that again."

There was nothing but steely determination in his eyes. "If anyone even *thinks* of harming you again, they'll be dead before they can complete the thought."

"It isn't just me I'm worried about."

A muscle in his jaw tensed. "I know." He said softly. "But *you* are who they always seem to go after. I doubt you need to be concerned about us." His eyes darted around my face, searching for any kind of reaction before he finally added, "I will make sure we're *all* safe."

I nodded.

"Come on." He started to stand up and pulled me up with him. "Let's get back before Lazarus comes looking for us." He half smiled. "He was as worried about you as I was."

I half laughed. "I didn't know he *could* be worried."

He started to walk out of the shelter toward the gate. "I've never seen him worry or care about anyone in… well, nearly six hundred years." He glanced back at me with a more genuine grin for a moment, before he looked ahead again and opened the gate. "I didn't think he had it in him anymore either, if I'm honest, but he cares about you."

I followed him through the gate and he latched it behind us. "Six hundred years."

Deiric locked eyes with me. "He's been through some shit too." He mumbled, and pulled me along with him when he turned to walk back toward the manor. "But that's his story to tell, not mine. And I don't think he'll ever want to talk about it."

Chapter 26

Mira

Two days later we needed to shift to Aris' manor to meet with Devlon and Garrick. We received word about the meeting's day and time less than a few hours after I witnessed what happened when Devlon responded to the second summons. The idea of shifting *still* made me anxious, but I knew I couldn't put it off forever. And it was absurd to be worried about shifting to one of our manors. I knew that.

Still I hesitated. Deiric had insisted that we all wear our fighting leathers. Lazarus, Deiric, Adriana, and I were all standing in the foyer, ready to go. Deiric stepped up to me and put his hand on my shoulder.

You can do this. He thought. *We're just going to Aris' manor. You know it will be safe there.*

He didn't explain *why* we had to wear our leathers, but I didn't really question it much. He assured me that he had an idea for how we were going to ease my mind and get us there safely. He didn't give me much hope when it sounded like I wasn't going to avoid shifting, but he assured me it would still be safe.

I took a deep breath, reminded myself that I wasn't shifting somewhere dangerous, and finally shifted us to the foyer of Aris' manor. Deiric gently squeezed my shoulder.

It will get easier. He assured me. Though I didn't feel that way at the moment, I did finally relax some.

Aris appeared before us in the blink of an eye, and I visibly flinched. He had been smiling, but that smile faded when he saw my reaction to his sudden appearance. He looked me over for a few moments, his eyes scanning for any reason that I *should* be jumpy, before a tight lipped smile found its way back to his face.

"Devlon and Garrick are here already, along with the blacksmith you requested, Deiric." Aris said and motioned toward the stairs. "They're in the usual meeting room."

A blacksmith? I thought. Adriana and Lazarus, from what I could tell, didn't react to the mention of the blacksmith, so it seemed I was the only one who was in the dark about his plans.

I told you I had a plan. Deiric thought.

A plan that includes a blacksmith?

Yes. He released my shoulder and I started toward the stairs, with Adriana keeping pace next to me and both him and Lazarus following behind. *I'm having real armor made for us.*

I stopped halfway up the stairs and glanced over my shoulder at him with a raised brow. *Armor?*

He just smiled, nodded, and nudged me forward again. I looked back ahead of me and continued up the stairs.

Devlon and Garrick were already talking when we walked in, and I wandered over to my usual seat at the table. Adriana walked over to sit to the left of Devlon, and Deiric and Lazarus took their usual spots behind me.

"We only have five more days before we have to take Adriana to the palace to see the king and queen." Devlon said by way of greeting.

I nodded. "I know."

Garrick leaned forward, resting both elbows on the table. "It seems that Deiric is already way ahead of us with ensuring that no one can just *kill* you, but would you mind giving us a little more detail about what happened?"

I had locked eyes with Garrick, but when he asked what happened I looked away. I opened my mouth to speak before Lazarus cut in for me.

"She took three stakes to the chest." He paused, and I watched as the color drained from each of their faces. "They also seemed to have learned of more of our weaknesses, and hit her with a dart that blocked her ability to heal, and essentially paralyzed her."

Devlon and Garrick shifted uncomfortably in their chairs, while I sank a little bit in mine, unable to look either of them in the eye while Lazarus spoke for me.

"All of this happened within seconds of us arriving, and before we could even get our bearings to know what was going on around us." Lazarus continued. "She attempted to shift us out but her magic gave out mid-shift. We had to rush her to my manor and wait for help to arrive."

"That explains why Elias requested we assign a mage to your manor." Garrick mumbled.

"I called on the blacksmith to make armor for each of us." Deiric spoke now, and everyone's attention fell to him. "I'm sure he can put something together rather quickly?"

The focus of the entire table, myself included, shifted to the man standing at the other end. He was rather burly, with shorter dark hair and a beard. There were a few gray hairs among the dark strands. He studied us for a moment and then merely nodded. He was dressed in plain clothing, but had a measuring tape in his hands, and a pencil behind his right ear. A piece of parchment sat on the table in front of him.

"I'll need to get measurements, and I can have all four pieces back to you within the next two days." He said flatly. "I have apprentices and helpers who will work around the clock to get it done."

"Thank you." Deiric replied. Devlon, Garrick, and Adriana looked back toward us. "I'd still prefer if the two of you, and maybe a handful of other mages would arrive first, to confirm that we don't have an ambush waiting for us, if that's alright?"

Devlon locked eyes with me for a moment and I forced myself to hold his gaze. "I'll have Tellus and another one of our magisters tag along." He looked tense, concerned even.

Garrick spoke next and I shifted my gaze to him. "I'll have Liam and Nedra come with me." His expression was similar to Devlon's, but also seemed to contain a little bit of frustration. I wasn't sure if that was because we'd need more people involved, or if he was frustrated about what happened. "And you're sure the prince was involved?" He asked me.

"The look on his face will be burned into my mind forever. So yes."

Garrick arched a brow, as if impressed I suddenly found my voice again, but he nodded. "Since we don't have any evidence other than *your* word, we won't be able to mention that to the king."

"I didn't expect you to."

"We're not questioning what happened." Devlon said softly.

I shifted my gaze to him again, and willed my face to be less angry, as I assumed that's what they saw in my expression to lead him to say that. "I didn't say you were."

A muscle in his jaw tensed. "You seem… irritated." He said hesitantly.

"I'm not irritated." I held his gaze. "I'm simply…" I considered what I was for a moment. Alive? Yes. *Anxious*? Fuck yes. Irritated? No. I didn't know how to describe what I felt. How is someone supposed to feel after something like that when they have to face it again so soon? I sighed. "I'm here." I glanced over at Garrick and then back at Devlon. "That's about as good as it gets right now."

Concern flashed across his face for a breath before it disappeared and his expression went flat and unreadable. "Let us know when you've got the armor ready, and we'll plan to go to the king as soon as we can after that."

I nodded.

Garrick shifted away without another word. Devlon leaned forward, glancing at Deiric, then Lazarus, and finally letting his gaze fall to me again. "Are you alright?"

"Physically, I'm fine." I mumbled.

"That's not what I asked."

"I think you know the answer to that question."

Devlon sighed and leaned back in his chair. "I will have more of my spymasters try to find out whatever they can about Ronan." He finally said after a few moments of awkward silence where we were just staring one another down. "We'll find a way to get evidence on him. Or we'll find a way to make sure he's… dealt with."

I arched a brow at him. He certainly never seemed like he was truly the violent type.

"Whatever the real reason for all of this is," Devlon said, "we will find out, and we *will* deal with it." A small scowl found its way to his lips. "It's a part of our treaty, remember? This is a threat to someone within the coven, and it should be dealt with accordingly. If you took three stakes to the chest, I'd consider that punishable by death."

"You didn't take me as the murdering type." Lazarus said from behind me.

Devlon looked around me at Lazarus. "I don't take kindly to anyone harming members of my coven. And I certainly don't take kindly to them harming the one person who orchestrated bringing balance back to our covens either." He rose from his seat. "Now, I think you need to get some measurements taken for the armor you're having made. I won't take up anymore of your time." He shifted away.

"So this is why we had to wear our leathers?" I asked as I stood from the chair and made my way past where Adriana sat to walk over to the blacksmith. Deiric was up and walking with me as soon as I started to move.

"Yes." He said. "I'll admit, I hate the idea of wearing something so restricting and clunky, but it is a good idea to have, just in case."

"Arms up." The blacksmith mumbled when I reached him, and he began to take measurements around my chest and waist.

Aris walked in now. “Three stakes to the chest and no one even thought to *tell* me?” He snarled at Lazarus. It would’ve been quiet enough for most people not to hear, but he clearly forgot that I could hear everything *he* could hear.

“We didn’t exactly have the chance to come here before now.” Lazarus replied just as quietly.

“You can put your arms down.” The blacksmith said quietly while he took a few more measurements. I was too busy listening to Lazarus and Aris to notice he didn’t need my arms up anymore.

“I wasn’t about to ask her to shift us here until she had to. Shifting here today took everything she had I’m sure.” Lazarus mumbled even quieter, but still not quiet enough to keep me from hearing him.

Aris sighed. “Still.” He mumbled. “You could’ve sent Leo, or *someone* to tell me so I didn’t just *appear* in front of her when you arrived.”

The blacksmith finished with me and moved on to Deiric next. I turned to look at Lazarus and Aris, locking eyes with the former. An emotion I couldn’t place flashed across his features for a fraction of a second before he looked back at Aris.

“We were a little preoccupied.” He snarled, then walked around Aris to come over to where we were standing. Aris turned and looked at me, nothing but concern on his face. He held my gaze until Lazarus appeared in front of me and blocked him from my view.

I looked up at Lazarus. “I am sorry for speaking for you.” He said softly. “I didn’t think you *wanted* to explain it all to them.”

“I didn’t.” I said quietly. “Thank you.”

His lip curled up into a half smile. He placed his hand on my shoulder, squeezed it gently, and then stepped around me to go toward the blacksmith and get his measurements taken.

I told you he cares. Deiric thought when he appeared beside me and wrapped his arm around my waist.

Chapter 27

Mira

Another two days passed, and I slowly started to wake up. I reached for Deiric, only to find the other half of the bed cold and empty. My eyes snapped open and I realized that it was *much* later in the morning than I would've thought. Why he didn't wake me when he got out of bed, I wasn't sure. I was tangled in the sheets, and about to fling myself out of bed when I heard the door knob turning and I looked up to see Deiric coming in with a steaming mug in his hands.

The corners of his mouth curled up into a small smile which didn't reach his eyes. "Good morning, love."

I pushed myself up in bed so I was sitting with my back resting against the headboard. "Why didn't you wake me earlier?" I asked, more concerned about losing half of my morning than anything else.

He sat down on the bed next to me and offered me the mug. “Liala made this for you.”

I studied him for a few moments, then reached out to take the mug. It was tea, and I could identify one or two herbs, but there were so many other scents wafting from the mug that I wasn’t sure what it might be.

“I didn’t wake you because I thought you could use the rest. You *rarely* sleep through me waking up and leaving the bed.”

“And Liala made this tea *specifically* for me?” I asked, a little hesitant to sip it without knowing why it smelled so strong.

“She thought it might help.”

“Help with what?”

A flicker of an emotion I couldn’t place flashed across his face before all I could see in his eyes was a little bit of concern. “You haven’t been sleeping well, and you have been on edge lately.” He stated hesitantly. “Liala went through something similar, although far worse, when Zane first brought her back here after the attacks. She managed to make this tea, which helped to…”

His voice trailed off while his eyes briefly left mine and he thought of how to continue that sentence. He finally looked back at me. “It helped to keep her calm and get through it until she *wasn’t* so on edge all the time.”

He studied me again, like I was a wild animal about to rip his throat out for even suggesting that I might need help. I still just held the mug, but otherwise my expression didn’t change. Finally, it hit me.

“And you’re giving me this tea now, because I’m guessing you know the armor is ready and we need to plan our visit to the palace." He nodded. "And you don't want me to panic like I did a few days ago." Another nod.

I brought the mug to my lips and took a sip. It had cooled down enough that it didn't burn me. His shoulders sagged with relief, and he didn't say anything else until I'd had several sips of the tea. It certainly didn't *taste* good, but I imagine that Liala probably wasn't concerned with the taste so much as she'd be focused on the effectiveness of whatever she put in it.

"Devlon scheduled an audience with the King for this afternoon." Deiric finally broke the silence. I looked up at him again. "We'll meet at Aris' manor and then they will go in first." He paused for just a few seconds, looking me over for any reaction, and when none came he continued. "They'll let you know when we can shift in."

Devlon usually went through me when planning these sorts of outings, so the fact that he went through Deiric this time bothered me a little bit. But what was more surprising was that the panic I expected to feel when he mentioned shifting there didn't hit me as hard as I expected. There was a lingering unease that was no more overwhelming than it would've been if I'd been asked to go there right after the treaty was signed.

I glanced down at the mug in my hands. I'd almost finished it, and I had to wonder what sort of herbs she put in here that worked so quickly and so intensely. I knew it couldn't be any form of magic, not even a simple spell. "What is in this tea?" I said softly.

"That's a question for Liala." He mumbled. "I don't know *what* it is. She just told me it would help."

I just looked up at him again and arched a brow. "When do we have to leave?"

"In an hour." He started, "If you don't think you can–"

"I'm fine." I finished the last of the tea. "But I think I should get up now and get ready."

A half smile rose to his lips now and he seemed at least a little bit hopeful that I wouldn't completely lose my mind in the palace.

*

We shifted into the palace on Devlon's word that we were safe to do so. We all wore the beautiful armor Deiric had crafted for us. It was a very heavy and sturdy steel that covered us from our shoulders down to about our navel. They painted it black, and had the insignia of the coven engraved on the front of it. While I found it mildly uncomfortable, I couldn't help but admire it.

The armor gave me the reassurance that at least if we *were* attacked on arrival I wouldn't take stakes to the chest again. I don't think, even with the calming tea that Liala made for me, I could've handled going to the palace without it. The shadows cleared from around us and we all bowed at the waist. We shifted directly into the throne room, as we had discussed, with Devlon, Tellus, and Quinn flanking us on the left while Garrick, Liam, and Nedra flanked us on the right.

We rose from the bow and looked straight ahead to where the king, queen, and prince sat on the dais. Captain O'Byrne stood at the foot of the dais, slightly to the King's right. The king was studying Adriana closely for a few moments.

"The armor is new." He observed. "I see we've foregone formal wear in exchange for that."

"Yes, your majesty." I said calmly. "For all of our protection."

He nodded, which I assumed meant he knew how our last visit had gone, at least perhaps a little more so now than he had when I watched him tear into Devlon the last time he was here.

The queen spoke now, shifting my gaze her way. She was wearing a much more simple gown today than the last time I'd seen her. It was very plain, but still just as beautiful. "Are you alright Adriana?"

Adriana nodded, but didn't speak.

"At least she's still *human* and *alive*." Ronan snarled.

I couldn't stop the scowl that rose to my face at his remarks. Still human. For fuck's sake he truly did think we were monsters. Who would turn a child?

The King turned to his son and scowled, but then looked back at me. "And where is her ladies maid?"

"She is back at the manor." Adriana finally found her voice and answered for me.

His gaze shifted to her. "How is your training going?"

Adriana looked up at me, and though I shouldn't have needed to encourage her, nor did I need to give her permission to speak, I nodded. She looked back at the king. "It is going well. I've started to learn how to shift."

The king raised a brow. "Have there been any… outbursts?" He asked after a few moments passed.

She shifted on her feet.

"If you are asking if there have been any nightmares resulting in flare ups of her magic, then yes." I said and his gaze shifted back up to me. "The first night she was with us there was an incident, but she has been fine since then, your majesty." I didn't need to read her thoughts to know that his words made her incredibly uncomfortable.

"Interesting." He mumbled. "How much longer do you expect this to take?" He glanced over at Ronan before looking back at me. "Some have expressed concerns with her staying in your company for too long.

"If things continue the way they are going, I expect her to master her magic by the Summer Solstice." I paused and he seemed pleased with that answer. "If not, it could take a year or more. It really depends on her."

He nodded somewhat dismissively. "I would like to receive monthly updates on her progress." He leaned back on his throne. "As for the issue with the falsified summons," He waved at his captain of the guard, "Captain O'Byrne is still working to investigate that issue and the moment we determine who was involved we will arrange for their execution."

"Certainly, your majesty. I will make sure to send monthly updates." I glanced at Devlon for a moment, who seemed to be watching everyone cautiously, then I looked back toward the king. "Could I make a request?"

The king raised a brow, but nodded.

"Would you allow me the honor of ending them?" I smiled, and there was nothing nice about it. Captain O'Byrne was gaping at me. The queen seemed horrified at the idea of the whole spectacle, though Ronan didn't appear surprised. If anything, there was a hint of amusement on his face.

The king stared at me for a few moments, his face unreadable and mostly blank. Finally, after what felt like an eternity, he nodded. "I suppose that could be arranged."

"Thank you, your majesty." And no sooner had I finished that statement did I go still as a statue when I heard the soft click of a crossbow being drawn somewhere to my left, high up on the castle wall. I didn't have to look behind me to know that Deiric and Lazarus heard it too.

I cleared my throat. "If that is all, your majesty, we should get back to resume her training today."

The soft clunk of the firing of the crossbow echoed throughout the chamber, loud enough for *everyone* to hear.

Lazarus was in front of me before anyone else moved and caught it. His hand sizzled where it touched the vervain at the end of the stake and he snarled a warning. The captain of the guard had drawn his sword and was scanning the walls on the left side of the room to find where the stake came from.

The king was furious. "Find them, and *kill* them." He snarled at the captain.

The captain didn't get the chance. Adriana simply *disappeared.* She shifted, though to where I wasn't sure. A few seconds later, she appeared in front of me again with the assassin held by the arm, crossbow nowhere to be seen.

I shot forward and grabbed him by the throat before anyone else had the chance to move, though I knew Deiric was *right* behind me, no doubt about to make the same move. The man was dressed in a guard's uniform, so he would blend in and be able to move about undetected. His gray eyes held nothing but rage. I didn't get even the hint of fear in his scent, despite that I held him up off the ground by the neck.

I tightened my grip. "You're going to tell me who you're working for and where the other two bastards you're working with are." I snarled, determined to compel the answers out of him.

He let out a strangled chuckle. "Fuck you." He spat.

I growled at him, baring my fangs and tightening my grip. Not a single person in the room moved an inch. I wasn't even sure if some of them were breathing. You could've heard a pin drop when neither of us were speaking.

"Go ahead and bite me you blood thirsty bitch." He spat at me. "You can't compel me. I drank vervain."

"Then you're of no use to me." I smiled as he struggled against my grasp, clawing at my wrist and arm to no avail. "And I made you a promise I fully intend to keep."

"You made no promises to me." He choked out.

I laughed, but there was no humor in it. Just murderous intent. The laugh unnerved him and I finally caught the slightest hint of fear. "Oh, right." I pulled him a little closer to my face, but didn't let his feet touch the ground. "Silly me." I drawled, a murderous smile still stretched across my lips. "I forgot. I had a little trouble speaking when we met. Stakes in my chest and all." I waved my arm rather dismissively and I huffed a laugh again. "Tell me, Deiric." I said sweetly over my shoulder. "What was it I promised to do to them again?"

He arched a brow, and a similarly wicked smile stretched across his features. "You know, I think you said something like, 'I'm going to kill them all. Slowly and painfully.'" He mimicked me, only making him look more terrifying.

I turned my gaze back to the man I was holding to find that all the color had drained from his face. "That's right." I don't know how, but I managed to smile even wider. "Slowly and painfully." I said softly.

I reached down to grab the dagger I had sheathed on my thigh and stabbed it through his throat, between my fingers where I held him. A steady stream of blood flowed from either side of his neck, then his mouth as he struggled to breathe. I simply dropped him, and pinned him to the ground with a thick casing of ice. He would eventually bleed out, but of course, I had to make sure he couldn't remove the dagger and hasten the inevitable.

I heard the rushing of footsteps behind us along the balcony at the second level of the throne room. Before I spun around, I noticed that the blood had drained from both the King and Queen's faces at the sight of what I'd just done. Ronan, to his credit, only looked *slightly* horrified. It made sense he would expect this sort of behavior from someone like me. But, I was obeying the king's order to find and kill him, even if it wasn't directed at me or specific enough to dictate *how.*

I spun around to see the source of the commotion behind me was the remaining two assassins lining themselves up on either side of the balcony and preparing their crossbows. Deiric and Lazarus made to move toward them, but I froze their feet to the floor.

"They're mine." I snarled.

In the blink of an eye, I was up on the balcony behind the one on the right. I yanked his crossbow out of his hands and chucked it over the railing. I heard the other one shuffling to face us, and I spun this man around in front of me. Seconds later, he took the stake that was meant for me, directly to the middle of his chest.

I sighed. "Well, that wasn't as slow and painful as I hoped." I pouted, and then chucked him over the balcony before running over to the last of the three assassins. Shock flashed across his features before he tried to fumble around for another stake. I snatched his crossbow and chucked that away as well, before I took the stake he grabbed and slammed it into his ribs, missing his heart but striking a lung. Then, just for good measure, I chucked him over the railing as well.

I shifted myself back down to the main floor of the throne room and walked slowly back over to Deiric, Lazarus, and Adriana. Deiric and Lazarus both had an impressed and vengeful smile on their faces, with nothing but pride shining in their eyes. Which was good, because I was certain they would not be pleased about letting me handle it myself. I let the ice holding them in place melt as I passed between them and they spun around to face the king again.

In truth, that ice never would've held them, but they allowed it to, and that was enough confirmation for me that if I truly wanted to handle it myself they would have let me, even though they wanted to kill them and savor it just as much as me. I locked eyes with the king again, who had now regained some color in his face but held his lips in a tight, unamused, line.

"I apologize for the mess, your majesty." I said nonchalantly, just as Adriana returned to my side, seemingly unphased by all the violence she just witnessed. "I can assure you, that given what I went through, their deaths are actually somewhat merciful."

"I would agree." Adriana mumbled.

A flicker of surprise danced across the king's face before he steadied his features in an unreadable and unamused look again. A wave of pride came over me for the fact that Adriana *was* unphased by all of this and seemed to agree with the method of punishment. A hint of a smile found its way to my lips.

I stepped forward, around the blood pooling by the first assassin, and pulled my dagger out. I wiped it on his tunic before sheathing it at my side.

"Don't you find that a bit wasteful?" Ronan drawled, as I moved back to where I had been standing next to Adriana.

I raised a brow and smiled at him. "Do you find it wasteful when you don't eat your spoiled meat, your highness? Or do you still feed it to the pigs?"

I was just as shocked as Ronan looked at my response when I heard the king let out a low chuckle. When my gaze shifted to him he collected himself and cleared his throat as though he hadn't just laughed at his son's expense.

"As I was saying, your majesty." I said flatly. "I think it would be best if we go, so we do not risk any additional danger to the princess, or myself, and so that we do not make anymore of a mess of your beautiful throne room." I turned only my eyes to face Ronan again for a moment, noting his disgust, before looking back at the king.

His captain of the guard sheathed his blade, and stood at attention, with a small smile finding its way across his lips. His thoughts revealed he fully agreed with the punishment I'd laid out for these three bastards, and I knew then that he had most certainly been informed of the details of what had been done the last time we came here. Devlon and Garrick surely would've had time to fill him in on the way to the throne room and I doubted they filled the king in on all of the bloody details.

"Yes." The king nodded. "I think that would be best." I nodded, and moments before I shifted us back home, he added. "Alesmira?"

"Yes?"

"You will protect my daughter?" His tone made it sound more like a demand than a request.

"With my life, your majesty."

He nodded and I shifted us home.

Chapter 28

Ronan

I sat down the glass of whiskey I'd been drinking. It didn't seem to manage to take the edge off of my frustration anyway. I'd been sitting in my chambers alone all evening after dinner, and despite that it gave me time to think, I was still at a loss. At least they didn't try to say I was involved in their attack, though I didn't know *why*. I knew they saw me. I knew my *sister* saw me. That had been a grave mistake.

Still, I wanted to throw the damned glass because if that gods damned vampire bitch hadn't ruined our plans, none of this would be necessary. But of course, *she* isn't the one who fucked up the attacks years ago. Still, she's managed to fuck up everything since then. Kieran swore he'd find her and convince her to work with us, though I had no idea how or why.

Neither of our plans seemed to work well. My plans to hire mercenaries to see how easily they'd be caught off guard proved they were much more aware of their surroundings than I thought. They caught on to the mercenaries before they even came close to killing any of them, and I still had yet to figure out how they were so organized so soon after the treaty's creation. I certainly didn't expect her to show up *here* and demand to see my sister before I'd found another way to catch them, but they never seemed to appear *anywhere* we knew about.

The warded manors they'd mentioned in our first meeting with them made sense, and it irked me that Kieran never mentioned them. I needed to speak with him. I suspected he had his own plans. He wanted to rule the mages and I wanted to expand the borders of our kingdom. I wanted the *world*. I should've expected some secrecy on his part, but I didn't expect to be missing so many important pieces. Clearly, even exploiting the weaknesses he'd told me about proved to be useless, or at least, useless in my plans.

It was late enough now that everyone else in the castle would be sleeping. My personal guards knew where I often wandered off to, but only those I trusted. Tonight, both of the guards assigned to my chambers were those in my inner circle. This would be my chance. I slipped out, nodding to them as I passed. They knew if anyone came for me to tell them I was not to be disturbed. I walked down the hall to the servant's passages and entered them.

I descended through the servant stairwells until I was at the lowest level of the castle. I made sure I was alone in the hallway before pulling on the torch that opened the passageway to the network of tunnels beneath the city. I pulled an unlit torch from my tunic, lit it on the one on the wall, and began to make my way toward the dungeons. I made sure to pull the hidden door shut behind me.

I knew these tunnels like the back of my hand. I've been down here so often lately that I probably could have navigated it without the torch. The smell of damp dirt and mildew became more pungent as I neared the hidden entry to the dungeons from these tunnels.

I set the torch in the sconce on the wall, and then listened to be sure there was no one on the other side of the door before I finally pushed it open. I looked left and right, to confirm I was still alone, and then made my way down to the last cell on the right. Once again, I closed the door silently behind me so no one would notice or suspect my presence. I looked in through the barred window of the cell door.

"To what do I owe the pleasure of your presence, your highness?" Keiran said from somewhere near the back of the cell. "I didn't expect to see you again so soon."

"She's killed my assassins." I snapped. "The dead man's blood didn't seem to stop them from escaping despite the three stakes we put in her chest. She killed them all today because we didn't have the element of surprise and they thought they could take her down anyway."

His wicked laugh echoed off the walls.

"I didn't come down here so you could laugh at my failure." I snarled. "Is there another way to capture her?"

He appeared in the window out of seemingly nowhere and stared at me wildly. I jumped backward, startled as I didn't even hear him move. His breath was absolutely rancid, his teeth had started to yellow, and the smell of him was so awful I could hardly breathe. He smiled wickedly at me.

"It's about time we do things my way, don't you think?" He had a crazy look in his eye, like this time locked away alone down here was truly driving him to madness. I wasn't terribly surprised by that, seeing as losing his magic last year seemed to almost drive him to madness then.

"I'm listening." I said and crossed my arms over my chest.

"We'll track your sister with her magic."

"That didn't exactly go well when you were tracking Alesmira that way, in case you forgot that." I narrowed my eyes at him. "I'm not going down a path that's going to lead to failure again. Give me something else."

"I don't know what she did to block us from tracking her, but I am certain your sister hasn't done that, and they won't expect it anymore. They think that the magisters were doing that, and they certainly don't suspect you're working with me."

He had a point. "Fine." I sighed. "How do I track her with her magic?"

"If you want to know how to do that you're going to have to give me something in return."

"What could you possibly want?"

"The ability to bathe more frequently." He snarled. "Basic hygiene."

I shrugged. "I'll see what can be arranged."

"You will see to it that it happens, or I will make sure that none of my people will help you."

There was no way he could get messages out of here, I was sure, but I shrugged again. "Fine."

"You'll have to track down Malachy." He smiled. "He knows the tracking spell. You'll just need something the princess used her magic on. Do you have anything like that?"

"She shifted one of the assassins today. Would one of his weapons or possessions work?"

"That will work perfectly. Get that to Malachy and tell him you need something to track that magic with. Then, whenever she uses her magic you'll know exactly where she is." He wandered back into the darkness of his cell. "If we find your sister, we find Alesmira."

"What do you want with her anyway? Why do we need her for all of this to work?" I asked.

"Well, right now we need her to train the princess how to use her Eldritch abilities, or tell us what she knows so we can do it. But when she's done with that I'd like my revenge." A murderous smile rose to his lips. "You can consider delivering her to me when you complete your conquest payment for my help. Then we'll take down Oíche from the inside out, and all will be right again."

"Where can I find Malachy?" I asked, ignoring his demands for the moment.

"He was in Edinborough when I was locked up in here, but he also regularly visits the castle ruins outside of Scottsdale. If he's relocated, you'll have to track him down on your own."

"Thank you." I turned to walk away.

"Don't forget our deal. I may no longer have my magic, but that doesn't mean I can't kill you if you betray me."

"Yes, yes. I remember." I sighed and rolled my eyes. He was never going to see the light of day again, but he didn't need to know that. I just needed to get my sister to summon the creatures I needed to help me conquer the rest of the kingdoms. Then I had no use for him, and had no intention of making good on our deal.

Chapter 29

Mira

A week had gone by since our visit to the palace and winter had finally come in full force. We had very few days where training outside was possible, without bundling the mages up to the point that they could hardly move. The only two who were unaffected were Aodh and Sorcha, but Aodh was officially deemed a master yesterday and received his tattoos, so he was free to go back home if he chose to.

There would be no coven meetings this month, with everything winding down for the winter and the holidays, though Garrick and Devlon assured me if they received word about any details for what Ronan was up to they'd let us know.

Today we were preparing for the winter solstice, which I also found out from Esme was Adriana's birthday. I was determined not to bring up anything relating to training, the issues with Ronan and whatever his misguided plans were. I wanted to keep the festivities free of any stress and frustration.

Zemora was gathering holly, pine cones, and evergreen branches to decorate the manor, while Eimear, Stella, and Adriana worked on drying orange slices and then weaving them into garland with cinnamon and cloves. Deiric and I were in charge of finding a yule log for the fire.

Deiric carried a saw while we walked through the woods, looking for the perfect down and dead tree to cut for the log. The first snow had fallen overnight, and it made the woods around the manor even more beautiful, while also being eerily quiet. Deiric pulled me along behind him, gently tugging on my hand each time I stopped to admire the scenery for too long.

"You seem… more cheerful today than I've seen you lately." He said softly, finally stopping to admire the frozen landscape with me.

I smiled slightly. "It's hard not to be a little more merry this time of year." I said quietly, admiring the icy parts of the stream and the way the snow glimmered around it. "It's so quiet and peaceful when it snows."

He sat the saw down against the tree next to him and pulled me into his arms, shifting my focus from the stream to him. Gods, his eyes were even brighter out here when we were in the snow. His hair was tousled from the wind and I'd forgotten just how damn captivating he really was.

His lips curled up into a sultry smile, which only made me more enthralled with him. I slipped my hands up around his neck and into his hair.

You keep looking at me like that and I'm going to abandon this ridiculous search for a yule log, take you back home, and strip you down so I can admire every *part of you. I'd rather spend my evening worshiping* you *than celebrating the re-birth of the sun.* He slipped his hand around the nape of my neck and pulled me in closer until our lips were almost touching.

You know, I'd forgotten just how insufferable you were. I smiled and gave him a swift and gentle kiss before staring up at him again. *Keep looking at* me *like that and I might just let you.*

He pressed his lips to mine in a hot and heavy kiss, instantly taking my breath and all other thoughts away. I forgot about the gods damned yule log, the snow around us, and all our other responsibilities. It was just him, this kiss, and whatever followed.

I melted into him, parting my lips to allow him to fully claim me and his tongue danced passionately with mine. I pulled at his hair and lifted myself up into him, needing more, needing to be closer to him. To leave the world and everything else behind.

The hand that wasn't on my neck slipped down to my ass, pulling me up into him as he nipped at my lower lip. Fuck the snow, and the cold. I'd have him right here.

He smiled into my lips and his other hand released my neck to slide down and lift my legs around his waist. Then he took a few steps and pressed me back into a tree a few feet away, while his hands slipped beneath my skirt.

He kissed down my neck, nipping as he moved lower. I let out a soft moan.

Gods I love it when you do that. Even his thoughts sounded breathless. He tugged at my underwear, then cupped one thigh with one hand and shifted himself so he could stroke me with his fingers through my underwear.

I gasped and tugged at his hair. *I want you. All of you.* I pulled one hand from his hair and reached to unbuckle his belt and pants. *Please don't make me beg.*

He groaned and kissed his way back up my neck. *But I love it when you beg me for more.* He let out a soft laugh and then claimed my mouth again.

You cruel, wicked man. I mocked, and finally got his pants undone just as he started to kiss down my neck again, but before I could try to pull them out of the way he sank his fangs into me.

I gasped, pleasure pulsing through me with each drag he took from me. I moaned and arched myself into him, slipping my hands up under his cloak and clawing at his shoulders through his shirt.

He pulled my underwear out of his way and thrust two fingers into me, and the combination of that and his feeding was nearly enough to send me over the edge.

He thrust his fingers in and out, his thumb tracing circles over my clit, pushing me closer and closer to the edge.

I leaned my head back against the tree, breathless and let out a moan. Just before I climaxed, he pulled his hand away, shifted his hips and thrust his entire length into me.

I cried out, but he quickly muffled my sounds with a kiss. *Gods I love you.* I arched my hips into him.

He retreated and thrust in again and my entire body was on fire with pleasure. I thought I might explode.

I slipped one hand out from his cloak and up into his hair while he settled into a steady and world ending rhythm. I pulled his head to the side and kissed my way down his neck before I sank my own fangs into him.

He gasped a moan and I shattered. Pleasure crashed over me in waves while I drank, and then he reached his climax with my name on his lips.

I retracted my fangs and licked up his neck, before kissing along his jaw and finding his lips again.

Gods, I love you. His thoughts were still just as breathless as if he'd spoken the words out loud.

I love you too.

He broke the kiss and leaned his forehead into mine. We stayed like that for a few moments, sharing jagged breaths before he finally pulled out of me and let my legs drop from his hips to the ground.

My legs were still so shaky that I nearly collapsed, only supported by the tree and the arm he still had around me.

He smirked, and buttoned up his pants with his free hand. "Interesting." His voice was breathy. "I don't think you've ever struggled to *stand* afterward before."

I huffed a laugh. "You've never fucked me against a *tree* before."

A sultry smile found its way to his lips again and he braced himself against the tree with his hand above my head. "Maybe we should do this more often then."

I looked from his lips to his eyes and bit my lip. "I don't think I'd have a problem with that." I breathed.

His hand slid down the tree, across my cheek and he lifted my chin before he gave me one quick peck on the lips. "We should get back to looking for the yule log before they start to think we got lost in the woods."

I groaned and rolled my eyes. "If we have to."

He just smirked and turned to go grab the saw again. "There's a tree over there that'll work." He glanced back at me. "We passed it earlier."

I arched a brow. "You mean to tell me that you saw one already and you just kept wandering around out here because *I* was having a good time?"

He picked up the saw and spun around to face me. "You have had a really shitty couple of weeks. I'd walk around out here in the cold all day with you if I get to see you look around with such wonder and happiness for once." He smiled, walked back over to me, and kissed my forehead. "Would you like to keep walking around, or do you want to go cut that tree into a usable log and head back?"

He was right, the last couple of weeks had rivaled the time *before* I met him for some of the worst weeks of my life. The tea that Liala had made at least helped me sleep more than I thought it would, and certainly helped calm me on days when I felt like I'd have another panicked episode like I had when we were summoned to the palace. I stood on my toes and kissed him. "I think I'd like to head back so we can do that against the wall in the bedroom with a little less clothes later."

"Oh we can do far more than that." The look in his eyes told me *everything* I needed to know about what our plans were for the evening, if we'd get that opportunity before we got pulled into the festivities.

Chapter 30

Mira

We got back with the Yule log just in time. Zemora and Leo were coming outside to prepare the fire pit. Zemora had her arms full with all sorts of things to decorate the log with before we set it on fire.

"It's about damn time." Leo called from the stairs while Deiric and I approached. "We were starting to think you got lost." He smiled.

"We got a little distracted." Deiric said with a sideways glance and smirk at me. He dropped the massive log into the middle of the fire pit.

Zemora came over immediately and started to lay holly and evergreen branches across it, while Leo brought over smaller pieces of firewood to put around it.

The sun was starting to set, and with the overcast sky, it was growing significantly darker with each passing minute. Liala and Zane came out now, carrying mead and whiskey for all of us to drink while we stayed up and celebrated the longest night of the year. Slowly but surely the rest of the crew filtered outside, with Aodh and Sorcha finally coming out last, hand in hand.

I arched a brow at Sorcha, and she just shot me a small glare before they took a spot near the fire. Leo had laid out small unsplit chunks of trees around the pit for us all to sit on if we wanted. Renwick sat slightly further back from the pit with his lute and a glass of whiskey already in his hand.

When Zemora was satisfied with the log she stepped back and looked at me. "Would you like to do the honors?" She smiled.

I glanced over at Sorcha and Aodh with a smile. "How about we all light it?"

Both their brows raised for a moment, then they each jumped up excitedly and smiled. "We'd love to!" They said, almost in unison.

I motioned for them to come up to the pit, and each of us took a spot around it. "Ready?" I asked them, and they smiled and nodded. "On the count of three." I smiled. "One. Two. Three." We all held up our hands and sent fire flying onto the log, holding it there until we could tell it was burning on its own.

The fire was nearly ten feet high at first, and we all had to take a few steps back, until it died down enough that it didn't burn us if we stood too close.

Sorcha and Aodh took their seats back, together, across the pit from Deiric and I. Liala and Zane began to pass out whiskey and mead, and each of us quietly tossed one of our thirteen wishes for the upcoming year into the fire. A tradition they could do every year if they wanted, that most of them found out about for the first time this year.

After a little while, Renwick began to play his lute, and we were all dancing and laughing like we didn't have a care in the world, which is precisely how I wanted this evening to be. Adriana was a little hesitant at first, but after finishing her first cup of mead, she loosened up and began to dance with Zemora and Stella.

Deiric spun me into him and kissed my neck. "If we're going to jump over the fire tonight, we should *probably* do that before you get too drunk." He whispered into my ear.

I laughed and spun around to face him. "*You* are going to jump the fire with me?"

He shrugged and smiled. "We're supposed to, aren't we?"

"I mean, it *is* a part of the tradition, yes." I put my arms around his neck. "But I didn't think that vampires really participated in that part."

"A little fire doesn't scare me." He kissed my forehead. "It's not like you're asking me to jump *into* it."

"Fair point." I stared up at him for a moment. "Let's do it then!" I grabbed his hand, which had found its way to my hip and turned to tug him along with me.

"Incoming!" He yelled past me, and Eimear darted out of the way just as we started to run toward the fire. Sorcha and Aodh jumped off of the log they were sitting on and ran around to follow us over it.

Deiric ran beside me and we lept over the fire, clearing it by more than a foot or two, and sending snow flying when we landed on the other side. He caught me when I stumbled and pulled me into a swift kiss when we were out of the way of Aodh and Sorcha.

"See?" He laughed. "If we waited any longer you would never have stuck the landing."

I rolled my eyes and sighed. "You know, even when I'm drunk I can still handle jumping over a fire. Have a *little* more faith in me." I grumbled.

He raised both brows. "Sure you can." He smirked.

He spun me around as Renwick began to play another song and everyone else took their turn jumping the fire. We danced and drank for hours. Everyone started to calm down the later we got into the evening. Eventually, Deiric and I were laying on the ground a safe distance from the fire, but still close enough to feel its warmth, and staring up at the stars. The clouds had cleared not long after dark and the sky was beautiful tonight.

*

I must have dozed off, because suddenly I was sparring with Aris. It was a beautiful summer day and we were back at my father's manor, the way it looked before the attacks. We almost never trained during the day, and we were moving so quickly it was like I'd been turned already. It had to be a dream, a weird manipulation of a memory with him.

Then, I heard a tiny laugh when Aris knocked me off balance and held his blade to my throat. Aris smiled at me and lowered his sword, before he looked over to his right. I followed his gaze and there was a little girl, no older than three or four, watching us. She looked up at us and–

Oh my gods. It was me. Her violet eyes, the black hair. I was looking at a younger version of myself, and my mother sat almost fifteen feet behind her, distracted and talking to Liala.

I looked down and grabbed the blade of my sword, then handed the hilt to little me. I realized then, I wasn't dreaming. I was seeing a memory… through my father's eyes.

Little me excitedly grabbed the hilt of the sword, and swung it around like I'd seen my father do many times. He laughed, and the sound absolutely warmed my heart. Aris was chuckling too, and my father knelt down with me, giving me some instruction on how to hold it and swing it.

He watched me as I walked over to Aris and tried to fight him like my father had been. Aris pretended to fight me back, but obviously let me win, without actually hurting him of course.

"Teron!" My mother's stern voice shouted, and he looked away from little me over to her. She looked furious, and was marching over to him. He stood and when she reached him she was seething. "Are you out of your mind?" She shouted. "Why on earth would you give a toddler a *sword*!"

My father chuckled again. "Relax Rosilin." He said. "She's just fine." He motioned over to me and they both looked. "She's having fun. She'll have to learn to use it eventually."

"She's a *sorceress*, Teron." She said firmly. "She doesn't need to learn to wield a blade, and certainly shouldn't be doing it when she's *three*."

My father rolled his eyes and shook his head, but kept watching me. "Let her have fun. And whether you like it or not, I *will* be teaching her how to use all weapons. She might need them one day." He looked at my mother again.

She frowned and looked a little sad. "She's in more danger than you let on isn't she?" She asked quietly.

He put his hand on her shoulder. "I told you we weren't ever supposed to allow for another Dhampir to exist."

My mother sighed and just looked over at me. "Well, she's here now. It isn't like we can *uncreate* her. I *was* taking a tonic so it isn't like we *planned* this."

"No, but we *can* train her to the best of our ability so that she can protect herself even if we can't." My father said softly.

They both watched as Aris and I "fought".

Someone shook my shoulders gently. "Mira?" Deiric's voice broke the hold of the dream and I opened my eyes. He was laying on his side next to me and looking down at me with concern. "Are you alright?" He asked. "You're crying." He gently wiped away a tear with his thumb while he cupped the side of my face with the hand he'd had on my shoulder.

I blinked and sat up, wiping my face with both hands. "I'm fine." My voice was barely a whisper.

"You fell asleep and you were *crying* while you slept." He mumbled, sitting up next to me and putting his arm around my shoulders. "That hardly seems *fine* to me."

I sighed, and smiled slightly. "I had the weirdest dream." I whispered.

"Do you want to talk about it?" He leaned in and locked eyes with me.

"Sure." I smiled, and I told him everything I saw. He sat and quietly listened, smiling at me while I described the memory of my first time fighting Aris with my father's sword. I didn't remember it myself, but I just knew that was the first time I ever held a blade, and I wondered if that might not have been my father's favorite memory of us. It felt like a gift from him, thanks to the veil being so thin this evening.

Chapter 31

Deiric

TRIGGER WARNING: Brief mentions of SA
This chapter is skippable.

Mira was already out of bed when I finally woke up. She had mentioned that she'd be working with Adriana today on more deadly shadow magic, but didn't explain what that really meant. It was unusual that I would sleep through her getting out of bed, but I didn't have any plans today, so it was a welcomed reprieve. I got up quietly, listening for any sign of her in the house, but I only heard the other mages.

I pulled on pants, a loose fitting long sleeved shirt, and washed up before I headed out of our bedroom. When I finally got downstairs, all the mages had wandered outside. I pulled on my heavy fur lined cloak and walked outside to see what they were up to. Since we lit the yule log, there was plenty of space outside near the fire that was warm enough to do their training today.

Mira had Sorcha, Zemora, and Stella on one side of the fire, practicing together, while she and Adriana stood on the side closest to the house. She had several things setup on this side, and a lot of them were obviously fueled by magic because none of the plants that were out there would have existed in this weather otherwise. They were already looking half dead with the chill in the air.

“Alright, first, I want you to channel the shadows you’ve seen me use that suck the life out of things.” Mira said sternly. “And you’re going to kill that plant.” She gestured to the beautiful tiger lilies she had conjured up next to Adriana.

“You want me to kill them?” Adriana asked, scrunching her nose like that bothered her, even though they’d die in the cold anyway.

“Yes. Would you rather kill the animals lurking in the woods instead?” Mira seemed mildly annoyed already, and I wondered if *she* should’ve slept in.

Adriana’s brows rose and her jaw dropped just slightly, but she shook her head. Her features leveled out to a look of concentration or maybe determination. She turned to face the lilies and summoned shadows, but the plant didn’t die.

“Try again.” Mira mumbled.

I leaned against the pillar at the top of the front steps and crossed my arms. I watched as this went on for nearly an hour before she managed to finally kill the plant.

Mira revived it. “Again.”

Adriana frowned, but they repeated the exercise with that and several other plants for another hour until Mira was satisfied.

"Good." She smiled. "Now you're going to mist them."

Adriana's brows scrunched together in confusion as she spun to face Mira again. "I'm going to *what?"*

Mira half laughed, but there was no humor in it. She raised one hand, and the plant in front of Adriana just… misted. Turned to dust as though it had never existed in the first place.

Adriana stared at it with a look of shock and awe for a few moments, before her face contorted in horror. "Does… Have you…" She couldn't even form a sentence, but I could hear her thinking, *have you killed a person that way?*

"Yes." Mira replied coldly. "I have."

My brows rose, and Adriana looked at her like she barely recognized her. I didn't even know she had the ability to do that, and I had certainly never *seen* her do it to anything other than the plant she'd just demonstrated the power on.

It struck me as odd that Adriana would be confused that Mira *would* kill someone. Surely by now she'd realize that Mira had no problem ending a life, especially in more gruesome manors. She demonstrated that right in front of Adriana in the throne room. So I assumed the look might simply be because *this* method of killing would be so quick and finite that they wouldn't even see it coming.

That's a little disturbing. I thought.

Mira glanced at me with one brow raised. *I don't use it often.* She looked back toward Adriana, but she continued her thought. *My mother didn't even train me with this sort of magic. I don't think she knew about it. I misted a man by accident when he tried to over power and assault me before I took on my alias.*

I gaped at her for a moment, then I thought back to the night we met. It made so much sense to me now, why she immediately put the knife to Alaster's throat when he so much as touched her without her permission. There was still so much about her past that I didn't know. So much she kept locked away and hidden from everyone, even me.

"When?" Adriana looked at her after a few moments of staring at the plant. "Who did you kill?" She was both confused and concerned. "Why don't you use that more often?" It was a reasonable question. It would prevent a *lot* of unnecessary fighting for sure.

"So many questions." Mira said almost boredly. "It was a long time ago. I've practiced it a few times since then on plants, like I'm having you do. Now, mist the lilies."

"You didn't answer my other questions." Adriana said defiantly.

"You don't need to know those details, Adriana." Mira crossed her arms under her cloak. "Mist the fucking lilies." She rarely cursed at the mages. Even the other three stopped to look at her with both her tone and instruction. She either lost all her patience or that memory bothered her more than she let on. I immediately regretted commenting at all and digging up the past.

It isn't your fault. She thought, but didn't look at me. *Just practicing this reminds me of the bastard. It took me a while to be able to recreate this particular form of my magic. It takes a lot of control.* She half laughed out loud, which prompted a concerned look from *all* the mages. *I guess that's why it manifested when it did. When I felt like I'd lost all control on the situation and the instinct and magic just took over.*

All the mages shifted their gazes to me, Adriana included. I guess they realized she was talking to me silently.

"Adriana." Mira's voice was stern. "Focus."

Adriana looked back at the lilies and held out her hand. Her face contorted with frustration as she focused on trying to mist them. After several minutes of nothing happening, Mira finally sighed.

"We'll try another day." She mumbled and started to walk towards me.

"I can do this." Adriana insisted, her stubbornness fueling her determination now.

"No Adriana. It's too much for you right now. We will try another day. It isn't a simple magic and you shouldn't force it if you can't do it right now."

Adriana sighed, but finally gave up and followed Mira toward me.

Mira waved her hand dismissively. "Practice your *less* deadly magic with the others for a few minutes and then you can have the rest of the day off if you'd like."

Mira locked eyes with me as she continued walking up the stairs toward me. *I'd rather not go over the details of that day, if you don't mind.*

I nodded. I didn't really expect her to. *You know you can talk to me about* anything *from your past if you ever want or need to, right?*

She stopped in front of me, just one step below where I was standing and smiled. *I know.* She sighed and gently brushed her hand against my cheek before resting her hand on the side of my face. *I'd rather not have to relive my least favorite moments of my past, but I appreciate that more than you know.*

I frowned. *Sometimes it is better to talk about it than bottle it up.*

She looked away for just a moment, dropping her hand back to her side, and then stepped up and around me to walk into the house. *That may be true, but I've gone this far without trudging through the depths of my past, and I'd rather keep it that way. Bringing it up now will just reopen old wounds.*

I turned and watched her walk into the house. I wondered how many other awful things she'd gone through that she hid under that strong and determined facade. Then it hit me. She had more in common with Lazarus than I would've thought. They both hid their heartache behind an impenetrable mask of either brashness and a careful display of their physical skills or an emotionless and aloof facade depending on the situation. You'd never know either was struggling at all unless you witnessed it, or they let you in. I was glad at least that she let me in, even if she didn't do it all the time.

Chapter 32

Mira

Somehow, this month they managed to coordinate all of the coven meetings to take place on the same day. It was a welcome relief for me, because I could get it all done at once and not have to travel out several times in one week. It also made coordinating the training of the mages in my absence much more manageable.

I wore a light cloak, just in case we'd need to move anywhere outside. My fur lined cloak seemed like it would be too heavy if all of the meetings took place inside. We were due to meet Devlon and the Solas magisters first. As we were getting ready to leave for the day, I reminded Liala what the goals were for today's training. The mages were all still eating breakfast while we set up things in the training room. I wanted them all practicing with our training swords.

Aodh and Gerald decided to stay with us, so they were going to jump in to partner up with one of the girls for this training session and help Liala correct them as needed. I had a feeling Aodh stayed because of Sorcha, but I didn't know what Gerald's motives for staying were, other than that he didn't really have a family to go home to.

I walked out to Deiric and Lazarus, who waited patiently in the foyer.

"Ready?" I asked them, and they both nodded. I shifted us to the castle that Devlon always hosted the Solas meetings at.

The castle was decorated for Yule, and even more breathtaking than it had been the last time we'd been here. True to their coven's name, the castle had numerous sky lights and massive windows to let in as much sunlight as possible, and the large room that we held the meeting in was probably the brightest in the entire structure.

It would be the throne room, if this were truly a castle. This place was warded even more than our manor was. No one could find it, and no one could get in at *all* unless they were a Solas member or they were invited. The large windows were lined with long dark green silk curtains. The color of the curtains seemed to change each time we were here. They were green now to match the evergreen branches and wreaths that decorated the rest of the space.

I walked up to the long table and took my place at the end, with Deiric on my right and Lazarus on my left, like we always did.

"Good morning." Quinn said as she came over and sat to my left on the longer side of the table. She smiled warmly at me.

Tellus sat at the far end on the same side as Quinn while Devlon took his place at the head of the table on the other end.

"Good morning." I said and returned the smile. We hadn't gotten off on a great start the first time we'd met, but since then she's become a welcomed ally. If I saw her more than once a month I may even call her a friend.

The other magisters filed in slowly and took their seats. When everyone had arrived, Devlon began the meeting. I sat quietly and listened as they all gave the updates for their regions. Those who arrived later were in other kingdoms in the area. We primarily functioned in Leinster, but the covens were not limited to this kingdom specifically.

Finally, it came time for Tellus to speak. He smiled at me. "I've got some interesting news about the prince to report."

I arched a brow and gave him my full attention. "I'm listening."

Every other head turned in his direction now too. They were all well aware of the ambush and most of what transpired that day.

"My sources tell me that he was traveling to Edinburgh recently, though we do not know why. Whatever his reasoning for making the trip was, it wasn't official business of the crown. He managed to evade my spymasters in that area, but we believe he might've been meeting with the mage he's been working with."

"Interesting." I said softly. "Is there any specific mage in Edinburgh that you think he might be visiting?"

Tellus shook his head. "Unfortunately no. The mages we know in the area were all unaware of the prince's presence there, and we have no reason to suspect any of them are lying. Whoever he was meeting is not associated with Solas, at least, not anymore."

"I'll send some of my contacts to the area to do a little more digging." Devlon said.

I nodded my thanks. "If you need anything from us, please let me know."

"I can spare a man or two as well if you'd like." Lazarus commented. It actually made me jump and glance back at him. He never spoke during these meetings, so it was shocking to hear his voice even though I knew he was right behind me.

Devlon nodded. "Are they capable of reading thoughts or compulsion?"

"One of them, yes."

"Good. If you have them meet me at Aris' manor in two days, I can shift them there and have Tellus coordinate."

Lazarus nodded. I looked back toward Devlon. He began going over what was going on in his region, and then the meeting adjourned.

Lazarus, Deiric and I stood together to leave, and Devlon walked over. "Might as well all arrive together, shouldn't we?" He smiled. "Since the meetings all lined up together this time."

I shrugged. "Sure."

I shifted the four of us to Aris' manor. Garrick had not arrived yet, which was not surprising because we were quite early. I looked around, and the foyer was uncharacteristically empty, though I could hear everyone throughout the house going about their business.

I glanced at Devlon. "Make yourself at home." I smiled, and then started to walk toward the hallway to the back of the manor.

"Where are you going?" He called after me.

I shrugged and continued walking silently.

"Is she alright?" I heard Devlon quietly ask Deiric.

"I think so." Deiric's reply was hesitant, like he couldn't be entirely sure. I didn't blame him. I didn't even think my intentions when I started to walk away.

I'm fine. I thought. *Just taking a walk down memory lane. You're welcome to join.*

"Yeah, she's fine." He said more confidently. "Like she said, make yourself at home. I'm sure Garrick will be here eventually."

Deiric caught up with me quickly. "You could've answered him yourself, you know."

I shrugged. "I haven't taken much time to wander around when we come here. I didn't want to offer him a *tour*, which would've inevitably been what he asked for if I lingered too long."

Deiric sighed, and kept pace beside me. I walked past all the doors that were once incredibly familiar to me. Everything looked the same, but so different at the same time. We finally reached the end of the hall, and I pushed open the door to the courtyard out back. It was mostly barren, aside from the bushes that stay green all year round. The fountain in the center of the courtyard was empty and dry, as would be expected for the dead of winter.

The dream I had the other night resurfaced in my mind. I found myself standing where my father stood in those moments, the open area beyond the fountain was perfect for sparring, even now. Nothing had changed, and despite how overgrown things must have gotten in the ten years it sat vacant they wasted no time cleaning it back up again.

Deiric stood next to me, quiet and patient, while I wandered around the courtyard for a few minutes. He didn't even complain about the cold. I listened quietly while he admired the space. While he wasn't actively speaking to me with his thoughts, I still heard them. I stopped abruptly and turned on my heel to head back inside, causing Deiric to nearly walk into me. He raised his brows and stumbled to the side to avoid the collision.

"Garrick is here." I said quietly. "We should get back inside."

"How do you know?" He looked at me incredulously. "I can't hear him, and if I can't I know *you* can't."

I smirked and raised my hand outside of my cloak, letting two tendrils of shadow slink around it like snakes.

He just looked more confused.

"I'm always feeling through the shadows to know where everything around me is." I smiled, dropping my hand beneath my cloak again.

"Is that how you always manage to know where everyone is and what they're doing when you're training them?" He smirked. "That's a bit of an unfair advantage if you ask me."

I shrugged and walked toward the back door. "What they don't know won't hurt them." I reached the door and glanced back at him. "Besides, even without the shadows, I would know where they are and what they're doing. My magic just extends my field of focus much farther when I decide to use it."

We walked in and met Garrick in the foyer, before we all headed upstairs to have both meetings. Devlon left after our joint meeting finished, which didn't take long, as usual, and the Oíche meeting was rather brief as well, with not much new to report from each Magister's region. They did seem to finally be getting the hang of their new positions. By the time we returned to our manor, everyone was preparing for dinner and I just wanted to have a nice drink and turn in for the evening.

Chapter 33

Mira

The next morning, after Deiric and I finally managed to pull ourselves off of one another to go about our day, I was outside with Adriana to once again practice shifting. She'd done well in the palace, and been doing well in short distances, but I wanted to see how far we could stretch it. Eventually, she'd need to travel across the country, which was harder than she probably expected.

Today, we'd be shifting beyond the wards, which Deiric and Lazarus didn't protest much, so long as we didn't leave the woods that we were all normally in anyway. I finally felt much less worried about shifting, thanks to Liala's tea *and* having done it a few times now without dangerous results.

Adriana was excited to see how far she could stretch it and I told her that if she succeeded enough here that we would go even farther and shift to our other warded manors. Or, at least the ones I'd been to anyway, which included Aris', Lazarus', and Silas' manors.

"Whenever you're ready." I said at last, standing next to her just beyond the front steps, with my hand gently on her shoulder. It was easier for her to shift both of us if we were touching, and I didn't want to add the variable of distance with her yet.

She nodded and shifted us out to somewhere in the woods. "This is where I was nearly discovered by Deiric during that challenge a few weeks ago." She smiled.

"Good. Next?"

She shifted us again, to another location in the woods. "This is where I found the Mullein."

We were just on the edge of the trees, with a nice open clearing ahead of us that would likely have been filled to the brim with the plant in the summer and fall. "Are we just visiting the places you found the herbs?"

"Well, these are the places I can picture the easiest. I committed them to memory after we did that challenge so I could find them again if I needed them."

"Good." I smiled and was a little surprised she thought that far ahead. "Let's move to the next location then."

She shifted us to each location where she'd found herbs, and then finally shifted us back to the manor where Deiric and Lazarus were impatiently waiting on the front steps.

"You're going to stress yourselves out with everywhere I go aren't you?" I asked, looking up at them with a raised brow.

They both nodded, arms crossed over their chests and unamused looks on their faces. I hadn't taken them with us because I didn't think they *wanted* to go along for these smaller shifts, but I knew they'd be pissed if I went to the manors without them.

"Well, you've arrived just in time. We're going to shift to a few of our manors next."

Lazarus frowned slightly. "Will she be able to shift all of us that distance?"

I shrugged. "I planned to shift the two of you with us if you decided it was important to go along."

"We'll come." Deiric said, without consulting Lazarus, though I don't expect that Lazarus would protest.

I gestured for them to come down next to us. They walked down the steps, taking up a spot to our immediate right and left. I directed Adriana to shift us to Aris' manor first. She did so, dropping us in the foyer. We startled a few people who were not expecting our sudden arrival, said hi to Aris when he walked out to greet us, and then I shifted us to Silas' manor.

Silas was not in the foyer when we arrived, but anyone that was startled just as those in Aris' manor had. I let her take everything in for a moment, let them all know we were practicing her shifting and that we would be back, and then she shifted us to Lazarus' manor.

Lazarus' manor was far less exciting, but he used it as an opportunity to check on Darragh and how things were going for a few minutes before Adriana shifted us back to Silas' manor just to prove that she could. When we arrived there she swayed slightly, which told me we'd reached the limits of what she was capable of for the day.

"I'll shift us home."

"I can do it!" She protested and I immediately shot her a glare that told her I wasn't going to allow it even if she could.

"You have already done enough today. This isn't a debate." I shifted us before she had the chance to protest. When we got back, I sent her into the kitchen to get some food and demanded she rest for the remainder of the day.

"It didn't take her long to wear herself out." Deiric commented. Lazarus walked off into the den.

I turned to face Deiric and shrugged. "She'll get used to it. She doesn't usually use *that* much power when we're training. It takes a lot to shift that far repeatedly."

"You never seem to be bothered by it."

"I've been doing it for nearly twenty years." The sudden realization of that made me feel a little old, which felt silly, given that I was now immortal and twenty years would probably feel like a month to me eventually. Deiric chuckled. "My magic has a much larger… 'well' if you will. I have more to pull from than she does." I said with a slight shrug of a shoulder.

He just shrugged and made a face that suggested he was barely interested in truly knowing *why* I could do far more than she could, even though I felt like it was pretty obvious as to why.

"When are you going to work on the eldritch abilities?" He asked hesitantly, looking over to where she was in the kitchen, retrieving some food. "Is she ready for that yet?"

I turned and followed his gaze. She was walking toward the dining room table now. “We could probably work on that soon.” I said softly. “I’m not sure when I’d consider her *ready*, but she’s progressing well enough that it wouldn’t hurt to try it.”

“Tomorrow then?” He asked.

I glanced over at him. “You seem oddly interested in those abilities.”

He smirked. “I just want to see what god awful creature she summons this time.” He looked me up and down before continuing. “It’s been a while since I’ve had to fight anything. Somehow, no monsters have appeared to take the place of those you’ve killed for us yet.”

I rolled my eyes and smiled. “Well I’m sorry that I’ve made your life so dreadfully boring lately.” I said sarcastically.

He slipped his arm around my waist and pulled me into him. “You have *definitely* not made my life boring.” A sly smile found its way to his lips. “If anything, you’ve made it *far* more exciting in many other, better ways.”

Xander made a grunt of disgust as he walked past us into the den. “You two *really* know how to remind us all that we’re so pathetically alone all the time. It's quite annoying.”

I shot him a half hearted glare. “I did offer to find you someone when I first came here, if you recall.” I said with a slight smirk.

He rolled his eyes, looking back at me over his shoulder as he kept walking toward the couch. “I will pass, thanks.”

I shrugged. “Offer still stands if you ever change your mind, or get desperate enough.”

He scoffed and then sunk down onto the couch.

"You're far too eager to play matchmaker for all of them." Deiric mumbled, his eyes dropping from mine to my lips and back again.

"I'm sure it isn't fun for them to watch *you* find a mate while they're all still alone. Well, except for Zane of course."

"They could find someone if they chose to. They just don't."

I arched a brow and gave him a look that suggested they don't because they don't want to be distracted, or bring them back here and risk people who *shouldn't* find our manor knowing its location, but I didn't push the topic. He merely rolled his eyes and pulled me along with him while he went into the den to get a drink and sit with Lazarus and Xander.

Chapter 34

Mira

We waited until the evening the following day to work on her Eldritch magic, and spent the first half of the day working on minor spells and magics. The Morrigan specifically referenced conjuring, and she had clearly summoned two horrifying looking beasts by accident during a nightmare. I hoped if we tried to summon them on purpose we might have slightly less horrifying results. I also hoped if she could open the portals to conjure these beasts that she could send them back.

Not knowing precisely what we might get, I made everyone other than the vampires stay in the manor while we practiced this. Every single vampire that was living with us at the moment was present and poised to fight whatever beast might come through. I felt like we were all at a bit of a disadvantage for my lack of knowledge in this particular type of magic and wished once again that my mother had passed on that knowledge to me before the attacks. We had no references to it in books, or any written form. It was passed down from one archmage to another, and my mother was the archmage of her generation who inherited the knowledge. I would have been the next, and potentially the *last* since I would be immortal, but she hadn't told me much of anything back then.

I had attempted to ask the Morrigan, but received no response. I guessed this was a '*figure it out on your own*' type of situation. She seemed to summon them when she was fearful, so I thought perhaps she summoned them on an instinct to protect her. I told her to meditate until she was completely calm, and then attempt to summon a creature that would protect her. What I didn't add was to make it a creature that hopefully *wouldn't* just kill us, but I assumed she'd know that.

We gave her plenty of space. We stood approximately twenty feet from her on all sides, with me standing between her and the manor.

I put a shield up around us, so that whatever she might summon wouldn't just run off, and then drew my sword. She had gotten quite skilled with meditation, so by the time I turned to face her with my sword drawn she looked like she was preparing to call on something already.

There was a brief flash of light, nearly blinding for all of us, and then when our eyes readjusted, a golden dragon sat next to her. It was nearly as tall as the manor, with massive bat-like wings spread widely from its back. Its long tail curled around Adriana where she sat with her eyes still closed, unaware of the beast lurking mere inches from her.

A hint of fear crept over me at the sight of it. It lowered its head in front of me and let out a low snarl. It had small spikes down the front of its face, which got larger the farther up its face they were. Beyond where its amber eyes stared back at me, the spikes were longer than my forearm, and continued down its neck.

"Lower your weapons." Deiric's voice was calm and low. His demeanor confirmed several of my suspicions about him since reading the journal he'd given me, though I never asked him about it or voiced them. He had definitely seen dragons before, and if my suspicions were correct, he *had* a dragon.

I crouched, very carefully and slowly, not taking my eyes off of the snarling beast in front of me, until I could lay my sword on the ground in front of me. Its eyes followed me while I moved, like it was deciding whether I was a threat or if it wanted me for dinner.

It huffed a breath in my face, and the force of the air hitting me caused me to stumble backwards, landing on my ass, but bracing myself up in a sitting position with my hands. I crawled backwards a few feet before I just stared up at it incredulously. If I hadn't literally *felt* it blow me back I genuinely would have thought this was all a hallucination.

After a moment, it raised its head back up to look around at us and I could finally see past it. I dared to take my eyes off of it and saw that Deiric was smirking at me. Adriana was just as shocked as I was. She stared up at it in amazement.

Dragons were supposed to be a myth, folklore, or a long lost legend. If they did still exist, you never saw them. Deiric's journal would have suggested they weren't myths, but that they disappeared a long time ago and hadn't ever returned. Where they'd gone, no one seemed to know, and it wasn't in the journal he'd given me.

After a few moments of evaluating its surroundings, the beast lowered its head and turned to Adriana, who tried to shrink back away from it only to bump into one of its large scaly legs. She yelped and now *she* looked as fearful as I had been.

The dragon cocked its head at her, but didn't react otherwise.

Hello Princess. A deep booming voice said– No. *Thought*. It was not meant for me to hear.

I looked at Deiric. He smiled and nodded. I hadn't had a thought, but I guess the look on my face held the question I meant to ask. He could hear it too.

I was riddled with confusion, not understanding how he heard *this* but didn't hear Macha when she talked to me. I would have to ask that later.

Adriana stared up at the beast still. "You– You can talk?" She stammered, out loud.

A deep wicked laugh thundered in my head. *Of course I can.* It said, *Only you and…* It looked around to Deiric and then me, *a handful of others can hear me.*

Adriana looked at me. I just stared at her in disbelief. She looked back up at the dragon. *I guess you don't speak truly, do you? You communicate with thoughts.* She thought.

That is correct. It replied calmly. *Normally only* you *could hear me, but the mated vampires can hear me and the thoughts of others because the blood magic that made them seems to mix very interestingly with their dragons' magic.*

With our what? I looked at Deiric like he would give me an answer, but he was carefully watching Adriana and the dragon. Either he didn't hear my thought or he simply ignored it. I wasn't *going to* ask about the journal, but we'd be having a chat later for sure now.

I looked back at Adriana to see that her jaw dropped, and she looked from Deiric to me, and then back again.

The dragon looked at me again. *This one created a shield, as though that would have stopped me from leaving if I chose to.* Its lips curled into what I suppose you could call a smile. *I could break it with half a thought.*

I dropped the shield, there was no sense in holding it if it was as pointless as my sword had been for this interaction. Deiric ran over to me and held out his hand. I took it, and he pulled me to my feet. A sly smile danced across his lips. I gave him a glare before I looked back at Adriana.

I think I'm supposed to send you back now. She thought.

The dragon snarled. *You will not.*

Deiric turned to face Adriana now. "If you can hear it, it has chosen to bond with you." Deiric said calmly.

Adriana's eyes widened, and then she looked up at the beast again. *Do you have a name?*

Cairbre. The dragon replied.

Are there others like you? She asked.

There are many. Cairbre looked around at each of us again. *They will return to this realm eventually.*

"Would anyone like to inform us of what in the hell is going on?" Zane said quietly.

Cairbre turned and snarled at him, and Zane rightfully stumbled back a few steps. I chuckled.

"She summoned her bonded dragon, whether she meant to or not. It's better than those nightmarish things she summoned when she first came here." Deiric said. "Dragons are only violent if provoked, so if you don't threaten him he won't eat you." He smirked at Zane.

Deiric jerked his head toward Adriana. "She's safer with *him* than with any of us. We should give them some privacy to get acquainted."

Adriana's face paled at that statement and Deiric chuckled. "Relax." He said calmly. "He's not going to eat you."

He's right. I'm not here to eat you. The dragon's deep voice echoed Deiric's explanation. *When you've finished with your questions, I'll be taking my leave to fly around and see what's changed in the last several hundred years since I lived in this realm.*

"We'll be inside." Deiric said and gestured for everyone to head into the manor.

I hesitated for just a moment, looking back at Adriana who still looked nervous. She nodded after a few moments and I let Deiric drag me into the house once I retrieved my sword.

"We need to talk." I said sternly the moment that the door closed behind us. I yanked my wrist from his hand and crossed my arms over my chest.

I guess I should've said that mentally, because Lazarus, Zane, and Xander all stopped in their tracks and turned to face the two of us with varying looks of concern and surprise on their faces.

A frown ghosted Deiric's lips for a half a second before he shot a glare in their direction. Zane and Xander walked away, but Lazarus leaned against the wall behind him and crossed his arms, determined to stand by and listen. Deiric looked back at me. "Upstairs." He mumbled.

I scowled at him, and I could see Lazarus raise a brow when I glanced over Deiric's shoulder.

Lazarus doesn't have a bonded Dragon and sure as shit isn't supposed to know half of what I know about dragons. Deiric's voice was stern in my head. *I'll answer all your questions, but not* here.

"Upstairs then." I snarled and pursed my lips in a tight line as I brushed past Deiric and made my way to the stairs.

Lazarus looked at me with a little bit of concern, and a question hung in his eyes, whether or not I wanted someone else present for whatever conversation we'd be having. I shook my head, and he sauntered off into the den while I continued past him and walked up the stairs with Deiric in tow just a few steps behind me.

When he closed our bedroom door behind him I spun on my heel and shot him a glare. "What the hell did he mean 'with their dragons' magic'?" I nearly shouted at him. "I've figured out by now that the journal you gave me to read was yours but there was no mention of mind reading coming from dragons." I looked over to where the journal still sat on the table beside the bed. I thought through everything I'd read in it, and realized that it also mentioned magic that the riders *got* from their dragons.

"Wait." I looked at him again. "You've had some form of magic this whole time and kept it from me?"

"Just, calm down for a second and let me explain." Deiric started.

I crossed my arms over my chest and stared at him with a scowl. "You'd better explain really fucking quickly." I was perhaps a little unreasonably angry, but I just stared down a gods damned dragon and had my suspicion that the journal he'd given me was actually *his* confirmed. I wasn't in any mood to listen *patiently*.

"I didn't know that my mind reading was courtesy of the dragons or how their bond and magic interacted with the magic that made *me*. Fiadh didn't mention anything like that, so I doubt at that time she knew. Especially considering I was still mortal when she bonded me." Deiric said rather dismissively.

"You–" I started and he put a hand up to silence me.

"Just, give me a minute to explain. Then you can ask questions." He arched a brow at me. "Is that alright?"

I sighed and nodded then sat on the bed, arms still crossed.

"Fiadh had a mate named Gaisgeach, which is why I'm marked with *two* dragon tattoos rather than one. However, Gaisgeach is not technically bonded to *me*. I don't know where they went, I just know that they left because the king at that time had ordered that the dragons be hunted. I haven't seen them in over six hundred years.

"Shortly after they left I was sent to Lazarus for training before I was inevitably transitioned. And no, I don't have any magic from her. I *did* when she was in this realm, but when they left that connection was severed. If she's even still alive, and she comes back to this realm, I imagine that I'd have access to that magic again, but it wasn't anything substantial."

"Being able to create wards, do simple spells, and infuse magic into a weapon isn't insignificant." I snapped. "If I recall, you also had access to fire magic. Is that all?"

He nodded.

"And what of his claim that *I* have a dragon?"

Deiric shrugged and walked over to sit next to me. "I'm not sure. Perhaps there's one in whatever realm he came from that already knows it intends to bond to you?" He offered, arching a brow and waving his hand suggestively. "That goes beyond what I know."

"By his logic, any of the vampires who can read minds would have dragons as well, would they not?"

"I suppose so, yes." He thought about it. "I'm not really sure how that works with the fact that they're not in this realm. Maybe it's like a predisposed thing. You're born innately being a dragon rider and you just don't know it until the dragon picks you? Somehow I guess the blood magic that created us manipulated it in a way that amplifies that trait when you turn."

I laid back on the bed and stared at the ceiling rubbing my face with my hands. I sighed. "I thought shit was complicated *before* and now we're adding dragons. Honestly, I'm starting to think that this is some kind of twisted dream I've been living in."

Deiric chuckled and turned to look at me from where he was sitting. His knee brushed my thigh as he shifted to bring one leg bent up onto the bed. "You are a sorceress *and* a vampire with a raven as a familiar who occasionally speaks to a goddess and you think that the dragons are the most ludicrous thing to have happened this year?"

"Well when you put it like that," I mumbled. I sat straight up and stared at him in horror as a realization hit me. "Holy shit, do you mean I might have to *ride* one of those things?"

He smirked. "Well, you don't *have* to do anything, but you might get the chance to if you ever meet the dragon that bonds to you."

I sat silently processing everything I'd read in his journal, that he just admitted to me, and that the dragon likely still sitting outside of the manor had shared. My head spun.

"How did they leave in the first place?" I mumbled.

"I'm not sure." Deiric said softly. "Either they created a portal themselves or perhaps someone with Eldritch abilities did so for them?"

"I really wish my mother had explained all of that to me before the attacks." I said softly. "I don't know of anyone else who knew anything about that, and it was never written down."

We sat in silence for several minutes, both too lost in our own thoughts to pay attention to each other. Our silence was finally broken by the unmistakable sound of massive wing beats outside. Adriana shifted into our room less than a second later.

We both jumped, not expecting her to appear in front of us.

"Oh." She raised both brows. "I guess I should have shifted to your door and knocked. I'm sorry!" She mumbled, looking at us sitting on the bed like she'd caught us in a much more compromising position.

"That would be advised in almost *any* other case." Deiric said sternly with a look of disapproval. "But you're here now, so out with it."

"He said you both have dragons. I've never seen them." It wasn't a question, and yet it came off that way.

"I haven't seen my dragon in over six hundred years." Deiric said.

"I'm just as surprised as you." I shrugged.

"He said they left through a portal, and they could come back through that same portal if they wanted to, but they didn't intend to until they *needed* to and there wasn't a push to hunt dragons anymore. I told him I didn't know of any reason we'd be hunting dragons." Adriana said softly. "Have I missed something? They've always been just folklore."

"Before I transitioned, the king at that time did send out an order to hunt down the dragons." Deiric explained. "He was irritated that the dragons and their riders were not a part of his chain of command, and that they refused to do his bidding."

Adriana was quiet for a moment. She was chewing on her lip, thinking. I blocked her out. She could sort it out on her own and I didn't need to listen to it. I had my own thoughts to sort out.

She looked at Deiric. "You have two tattoos."

He nodded.

"How did you–" I started

"After my nightmare, he and Zane were in here keeping watch over me while you made my tea. He didn't have his shirt on."

"Right." I mumbled and looked away.

She shifted her cloak so it was over her shoulders and revealed the tattoo now marking her right forearm. "Why do you have two tattoos, and I have one? And why is mine different?"

"My dragon's mate is linked to me, through her. Each dragon decides how they're going to mark you. It's different for everyone."

"Interesting." She mumbled and went back to thinking. "He's going to call on the other dragons when he's ready." She shrugged and turned to leave. "I guess you'll get to meet your dragon then." She glanced back at me and smiled. "Whoever he or she is."

She seemed far less freaked out than me, which was surprising. She walked out and closed the door behind her.

"Did she seem unnervingly calm about all of this to you?" I asked Deiric.

He huffed a laugh, still looking at the door. "I guess." He finally glanced over at me. "She's taking it far better than you."

I gave him a brief glare. "To be fair, you gave me your journal and tried to pretend it wasn't *your* journal. Not exactly a lie, but certainly not the whole truth, so I had other reasons to be upset than finding out *everything* I thought I knew was wrong."

"Fair." He mumbled.

Chapter 35

Mira

The following morning, I woke to Macha banging on the window, which we'd kept closed because it was far too cold outside to leave it open. When I finally jolted awake she perched calmly on the windowsill.

Deiric groaned behind me and pulled me into him, nuzzling his face into my neck and shoulder to block out the earliest rays of the morning sun while I glared sleepily in Macha's direction.

A man approaches the manor from the east. He is armed.

I rubbed my eyes and stared at her blankly for a moment wondering if I'd heard her right.

You did. An armed mercenary approaches, and I do not know what his purpose is but he doesn't seem like he's getting turned away by the warding.

"Shit." I said out loud.

Deiric barely moved, but mumbled, "what?"

"There's a mercenary in the woods."

He pushed himself up, bracing one hand in front of me, one underneath his chest and glanced in Macha's direction. "Please tell me this is some kind of joke."

Macha just stared, unmoving.

"Shit." Deiric grumbled, and got up to get dressed much quicker than I would've expected for someone who'd just woken up.

He is still a good distance away, but I can lead you to him. Macha said.

I started to get up and get dressed as well. "She said she can lead us right to him."

"You are staying within the wards." Deiric scolded as he buttoned his pants and reached to grab his boots.

"Like hell I am." I said while I started to fumble with a corset.

"Mira." He stood up and gave me a look that said there was no way he was letting me go along.

"It's one mercenary, who is probably not going to expect us to run up on him. I'm going with you." I insisted and pulled on my own boots.

He gave me an exasperated sigh, but patiently waited while I strapped on my weapons and grabbed my cloak. We made it down the stairs and halfway across the foyer when Lazarus appeared in the doorway of the dining room.

"Where the hell are you two off to in such a hurry?" He said, sounding more than a little annoyed to see us armed to the teeth and heading out without him. He wasn't dressed in armor, for once, and seemed to have just stumbled downstairs without dressing beyond his loose fitting pajamas yet.

"There's a mercenary near the edge of the wards." I explained. "Macha is going to take us to him."

Lazarus raised a brow and crossed his arms over his chest. "You're going to go beyond the wards for a mercenary and you didn't think to even tell anyone?"

"It's *one* mercenary. I've already–"

"I don't care." He scowled. "It could be one or ten. *You* shouldn't be going out there."

I snarled at him. "I'm perfectly capable of handling *one* mortal when I have the element of surprise." I glanced toward the door, then back at him. "Now, if you'll excuse us. I'd like to go find him before he gets any closer."

Without another word, Deiric and I walked out the door, and Lazarus didn't yell or run after us. Though I suspect that was only because he certainly wasn't dressed appropriately *or* armed.

We followed Macha nearly a hundred yards beyond the wards when we finally saw him. He wore a navy cloak. A cloak that resembled one I'd seen before. I presumed that meant he wasn't a sorcerer, as the other mercenary I killed hadn't been either.

Deiric and I flanked him, with Deiric approaching from behind, ready to strike, and me approaching him directly. I emerged from the trees in front of him like a dark shadow, with my hood covering my face. I intended to spook him, more than threaten at first.

It had the desired effect, as shadows continued to swirl around my feet. He stopped dead in his tracks and stared at me. The faint scent of his fear wafted toward me on the morning breeze. I smiled wickedly, which resulted in him lowering into a fighting stance, as though he had any chance. I could see Deiric lurking just behind the tree over his right shoulder.

"What is your business here?" I demanded.

"I'm just passing through." He said, trying to keep his face expressionless.

"Just passing through when you're armed with a stake?" I tilted my head to the side, as I let the shadows tell me exactly what he hid beneath his cloak. "Or several, actually."

His throat bobbed in a nervous swallow while he considered his options. "You can't compel me." He said as calmly as he could. Which confirmed he knew exactly who I was, and who he was after.

I let out a low chuckle. "Ah, yes. Drinking vervain so that we can't get answers out of you." I waved my arm in a grandiose gesture of boredom and disinterest. "How clever." I smirked.

He shifted on his feet, backing up a few steps closer to Deiric without even realizing that he was closer to someone who'd sooner slit his throat than let him leave here.

"State your business here." I said coldly.

He scoffed. "You're not going to get any answers from me."

"Oh we will." Deiric smiled and stepped out of the shadow of the tree behind him.

It was far too entertaining to watch the man nearly jump out of his skin and try to turn so he could see the both of us. The scent of fear in the air now was nearly intoxicating and enticing a primal part of me that I hadn't encountered much yet.

"Stay back." He said. He reached for one of his stakes, and his hands were shaking just as much as his voice. I assumed that he was after me, and I couldn't imagine them sending someone who was so easily spooked by vampires to hunt one.

Deiric and I took a few steps closer to him, and he backed away from us, waving the stake like he actually had a chance to harm us with it. It took all of my self control to keep myself from launching at him to make him my next meal. Deiric didn't seem to be affected by his scent at all.

Deiric was in front of him in a fraction of a second, before the man could register him there, he'd grabbed the stake and knocked the man unconscious with a blow to the back of his head with the blunt end of it.

Lazarus appeared next to him a moment later. "I see you got to have all the fun without me." He frowned slightly.

"We need to lock him up somewhere until the vervain has worked its way out of his system." I said as I walked over to Deiric. "He might have insights into who hired him and where we could find them."

"We shouldn't keep him here." Deiric looked over at me. "We don't need anyone tracking him here. And we certainly don't need him getting beyond the wards on purpose."

"We could take him to my manor?" Lazarus suggested.

"I don't think he should go to any warded manor. Do we have anywhere that *isn't* warded?" I asked.

They both shook their heads. I suspected as much, but never really bothered to confirm it for myself anymore.

"What about Devlon? Would Solas have anywhere that isn't warded?" Lazarus suggested.

"Give me a few minutes." I said, and shifted myself to Devlon before I could think better of it. I was surprised to find myself in Aris' manor, outside of one of the bedroom doors on the second floor. I reached up and knocked on the door. It was still early, and I realized I'd probably be waking him up. I waited patiently for a few moments, and then knocked again.

I finally heard someone stirring on the other side of the door and after a few more minutes of waiting, the door cracked open, revealing Devlon, shirtless, and poking his head out the door. I raised a brow at him.

He looked at me like I had three heads. "First of all, do you have any idea what time it is?" He snarled, his eyes still foggy with sleep. "Secondly, what the hell are you doing here?"

I smirked. "Well, for your second question, I could ask you the same thing." I said slightly amused. "The first question, yes, I do know what time it is, and I'm sorry to bother you so early."

"You didn't technically answer the second question." He grumbled.

I sighed, and was about to tell him he needed to answer me first when I heard a female voice beyond the door asking him who it was. I chuckled, and let a knowing smile find its way to my lips. "Well, that answers that."

He scowled at me.

"What, I'm not judging." I crossed my arms over my chest, still smirking at him. "I'm here because I needed to find out if you had anywhere to house a prisoner while we wait for the vervain to leave his system."

He opened the door, and made to step outside of the bedroom, which prompted me to take a few steps back into the hall. He shut the door behind him. "A prisoner?"

"We found a mercenary lurking just outside of our wards, and we don't know what his reason for being there was." I said with a shrug. "He was wearing a cloak similar to a mercenary that had hunted *me* before we started working together. If we can compel him, we might be able to get some answers from him about who is hunting us, or maybe even who Ronan is working with."

He looked away, and I could see the wheels turning in his head as he thought, though I did my best *not* to invade his thought process at that moment. It felt like a breach of trust sometimes.

"We do have somewhere we could probably hold him." He finally said, locking eyes with me again. "Give me a few minutes to get dressed and I can come with you to collect him."

"Take all the time you need." I gave him another knowing look, and he just scowled at me.

"This isn't what it looks like." He mumbled as he turned to walk back into the bedroom.

"Sure it isn't." I smiled again, and he rolled his eyes before he finally walked into the room.

I stood patiently and quietly while I heard him whisper a quick explanation to his female companion before he got dressed and came back out the door.

"Let's make this quick." He said sternly. "I *do* have other things to do today and I'd like to get back here before lunch."

"Interesting." I mumbled, and then shifted the two of us back to Deiric and Lazarus.

When we arrived, Deiric had bound his hands and ankles, and they were both standing over him where he still lay unconscious on the forest floor.

"I imagine he'll be ready to talk by tomorrow morning, depending on how long the vervain takes to get out of his system." I said as I looked down at him.

Devlon walked over and examined the cloak, and the man for a few moments. He was rather unremarkable, with dark brown hair that was tousled on top of his head. He had a little bit of a scruffy dark brown mustache and beard, and he was of average build, with nothing else about him that would indicate who he worked for or his origin. There were no symbols on the cloak either, but it was definitely the same fabric and style of the cloak that had been on the mercenary that Deiric and Xander had dealt with when we'd killed the Lanzani.

Devlon grabbed his arm. "Meet me at the manor tomorrow morning and I'll take you to him." He glanced up at me.

"Staying with your new friend again?" I smirked down at him.

"Aris didn't tell you then?" He raised a brow.

The confused look on my face must have confirmed that Aris had not told us whatever it was he was referring to. He just smirked up at me for a moment and chuckled. "We meet at that manor for all of our joint meetings, so we decided to move in several of our mages as well, to make it more of a joint manor for all coven gatherings."

I raised both brows. "Are you saying *you* live there now?"

He still kept that smug smirk on his face. "Is that so surprising?"

"And your lady friend?" I smirked again.

"That's none of your business." He arched a brow in return at me, and then looked back down at the unconscious man he was holding onto. "Just meet me there tomorrow morning, at a more reasonable hour, and I'll take you to him." Then he shifted away.

"A joint manor?" Lazarus mumbled. "That's a twist I didn't see coming."

I shrugged. "At least we know that we can trust them." I glanced at Deiric. "I don't think it's a bad thing."

Deiric shrugged, then a seductive smile found its way to his face as he walked over to me. "You seemed to enjoy playing the part of the dark, scary woman of the forest to scare the shit out of that man." He slipped a hand around my waist. "I think you play the part quite well."

"Oh for fuck's sake." Lazarus grumbled and started to walk away. "Is that all you two do?" He got a few steps away and then mumbled, "please don't actually answer that question," under his breath.

"Jealous are we?" I called after him, looking over Deiric's shoulder at where he stalked off toward the manor.

"Not at all." His voice was quiet, as he continued walking away, but I didn't have any problems hearing it.

"I feel like I need to play matchmaker for that poor man." I whispered to Deiric.

Lazarus stopped in his tracks and glanced back at me. "You wouldn't dare." His voice was sinister, and cold, but I saw the faintest glimmer of a smile on his lips, even at this distance.

I smiled wickedly and Deiric tried to stifle his chuckle. But I would. In fact, I would be honored to, if Lazarus ever deigned to let me. After all, there wasn't a real rule against turning women. Especially now, and he deserved a little bit of happiness. There was no sense in letting him sulk for all eternity.

Chapter 36

Mira

We walked back to the manor hand in hand, enjoying the few moments we had alone. When we were just about to clear the tree line to walk to the front door I heard wingbeats in the distance, and then saw Adriana burst through the front door in her fighting leathers, a wide grin plastered on her face and her braided hair bouncing behind her as she ran.

Deiric released my hand and grabbed my waist, jerking me back into him as Cairbre landed between us and the manor so swiftly that I hadn't seen him coming. The ground shook under his weight. He crouched down while Adriana climbed up onto him, still grinning from ear to ear.

It took me a few moments to register what was happening. "And what the hell do you think you're doing?" I called up to her.

She glanced over, having apparently not seen us until now. She had both brows raised and looked genuinely shocked for a moment. I assumed she thought we were still in bed. Her expression softened and she smiled down at me. "I'm going to learn how to ride him!"

Don't question the dragons. Deiric warned silently, knowing I was about to shut down the idea.

"We were supposed to train today." I said up to her, avoiding my immediate 'absolutely not' response I had planned at Deiric's instruction.

"We can train when we get back." She smiled.

Cairbre looked at me and barred his massive teeth. A warning to back off. I nodded at him and backed up a step. Before she could even say goodbye he launched them into the skies. The blast of wind from his wings caused Deiric and I to stumble backward. I couldn't help but be impressed that she didn't fly off immediately.

I looked toward the manor again to find all of our mages staring at us wide eyed with their jaws practically on the ground. It was Zemora who spoke first.

"Either I hit my head *really* hard, I'm still dreaming, or there was just a gods damned dragon here."

I smiled. "Well, I don't know if you've hit your head or not, but you're not dreaming, and that was in fact, a dragon."

"Since fucking *when* do we have *dragons?*" Aodh shouted incredulously.

"*You* do not have dragons." Deiric said sternly. "Adriana has a dragon."

"How did *she* get a dragon?" Sorcha asked.

"She has the gift of being able to conjure beings from other realms." I explained. "She summoned him last night and apparently he's decided to bond with her."

Deiric and I started walking toward the front of the manor again. "You know what." I smiled and glanced over at Deiric. "Perhaps *Deiric* should lead the training today. He can tell you everything you need to know about dragons."

He gave me a pointed look, and did not seem amused at the idea.

"What? If we're going to have dragons around, it would be important for them to know how to act around them, and what to expect." I shrugged. "You obviously know what you can and can't share with them."

A muscle in his jaw tensed as he thought it over. Finally he nodded. "Inside." He grumbled, and we all filed back into the house.

*

Adriana was gone for longer than I would have thought, but I tried not to worry or think about it. After we finished their lessons on dragons, or at least as much as Deiric was willing to share, we all took to sparring. The mages sparred with magic, while we sparred with our swords. Deiric and I were in the middle of our match when I heard wingbeats in the distance.

We both stopped and sheathed our swords, looking up to the sky to see if we could see where she was coming from.

"Make room." I shouted, and everyone stopped sparring to look at me. "Adriana is coming back."

They frantically moved out of the way, either up onto the front porch of the manor, or into the trees. Deiric and I hadn't moved yet. We were still looking up to the skies to try to see them.

Brace yourselves. I heard Cairbre say.

Deiric, seeming to understand whatever the hell that meant, grabbed me and spun me into him before slipping his arms around my waist. I instinctively put my arms up around his shoulders and neck, but stared up at him in confusion because it sounded like they were headed straight for us.

Something slammed into my back. I grunted, getting thrown against Deiric as Cairbre's claw wrapped around us snuggly and we were lifted off the ground.

"Shit." I managed to gasp out as I clutched Deiric like my life depended on it and smashed my face into his chest. The bastard chuckled, seemingly unbothered by the fact that we were now in a dragon's gods forsaken claws, flying the gods only know how high.

"Relax" He mumbled.

"What if he drops us?" I grumbled into him, likely barely audible in the wind blowing around us.

Do not insult me, witch, or I will drop you out of spite. Cairbre's voice boomed in my head. That got another chuckle from Deiric and if I hadn't been holding onto him so tightly I'd have punched him.

I dared to open my eyes and look up at Deiric, which was a mistake and a half given that looking *up* at him actually resulted in also looking *down*. Good gods. We were at the same height as the clouds. I squealed and put my face into his chest again.

Of all the things I thought you'd be afraid of, heights certainly wasn't one of them. Deiric thought.

Well, I'm sorry. Not all of us have ridden a gods damned dragon before, and my feet have always been firmly *planted on the fucking ground.* I snarled in my mind at him.

He almost imperceptibly squeezed me a little tighter. *That's not true. You've ridden horses.*

Horses are massively different from dragons and you know it. I snapped.

He chuckled again. *You know, if you'd relax and realize that even if you fall you could shift yourself to safety it wouldn't be half as scary.*

I considered that for a moment, and then dared to look up at him again. *And what of you? If you fell, you'd just hit the ground.*

He smirked. *I won't fall. I know how to ride dragons, remember?*

I scowled at him.

Diving. Cairbre said, and that was the only warning we got before he tucked his wings in and we began a *very* quick descent that left my stomach up in the clouds.

His wings spread wide again to slow us down and I felt his hind legs hit the ground first. He sat us down on the ground with surprising gentleness. I only realized then that I was actually trembling slightly.

Best of luck. Cairbre muttered and then he and Adriana took to the skies again. He didn't even give her the chance to say anything to us. When his massive form disappeared from behind us, we turned to find two other dragons sitting in the large open field he'd dropped us on.

Deiric and I released each other and he smiled toward the beautiful but slightly smaller blue dragon that stood on the left. It was stunning. Its blue scales shimmered in the afternoon sun. Its long tail had large spikes down the length of it with even more threatening looking spikes at the tip of it, which more closely resembled a spiked club. Its wings were tucked closely to its sides and it stood like a statue for a few moments while it sized us up. Its green feline-like eyes felt like they stared directly into my soul.

Fiadh. He started to walk toward her. *It's good to see you.*

The female lowered her head as he approached, and he gently put his hand on her snout. *You haven't aged a day.* She replied.

He smiled. *The benefits of immortality, I guess.*

The other dragon huffed, and I shifted my attention to it. It was significantly larger than Fiadh and studied me closely. Its golden eyes were the most stunning things I'd ever seen and they almost seemed to glow. This dragon's scales were so dark they appeared black, but in the sunlight they shimmered a deep violet hue that was mesmerizing.

I wasn't even consciously aware that I'd started to approach it. My feet seemed to move with a mind of their own. It cocked its head at me and continued to watch me closely. It towered over me, certainly larger than even Adriana's dragon. Power seemed to radiate off of it.

Alesmira. The dragon's voice boomed in my head.

I stopped in my tracks and stared up at its face incredulously. The spikes on his head looked even more threatening up close. *You know my name?* I asked.

He lowered his head and huffed right in my face. The warm air from his nostrils blew the tendrils of my hair that had escaped my braid out of my face. *I've known your name for centuries.*

I was feeling brave. *Do I get to know your name?*

You already know my name. The dragon grumbled.

Gaisgeach. It clicked then. Fiadh's mate. Of course. I could feel Fiadh and Deiric's eyes on us.

Gaisgeach nodded ever so slightly with that massive and terrifying looking head of his, hovering just inches from me.

I'd prefer if you called me Mira.

He angled his head so I was staring right into one of his golden eyes. *I will call you whatever I see fit to call you, Alesmira.*

I shifted on my feet anxiously, a movement he certainly noticed.

Assuming you choose to accept me. He said quietly, and then turned his snout back toward me, inching just a little bit closer.

My mouth dropped open, and then I slammed it shut. *If* I accepted him. Yes, because I guess I could just refuse him. Though I don't know who in their right mind would tell a dragon no, even if Deiric hadn't given me the warning earlier.

Give us a moment. Gaisgeach said to Fiadh and Deiric, who I heard turn and walk away to give us some space. *You're nervous.* He grumbled, like he was slightly annoyed.

I didn't know dragons were even real *until last night.*

That isn't true. His head tilted so I was staring right into one of those golden eyes again.

I sighed and tried to force my body to relax and my heart rate to slow down. *I suppose you're right. I did suspect after I read that journal that it was Deiric's.*

A slight tilt of his head in a nod.

I thought I was just a little ridiculous to think that though. But I can't really deny that anymore.

No. You can't. He was surprisingly patient with me, despite his initial annoyance.

What now then? I asked, staring up at him.

That is up to you. He said, and turned his snout back to me. *If you choose to accept me, you'll become a dragon rider. I'm sure we can overcome your ridiculous fear of flying.* I heard a soft laugh.

I made a face of disapproval of his taunt, but didn't back away. *Alright.* I instinctively reached out to touch his snout, and I could've sworn his lips curled up into a semblance of a smile.

Very well then. He thought, and the moment that my hand touched him, I felt a wave of unfamiliar energy cascade over me. There was a tingling and stinging feeling along my lower back and up around both of my sides, which prompted me to jump just a little and hiss.

Another low chuckle rumbled in my head, and then he lifted his head. He lowered himself to the ground. *Surely you're not going to fly in* that?

You expect me to fly right now? I stared at him incredulously.

I realize you can shift yourself home, but yes. You'll fly.

I arched a brow at him, but waved my hand, replacing my usual blouse, corset, and skirt with my fighting leathers. *Better?*

That will do.

I heard Fiadh approaching again behind us, but didn't hear Deiric's footsteps with her. I turned to see him already sitting on her back, right where her neck met her shoulders. The only place where there didn't seem to be spikes on her spine. I wondered how much of our conversation he'd heard.

I heard all of it. Fiadh wasn't listening, but I wanted to stay close by and make sure you didn't insult him and get eaten.

Gaisgeach snarled at him. *I would not let harm come to her, even if she refused me or insulted me.*

I carefully climbed up onto Gaisgeach and sat at the base of his neck, like Deiric sat on Fiadh. *Please take it easy on me.*

He huffed. *I will do whatever I see fit. If you fall, shift your sorry ass back onto my back.*

I shot him a glare, which he ignored. He stood up and his long neck twisted in what seemed like an unnatural way to me as he glanced back at me. *Hold on tight* Mira.

I would have been happy he finally used the name I preferred if he hadn't emphasized it that way and then promptly launched us into the air. I grabbed frantically for something to hold onto.

I nearly slipped off his back before we were hardly airborne at all with the sudden movement, but managed to grab a hold of a smaller spike and hold on. I supposed it wasn't that much different than riding a horse, except there wasn't a real saddle, and there were no reins. I was entirely at his mercy for where *he* wanted to go.

I heard Deiric and Fiadh launch into the air behind me, but didn't dare look over my shoulder to see him when I was too busy trying not to think about how high we were rising, and how gods damned fast we were moving. When we finally leveled out and I could think straight again I slowly started to relax.

Not as bad as you thought, is it? Gaisgeach tilted his head to glance back at me briefly before he looked ahead again.

When we're just cruising along like this it isn't awful. I begrudgingly admitted. I caught a glimpse of Fiadh and Deiric sailing beside us, and looked over to see him smiling at me.

Admit it. Deiric thought. *It is rather fun, isn't it?*

I watched him, realizing he wasn't even really holding onto anything. *Well, at the moment it isn't terrifying.*

I guess I'll take that. He looked forward again, at wherever it was we were flying to.

*

By the end of the evening, I finally decided that flying wasn't quite as awful as I thought. There were certainly still moments where I absolutely panicked and almost slipped right off of Gaisgeach, though. Deiric admitted to having a few close calls himself, since it had been so long since he'd ridden or even seen Fiadh. We left the dragons at a cave they'd decided was safe and secluded enough for them, which was surprisingly close to the manor. I shifted us to the foyer, and we snuck off to our bedroom when it appeared that no one was looking for us or noticed our arrival.

Once we were in the room and the door was closed behind us, Deiric pulled me against him. His eyes glimmered with curiosity as he surveyed me, one hand traced down my right arm.

"I wonder…" He smirked. "Where did your tattoos end up?" His curiosity switched to something a little more hungry and fierce. He tugged at my leathers, carefully beginning to peel them off of me as his lips grazed mine.

I smiled and tugged him closer to the bed while I backed towards it. "I guess you'll just have to find them." I whispered and started to try to pull off his leathers as well. We both kicked off our boots and got our shirts off, before we reached the bed. He pressed a quick kiss to my lips before spinning us around so he could sit on the bed and look up at me.

He traced his fingers along the tattoos of dragons now etched into my skin, from my hips to my ribs. One on each side, wrapping up and around me, their wings splayed behind them in two stark silhouettes.

I straddled him on the bed, sitting myself on his knees. "If you're quite finished *looking*…" I mumbled, and leaned in to kiss him.

I felt him smile against my lips as his left hand slipped around my waist and his right hand cupped my neck, pulling me against him and deepening the kiss. In the blink of an eye, he had spun us around and laid me down on the bed.

Our bedroom door burst open. "How did–" Adriana started. "Oh gods!" She gasped.

Deiric broke the kiss to turn and bared his fangs in a snarl at her over his shoulder. I imagined it would scare the hell out of her. I didn't even lift my head to look her way, but I heard her quickly shuffle herself back out of the room and yank the door shut behind her. Beyond the door, I heard a chuckle, and then Zane's voice not far down the hall.

"I'm pretty sure she told you to always knock first." His amusement was evident by his tone, and I heard Adriana let out an exasperated sigh. "Surely you've now learned your lesson."

She scoffed. "I didn't exactly expect them to be–"

"Adults, partaking in *adult* activities?" Zane mocked.

"It's not like I could *hear* anything beyond the door." She protested.

I could perfectly picture the smirk I knew was on Zane's face. "And why do you think that is, little sorceress?"

I heard her start to speak, and then I assumed she made the connection that we had a shield around our room so that no one could hear us, before she finally grumbled and stormed off.

Deiric looked back at me, his fangs still out.

"I think the fangs were a little bit of overkill. She's probably scarred enough with what she interrupted, let alone having you snarl like that."

He huffed a laugh and moved to kiss down my neck as though nothing had happened. "Perhaps she needed a little bit more of a reason to leave us be. She'll never storm in here again after that."

I felt his fangs graze where my neck met my shoulder and I let out a soft sigh. I arched my neck to allow him easier access to it. His lips curved into an approving smile and his hand slipped into my hair before he bit me.

I clawed at his back, pulling him down on top of me and arching up into him. Each drag he took from me just fueled the heat and never ending need inside of me. My left hand found its way into his hair, and I pulled his head just slightly to the side while he fed from me. I kissed down his neck before I bit him too.

His entire body tensed and he moaned. The hand that wasn't in my hair slipped up to cup one of my breasts. I realized now that we both still had our pants on, and my bra was an unwelcome barrier between us. Half a thought from me had all our remaining clothing disappearing from both of us.

I felt him against me now, hard and ready. The hand that had been in my hair slipped down my back, under me, until it found its way to my thigh. He pulled my leg up and around him.

He lifted his head from my neck and looked down at me. I pulled away from him at the same moment and looked up at him to see my blood still glistening on his lips. He had a wicked smile on his face.

He closed the distance between us and our lips collided in a passionate fury of tongue and teeth. His fangs grazed my lower lip and I moaned into his lips. The taste of our blood mingled as we devoured one another.

He adjusted himself and thrust into me. I gasped and rocked my hips into him, then flipped us over so that I was on top of him. I felt him smile against my lips and his hands shifted down to my hips. I rode him in a rhythm that brought me right to the edge, the moans and noises I made getting higher pitched with each movement. His hips moved in time with mine, and he kept me moving in that same rhythm until every part of me shuttered when I climaxed.

He shifted us around so I was face down into our pillows and he was behind me. "Gods." He whispered in my ear when he bent down over me. "I love the noises you make. I could never get tired of hearing that."

Then he grabbed my hips and shoved into me again. I gasped into the pillows, clutching the sheets with both hands. I wasn't sure I would ever understand how every single touch from him lit a fire in me that I simply couldn't control. It was passion, lust, a level of bliss beyond anything I'd experienced before we met.

He settled into a maddening rhythm, before his hands slipped down my sides and he pulled me up and back into him. His right hand slipped down around me to stroke my clit, while the other hand teased at my breasts. I moaned, breathless, and slipped one hand up over his head into his hair while I leaned my head back onto his shoulder.

He kissed down my neck, and bit me again. I gasped his name, and he shuttered into me, reaching his climax at the same moment I came to my own again while he drank from me. When he finally released me and withdrew his fangs, we both collapsed listlessly onto the bed.

He pulled me into him, with my back against his chest while we both caught our breath. "You are… just incredible." He mumbled. "I love you."

"I love you." I breathed.

Chapter 37

Mira

The following morning we left Liala in charge of overseeing the sparring of the mages, and Adriana continued to work with Cairbre. Fiadh and Gaisgeach assured us they'd be close by and hiding somewhere they'd be unnoticed. I didn't think that two massive dragons could truly be *that* hidden. However, it wasn't my place to question them.

I shifted Lazarus, Deiric and I to Aris' manor to meet Devlon around noon. He was waiting impatiently in the foyer when we arrived, no sign of his female friend or who she might be.

"I said in the morning." He seemed only mildly annoyed while he walked over to us.

"You said at a reasonable hour. I didn't know what 'reasonable' was to you so I waited until noon." I said with a dismissive shrug.

He gave me a slightly more annoyed glance and then shifted us to wherever it was he had the mercenary. We were somewhere stone and dark, which I assumed might be below our usual meeting place for the Solas gatherings.

A man I didn't recognize jumped to attention when we appeared, looking like he'd been half dozing off sitting on the stool by the door.

"He's been quiet." The man said. He had dark hair, and was wearing a plain shirt and pants. Clearly not an armed guard, but I assumed he likely had magic of some kind to be standing there without any weapons at all.

"Thank you. We'll take it from here. I'll get you when we're finished." Devlon dismissed him, and the man nodded before walking off toward the stairs a few cells beyond us.

Devlon unlocked the door with a wave of his hand and then pushed it open.

Inside the cell the man we'd collected yesterday sat, shackled, on a cot near the back wall. It was a small cell, cramped with the four of us now joining him in it. He had a chamber pot, and an empty tray sitting near him. Overall, the conditions of this cell weren't awful. It only stank of mold and mildew from being below ground and a bit damp.

"Are you ready to talk?" Devlon asked.

The man looked up at us and glared. "I imagine you're going to make me."

I stepped closer and leaned down to lock eyes with him. "You're going to answer all of our questions truthfully, and without hesitation. Do you understand?"

He nodded.

"What were you doing in the woods yesterday?" I asked as I stood up.

"Tracking the princess."

"How?"

"We were given a charmed compass, which led us in the direction of anywhere she'd used her magic. I was following the compass and it led me to that area of the woods."

Interesting. I had always wondered how that other bastard had tracked me, but I hadn't considered they might use the same process for the princess.

"Why the princess?" Deiric asked from behind me.

The man looked at Deiric. "Malachy has requested that she be located."

"Malachy?" Devlon asked, as if to make sure he heard him correctly.

The man nodded.

"What does Malachy want with her?" Devlon seemed to know the name.

"We weren't told *what* he wanted, only that he wanted her, alive and unharmed."

"Who does Malachy work for?" I asked now, hoping to get other names.

"I don't know."

"How many of you are there?" Lazarus asked.

"Three, including me."

"Where were you to take her, once she was found?" I asked.

"We were to take her to the palace, but not to enter through the front gates. There are a series of underground tunnels that we've all been given a different entrance to. We were told exactly where to deposit her within the cells of the dungeon."

"The dungeon." I mumbled while I thought it through. Why would they want the princess in a dungeon? What purpose would that serve?

"Were you to collect anyone else?" Devlon asked.

The man looked at me, a glare on his face. "We were to retrieve the female vampire with violet eyes, if she was with her when we found her. If she wasn't, we were ordered to watch and wait until we could collect them both."

"And what did they want with me?" I arched a brow and studied him closely.

"I don't know. You were to be separated into two different cells."

"So I was to be taken alive as well?"

He nodded. "We were instructed to disable you with the dart I was carrying, and then get you back before that wore off."

I tried to hide my surprise, but I heard Deiric and Lazarus shift a bit on their feet behind me. I stepped back between them, not daring to turn my back on the man, even though he was shackled and stripped of all his weapons. I finally glanced at Devlon. "What have you done with his weapons?"

"They're upstairs, under lock and key with Tellus." He explained.

"I have no further questions at the moment, but I'd like to see his weapons." I turned and walked out of the cell, with Deiric and Lazarus on my heels.

Devlon walked out behind us and locked the door. He walked around us and we followed him up the stairs at the end of the hallway. He sent someone back down to guard the cell before leading us to where Tellus held his weapons.

We followed him in silence until we entered a different hallway and he finally glanced back at us. “It seems odd that Ronan wants both of you. And even more odd that he thinks the King wouldn’t hear of it.”

I kept my face unreadable. “Her training isn’t completed, perhaps he intended to have me finish it. I’d sooner stake myself than do anything for him.”

I could feel Deiric’s glare piercing the back of my head, and Lazarus too. I hadn’t even considered what sort of reaction that comment might bring from them, but the rage I felt coming from both of them was palpable.

Devlon huffed a laugh. “Good to know our most powerful coven member would sooner kill herself than ally with the enemy, *but*.” He stopped at a door and turned the knob to enter without knocking as he glanced at me. “I think that all three of us would agree that we’d rather put ourselves in front of that stake than see you dead.”

I arched a brow at him. “I wasn’t aware that you cared.”

Before he pushed open the door he gave me a sad smile. “Whether or not you see yourself as valuable to us, you’re more important than you realize. You’re more than just a weapon, and the most powerful among us. You’re the embodiment of freedom and choice, especially to those in Oíche.” Then he pushed open the door and walked into the large open room.

Tellus was sitting at a desk, writing on a piece of parchment in front of him. He glanced up from what he was doing, his eyes pausing on each one of us. He looked almost bored. “I expected you a few hours ago. What took so long?”

He asked, finishing whatever it was he was writing before sitting down the quill.

“Devlon said to arrive at a reasonable hour. It seems I waited a little too long.” I glanced at Devlon with an apologetic half smile before looking back at Tellus. “My apologies. Could we see his weapons?”

“There’s no reason to be so formal about it.” Tellus rolled his eyes and slid his chair back before pushing off of the desk to rise from his seat. “I put them over here. We haven’t really examined them, just locked them away.”

He reached into his pocket, dug out a key, and walked over to a small chest of drawers along the right wall. He put the key in, unlocked it, and slid open the top drawer, then gestured for us to look inside. He took a few steps back to give us room.

Lazarus walked over, while Deiric, Devlon, and I remained unmoved. He picked up a stake, which resulted in his fingers sizzling where he touched the vervain on the end of it. His grumbled curse was his only reaction before he set it back down. Then he trifled through the drawer until he finally stopped and pulled a dart out. He turned and showed it to us.

“He didn’t lie,” was all he said.

“You expected him to, even though I compelled him?” I asked as I walked up behind Lazarus so I could peak inside the drawer myself. There was a crossbow, multiple stakes, several of those darts, and various daggers.

“I wasn’t sure if the vervain had actually left his system or if he was just lying for the sake of getting us to leave him alone.” Lazarus looked back at the drawer.

"What exactly is in that dart?" Devlon asked from behind us. I looked back at him and he hadn't moved from where he stood just inside the door.

We were all silent for long enough that Tellus finally spoke up. "We're not going to use it against you, and quite frankly if they know about it there's no sense in hiding it anyway. We'd be of more help to you if we know what we're up against."

I looked over at him, and he had a rather grim look on his face.

"Dead man's blood." Lazarus finally mumbled, and looked up from the drawer to lock eyes with Tellus. "Depending on how much of it is used, it can completely disable us for an unknown amount of time. It depends on the vampire, their age, strength, and a lot of other variables, but it is much worse than vervain, which you already knew about."

Tellus' brows raised. "How do you suspect they found out about that?" He asked, a little taken aback by the substance, I guess.

"Anyone's guess." Lazarus shrugged, still holding his gaze. "Thcy could've taken someone in the attacks years ago and experimented with what might disable or kill us. I don't know if anyone ever actually checked to see if everyone *we* had died in those attacks. Takc Aris for example, he wasn't killed, but none of us knew he was still alive until Leo found him."

A muscle in Tellus' jaw tensed, and his lips pursed. He looked a little irritated now. "Did they really not care enough to do an actual death roll for everyone you lost? Confirm there weren't any who were captured or escaped?"

Lazarus just shrugged again. “They might’ve done that for those with magic, but they didn’t really care about us after that. They wouldn’t have been able to tell anyway. Stake us, and we turn to ash. There’s not much left as far as identifiable material except *maybe* our clothing.”

Tellus grimaced and looked away.

“In their defense,” I started, and all eyes turned to me. “I doubt that anyone was thinking clearly after those attacks, and I’m certain they wouldn’t have expected them to take prisoners. We couldn’t have expected them to know how many of us would’ve been present on those days and then count the piles of ash.”

Lazarus' brows raised as he turned fully to face me. He hadn’t considered that I guess. I was surprised I even thought of it just now, but it made sense. I doubted that Garrick and the other remaining magisters were so cold that they didn’t care about us at all.

“Maybe.” Lazarus said quietly, and then brushed past me to walk over to Deiric. “We should get back and check on Adriana.”

I looked at Tellus, then turned to face Devlon. “I hope that you won’t tell anyone what that does to us, and that you won’t question me if I take this with us to dispose of it?”

Devlon waved his hand dismissively. “You can do whatever you’d like with all of his weapons. Whatever was discussed in this room won’t leave it. That secret will die with us.”

I nodded, and with a wave of my hand, I sent everything back to our manor. “Thank you for your help. What do you plan to do with him now?”

Devlon shrugged. “I suppose we could keep him, at least for a while. He hasn’t done anything to merit killing him, and we might be able to use him to identify others he was working with."

I nodded again. "Keep me posted if anything changes." Then I shifted Lazarus, Deiric and I home. I spent the rest of the afternoon mulling over what we had learned. The prince wanted *both* Adriana and me. I couldn't help but wonder why, and what he might be up to, but I came up empty. And why me specifically? It made no sense. Any mage could train her with her regular abilities, and his distaste for vampires made me the least likely candidate to do the training.

Chapter 38

Mira

That evening, I was laying awake long after Deiric had fallen asleep. I was stuck on the fact that I didn't know what they wanted me for. It made sense now, why they didn't try to kill me the day they ambushed us, but it still drove me a bit mad. When Deiric seemed to be sleeping soundly enough I slipped out from beneath his arm and snuck into some clothes. I had an idea and hoped it might get us closer to getting all of our answers. Then I shifted to Aris' manor. To Devlon.

I was shocked to find myself in the kitchen of the manor, with Devlon sitting at the table and reading. He jumped, not expecting me to appear before him, and then glanced up at me from his book.

"It is the middle of the night." He said plainly.

"And yet, you're sitting almost in the dark in the kitchen and reading a book." I said in response. "Looks to me like you can't sleep either."

He sighed, marked his place, and closed the book. When he sat it on the table, he leaned back in his chair and looked at me. "We caught one of three mercenaries. That means there are two more out there. I've been trying to decide how we'll track them down, aside from just hoping they'll appear by you."

I pulled out a chair and sat at the small table with him. "I guess we both have the same idea then."

He studied me for a few breaths. "You look like you have a plan already."

I smiled. "I do actually, but I'll need your help."

He crossed his arms over his chest and had a doubtful look on his face. "Why me exactly?" He asked, chewing his lip for a moment in consideration. "You've got the entire Oíche coven at your disposal, and yet you're here with me."

I shrugged. "You are holding the mercenary in one of your cells."

"That I am, but it doesn't mean you have to work with me on this." He paused, again looking me over. "Why?"

"Because I've decided that I trust you, and that I think it would be better to have *you* and maybe Tellus in on this rather than Garrick and Oíche." I paused, and then I took the time to study him. He still didn't look convinced. "I plan to use myself and the princess as bait."

His eyes widened for a half a second in surprise, the only sign it caught him off guard. "You trust Tellus and I to watch your back more than you trust the Oíche magisters?"

"I didn't say that."

"Yet you just said that you think we'd be better for this plan of yours."

I nodded. "You managed to build a rebellion without anyone noticing, and I'm sure you've gotten far better with being stealthy through that experience. Plus, if this works we'll have two more mercenaries to toss in your cells."

He leaned forward and propped his elbows on the table as he leaned closer to me. "So what is your plan exactly?"

"We'll go to *practice* outside of the wards. You, Tellus, Deiric, and Lazarus will stay hidden somewhere, assuming that one of them will come. I imagine we'll have to do this a few days in a row to summon them, since they seem utterly human and have no magic."

He nodded.

"When they appear, you'll have to spot them and take them down before they can get to us." I stared at him coldly. "My life sort of depends on it."

"Deiric and Lazarus aren't going to like this idea." He leaned back in his chair.

"I know. But it's the best way to draw them out."

"Are you sure it's worth the risk?" He asked, not even seeming phased by the idea.

"I want to know precisely what they wanted with me, so yes."

"And you don't trust just doing this with them?"

"I do, but like you said, they won't like it." I leaned back in my chair. "We'll have to bring it to them together."

He frowned. "I'd rather not make them hate me."

I smiled. "You said this morning that you'd take a stake for me. I don't think they can hate anyone who feels that way."

He arched a brow. “When do we bring it to them?”

“I can bring them by tomorrow.”

He nodded.

“Does that mean you’re in?”

He smiled a little wickedly. “I’m in. I’ll talk to Tellus in the morning.”

“Fantastic.” I returned a similar smile. “I’ll bring them in the afternoon so we can discuss it.”

“Get some sleep.” He said dismissively, and picked up his book again.

“You should too.” I said, and then shifted myself back to the manor.

I didn’t get more than one step in the foyer before Deiric and Lazarus appeared in front of me. Both only wore pants, and both looked absolutely furious with their arms crossed over their chests.

“Where the hell did you go?” Lazarus snapped.

I raised both brows and took a small step back, mostly in shock that they both discovered that I had left. “I couldn’t sleep.”

“You shifted here.” Deiric seethed. “Where were you?”

I gave them a small frown. “I was gone for maybe five minutes and you’re both ready to snap at me.”

“Did you *really* think I wouldn’t wake up?” Deiric snarled. “You shifted out of the bedroom. I know you didn’t just slip out because you couldn’t sleep.”

Well, I guess there went my element of surprise for the plan I’d concocted to catch the other mercenaries. I wasn’t a good liar, at least, not when I didn’t plan to lie. “I went to talk to Devlon.”

"In the middle of the night?" Lazarus was not amused, and his voice, while it remained low, was more menacing than I'd ever heard it.

"I couldn't sleep. Apparently neither could he. And I had a plan that I wanted to run by him first."

"Without us?" Deiric snarled again. I don't think I'd ever seen him this pissed. Even when I'd forgotten to feed he wasn't truly pissed. Annoyed, yes, but not pissed.

"Well, seeing as you wouldn't like my plan, yes." I shrugged and crossed my arms over my chest. "He agreed to it. I was going to take you two over to discuss it with him tomorrow afternoon."

"And this was so important that you had to go in the middle of the night?" Deiric was *not* happy at all. Maybe even a little jealous? I couldn't tell. If it was jealousy I sensed, it was absurd. I had no desire for anyone but him.

"Well, it wasn't *that* important, but there aren't exactly a lot of moments where I get to go and talk to people by myself, so the middle of the night when I thought it through felt like my best chance."

Deiric's brows rose and his face softened some. They never let me go out by myself, so having private conversations was a little challenging. I could set up a sound shield around myself and whomever I would be speaking with, but still.

"I was gone for five minutes." I said flatly. "Maybe ten. I wasn't shifting into danger. I was shifting to another warded manor to have a brief discussion with someone who literally said he'd take a stake for me this morning. You had nothing to worry about."

"You could have said something." Lazarus said with a scowl.

"And if I said something, would you have let me go by myself?"

"Absolutely not." Lazarus said.

"Exactly."

"What's the plan then?" Deiric asked, changing the subject before I could finish the step I started to move around them and walk upstairs. "Obviously Devlon approved, so you might as well save us the anticipation and tell us now." He didn't seem quite as pissed, but was still clearly annoyed.

So I explained, as casually as I could, and the looks on their faces told me their answer before they said it out loud. It was a resounding no.

"I don't like the idea of them being out there, searching for us. I'd rather we track them down *before* they come here."

"So you'd put yourself in harm's way just to catch them?" Lazarus snarled.

"They might know something. The more we know about why they want her or what their plans are the better. Unless you just wanted to double up on patrols around here and catch them all before they come knocking on our damned door. They're not going to capture others. They're going to kill them."

"She has a point." Deiric mumbled.

Lazarus glared at him in disbelief. "You'd go along with this?"

"If we have enough people to keep them from actually harming her, yes." Deiric held my gaze. "She has a point. We shouldn't just sit idly by while we wait for them to show their faces here."

I shrugged. "Sleep on it and tell me your actual answer in the morning." I said and walked around them both to head upstairs. "I'm *actually* going to bed now that I've got a plan." I walked up the stairs without another word.

Deiric joined me in bed a few minutes later. He slipped his arm around my waist when he slipped in behind me. "I realize that I would've said no, but you could've at least left me a note for where you were headed." He mumbled. "You just disappeared."

"Would a note have actually helped?"

He sighed. "I'd still be upset, but at least I would know where you were."

"Did it upset you that I went to see another man in the middle of the night, or was it just that I left at all?"

"You left without telling me where you're going when we know that there are people out there trying to take you from us. I trust you enough to know that if you're going to meet someone else, I don't need to worry, but going somewhere alone *really* isn't a good idea."

"Eventually, you're going to have to let me go places alone." I said softly. "You know that right?"

"When I know people won't try to kill you, you can go wherever you want by yourself." He whispered. "Now get some sleep."

I sighed, but I didn't really blame him.

Chapter 39

Mira

For the next few days, Tellus, Devlon, Deiric, Lazarus, Adriana, and I would meet at a clearing we picked in the woods late in the afternoon after we'd done some training with our dragons. Adriana and I trained various forms of her magic, and even fought, practicing some close contact combat with magic. The first two days we brought the training swords and I also taught her how to fight hand to hand. By the fifth day, we finally found our marks.

I heard them approaching behind Adriana. Devlon and Tellus jumped in before I even had to say anything. Either they'd seen them approaching, or they had some kind of magic setup to notify them of their arrival, because I knew there was no way they heard them. They didn't even use their magic, aside from shifting behind them. They merely held two short blades to their throats and the men begrudgingly yielded. They were not in positions to fight back.

"Well, that was easier than I thought." I said with a smirk. "You two make a pretty effective team."

Tellus smirked right back at me. "We had *years* of practice before Devlon got far too involved in politics." He rolled his eyes a bit when he glanced at Devlon.

I had wondered what seemed to have pulled them apart. They acted like close friends since the treaty had been signed, but their interactions before that were tense at best. It made sense now. Devlon moved into the political aspects of the coven to save it, that much I knew. He didn't have a plan beyond that though. Tellus had the grit and the vision, leading the quiet rebellion.

Devlon didn't even appear to be slightly offended and just half shrugged. "We'll make sure they're ready when you come to interrogate them."

I nodded and without any further discussion they shifted away. If they didn't have Deiric and I to compel them, I wondered who would be performing far more… barbaric interrogation. Tellus, I suspected, though I didn't think either of them had it in them to torture people for information like I knew *I* would. And in that moment, I realized just how dark my soul had become. I never once questioned what I'd done in the years I was a mercenary to the people I'd tortured or killed.

"Are you alright?" Adriana asked, breaking me from the thoughts that were plaguing me. I blinked and looked at her for a moment. Had she said something before that? I wasn't sure. I gave her a half hearted smile.

"I'm fine. Just thinking, that's all."

"It didn't look like *good* thinking."

A slight frown formed on my lips before I could stop it, then I shook my head. "It's nothing you should be concerned about."

Deiric and Lazarus emerged from the trees behind me and I shifted us back to the manor to resume her training. Stella, Sorcha, and Zemora were all practicing as I'd requested, fighting one another with their various magic types and practicing dodging, shielding, and attacking.

"Go practice with them." I said to Adriana, who looked at me with confusion, still holding the practice sword in her hand. "With magic." I specified and nodded my head in their direction. "We'll all resume hand to hand training tomorrow."

She was nearing a point where I could say she'd mastered her magic, but I wanted her to successfully master misting first, which had some slow progress so far. She nodded and handed the training blade to me before going over to join their group. Their training and the dragons got me thinking. I turned to face Deiric.

"I think that we should practice." I said with a half smile.

Lazarus looked between us, just as confused as Adriana had been. "With training blades?" He asked.

Deiric smirked. "No." He glanced briefly at Lazarus before locking eyes with me again. He knew exactly where my mind had gone just now when I'd watched Adriana go to train with the other mages. "With magic."

Lazarus snorted. "You don't have–"

Deiric summoned Fiadh's fire in his hand.

"What in the actual fuck." Lazarus stumbled back a step, well and truly shocked. More so than I'd ever seen him before.

I chuckled and Deiric's smirk grew into a more wicked smile. "I was wondering when you'd ask to see it."

"He gets magic from his dragon." I said to Lazarus without looking away from Deiric. "I would too, but I don't really need it." I summoned a little fire of my own. "On with it then."

The small flame floating in his hand grew and flew at me in a massive blast of fire that sent Lazarus sprinting toward the manor, while the mages nearby stopped and gaped. I switched fire for water and the resulting steam made it hard to see for anyone in the vicinity.

"You did that on purpose." Deiric snarled.

"So what if I did?" I smiled and sent a blast of fire at him similar to the size he'd sent at me, careful to make it a fire that wouldn't burn or harm him if he didn't block it.

He hissed and blocked, almost too late. I let a massive gust of wind blow the steam out of the way so he could see again.

"You'll have to fight in less than ideal conditions at some point. You're going to have to really pay attention to your surroundings without being able to see what's in front of you at all times." I smiled. "You managed to block that, so you're not too rusty I guess."

Go easy on him. He hasn't practiced at all. I heard Fiadh's voice in my head.

I may be out of practice but I'm not completely useless. Deiric snapped back at her.

And you're of no use to me burned alive either. She snapped right back.

I wouldn't let it burn him. I said sweetly. Though, truthfully, I would if I needed to do so to remind him just how quickly he *could* be hurt if he didn't pay attention and react quickly enough. He had the reflexes and superhuman speed to do it, after all.

He sent another blast right for my face and I smirked before blocking it with a small shield of shadow.

"You know, it would be far more interesting if you just used fire too." Deiric said with only a hint of annoyance.

"Maybe, but I prefer the shadows. You know that."

"Perhaps you need more practice with the other elements?"

I arched a brow at him. "Fine." I smiled again. "Only fire. Bring it on." I set up a shield around us so that he didn't accidentally light the house or the mages on fire, and we began a fun dance of fire and fists.

He sent fire hurtling toward me in various forms, a ball of fire, a massive blast, or smaller whip-like flames and I sent all of it right back, dodging, deflecting, or simply returning the magic he threw at me. To my surprise, he kept up fairly well and I didn't even have to hold back much.

He was right, for once, I was rusty with fire. He almost landed several blows to me when I didn't deflect well enough.

"I told you. You need to practice the other elements more." He said with a wicked grin when he nearly singed off my hair.

Easy. Gaisgeach said quietly, like he could feel the burning rage that rose in me with Deiric's comment. I wondered for a moment where they were so that they could hear us.

We're not far. He said almost immediately. *We keep close in case we're needed, out of sight among the clouds.*

We resumed our fighting for a few more minutes, until I could tell Deiric was nearing his limits for having not practiced in so long.

"That's enough for today." I said finally and removed the shield I'd put up. "No sense in burning yourself out just to prove a point."

"I do know how much I can handle you know." He said with a slight scowl, his breathing only slightly labored, but the hint of sweat on his brow told me enough.

"I'm sure you do, but *I* don't see a reason to push it."

He shrugged and headed toward the front door. Lazarus was still looking at him like he had three heads, as if he couldn't possibly fathom Deiric ever having any kind of magic. The mages wisely had already gone back to practicing themselves.

Macha swooped down from the roof and landed on my shoulder. *Since you seem a little preoccupied, I thought I'd remind you tonight is a dark moon.*

I turned to look at her and smiled. *For once, I'm glad you reminded me.*

You can repay me for reminding you by making sure your new beast doesn't eat me. She said flatly.

I chuckled. *I don't think he'd eat you. I imagine he prefers larger meals.*

I do. Gaisgeach said. *Birds are not worth the effort, and their feathers are less than appetizing.*

Macha shook her wings in annoyance and cocked her head at me. *I'll be out here when you're ready to leave.*

You're coming along this time?

If you'll have me, yes.

I nodded and she flew back up to her usual perch.

Chapter 40

Deiric

I found myself lying awake in the early hours of the morning deep in thought. Sleep at this point entirely escaped me. I looked down at Mira, who was sleeping soundly with her head on my chest and her arm around my waist, completely unaware of the thoughts swirling in my mind. She willingly put herself and Adriana in harm's way for several days just to capture the two remaining mercenaries that hunted them.

I couldn't help but wonder what on earth was so important for *Mira* to be captured too. She seemed to have her own suspicions which she didn't share with me, but I was at a loss. Unless Ronan wanted her training to continue after he secured her somewhere else, but that left the question of what he planned to do when the king found out, and what sort of plot he was running there.

I sighed and lifted my left hand up to toy with the fire magic I could channel from Fiadh. I let the flames dance around my fingers for a few moments, admiring them.

You're up early. Fiadh's voice floated into my head, with a mildly annoyed tone to it. *Shouldn't you be sleeping?*

I could say the same for you. I let the fire I was playing with fizzle out and lowered my hand to Mira's arm where it rested across my stomach.

I sleep when I feel like it. I don't need to sleep all night like you do. Fiadh snapped. *What troubles you?*

That is a long list.

She sighed. *Enlighten me.*

Well, I'm concerned about what the prince's plans are for Mira and Adriana. I started.

Yes, that's old news, we're all curious about his plans. What else? Her tone was more dismissive than I remembered her ever being with me all those years ago.

Are we mated because *of the two of you, or is that simply a coincidence?*

I heard her snort. *While it is certainly an* odd *coincidence, our choice in mates is unrelated, unless you consider both of us going for a powerful mate as a stroke of fate.*

I half laughed at that. Though I don't think power was what drew me to Mira in the first place. *Did you or Gaisgeach know she was my mate?*

No. Fiadh said rather matter of factly. *But even if I did I wouldn't have shared that with you.*

How are you still... alive? I asked hesitantly. She'd told me once that when a rider dies, so does their dragon. Technically, I died when they turned me.

Your humanity may be no more, but you were never dead. *You were merely in a state of transition.* She paused for a few moments, and just as I was about to ask another question, she continued. *Do not think that it didn't pain me, even in another realm. I could* feel *your human death. Had you not completed the transition, I would have died as well.*

And how is it that my magic didn't work for all those years, but you felt that?

She sighed. *The bond between us as far as our lives are concerned is far different than the magic we share. If we are too far apart, you won't be able to draw that power from me.*

I gently began to run my fingers through Mira's hair. She snuggled closer to me at the touch, but didn't stir otherwise. She remained blissfully unaware of my silent conversation with Fiadh, and all the concerns brewing in my head.

Why are you here now? The question I'd really wanted to ask, but was afraid of the answer to. They wouldn't come back without cause.

The princess finally summoned Cairbre, and he determined that the world was safe again, at least for now.

I stopped running my fingers through Mira's hair abruptly and arched a brow, despite that she couldn't see me. *What does that mean exactly?*

War is brewing.

War? With who and for what? I asked, my breath hitching for a moment and my body went rigid. We just battled to allow the damned coven to exist again. We're going to have to go to war *again?*

There are forces at play that are beyond even you, and I will not elaborate further. I've already said too much.

We are here again because we were called to be, and the fates would not be in your favor otherwise. That is all you need to know.

But– I started, but Mira stirred.

She looked up at me with heavy, sleep laden eyes. "Shouldn't you be sleeping?" She asked, her voice barely a whisper.

"Shouldn't you?" I replied with a half smile that I knew didn't meet my eyes.

"You were talking to Fiadh, weren't you?" She mumbled.

"How did you know?" I asked.

"Lucky guess." She half smiled, then shimmied herself up so she was able to lay a gentle kiss on my lips. "You should get some sleep, love. You can talk to her at a more reasonable hour."

She has a point. Fiadh cut in.

"I haven't been sleeping well lately."

"Hmm." She lazily lifted herself up and straddled me before I could stop her, positioning her hips right over mine. She leaned down until her lips almost brushed mine again. "I think I know what might help you with that." She had a smile on her lips as she stared down into my eyes. Her hands found their way to my chest, and then one slipped up into my hair.

I slid my hands up her thighs to her hips and found a wicked grin rising to my lips. "Oh really?"

She nipped at my lower lip and then rested her forehead against mine. "Unless you'd rather just lay awake all night…" She rolled her eyes coyly and started to lift herself off of me to lay back down next to me.

I grabbed her hips now and held her in place. "I couldn't think of anything I'd rather do." I said softly.

*

When we finally woke up again, it was already mid-morning and it sounded like the rest of them had gone about their day without us. Mira was laying in front of me, curled into me and still completely naked. She interlaced her fingers in mine and glanced over her shoulder with a smile.

"Don't get any ideas." She said softly. "We *do* have to get out of bed at some point. I just left a note on our door to leave us alone until noon." She smiled.

"How did you manage that?" I asked softly, kissing her shoulder.

She rolled onto her back and looked back at me. "I don't *have* to train them in the mornings and I figured Fiadh and Gaisgeach wouldn't complain about a day off from training *us* to stay on their backs."

Someone banged on the door.

Mira snarled. "The note clearly says not to bother us before noon."

"Yes, well Devlon sent me to tell you they found Malachy, and they'd like to move *today*." Aris said from the other side of the door. How he got here, I didn't know. Unless he'd run all the way here this morning.

Mira pulled the sheets up over herself. "You can enter and explain."

"Mira, shouldn't we at least–" I didn't even get to finish suggesting that we get dressed before Aris had opened the door. Mira was sitting up with the sheet wrapped around her, leaving me still laying down and exposed from the waist up.

The look on his face suggested he regretted listening to her. “You could’ve gotten dressed first.” He mumbled.

She shrugged. “It isn’t like you caught us in the act.” She surveyed him for a moment while I looked back and forth between the two of them. “Explain.”

“One of Tellus’ spymasters tracked Malachy down, and determined that he goes to a set of castle ruins once a week, like clockwork. If that schedule still holds true, he’ll be going today.” Aris explained rather matter of factly, gave me an incredulous look, which I merely shrugged at, and then looked back at her. “They’d like us to meet at my manor in an hour.”

“That’s rather sudden isn’t it?” Mira asked, a hint of annoyance in her voice. “What about interrogating the other mercenaries?

Aris shrugged. “At least you’ve got an hour to finish up whatever it is you were so busy doing in here.” He smirked. “He didn’t seem concerned about interrogating them now that they’ve found Malachy.”

“Sleeping.” She seethed. “We were *sleeping.*”

He arched a brow and his smirk grew into a grin. “Sleeping because you were up half the night doing other exciting activities I’m sure.”

She chucked a dagger I didn’t even realize she kept under her pillow at him. He caught it midair and just shook his head.

“You must be tired if your aim is *that* bad.” He smirked again.

“I wasn’t trying to hit you.” She shrugged one shoulder. “That was a warning.”

He tossed the dagger back at her. She caught it and stuffed it back under her pillow. "We'll be there." She mumbled. "Please close the door on your way out."

He nodded, stepped back out of the doorway, and pulled the door shut behind him.

She sighed and laid back onto the bed next to me. "So much for training at *all* today."

I was still stuck on the dagger she'd pulled out from the pillow, how I hadn't ever noticed it, and why she felt the need to sleep with it.

I tried desperately to hide the smirk rising to my lips. "You sleep with a dagger under your pillow?" I couldn't hide the amusement from my voice, because for some reason, that kind of turned me on.

She looked over at me, studying my expression before she finally narrowed her eyes at me. "Oh no, don't you go getting *any* ideas because of that either." She grumbled, and then slipped from the bed to walk to the bathing room. "We only have an hour before we need to be there and I don't want us to be late."

I just sighed and begrudgingly got out of bed myself to get dressed.

Chapter 41

Deiric

We told Gaisgeach and Fiadh to stay back at our manor. Mira made it very clear to everyone at the manor that the dragons would be a secret until it was relevant to mention them. Gaisgeach and Fiadh protested heavily that we *shouldn't* go alone, but after I assured both of them we'd be perfectly safe without them they finally agreed to stay back and stay hidden.

All of the magisters from both covens were gathered at Aris' manor when we arrived. His manor became our base of all joint operations and housed members of *both* covens. This recent change had been prompted by our last visit here, where Devlon did decide to make himself at home, *literally*, as Mira had suggested. It seemed odd, seeing all of them here again. I didn't know what to make of it, if I'm honest. I knew that Devlon said they'd done this when we saw him in the woods that day, but I didn't believe it until I saw it myself.

All those years in hiding, all those years fighting, and now here we all stood, working together as a well oiled machine. Our spymasters worked together, our *people* worked together, and we were about to go track down a rogue mage as one unit, rather than separate covens. It was downright mad.

Mira smirked, no doubt following my train of thought, though she didn't seem to have a readable thought in her head at the moment. I only knew the smirk resulted from *me* because no one else was talking, and to my knowledge, was *thinking* anything coherent either.

"We need to move." Devlon walked over to us. "If we don't move now we might miss him."

Mira nodded and as one, we all shifted. We arrived at the edge of an unfamiliar thicket of trees. Far enough from the edge of them that we would be undetectable to anyone near the castle ruins that we could see just over the hill. There was a rustling to our left in the brush and then a man wandered into view.

He was tall, lanky, and wore a long sleeved tunic and black pants. His clothing was rather plain and inconspicuous, which, if he was a spymaster, I guessed was the point. His bland blond hair was tied back in a ponytail at the base of his head, and his blue eyes looked dull and bored, like he had far better things to do. His expression matched them.

"You're certainly cutting it close." He mumbled, glancing at Devlon before looking around at the lot of us.

"We have plenty of time." Devlon replied sharply.

Mira surveyed him, her expression blank and unreadable. *He's not quite what I expected.*

I nearly chuckled at her thought, but managed to stifle it to just a smirk. *This is his illustrious spy master?*

I noted the slight shrug of her shoulders, but Devlon didn't introduce us.

"He should be arriving any minute now." The man continued. This must be the spymaster then, otherwise he wouldn't know Malachy's schedule. I looked back over toward the castle ruins. There certainly didn't appear to be anyone else here. It was almost too quiet and deserted, and it made me a little uneasy.

"Have you gone in and investigated what is within the ruins yet?" Mira asked. I turned my focus to her, and then this unnamed sorcerer again.

He shook his head. "I didn't want to spook him, or run into anyone who could get word to him that we'd found the place. All I've done is observe. This seems to be the only time he's alone where we could successfully capture him without causing an uproar or endangering innocent people."

Mira's lips pursed into a tight line and something told me she had a gut feeling too, but she kept her thoughts shielded and unreadable. Her gaze shifted to look back over toward the ruins while everyone spread out around us so they could see as well. Even though we were working as one, it seemed that we didn't mingle much. Everyone from Oíche took the space to our right, while everyone from Solas took the space to our left.

A few minutes passed and then, emerging from the tree line, was a man with light brown hair, dressed in a plain tunic, pants, tall black boots with a thin gray cloak over his shoulders.

Shit. Mira thought, so bluntly that I jerked my head around to look back at her again. Her expression was no longer blank, in fact, her face had gone pale, and her eyes were wide. Even her heart rate seemed to pick up. I desperately hoped this wasn't the beginning of her going into a complete panic again. Not here. Not in front of all of them.

She locked eyes with me for a brief moment. Enough to tell me she recognized this man, and while she didn't give me any idea as to how, I didn't doubt that for a moment. Her nostrils flared, like she was scenting the air for something specific.

"What's wrong?" I whispered and every head turned in her direction.

She knelt down to the ground, and lay a hand on the bare earth in front of her. After a moment, she hissed and recoiled her hand from the ground as though she'd been physically burnt by it. She stood up and looked toward Malachy again as he approached the ruins. She frowned and looked at me.

"This isn't just a castle ruin." She said flatly, a tinge of fear even edging her voice. "It's a prison." She turned and watched him walk toward the entrance. "And he's carrying blood."

I locked eyes with Lazarus, who was standing just beyond her left shoulder. We both took in a deep breath, and sure enough, so faint it would've been missed if we weren't looking for it, the scent of stale blood was there. It clicked then and I knew without a shadow of a doubt that this was the man from the nightmare she'd had all those months ago.

I looked at Devlon, and the Solas mages, whose brows nearly rose to their hairline. Clearly, they were not aware of this *prison.*

"A prison?" Devlon asked.

She nodded subtly and slowly. “There are wards around it. I can’t see beyond it and it burned me for trying. If we go in, we’ll have to be brought out by one of you. Otherwise we’ll be stuck in there.”

“We can’t just remove the wards?” Garrick asked from somewhere behind me.

Her face went rather grim. “No.” She looked over in his direction. “These wards were created with blood magic. We’d have to kill every single magister who created it, and their entire bloodline in order to destroy them.”

“Whatever we’re going to do, we need to do it now.” Lazarus watched Malachy carefully as we discussed what to do. “He’s reached what’s left of the front door, and if we don’t get down there quickly we’ll lose our chance.”

The only other way to remove the wards would be for the old magisters to do it themselves, and their magic is gone. Mira added mentally, and I realized she was furious with herself now for the decision she’d made about their punishment. If she’d allowed them to keep their magic and just imprisoned them in cells that blocked it, this could’ve been avoided. We could’ve compelled them to remove it.

We all shifted closer, to just outside the wards, and began to walk toward the ruins. Mira paused at where I guessed the wards were. There was the slightest hesitation, like she’d misjudged what she read when she encountered the wards with whatever magic she used back in the trees.

Garrick stepped up next to me and then stepped forward through it. The only confirmation I got that this *was* the limits of the wards was the grimace on his face as he passed through them and it clearly didn’t feel pleasant. As if to test Mira’s theory, Tellus almost immediately reached beyond the invisible wall, grasped Garrick's arm and yanked him back through.

Garrick stumbled and looked like he might be sick, doubling over and bracing his hands on his thighs for a moment. "Shit." He breathed.

"It's keyed specifically to members of Oíche." Mira explained. "It will lock us in, and hurt like hell coming back out."

"We will pull you all out." Devlon said, like he needed to reassure her. Then he walked through the wards himself. Before he proceeded, he backed out just to confirm for himself that Mira was correct, and breathed a sigh of relief.

"Let's move." Mira said and, without hesitation, walked right through the wards.

I followed less than a step behind her. Saying that the experience was unpleasant was an understatement. I could *feel* the magic move through me, and it burned in a way that was hard to put into words. The rest of the group crossed behind us and we spread out as we approached the entry. Devlon, Garrick, Tellus, and Liam went in first. Mira drew her sword. Lazarus and I followed suit before we entered the castle ruins. I still found it rather ironic that she went for her weapons first, when she had an arsenal of magic far larger than any of us did. Perhaps all those years as a mercenary where she couldn't use her magic were just too hard to shake.

The first portion of the castle was still mostly open to the sky. The roof had deteriorated and fallen in some areas, while in others I don't think there had ever been one. We crossed through the courtyard and then entered what would have been the foyer of the castle, which was where we'd watched Malachy move less than two minutes ago.

We listened closely to everything around us as we all went further into the space, some of the magisters breaking off to clear rooms and confirm he wasn't there. Lazarus and I stayed less than a step from Mira on either side of her, prepared to jump and defend her at a moment's notice.

In the dim light of the castle, I was thankful we had the ability to see better in the dark, but I was even more thankful for the armor we wore. I knew that at least with this no one could *kill* her in the dark. Unless they tried to behead her, but we'd be able to block that before they could.

We followed a safe distance behind Devlon and Garrick. There was a scuffle ahead of us, followed by shouting and cursing from Devlon, Garrick, and who I presumed to be Malachy.

"We've got him." Devlon called out.

The other mages continued on their mission to clear the remaining rooms while the three of us caught up with Devlon and Garrick. When we reached the large stone room they'd caught him in, he was restrained with chains that blocked his magic and they had him on his knees. I hadn't even seen the chains on them when we arrived, but I assumed they had to have been carrying them under their cloaks. Garrick and Devlon each held one chain in their hands.

His hazel eyes gleamed with a wickedness that nearly sent shivers down my spine. He smiled just as wickedly when he saw Mira that I was tempted to behead *him* just for that look.

"The legendary *elder mage*." He spat her title with a sneer. "We've been expecting you." He mumbled. "Well, technically we were looking for the princess, but we needed you too." His smile widened. "How lovely to meet you."

Mira glared at him.

"He's mad." Devlon scowled at him. "He seems to think that he's still won somehow."

He chuckled, the sound was deep and menacing. "How is the princess's training going?" He drawled. "Has she practiced her eldritch abilities yet?"

Mira, to her credit, did not react. The same could not be said for Devlon and Garrick, but he couldn't see their faces, so I supposed it didn't matter.

"She doesn't have Eldritch abilities." Mira said menacingly, and slowly.

"Liar!" He snapped and scowled. "We've known about those abilities since her birth." He smiled again. "Well, a select few of us anyway."

"He's stalling." Tellus said as he came up behind us. "There's probably some kind of trigger on this ward that would notify others when we arrived. We need to move."

Then, I heard something. It was faint, like it was barely a whisper.

Mira shushed everyone in the room. All three of us leaned forward and listened. There was a dark passageway behind the three of them that we hadn't bothered to look at or care about until now. It was a stairwell that led down below ground somewhere.

"Mira?" A voice I didn't recognize came again from the depths of that passage.

"Shit." Lazarus said aloud and lunged for her, but it was too late. Mira was already moving.

Chapter 42

Mira

There was no mistaking that voice. It wouldn't have mattered if it was ten years since I'd heard it or a few days. The moment the realization hit me, I was moving, damning the consequences of flying into the depths of that passageway alone. Lazarus and Deiric sprinted after me.

"Mira." Deiric grabbed for my elbow, and I felt his fingers graze me, but I pulled away before he could stop me. I heard my name again and stopped in front of the door it had come from. I placed my hand on it and undid the lock. It felt like far too simple of a spell. I guessed with the warding, they figured none of us would be stupid enough to come in and get someone out.

I hesitated before I shoved the door open. This could be a trap. I just sprinted down into this tunnel without warning. Deiric and Lazarus stood behind me now, on either side, but neither moved to stop me. I sheathed my sword, and shoved the door open.

There, in the back of the cell, was my father. He was leaning back against the stone wall, shackles on his wrists and ankles. He was filthy. His gray eyes looked tired and wary, but relieved to see me at the same time. Otherwise, he appeared the same.

He was so incredibly weak. I could tell. And I stood there frozen in disbelief. Lazarus stepped around me and walked in. I unlocked the shackles, another simple spell, and Lazarus leaned down to help my father to his feet. He pulled his arm over his shoulders and supported him almost completely.

Deiric tugged at my elbow. "We need to move." I glanced over at him, and his eyes locked with mine. "*Now*."

I yanked him aside. I motioned for Lazarus to go first and take my father out. He seemed delirious despite having recognized me and knowing my voice enough to call out to me. Still, he seemed just as shocked and frozen as me.

Deiric and I followed right behind them. Tellus and Liam waited for us at the top of the stairway and then followed us all out in silence. When we reached the wards, Malachy was nowhere to be found, but Devlon and Quinn were there.

"I sent Malachy back with the other magisters. They're taking him to a cell." Devlon explained. He reached through the wards to grab one of us and pull us through.

Deiric nudged me forward first, and Devlon pulled me out. The wards definitely hurt more the second time I passed through them. I hadn't seen him reach beyond me, but Tellus pulled Deiric through right behind me. Devlon and

Tellus both reached in again to pull Lazarus and my father out, before finally pulling Liam out as well.

Devlon didn't say a word, but he, Tellus, and Quinn shifted us all back to Aris' manor.

"I didn't expect you–" Aris' voice cut off abruptly. "Shit. Teron?" His voice sounded just as confused, shocked, and distraught as I felt. "How?" He asked next.

"Doesn't matter how." Lazarus grumbled. "He needs to feed. Now." The urgency in his voice said everything Aris needed to know.

Aris took my father's other arm and they walked him away to a room off the foyer. Aris barked orders to someone in the direction of the kitchen, before they closed the door behind them.

I was vaguely aware of Devlon talking to Tellus, Quinn, and Liam, but I didn't hear what he was saying. I was too busy staring at the door that they'd taken my father through. I found myself asking the same question that Aris had. *How?*

None of this made sense. He was held captive. For what? And how was he still in at least relatively decent shape? His body condition didn't seem to have changed, though he might've looked tired, filthy, and utterly devastated. He didn't say a word to me after he saw me. There was recognition in his eyes, but nothing else.

He had clearly been drugged, vervain if I had to guess. The dream I had… I thought back to it. I had this feeling of not wanting to drink the blood for some reason. I suspected vervain was the reason the more I had thought about it. It also smelled stale so certainly not something I would've ingested unless I had other options. My mind raced.

Deiric stepped in front of me, blocking my view of the closed door and refocusing my attention on him. "Mira." He said calmly.

I searched his face like it would give me answers, but I knew he had none. "He's alive." I finally breathed.

He merely nodded.

I wanted to pace. I wanted to scream. Part of me wanted to cry with relief. The emotions rushed into me all at once. Twelve years. It had been *twelve years* and I thought he was dead all this time. Finally, my emotions leveled out and all that was left was cold, hard, rage. He'd been held captive for *twelve years*. Those fucking bastards.

"I'm going to *slaughter* them." I snarled.

Deiric smirked. Actually fucking smirked. "And just like that, she's back." He chuckled. "I thought I lost you there for a few minutes."

"Those bastards." I growled.

He squeezed my shoulders. "Easy." he cooed, like I was a wild animal who needed taming. "We need to figure out what they're trying to do first. What their goal is." He said calmly, the smirk long gone now that he saw the raw bloodlust in my eyes.

"I should have killed them *all*." I was seething. There was nothing that could calm me. I wanted to rip all of their throats out for whatever they might've done to him, for how long he suffered.

There was a half laugh from behind Deiric. "She is quite a handful, isn't she?" My father drawled. I glanced over Deiric's shoulder and there he stood, leaning against the threshold of the room they'd shuffled him into, arms crossed over his chest, with Lazarus standing to his right and Aris leaning against the wall to his left. Already back on his feet, somehow seemingly unphased by everything.

I should've expected it wouldn't take that long to find him someone to feed on to recover even a fraction of his strength, but I didn't expect to see him up and *normal* looking so quickly. His clothes were still torn and tattered. He was still filthy, but he looked exactly like he did that morning before my entire world crumbled around me.

Deiric released my shoulders, but I didn't move. I just stared at my father, an angry snarl still plastered to my face, my fangs still out, and rage boiling in me like a volcano readying to erupt.

"Seems like I've missed a lot while I was… " his voice trailed off while he looked away for just a moment as though he couldn't bring himself to say while he was locked away and dealt with the gods only knew what for twelve years. He looked back up at me and smiled, a bit smugly.

"Perhaps you'd like to introduce me to your *mate?*" He had the nerve to raise a brow and look mildly disappointed with me.

Deiric turned so he could see both my father and me. He was carefully evaluating my reactions, and watching my father as well, like he didn't know how this was going to go.

I snarled at him, and my hands curled into fists at my sides. I could see Deiric's raised brows out of the corner of my eye as I stared down my father and started taking a few steps in his direction. The look on my father's face wavered slightly, like he might've realized he made a mistake with the tone of his comment and my current mental state, but it was Deiric that stopped me.

You're only angry right now because you want to kill them all for what they did to him. Breathe. He said softly in my mind.

I halted, and only slightly turned my head in his direction.

Breathe Mira. He urged and walked toward me to grab my arm.

I looked back at my father, who absolutely realized he'd made a mistake in taunting me at this very moment. He also looked confused, like he couldn't understand how Deiric had stopped me. I guessed by that look that he'd shoved off Lazarus and Aris trying to catch him up and demanded to just *see* me. But no one should see me right now.

I shifted Deiric and myself outside, where everyone always sparred in the courtyard. He didn't ask any questions. He drew his sword and prepared to fight. I spun around and drew mine, and we both lunged for one another.

Chapter 43

Teron

Aris and Lazarus hauled me off to a room just off of the foyer and moments later a woman was rushed in for me to feed on. I didn't even see her face, nor did I really care. When I was replenished enough to function mostly normally I stopped and looked up at Lazarus, who was looking off toward the door and carefully listening to what was happening outside of the room.

"I'd like to see her." I demanded.

"Now is really not a good time." Lazarus replied, still looking toward the door and listening.

"I didn't ask if it was a good time. I would like to see my daughter."

"Teron, she's probably in shock, and if I know her at all she'll go from shock to bloodlust faster than you'd think." Aris said calmly.

I looked at him with a scowl. "I seriously doubt that."

"She's not the *girl* you knew when you were captured." Lazarus snapped. I looked back toward him again and found him glaring at me. "She's been through hell."

"And clearly transitioned, which I thought would never have been allowed." I snapped. "You will take me to her, or I'll find her myself." I started to rise from where they'd sat me down to stalk toward the door.

Lazarus smiled wickedly. "Fine." He shrugged and stood to lead me back out to her. "Don't say we didn't warn you."

Something in his tone bothered me. Something about the fact that he seemed to think he knew her better than I did, and might actually *care* how she'd react to seeing me made me even more furious. For a man who absolutely hated her when he found out she existed, this entire conversation was surprising to me.

They led me out to the foyer to where Mira stood with a tall and muscular vampire I'd never met. I recognized him though. He was with her when she found me. Their scents co-mingled and nearly stopped my heart right there. They were mated. She had a *mate*. Gods, I knew it had been years but I'd lost track. How long was I in that gods forsaken cell? And what the fuck happened while I was in there?

There was nothing but rage in her eyes, and she stated that she was going to slaughter them. I raised my brows. I didn't think she'd ever be capable of being one of us, let alone threaten to slaughter people. Lazarus was right. I barely recognized her. She had to be in her twenties now.

The man holding her acted like those words brought back the woman *he* knew, but then her eyes went dark and the fangs came out. I never thought I'd see her as a vampire, but that nearly took the breath out of me. I wondered if this was all some sort of weird and cruel dream or hallucination for a moment.

I leaned back against the threshold behind me and crossed my arms over my chest. I chuckled and started speaking before I knew what I was even saying.

"She is quite a handful, isn't she?"

Her gaze shifted to me, and held me in place like she'd turned me to stone. She must not have heard us come back out of the room. Her eyes were nothing but pits of black boiling with bloodlust and rage. He released her, and turned to look between us, clearly monitoring the situation like he'd seen her bloodlust before and knew just how delicate of a line this was we were walking.

I couldn't stop myself. "Seems like I've missed a lot while I was…" My voice trailed off and I glanced away, suddenly regretting speaking at all. Then I looked back over at her and finished. "Perhaps you'd like to introduce me to your *mate?"*

She had to know that I would know the moment I scented them together, or scented her at all. I was a little irritated to find out she had a mate and I'd never even had the chance to *meet* him before they solidified that bond. Rare as those bonds tended to be, I knew I couldn't have stopped it, but seeing her bonded to someone without knowing him just rubbed me the wrong way. And he certainly didn't look like what I would've picked for her.

I watched as she curled her hands into fists and started to stalk toward me with the bloodlust still boiling in her eyes. *Shit*. I'd made a huge mistake. I knew better than to poke a vampire's temper when they're like this, especially a *new* one. Clearly my time in that cell had done nothing but make me forget some of the more important things. I had no doubt I could fight her off if she actually attacked me, but then again, I wasn't at my full strength and she certainly had murder in her eyes.

She stopped suddenly and angled her head back toward her mate, like he'd spoken to her. I'd never seen anything like it. Mates couldn't communicate telepathically. She looked like she was listening to him, but he didn't say a single word. She took a deep breath as he neared her and reached to grab her arm. She took one last look at me before they disappeared in a puff of shadow.

"Honestly Teron, taunting her choice in mate when she's clearly ready to kill someone?" Aris was rubbing his temples where he leaned against the wall to my left. "Have you gone mad?"

I glanced at him and opened my mouth to speak when Lazarus cut me off.

"Out of all of the vampires she could've ended up with, *Teron*," the way he said my name made me want to spin around and hit him, but I knew better than that. "Deiric is probably the most honorable of us all. You couldn't have asked for a better match for her."

I turned and locked eyes with Lazarus now, who had also turned to face me directly.

"And if you have a problem with them, you can go through *me*." The look on his face, and the tone of his voice told me everything I needed to know about Mira's relationship with *him* too. I could do nothing other than raise my brows at his tone and stance.

He stood here, ready to fight me over my opinion of my own daughter. A daughter whom I knew he'd hated with every fiber of his being before the attacks. What on earth had changed over these last few years? Why was he acting like more of a father to her than I felt like at the moment?

I failed her. Failed miserably to protect her all those years ago and I knew they kept me locked in that hell hole to use me against her when they one day tracked her down. Or at least that's what they claimed anyway. I doubted she'd actually survived but they seemed certain of it. Tried to convince me hundreds of times to work with them and seek her out myself on their behalf.

Now, here I was, my second having taken over my manor and Lazarus staring at me just like he had all those years ago when he found out that I'd created her. He hadn't cared then that she was an accident. He was furious I had the nerve to fornicate with a sorceress.

After a few moments of awkward silence, I heard the sound of metal striking metal, and I knew where she'd shifted them. They were outside sparring. I turned and shifted on my feet so I stood tall in front of Lazarus, who still towered over me.

"Would either of you like to fill me in then? How long was I in that cell?"

"It's been nearly twelve years." Lazarus said flatly. "A lot of what happened is her story to tell. Not mine."

Aris pushed himself off the wall behind me and started walking toward the back of the manor, gesturing for us to follow. "Lazarus is right, but I can give you some of the important pieces if you'd like. She can fill in the gaps for you later."

I stared at Lazarus with a scowl for one final moment before following Aris with Lazarus in tow behind me. It felt like neither of them trusted leaving me alone here. Part of me didn't blame them. I hadn't been around this many humans in… well I guess nearly twelve years.

We walked to one of the back rooms of the manor where we could see them sparring through the window. It almost felt inappropriate to watch, but I was relieved to lay eyes on her again and confirm for myself that she was really alive, and in front of me.

And my god, she was holding her own, blow for blow with this vampire. Deiric, Lazarus had said his name. Their sparring match was like a wicked dance, and they knew each other's movements well, yet neither dealt any serious blows to one another.

Aris calmly explained what happened the day of the attacks. That she'd taken an alias and begun hunting monsters. She became one of the fiercest and most revered mercenaries in all of Leinster. She had been on her own entirely for ten years before Deiric stumbled across her by accident one day.

She'd bargained with him and made the daylight rings he and his men were supposed to be getting the evening after the attacks. I remembered Sidra telling me she and Mira were to make rings that evening. Still, that bargain seemed like an idiotic idea. What could she have been thinking?

Aris explained how she'd been taken down right after that, and how she'd demanded that they let her be taken. She didn't want them dying for her, not like everyone here had. It killed me to think she didn't value her own life at all. It also irked me that she'd come up with such a ludicrous plan too.

Even worse, that her mate allowed it. Surely he had to know by then what she was to him.

But then he explained her escape, and how she fought to turn the people against Solas and in support of us instead. She asked to be turned and took the transition so well she had all of them surprised. She infiltrated a Solas party like an expert assassin and set the plan in place for an alliance, which ultimately led to victory in battle.

A battle which Lazarus explained she'd nearly burnt herself out to end when someone came moments from killing her beloved. Her mate. Who she still danced with outside, sparring like a well oiled machine. Now she was an Elder Mage, as they called it, and a part of both covens. We had an agreement with Solas, and we worked together regularly. That, at least, impressed me. I couldn't have seen that part coming.

Lazarus nearly brought me to my knees when he told me what had happened just recently, and what we were now facing. She'd taken not one, but *three* stakes to the chest, which explained the absurd metal armor that they all wore today.

I could barely recognize her. Nothing I was hearing made sense to me. My daughter, the girl I knew the day I was captured, was a far cry from the woman she was now. Still, I was worried, and found myself wondering how I could keep her from more heartache, and more danger.

I watched quietly now, they'd finished catching me up with what they decided to share. She disarmed Deiric, and in one swift motion he'd spun her around with her back to his chest. She let him, I knew that she could have blocked that without a second thought after the rest of the sparring I'd just witnessed.

Her laugh was music to my ears. The embrace he held her in was not meant to hold her as though they'd really been in a fight. It was intimate, and his head was tilted down next to her neck. I couldn't see his face, but the smile on hers was contagious. I found myself smiling as well. She was alive. She was alive and, despite the hell she'd been through, she looked happy.

They were a blur of movement and then she had him pinned on the ground beneath her, and was leaning down into him. Suddenly, this felt far too intimate to watch and I turned from the window. Aris and Lazarus followed suit swiftly, like they too knew where that encounter might be going. They surely knew better than I would.

"Give her some time." Aris said softly as we walked back toward the foyer of the manor. "It's probably going to be a bit of an adjustment to get used to having you around again."

"We need to debrief you anyway." Lazarus' voice was all business. "We need to know everything that happened and anything you know about their plans or who else is involved."

"Could I at least get cleaned up first?" I asked hesitantly. I was certain I smelled awful, though no one made any comments.

Lazarus nodded and Aris motioned for me to follow him.

*

By the time I'd cleaned up and dressed in what Aris had provided, Deiric and Mira had come back inside. They were sitting in the front room on the second floor, where we'd held the coven meetings that Mira wanted so badly to be involved in and always eavesdropped on. Lazarus was sitting with them, and they were all very quietly chatting before I walked in with Aris.

Both Deiric and Mira's gazes fell to me when I strode for the chair on the side of the table closest to the door I came in. I really would've preferred that she not be here for this.

"I'm not leaving." She said boldly as she stared me down from her seat. Deiric had his arm protectively around her back, as though I was something to be feared or concerned about. His lips were pursed together in a tight line while he surveyed me quietly.

I didn't say anything, but couldn't help but think how this would probably upset her and she didn't want to hear half of it.

"She can handle it." Deiric said sternly.

Mindreaders. It hit me then. They could both read minds.

They nodded almost in unison. Suddenly I wasn't sure if they were here because they wanted to be, or if they were here to make sure I didn't hold anything back.

"Both." Mira said.

I frowned, but gave no other reaction. Neither Lazarus or Aris asked what I'd been thinking. They ignored the interaction entirely.

"Tell us everything." Lazarus said as Aris sat down next to me.

Mira flicked her wrist in a way that made me a little bit uncomfortable. "There's a shield around this room so no one else can hear us. We need *every* detail. No matter how insignificant you might think it is."

Yes, I definitely didn't recognize her at all. The little girl I knew was gone. Maybe she died that day with her mother. I didn't know, but this was a full grown woman sitting before me. One who had probably seen more in her twenty seven years alive than I'd seen in my nearly eight hundred. Her gaze was cold and calculating, but there was a trace of care and concern underneath it.

So I sighed, and I started from the very beginning.

Chapter 44

Mira

Gods. He had been through hell. And I could hear him surveying me every moment he paused, watching for a reaction that would cause him to pause or stop so he didn't upset me. Unfortunately, at this point nothing could.

They wanted my mother that day, not me. The attack was too messy and, someone not involved in whatever this particular movement was, shot her before the person who was supposed to take her got to her. She didn't survive her resulting injuries long enough for them to take her and heal her. He didn't say *why* they wanted her, but given her knowledge of Eldritch magic, I could make my own guesses.

They wanted *her* to train the princess. I imagined the king couldn't have been involved. He seemed entirely oblivious to the prince's plots, so I wondered again what

Ronan's end goal was. Nothing seemed to add up in that regard.

My father was captured to use as a bargaining piece, as leverage against me or my mother. They'd actually meant to capture us both, but it didn't work out that way. When my mother was dead, I became their focus. They'd carefully crafted their story with the other magisters, and it was only one who had the real knowledge of this movement, this plan, but my father didn't know which one it was. He also didn't know what their plans were, other than my mother or myself were required for some reason.

He explained the conditions he was kept in. He was tortured for information on me several times, which he could not provide even if he wanted to, because he didn't know. He was kept drugged, with small weekly rations of blood mixed with vervain, that he only sometimes drank. Malachy, whom we'd captured, was his assigned warden and in charge of keeping him alive while they searched for me.

When he'd finally finished explaining everything up until the moment we found him, we were all silent. I was deep in thought, as was Deiric next to me. The silence stretched on for several minutes.

"I hear you were a formidable mercenary." My father said, which prompted me to look up at him. He had a small and cautious smile on his face.

I nodded slowly.

"What sort of beasts did you kill?"

It was a simple question with an answer a mile long. "Probably one of everything you can think of right now." I said quietly.

He arched a single brow.

"Her stubbornness nearly got her killed with a Lanzani." Deiric mumbled.

I elbowed him and he jolted, but didn't release his arm from around my back.

My father chuckled. "That doesn't surprise me in the slightest."

"I believe it was right after that when she demanded to be transitioned." Aris commented quietly.

I shot him a glare and he quickly shut up.

My father's gaze shifted to Deiric, studying him quietly for a few moments. Deiric didn't even flinch. Though my father's gaze wasn't as cold and calculating as I would've expected it to be. It was more contemplative.

"I've heard nothing but good things about you." My father said, "I'm surprised that I've never met you."

His thoughts gave away nothing. He was much more guarded now, which wasn't surprising knowing we could both hear them.

"I was with Lazarus for a long while, and then Killian, before we moved to my manor." Deiric explained.

My father's brows raised just long enough to be noticeable. He didn't know Deiric was an elder, so clearly he hadn't heard much about him. I wondered what had been said while we were outside. I didn't think there was a single vampire my father *hadn't* met so the fact that he didn't know Deiric at first was a surprise to me too.

"If you have questions for me, feel free to ask them." Deiric's voice was colder now, with a hint of annoyance that my father's mind seemed blank or guarded.

"Were you already mated when she was attacked the night she made your rings?"

"Yes."

A brief bout of rage flickered in my father's eyes, but he didn't react otherwise. "And you didn't stop her from creating them?"

Deiric shifted slightly in his seat, but not enough to be noticed by anyone other than me. "In case you haven't noticed, she doesn't take *no* for an answer very well."

My father arched a brow, but before he could say anything else Deiric continued in a tone so final and mildly threatening that I doubted my father would speak again.

"Every single thing comes down to her choice. Even if I want to question her actions, or her choices, she wouldn't tolerate it." He pulled me closer to him, enough for everyone at the table to notice. "I respect every single choice she's ever made, even if they drive me mad because they put her in an unnecessary amount of danger. You'd do well to learn to respect them too."

It took everything I had not to let my jaw hit the floor. The surprise and little bit of fury that flashed in my father's eyes didn't go unnoticed, but neither Lazarus or Aris reacted. I wondered what choice Deiric seemed to think my father *didn't* agree with or respect. I wondered if there was something Deiric picked up on in his thoughts that I had missed.

Sensing my question, Deiric thought. *He is conflicted about a lot of things. He doesn't understand what you saw in me, and doesn't like that you've been put in harm's way so many times while with me. He believes that it is my fault and that I coerced you into deciding to be a part of each of the moments where you were in danger.*

I really had a lot to learn, or I guess a lot to work on. Somehow I couldn't read any of that, but Deiric seemed to do so with ease. With six hundred plus years of practice, I supposed that made sense.

Of course he does. I leveled a glare in my father's direction, and when he locked eyes with me there was the faintest glimmer of a question there. Suddenly, I was fifteen again and facing down the man who never seemed to be impressed with me. My patience snapped slightly and I settled back into who I was now.

"You weren't there." I seethed. And his eyebrows raised just a hair in surprise. "You do not get to question a single choice I've made in the last twelve years." I said it so slowly and menacingly he shifted backward in his chair a bit too. "You don't get to question *anything* at all actually."

I leaned forward and stared directly into his *soul* as I uttered my next words. "I am relieved you aren't dead, but if you mean to sit here and question any choice I've made that kept me alive. Any choice I've made that brought me even a sliver of happiness over the last several years, you will remain dead to me." I paused as I watched the hurt settle in his eyes. "Do you understand me?"

He nodded slowly.

"I'm not a naive little girl anymore that you get to mold, keep hidden, and protect." I snarled. "I'm a grown woman who can protect myself, and who is sick and tired of people who doubt her and underestimate her."

He nodded again.

I looked over at Aris. "Do you have space here?" I asked calmly.

He raised a brow at me and sat up in his chair. "I'm sure we could make room." He said hesitantly.

"Good." I said flatly.

Mira. Deiric thought.

"He can stay here then."

"You don't have the authority to tell me where I'll be staying." He snarled in response.

I shot up from my chair. "I have the authority to do what I gods damned please and that includes deciding where you'll stay."

He stood now and glared down at me. "I outrank you."

"Sit down." Lazarus snapped.

My father smirked at me. It took him a moment to realize that Lazarus was actually speaking to him. His gaze shifted slowly from me to Lazarus, confusion swirling on his face.

"I said," Lazarus seethed. "Sit. Down."

"I–"

"She outranks all of us, but even if she didn't– I outrank you. Sit the fuck down."

Lazarus didn't even need to rise from his seat. My father obeyed.

Mira, are you sure–

I leveled a glare at Deiric who simply put his free hand up in defeat. *So much for not questioning my choices.* I thought, and saw his smirk out of the corner of my eye as I looked back down at my father.

I only question you when I can tell you're acting out of emotion at first and I don't want you to do something when you're upset that you'll regret. You know I respect and stand by whatever you decide no matter what.

"Mira." My father said softly. It was still a plea. One he could've gotten further with it he hadn't had a condescending tone behind it.

"My decision is final."

Chapter 45

Mira

We shifted directly into the foyer of the manor. Zane, Leo, and Xander were all waiting for us in the den. They all stood as one and started to file into the foyer to find out what had happened. I was still fuming a bit from the discussion with my father, and I gathered by the way they approached that they could feel the tension wafting off of me.

"This doesn't bode well." Xander muttered as they approached us.

"We caught Malachy and they're taking him to the Solas prison. We'll interrogate him tomorrow." I seethed, unable to keep the annoyance I felt from my voice.

"You don't seem thrilled, despite that it sounds like it went well." Leo said, studying me carefully.

"We also found her father." Deiric said from behind me. Leo arched a brow while Zane and Xander looked rightfully confused. "Alive."

"Alive?" Leo's brows both raised and he practically gasped the word. "How the hell was he *alive?*"

"They held him captive all this time, apparently." Lazarus mumbled and started to walk toward the dining room.

Leo, Zane, and Xander stared at me for a few moments. Liala came rushing down the stairs, just as flabbergasted as the rest of them which told me she must've heard what he said. She halted when she reached Zane's side.

"And how are *you*?" Leo asked hesitantly.

I shrugged. "He's alive." I turned to follow Lazarus into the dining room.

"And yet he's not here?" Liala said softly, almost so softly that I wouldn't have heard her unless I had enhanced hearing.

"No. He won't be coming here." I mumbled and walked through the threshold into the dining room, where I found Lazarus already pouring another glass of whiskey to hand to me.

"I figured you could use this." He handed me a nearly full glass.

"Thanks." I took the glass and sat at the table. Lazarus took up a seat across from me and took a small sip from his glass. I just stared into mine.

"It only helps if you actually drink it, you know." Lazarus mumbled. The rest of them filed into the room behind us, taking seats around the table. Deiric slid in next to me with a glass of his own.

"You see your father after twelve years, discover he's alive, and you don't want to bring him back home with you?" Xander finally asked, after several minutes of an ever growing very awkward silence. It occurred to me now that none of them had any of their family around them. I imagined they missed them greatly and this probably seemed absurd to them.

I finally took a long sip of my whiskey, and sat the glass down, but didn't let go of it. "It's complicated." I didn't look up from the glass as I spoke.

"So… uncomplicate it?" Zane said with a smirk, which I only saw because I shot him a brief glare. He didn't shrink away from it though.

"We didn't exactly have the best relationship *before* he died, but didn't die." I snapped. "And nothing has changed." I half laughed then, and looked back at my glass. "Well, that's not true. I've changed. And I'm not going to tolerate his bullshit anymore. So he won't be coming here."

"That's a little harsh don't you think?" Zane asked. "If he was held captive, I'm sure he'd have been through hell. You could cut him a little slack."

"Leave it Zane." Liala snapped. "If he acted the way he did toward her to me, I wouldn't want to be around him either."

"Oh he *loved* me." Deiric said sarcastically, and took a sip of his whiskey.

"I'm sure that was a fun thing to explain." Xander smirked, and I glared down the table at him.

"We didn't really have the chance to explain much of anything. He scented us before we could. Not that it mattered." I rolled my eyes. "You would think, after Lazarus and Aris clearly filled him in on important events he'd know better than to throw judgemental looks and thoughts around, but I guess he couldn't help himself." I scowled. "Nothing I've ever done has been good enough for that man, not even saving his sorry ass, apparently." I mumbled.

Xander's smirk faded to a frown, and the entire table went silent. I finished my glass, and Lazarus got up to grab the decanter and refill it.

I have no problem burning him the next time I see him, if he makes you feel so insignificant. Gaisgeach said. *Clearly, he doesn't realize the power you wield.*

The corner of my mouth tilted up for a fraction of a second in a small flicker of a smile. *We don't need to burn him.*

I heard the doors to the back room of the manor open and the mages started filing out with Eimear and Renwick. I cringed knowing they were sure to ask how things went as well. Lazarus topped off my glass, then his own, and Deiric's before just sitting the decanter on the table in between us and then sitting back down.

"You're back!" Adriana said excitedly as they all filed into the kitchen and dining room. I assumed Gaisgeach or Fiadh must've told Cairbre and he let Adriana know. The timing was suspicious at best that they came out the moment we all sat down and Gaisgeach popped into my head.

"We're back." I said and half smiled at her with a slight raise of my glass before bringing it to my lips for another sip.

"That bad huh?" Sorcha asked and leaned against the wall behind where Zane and Liala sat.

"We got Malachy, so you could call it a success." I said and watched as the rest of them decided to head toward the kitchen to help Eimear and Esme cook. Adriana came and sat at the table with us, taking the spot next to Xander across the table from Zane.

"It isn't a success if you're all sitting here and drinking whiskey like someone just killed your dog." Adriana mumbled.

I smiled wickedly. "Very observant." My voice was riddled with sarcasm. "Turns out, my father isn't dead. He's still a bastard though."

Lazarus nearly spit out his whiskey and Xander stifled a laugh. Even Deiric smirked. Adriana rightfully looked both shocked and confused. Zemora spun around from whatever she was doing in the kitchen and looked like she couldn't believe me for a moment.

"That explains why I only saw your mother on Samhain!" She mumbled.

I flinched at the thought of it. If I'd known sooner, perhaps he wouldn't have had to rot in that cell for all these months. Deiric slipped his hand under the table and gently squeezed my thigh. His silent reminder that it wasn't my fault and none of us could have known.

Even if you had known he wasn't dead, you would not have known where to look for him. Gaisgeach jumped in.

"Sorry." Zemora mumbled and turned back around to what she was working on.

"You were too pissed to notice, but you did actually scare him a little bit when he heard you mention you wanted to slaughter the people who did that to him." Deiric smiled slightly as he lifted his glass to his lips. "If that makes you feel any better."

I half smiled and locked eyes with him for a moment. "Funny, I didn't think he knew *how* to be afraid of anything, let alone me." Then it hit me. "Oh wait till he sees Gaisgeach." I was grinning now. "He'll shit himself."

"Oh, I'd pay to see that." Lazarus said with a smirk as he took another sip of his drink. "I'm certain he's never been face to face with a dragon of any kind before."

"Have you, besides when you met Cairbre?" I turned to him and asked, curiosity getting the best of me. He hadn't met Gaisgeach at all yet.

"I've seen them. We never fought them." He glanced around the table before looking back at me. "Teron has always been a bastard. Don't let his bullshit opinion of you upset you."

"I don't intend to." I said flatly. "Not anymore anyway."

"Good." Lazarus locked eyes with me and smiled.

"Maybe Aris can talk some sense into him." Leo said quietly. "They were close before all this right?"

I looked over at Leo. "As close as one can be with someone like him, sure." I shrugged. "I'm not holding my breath." I glanced around the table again. "You'll get to meet him and see what I mean if you tag along to any of the meetings."

"If you're all just going to sit around drinking and talking, perhaps you'd like to move to the den so we can eat at the table?" Eimear walked over to stand behind Renwick, who had taken the seat at the head of the table. She arched a brow and put her hands on her hips like she was our mother scolding us for being in her way.

I rolled my eyes and started to rise from the table. "Yes, mam." I mocked.

She scowled at me while half of the guys tried to stifle their laughs. "Don't call me that."

"Well you *are* acting rather motherly." I smirked and slipped my free hand into Deiric's as he rose and turned from the table. "It was only fitting." I started to follow Deiric out.

She crossed her arms and frowned. "Move along then. We need the table."

Lazarus grabbed the decanter and followed us into the den where we passed it around to the others who grabbed glasses on the way out of the room. Deiric and I took the couch, Lazarus and Leo grabbed the chairs and the rest of them sat on the floor around the coffee table. Leo gave us some of his updates from his travels for the week and his connections from the towns around us. Then we discussed our plans for interrogating Malachy.

Chapter 46

Mira

The following afternoon, after we'd done some training with the mages, Deiric, Lazarus, and I shifted to the Solas castle where Devlon and Tellus met us almost immediately in the foyer. They were both smiling and seemed quite pleased with themselves when they approached us.

"You'll be delighted to know that we won't need your help for his interrogation, because we're already finished." Tellus said while he adjusted the lapels of his jacket. "Apparently, all we had to do was threaten him with having his magic stolen by you and he sang like a bird."

I snorted. "You're kidding right?" I didn't even try to hide my doubt. I crossed my arms and looked at them like they were a bit nuts.

"I wish I could say we were, but he wasn't so tough when he realized how dangerous you could be after finding your father alive down there." Devlon looked me over for a moment. "Though, it seems that you had a less than ideal reunion since he's living with us now."

I frowned just slightly. "It's complicated."

He chuckled. "How many times have you said that in the last twenty four hours?"

I scowled at him. "Enough."

He shrugged. "He was working with Kieran, who seems to still be calling all the shots from his prison cell in the palace dungeons. I'm sure we can all guess who's relaying these messages for him." He shifted his weight and cocked one hip to the side, while he waved his hand in feigned annoyance. "Though Malachy *didn't* identify the prince specifically."

"Was that all he gave you?" I asked rather boredly. Knowing which former magister was running this circus didn't really help us much. We needed their plans. We needed to know what they stood to gain with Adriana.

Clearly, they were interested in her eldritch magic, but to what end? Deiric and Lazarus seemed to be as still as statues behind me, though I didn't look to see if they'd given any reaction at all yet.

"No." Tellus continued for Devlon. "He's also working with Finn and Oisin, who are two rogue mages that left the coven when we took over. We don't know where they are yet, nor what role they played, but we already sent our spymasters out to find them."

"He didn't know?" I asked and Devlon shook his head, looking a little defeated and annoyed.

"They apparently keep things compartmentalized so that if one of them is captured, they won't be able to get enough useful information to figure out their next move. I guess that's part of the reason why they managed to go this long without detection." Devlon explained.

"So we're stuck with two more names, no real plans, and another prisoner." I said.

They both nodded.

"Do you have any ideas for why they'd want or need the princess and her abilities? I can't see what they'd stand to gain." We still hadn't told them about the dragons, and I didn't see a need to yet.

They shrugged in unison. "I mean, if she can conjure beasts, maybe the prince intended to use them for his own gain? Or use her magic for his own gain? Honestly, your guess is as good as ours." Devlon said.

"The fact that they also want *you* tells me that if they succeeded in taking her before she was fully trained and had mastered it they wanted to make you train her until she did." Tellus added.

"And then kill me I'm sure." I scowled.

"More than likely." Devlon didn't hide the distaste from his expression as he said it.

"The Morrigan seemed convinced that Adriana would be queen one day." I said, and their brows rose. "She wouldn't have said that if it weren't important. I'm assuming that by getting us involved, either the prince will have to die, or be punished for treason. We don't seem to have enough evidence to take to the king to convince him he's acting treasonously, so I guess he's going to die." I said with a shrug.

Devlon choked back a laugh, though I think it was more out of shock and how nonchalantly I hinted at killing the prince. Deiric and Lazarus still stood silently behind me, I guess just taking it all in. "And how do you expect Ronan will *die*?" Devlon finally asked after a few moments of awkward silence.

I shrugged. "I can't see the future, but I'd certainly be happy to do the honors myself if given the chance."

"Then you'd be put to death for treason." Tellus said flatly with a slight frown while he looked me over as though I was suddenly a threat.

I considered that for a few seconds. "Not under the right circumstances." I shrugged again. "But that's neither here nor there at the moment. Until we know what he's planning, we're just stuck."

"We'll keep you updated with what our spymasters find out." Tellus offered.

"Could you provide a description of the two of them so we can have our spymasters on the lookout as well?" Lazarus asked.

"I haven't seen them personally, but I'll find out and get that over to you as soon as I can." Devlon didn't even bat an eye at the request.

I could see Lazarus give him a curt nod out of the corner of my eye. "Well, if you don't need us for the interrogation, then we have plenty of other things to do this afternoon." I said dismissively. "I'll see you at the next meeting?"

Devlon nodded, and I shifted us back to our manor.

"That was far too easy." Deiric mumbled, and I turned to look at him. He looked like he didn't believe a word of what they'd just said. "We still could've compelled him to confirm it was the truth."

"If he at least got us names, I doubt he'd lie about the rest of it." I strode toward the front doors. *Gaisgeach, are you up for a little bit of practice this afternoon?*

He huffed, and then grumbled. *I was wondering when you'd find time for us today.*

I smiled, despite that he couldn't see me. *We do have other priorities you know.*

Oh, sure. Tracking down the rogue mages and the prince's plans. How riveting.

It isn't like we *can help figure out what sort of hell will break loose with that bastard running around.* Fiadh butted in and seemed mildly annoyed at her mate. I couldn't help but chuckle.

"I'm assuming there's an entire conversation happening that we're not a part of?" Lazarus asked, and when I glanced at him he was gesturing toward me with his hand and looked immensely confused.

Deiric just nodded. "Well, that *you* aren't a part of. I can hear every word."

Lazarus shook his head and walked away. "The more weird animals that find their way into this mess just make it even more bizarre to be around you two sometimes." He mumbled as he strode for the stairs.

He's pleasant. Fiadh commented.

He's probably just frustrated that he *doesn't get a dragon.* Deiric thought with a smile as he walked over toward the front door with me.

Adriana came running down the hall. "Are we flying?" She asked excitedly. "Cairbre said you were talking to Gaisgeach about it."

"We are, if you'd like to come along." I smiled. "I could use some practice *not* flying off when they do more than just fly in a straight line."

"It's not quite like riding a horse when they're spinning and jerking you around." She smiled. "It is still really fun though." Then she looked confused for a moment and looked at Deiric. "Why *don't* we use saddles?"

If that witch even thinks of putting a saddle on any of us I'll torch her myself. Gaisgeach snarled.

I bit back my laugh. "I don't think they like saddles." I considered it for a moment. "And honestly, I don't even know where or how we'd get one made to fit them."

Insult us like that again and I'll fry you *too.* Gaisgeach snarled again.

That wouldn't be very wise. You'd die too. I thought, and he merely huffed.

We are on our way. He grumbled.

Chapter 47

Mira

Almost a week had passed since we'd discovered who else Malachy had been working with. Deiric and I were training with his magic again, after I'd worked with Adriana earlier in the morning. We decided it would be better to train up on the cliff he'd taken me to on my birthday. We wouldn't be disturbed and we were less likely to catch anything on fire. I also argued this was better because of the altitude. If we'd be using this magic from the backs of the dragons as well as the ground, we should be used to both.

We were nearly thirty minutes into a rather brutal sparring match when Gaisgeach flew overhead and landed on the edge of a neighboring cliff.

Other dragons are coming.

His arrival was distraction enough that Deiric almost caught me off guard and burned my left arm. I snarled at him and sent a blast of fire right at his chest, which didn't burn him but *did* blast him back a few feet and knock him on his ass. Gaisgeach's resulting chuckle in my head was worth it, although Fiadh flew up from below the cliff and chuffed a blast of hot and awful smelling steam right in my face that sent *me* staggering back a few steps.

I glared at her while she looped up above us and landed next to Gaisgeach. I looked over at Deiric. He had a smug smile on his face where he still sat on the ground, one arm propped on a knee and his other arm holding him upright to look at me. I just rolled my eyes and looked back at Gaisgeach.

Other dragons? I asked.

He craned his neck and looked down at me. *Yes. There are hundreds of us, you know.*

I arched a brow. *And what do other dragons coming have to do with us?*

He blinked, perhaps the only sign of his surprise that I questioned him this way, before he huffed a sigh. *You know some of the other riders that aren't... human.*

"Alaric."

"Alaster." Deiric added as he walked up to stand beside me.

Gaisgeach nodded. *Bring them to the field you met us in tomorrow.* He flew off without another word.

Fiadh glanced over at us. *Hit him like that again and it won't be steam I hit you with.*

I raised both brows. I assumed she didn't mean *fire* because that would surely kill me, and in turn kill her mate. I wasn't eager to find out. I could've sworn I saw the edge of her mouth curl up in a smile before she flew off after Gaisgeach.

"She gets a little touchy sometimes." Deiric whispered from behind me, close enough that his breath tickled the back of my neck.

I jumped, having not realized he'd come that close to me, and spun around to face him. "Touchy is putting it mildly."

He shrugged one shoulder and smirked. "We should probably go talk to Silas sooner than later." He looked me up and down for a moment. "But," his smirk grew into a much larger grin. "I'd like the chance to get you back for that hit first."

I rolled my eyes and took a few steps back. "Go ahead and try." I motioned for him to attack first, and he didn't hold back this time.

*

By the time we finally decided to go talk to Silas, we'd managed to singe bits of each of our leathers, but he did not knock me on my ass like I'd done to him. While I was a little bit smugly satisfied that he *didn't,* I was also a little bit worried because he should have been able to. We needed to train far more often.

I shifted us to Silas' manor and managed to startle the three women who were gathered in the foyer. Whatever conversation they'd been having quickly silenced when they turned to look at us. I didn't recognize any of them, and they were very obviously human based on their scent. Judging by their more scandalous dresses, and the fact that one of them had a chiffon scarf tastefully tied around her neck I knew they likely *weren't* mages and were here for other purposes.

I couldn't stop the slight disapproving frown that rose to my lips. It wasn't necessarily unusual for them to find willing participants to drink from but it was rather unusual for them to end up at the manor itself. At least, at the ones I'd lived in anyway. The women seemed confused by my presence, but immediately zeroed in on Deiric. The smiles that rose to their lips as they looked him over made my skin crawl.

I, not so casually, stepped in front of him and bared my fangs at them in a snarl when their attention shifted back to me. I took far more pleasure in the shock on their faces than I should have as they all scurried off down a hallway.

"Come now, Mira, I'm sure you have better manners than that." Silas cooed as he entered the foyer from a door off to the left of us. "That's hardly a polite way to interact with our guests."

I looked in his direction and shot him a glare. I opened my mouth to speak but Deiric cut me off. His right hand gently rested on my hip as he stepped around to stand to my left.

"We need to talk." He said flatly. "Somewhere," he glanced around us at the other various people who wandered in and out of the foyer occasionally, "more private."

Silas arched a brow at him, but then looked back at me. His expression softened as he approached. "It's good to see you…" His voice trailed off when he finally stopped a few steps from us. "Whole again."

Right, because the last time he saw me was… less than pleasant. I remembered hearing his voice, and that it was Elias that healed me. I wondered what I looked like then. I didn't even really want to imagine it. He studied us for a few moments, and his thoughts were a cluster of intrigue and concern.

"What fresh hell did you just crawl out of that you both smell like sweat and burnt leather?" He wrinkled his nose as he fully took in what we smelled like.

"Silas." Deiric's voice was full of warning. "Somewhere, private?"

Silas rolled his eyes. I glanced beyond him to find Alaric lingering in the doorway he'd come out of, watching us closely.

"He can come too." I gestured to Alaric. His brows rose, but he closed the distance between himself and Silas rather quickly.

Silas shrugged one shoulder. He motioned for us to follow him as he turned around and walked toward the stairs. "This way."

We followed him up the stairs and down a hallway to what seemed to be a private office. There was a large wooden desk in the center of the room with large windows lining the wall behind it. There were a few rather plain wooden chairs in front of it. The left wall had another door in it, that I would have assumed to be a closet if it hadn't been left ajar to reveal a bedroom beyond it.

Alaric closed the door behind us and Silas took the seat behind the desk. Alaric went to stand behind him just off to his right, while Deiric and I sat in two of the chairs in front of the desk.

"Out with it then." Silas said dismissively and waved his hand at us from where he slouched back in his chair.

It was at this moment that I realized two things. The first is that he had yet to call me 'little wicked one' since we'd arrived. He called me by my name, which was an odd change. I didn't know how I felt about the lack of his normal teasing. I almost missed our banter. The second was I had no idea how to even begin to discuss this with him. Deiric and I hadn't decided or discussed *how* we'd bring this up to him. What was I going to say, 'do you know dragons aren't myths?'. Surely not.

Alaric stifled a chuckle, and I looked at him with a small glare. I knew he could read my thoughts, and I was kicking myself for letting my guard down and letting that thought through the shields I'd so carefully been practicing putting in place.

"We will need to borrow Alaric and Alaster tomorrow." I finally spoke up, looking directly at Silas again.

"Borrow them?" Silas huffed a laugh with a bemused look on his face. "For what exactly?"

"To meet their dragons."

Silas' brows furrowed in confusion and he looked at Deiric, as if he would give him a better answer, but Deiric didn't react. "Dragons?" He finally breathed. "Did your near death experience kill off part of your brain?" He glanced at Deiric again and then just stared at me in disbelief. "This must be some kind of joke."

I opened my mouth to speak, but then the flicker of a flame caught my attention and I turned to look at Deiric, who had summoned fire at his fingertips. "She's not joking."

I don't think I've ever seen Silas well and thoroughly shocked. He was rendered entirely speechless, his jaw slightly agape as he stared at the fire in Deiric's hand. The last time I'd seen even a glimmer of this much shock across his features was the first night I met him when he *scented* the mating bond on Deiric and I, but even then, he hadn't been speechless.

"Clearly, I am missing something." He finally mumbled after studying Deiric for longer than necessary.

"Before we met," Deiric began to explain, "before we transitioned, I had a dragon. They were well hidden back then, but they all completely disappeared almost two years before I came to train with you, under Lazarus." He glanced over at me. "They've come back now, thanks to Adriana, and Mira has a dragon now as well." We both looked over at Silas now.

"Dragons are a myth." Silas said flatly, like saying it would make it true.

"I thought the same thing, if it makes you feel any better." I cut in. "Apparently, dragon magic blends very interestingly with blood magic." I gestured toward Alaric and Deiric. "It's why Deiric, Alaric, Alaster, and I can all read minds."

Silas glanced back at Alaric, who looked rather stoic and unaffected by this entire discussion. I was actually quite surprised to see he didn't seem to be nearly as shocked as Silas, but I couldn't read his thoughts and wondered if he was just better at hiding it.

Silas looked back at Deiric now. "So you're telling me, he's got a dragon, and he'll be able to do whatever it is that you just did and have fire magic?"

Deiric nodded. "If he decides to accept the dragon, yes."

"We are trying not to tell many people about the dragons, until we absolutely need to." Silas looked back over at me. "Everyone in our manor knows because we couldn't really hide the dragon that Adriana conjured up and brought there, but we have not told the magisters, and we intend to keep it that way for now." I glanced up at Alaric and then back at Silas. "We're only telling *you* because we knew you wouldn't just let them go off with us without knowing why, and it will take a while for them to figure out how to use the magic from the dragons, let alone how to ride them."

"And you think there's a reason they'd need to learn that quickly?" Silas' concern was written all over his face. For someone who couldn't read minds, he was quite good at reading people and reading between the lines of what I was trying to say.

I nodded. "I'm not sure what is brewing with the prince, but I have my suspicions that we should be ready for anything." I glanced at Deiric, who also nodded. "The dragons coming back *now* combined with recent events leads me to believe it is all connected for some reason and it likely isn't a good one."

Silas put his elbows on his desk and rested his chin on his hands while he considered everything we said. I could see the wheels turning in his head as he thought, though I refrained from reading exactly where his mind was going.

After a very long and awkward pause, Silas finally shrugged his shoulders and sighed. "Take them as often as you need to. The only problem you'll run into is that Alaster doesn't have a daylight ring."

"That's fine." I cut in before anyone else could. "It's better that they train with the dragons and fly at night. It will be less visible that way, otherwise we'll be waiting for cloud cover to hide our movements." We would need to coordinate getting him a daylight ring, but we could worry about that later.

Chapter 48

Mira

I shifted Deiric and I back to Silas' manor the following evening, just as the sun was setting. We both wore our fighting leathers, as we had the day before, but a different set today. A set that wasn't scorched from our sparring the day before. We arrived in the foyer just as Alaric and Alaster were walking in to meet us. I didn't know if Alaric had filled Alaster in on why he was being summoned or not. I hoped he had.

Gaisgeach and Fiadh were less than amused that we had to do this under the cover of night. They agreed with me that this was safer anyway, but they still didn't seem very thrilled about it. Despite that, we agreed that they would already be in the field when we arrived.

"I trust you'll bring them back in one piece?" Silas said from behind us.

I flinched just slightly, having not heard him behind us. Deiric placed his hand on my lower back gently the moment he saw me move. A lot of time had passed since that ambush, but surprises when we shifted places still made my heart stutter for a moment.

Silas must have noted my flinch as well. He walked slowly around us and gave me an apologetic glance as he walked past us toward Alaric and Alaster. When he turned to face us finally, Deiric spoke before I could.

"I can't make any promises that they'll come back in one piece." He said softly. "That depends on how this… meeting goes."

Silas seemed intrigued, but didn't ask any further questions. I guess he inferred what Deiric didn't say. The dragons make their own choices, and we don't control them. I didn't know what might happen if either of them refused to bond their dragons, or what that would mean for them. I didn't want to think about it.

Silas finally let out a sigh and shrugged. "Best of luck then. I'll expect them back by dawn, for obvious reasons." Then he turned and walked between them, down the hallway they had come from.

"Is someone going to tell me *why* I've been summoned and why I might not come back in one piece?" Alaster demanded.

I smirked. "Oh, you'll find out soon enough." And I shifted the four of us before he could ask another question.

When we arrived in the field Gaisgeach and Fiadh were right behind Deiric and I. Alaric didn't appear to be concerned, but Alaster stared up at them like he'd get eaten.

"Fucking gods." Alaster mumbled. "Are those dragons?"

I couldn't stop myself from laughing. I understood now why Deiric was so amused with my reaction to meeting Cairbre. It was rather funny to watch someone lose their mind when confronted with a creature they'd always thought was a myth.

"Fuck you." Alaster snapped at me.

Gaisgeach snarled at him, low and threateningly. He lowered his head so he was just behind my left shoulder.

"You should probably be careful how you talk to her. Gaisgeach is the burn first, ask questions later type." Deiric smiled.

As though he needed to, Gaisgeach said, *Whether you're bonded to Enda or not, I will rip your puny head from your body if you insult her again.*

Alaster's eyes went wide and his eyebrows practically reached his hairline. "They can talk?"

We can. A feminine voice I had yet to hear. Enda, I would guess. She approached behind Alaster, who spun to look at her incredulously. She was about the same size as Fiadh, and a deep green color. Her scales reminded me of emeralds, and her golden eyes were glistening in the faint moonlight.

"I'm guessing you didn't decide to tell him anything then?" Deiric said to Alaric, who merely smiled and shrugged a shoulder in response.

"He wouldn't have believed me if I tried." Alaric didn't seem to be bothered by any of this, which I still found a little surprising. He hadn't ever really reacted to much of anything in all the time I'd known him, but still.

He turned to look at Alaster now. “Turns out, we can read minds because we have dragons that are, or *will*, be bonded to us. I would guess that this one is yours.” He gestured to the Enda.

Enda tilted her head in a brief nod. *If you choose to accept me, anyway.* She said, and she studied Alaster for a few moments, who seemed to be too awestruck to speak. *I would advise you to watch your tongue. I would hate for Gaisgeach to eat you before we've been properly introduced, and it would be incredibly inconvenient for me to bond you and then die because of your stupidity.*

I managed to stifle my laugh this time before it bubbled out of me.

Another large and dark form approached behind Alaric. He turned to face it as it approached. This dragon's scales were a deep shade of brown. Had there been no light from the moon I would've suspected it was actually black, but the moon illuminated everything enough that I could see the brown hue to its scales. Large emerald eyes studied Alaric closely.

“Perhaps we should give them some privacy?” I suggested quietly to Deiric. “Let them get acquainted?” Deiric nodded.

Enda and Dáire will let us know when they're ready for us. Gaisgeach said as Deiric and I turned to walk toward him and Fiadh.

*

Several minutes later, Deiric and I were laying on our backs at the edge of the field, with Gaisgeach and Fiadh laying not far from us while we waited to be summoned back to Alaric and Alaster.

It was quiet, aside from the soft noise of the grass swaying in the breeze. It was a surprisingly clear night and we were admiring the stars when the sudden whoosh of wingbeats broke the silence.

Both Enda and Dáire flew over us, and I couldn't tell which one, but either Alaric or Alaster were yelling in excitement. I chuckled.

"Clearly they're taking the flying bit much better than I did." I mumbled.

"Well, one of them is."

I watched as they flew around above us, and then Enda suddenly dropped into a dive. It took me a few seconds to realize that she was diving for Alaster, who had fallen off. "Shit." I breathed, but before I could intervene she'd caught him and thrown him up onto her back again.

They won't let them fall, just the same as I wouldn't let you fall. Gaisgeach grumbled. *My life depends on catching you, just as theirs depends on catching them now.*

I hadn't thought of that, even though I knew that to be true. Still, if I'd fallen like that I'd never want to fly again, I was sure.

You could save yourself too. Your fear is absurd.

I shot Gaisgeach a glare and he rolled his eyes in return.

There will be more of us arriving soon. Fiadh said softly. *Bonded to humans. They will find their riders themselves.*

Humans? I couldn't keep the surprise from my thought. If the dragons can live this long bonding humans didn't seem like a wise life choice.

Our magic would extend their lifespan to match ours. In your case, you will be likely to outlive us. Gaisgeach explained.

The thought of that left me rather conflicted. I didn't know them very well yet, we'd only been bonded for a short time, and yet, I couldn't imagine being without him, without both of them, already. Gaisgeach was a constant presence in my mind, even if he wasn't nearby.

I glanced over at him, and the knowing look on his face said he heard everything I was thinking, even if I wasn't consciously pushing the thoughts to him. That, in and of itself, the fact that I could read his expressions already despite that there wasn't really a single human feature about him struck me like a blow. I would outlive him, just like I would outlive *everyone* who wasn't one of us.

"You should get some rest." Deiric said softly and put his arm around my shoulders to pull me closer to him. "I don't think you need to stay awake and be worried with these two next to us."

"I'm fine." I said just as quietly, staring up at the stars again. "Surely they won't be up there flying *all* night."

Deiric huffed a laugh. "I doubt it."

We had flown with Adriana earlier, or I would've suggested that we should be up there too, but for the moment, I was perfectly content to stay here.

"You'll have to teach them how to handle their magic." I mumbled.

"I know."

"Probably wouldn't be a bad idea to teach Adriana too."

"And you." He paused for a moment, his hand tracing idle circles on my shoulder. "Though, I think you already know how to do it, you just haven't ever *tried* to pull any magic from Gaisgeach. It is the same as what you've taught Adriana."

"Mm." I found myself almost dozing off already as we laid there together. It was unusual lately that I felt so calm, so peaceful. Under the stars, in his arms, with our dragons laying on either side of us I hadn't felt more safe. Even more than what I felt within the wards.

I snuggled closer into Deiric, slipping my hand around his waist. He kissed the top of my head, and I drifted off to sleep listening to the slow and steady rhythm of his heartbeat. Even the slight chill of the spring air didn't keep me awake.

*

A few days later Alaster had his daylight ring and we'd gone back to meeting during the day for them to practice with the magic they got from their dragons. We always met in this field, which seemed the safest place for us and for the human riders to meet. As the dragons arrived in our world and found their bonded humans, they would bring them here and Deiric became their teacher.

It was an interesting challenge of time management for me, making sure I had time to train Stella, Sorcha, Zemora, and Adriana with their natural born magic while I came out here to observe Deiric teaching them how to use their dragon magic. I didn't participate in his lessons, but it seemed like a good thing to learn in case I might ever need it, though I doubted a day would come that I *would*.

There were too many now for me to remember all of their names right away. I decided I would only commit their names to memory if they would be close to us, or around often enough for it to matter.

I watched as Deiric walked down the line of riders in front of him. Alaric and Alaster kept close to one another and the humans gave them a *very* wide berth. Each person he passed played with their fire in various ways. Some of them imbued their weapons with the magic and others just practiced using it in general. It was odd to see Deiric doing the teaching. This was usually my job. He turned to me with a satisfied smile on his face.

"You know, you could at least *try* to pull magic from Gaisgeach." He said as he walked by me again.

I shrugged. "I could."

He glanced at Adriana, who stood just a few feet away actively practicing playing with the fire she could summon from Cairbre. She took to this well, thanks to her work with me and using her shadow magic. She did however often misjudge how unpredictable fire could be.

"Be careful with how much you summon at once." Deiric commented, looking her up and down for a moment. "You'll burn yourself out if you pull too much and you look like you're on the brink of that now." I looked over at her and he was right, she was sweating and looked drained. "Take a break." He kept walking back down the line of the others he was training.

Adriana sighed, defeated, and sank down to her knees on the ground with a frown. "This is so much harder than I thought."

She looked over at me and I smiled. "You seem to be doing quite well with it from what I can tell. You have always had a tendency to pull too much power though."

She shot me a look that said I was wrong, but we both knew better. That was almost always her biggest struggle with the shadows too.

"I'm sure you'll get it with more practice!" I tried to be encouraging, because I could tell she was far harder on herself with this than she'd ever been with the shadow magic. For some reason, this seemed more exciting to her.

"Cairbre is always frustrated with me." She mumbled. "He says I'm too frivolous with *everything*."

There was a chuff from somewhere behind us as Cairbre walked up to her. *That is not what I said.*

Adriana rolled her eyes. *Sorry, I was paraphrasing.*

I chuckled.

Are all young people like this? He gave me an exasperated look.

I merely lifted one shoulder. *From what I can tell, yes.*

He visibly rolled his eyes.

Better to be eager and frivolous than terrified of flying. Gaisgeach cut in.

Fuck you. I shot a glare at Gaisgeach where he sat by the edge of the field. I could have sworn smiled slightly. He made a noise that I assumed was similar to him huffing a laugh like Deiric would've at the comment.

I looked back at Adriana. "On a different note." I said, shooting another look toward both Gaisgeach and Cairbre that told them I didn't want to hear their input, "I have one thing I think you should try now, because I am fairly certain it will work."

Adriana arched a brow. "What?"

I waved my fingers and a tiger lily appeared between us. "Mist it."

She sighed, put up her hand, and a wave of her fingers had the plant turning to dust. She gasped, and looked at me like I'd suddenly grown an extra head. "Holy shit!" She exclaimed. "I actually did it!"

I smiled. "You actually did it."

Chapter 49

Deiric

We were coming up on one year since we'd signed the treaty. One whole year since the battle where I'd been moments from death and Mira had ended the fight with one swift blow of magic that honestly left most of us a little rattled. I wasn't sure if she realized just how much she made most of the people on that field fear her that day. Thankfully, none of them noticed her falter at the very end, and even though Elias knew, he never mentioned it.

Mira still lay quietly sleeping next to me, unaware that I'd already woken up and was now laying with myself propped up on an elbow, admiring her while she slept. It was a welcome reprieve to see her so peaceful when I could tell, no matter how good of a face she put on, she was still not herself. I shouldn't be surprised that she had a lot of them fooled. She'd been good at masking when we first met, but this was a whole other level of it.

She locked all her emotions away, never letting anyone but me see them, unless she had to. Her panic was harder to hide, given that it made her body freeze up even with her best attempts to stop it, but her general unrest, stress, and anxiety were well hidden. I was sure if it wasn't for the tea Liala still made her, which she drank nearly every night, that she wouldn't sleep at all. I still wondered what was in it that could work so effectively. Mira didn't seem to know, nor did she question it, but the tea certainly made her relax.

Her hair was sprawled out on her pillow, haphazardly strewn between us, and I was being extra careful not to lay on it right now. She wasn't even wearing her nightgown. Neither of us were wearing clothes. We hadn't bothered to put them on when we finally managed to keep our hands and mouths to ourselves long enough to fall asleep last night.

A cool spring breeze floated in through the open window, carrying Macha to the sill with it. The sound of her landing didn't stir Mira, but the cold air brushing her bare chest did. She shivered, pulled the blanket over her and shimmied herself back into me.

"Good morning, love." I whispered and kissed her cheek.

"Good morning." She mumbled, but didn't open her eyes. Macha cawed, and her eyes just barely opened to glare at the raven. "Surely whatever it is you've brought us isn't so urgent you have to give it to me now?"

Macha responded by flying over to the bed, dropping a rolled up piece of parchment in front of Mira and then flying back out the window. Mira's exasperated sigh suggested that this wasn't actually urgent, but obviously Macha wasn't going to keep carrying this around.

I reached around her and picked it up before I rolled over onto my back and untied the ribbon around it to open it up and read it. It was a rather simple note. An invitation, actually. We were being invited to our joint manor to attend a party to celebrate the signing of the treaty.

"Looks like you'll need a new dress." I said with a smile as I glanced over to Mira again. She hadn't moved.

Another sigh left her lips and she rolled over to face me now with a slight frown. "A new dress?" She mumbled, and then looked at the invitation. "What for?"

"A party to celebrate the anniversary of the signing of the treaty apparently." I passed the note to her. "Devlon is planning it at the joint manor instead of the castle. Sounds like it'll be a more intimate gathering than the party at the palace had been."

"Something tells me he doesn't know how to throw an intimate or small gathering, so I doubt that."

I took the invitation back from her and sat it on the table by my side of the bed before I rolled on my side to look at her again. "I feel like we could all benefit from a fun party, regardless of its size." I studied her while she stared at the ceiling. "Are you alright?"

Her gaze flicked to me for just a moment, before returning to the ceiling. "I'm fine."

"You don't have to wear that mask with me, you know." I said a little bit scoldingly. She'd known that for a long time, even mentioned how much she appreciated that.

"I don't know how to describe how I feel." She mumbled after a few minutes passed where I looked at her disapprovingly and she just stared off into space.

"Do you want to talk about it?"

Her gaze flicked to me again. The intensity behind her gaze rooted me to the spot. "I don't think you *want* me to talk about it." She mumbled. "None of it will make sense."

"It doesn't have to make sense."

She frowned slightly. "I know that fate plays a part in everything, and everything happens for a reason." She started. "I just don't understand why I always seem to end up drawing the short straw, so to speak. I always get dealt the shit hands."

I wanted to jump in and tell her that wasn't true, but I feared that would stop her. She wasn't dealt a shit hand when she found us, and she certainly wasn't dealt a shit hand when she was bonded with Gaisgeach, but those were the only two *good* things I could think of.

"I thought everyone was attacked years ago because of me, and maybe I was the reason they chose, the carefully crafted reason, but still." She stared at the ceiling again. "I thought my entire family was dead, but through some stroke of luck, or I guess weird fate, my father was never dead. We've been living well for months and he was still rotting in a cell. That makes me feel shitty." She rolled onto her side and looked at me.

"I am always the gods damned target for their schemes. They hunted me for years, they attacked me in the woods, they staked me in the castle, and they still come after us, come after Adriana, and me. They were going to use my father for leverage, knowing that I would probably do anything to free him when I found out he was alive, even if our relationship is strained and complicated."

Her face contorted in disgust. "Hell, it's only a matter of time until they realize I have a mate they could exploit. I've already run myself ragged being stressed about *that*."

I was also shocked that I had yet to become the focus of their schemes, but I hoped that was just because they still didn't know about me, or didn't know who I was. I planned to do everything I could to keep it that way.

"I can't sleep, because I lay awake thinking of what they're going to do next. If it weren't for that mysterious damned tea Liala crafts for me, I wouldn't sleep at all." She studied me for a few moments. "And now, it feels like we're preparing an army of dragon riders, and gearing up for a battle. It feels like a war is coming and I just don't know what it will be about or for this time, and losing anyone else would absolutely kill me."

A slight frown found its way to my lips before I could stop it. She noticed it and her lips pursed into a tight line. "You know something. We are preparing for a war aren't we?"

I nodded. Fiadh had said war was coming, but I didn't voice that after our late night discussion.

"Adriana will be queen." She said softly. "The Morrigan said as much."

I nodded. "Which is probably the outcome of the war, so at least you don't have to worry about her." I tried to offer her a small smile, but I knew it didn't help.

"I'm worried about you." Her voice faltered slightly. "I'm worried about Lazarus, Eimear, Liala, Zane, Xander." She drew in a shaky breath. "I'm worried about *everyone*."

I cupped her face with my hand. "You can't worry about *everyone* all the time." I said softly. "We can't spend all day today worrying about tomorrow, or even next month's problems. We can only worry about *today.*" I smiled a real smile this time. "Besides, we need to celebrate our one *good* victory at a party and you need a new dress. You should worry about *that* first."

She snorted, but I could tell that worked. She was on the verge of tears and now her face contorted into a slightly disgusted smile. "A new fucking dress." She mocked. "Yes, I'm so concerned about finding one of those."

"We could have one made?" I suggested.

"How on earth would we have one *made?*" She looked genuinely confused. "I don't know a seamstress, and we sure as hell can't ask Adriana to have the royal seamstress make me something."

I smirked. "I am pretty sure Silas knows at least one, if not several."

She scoffed and rolled her eyes. Surely remembering the dress he gifted her last year.

"We'll go this afternoon." I said, without giving her the chance to argue. "I'm sure Silas will be thrilled to get to have his seamstress make you another jaw dropping gown."

Another snort and roll of her eyes, but she smiled. "Fine, but I want it to be absolutely scandalous so it reveals *all* my tattoos."

The thought of her in such a revealing dress in front of everyone made me cringe, but I nodded. Then I found myself wondering how on earth that would even be possible. I figured that the seamstress would know just the thing.

Chapter 50

Mira

I decided if *I* was going to have a new gown made for me, that Eimear and Liala needed one too. I shifted Eimear, Liala, Lazarus, Deiric, and I to Silas' manor that afternoon. I had sent Macha with a message to Silas to let him know we'd be coming. His reply was swift and welcoming without question.

He was waiting in the foyer for us, with Elias and not one, but three women with measuring tapes over their shoulders and a vast array of colorful fabrics strewn about the tables and chairs around the room. Silas smiled, and there was a hint of a taunt to it, which I suspected was directed at Deiric. Clearly, he didn't realize this was Deiric's idea.

Eimear didn't wait for him to say anything before she darted across the room to admire a beautiful lavender shimmering fabric that had been tossed over the back of a chair. "Oh this is stunning." She breathed.

One of the women walked over to her with a warm and welcoming smile on her face. "I had a feeling you might like that one. Silas described you and your tastes to us, and that fabric was at the top of my list of choices for you." She took the measuring tape off of her shoulders and looked Eimear up and down for a moment. "My name is Layla. May I take your measurements while you describe what sort of dress you'd like?"

Eimear nodded excitedly and turned to face the woman. They began chatting quietly with one another as she started to take measurements and write them down on the paper next to them.

"I'm surprised you asked for my seamstress' help." Silas said as he walked over to the rest of us.

Deiric's hand rested on the small of my back. "It was my idea, actually." He said with a slight smile as Silas shifted his gaze to him with a raised brow. "I assume you got the invitation to the party as well?"

"It came this morning." Elias said from where he still stood by the back of the foyer.

"She has a very specific design in mind." Deiric continued. "She'd like to show off her newest tattoos." He smirked.

Both of Silas' brows raised at that, and he looked back at me again. "Interesting." He said, looking me up and down. "Mika is the best around." He gestured toward the blonde woman who approached us now. "She'll create something stunning for you I'm sure."

I nodded. "Thank you." I started to step around him to meet the woman near one of the stacks of fabrics that caught my eye. Deiric followed behind me.

I saw Silas glance at Lazarus before I turned away completely to look at Mika. "And to what do I owe the pleasure of a visit from you?"

I didn't have to be looking at Lazarus to know he scowled a little bit. "I'm here for her." He grumbled. "You know that."

Silas scoffed. "As though she'd need protection *here*."

"I don't take any chances when it comes to her safety." Lazarus snarled. "*Anywhere*."

I wanted to say that made me feel safe, but it only made me a little more uneasy. He had to know I was safe here. I still didn't really understand his incessant need to protect me *everywhere*, but it had only gotten worse since we were attacked at the castle. One day, I would ask him about that. For now, I shifted my focus to the task at hand.

Mika took many measurements. She was very thorough. I explained to her where all of my tattoos were and that I really wanted something that would show them all off. I recognized that it would probably be quite hard, but she seemed to believe it would be easier than I thought. She did say that it might end up being two separate pieces, but she would see what she could do. I opted for a beautiful midnight blue shimmering fabric that felt like the softest silk.

We were all told that our gowns would be ready in plenty of time for the party, and that we would meet them back here to try them on to get any final adjustments made. Eimear was absolutely ecstatic. She was bubbling on about how she'd never had a dress made specifically for her.

All her dresses had just been gowns she'd found when she went into dress shops. Deiric and Silas assured all of us that they would be paid for and it was no problem. It was the first time in quite a while that I realized I hadn't questioned where or how they managed to have money for this.

I knew they still did take care of monsters and beasts on occasion, but we weren't really paid for that, so they must have also been taking up bounty hunting, or something else. Perhaps they had some wealth built up that I'd never have known about. That never occurred to me before. Regardless, we returned to our manor long before sunset, which gave us plenty of time to spar.

Adriana, Zemora, Stella, and Sorcha were taking advantage of the pleasant spring weather outside when Eimear and I joined them. They were sparring with their magic while Aodh watched and guided them as needed.

"Adriana." I called out to her as I approached, a training blade in my hand.

She stopped halfway through sending a blast of shadow toward Zemora and looked at me. She opened her mouth like she was about to speak, but then took in the training blades in my hands and looked at me quizzically. "Shouldn't I be focusing on my magic?"

I hadn't told her she was close to mastery and I wouldn't yet. "You're doing well with it." I said with a shrug. "We can stand to focus on a sword for today." I glanced over at Eimear who just smirked. "Eimear can show the rest of you how to throw knives."

Eimear's face lit up with excitement. Despite her lack of enjoyment in learning with me last year, she did start to find throwing knives quite fun over time. I think that had everything to do with the fact that she could use that skill when she went to some of the taverns in town and earn a little bit of money betting with the locals when she challenged them.

She'd gotten quite good at throwing darts too, it seemed. She turned and went into the house to retrieve the knives while Zemora, Stella, and Sorcha stepped to the side to give Adriana and I room.

I handed a training blade to Adriana and spun the other training blade in my hand. I really disliked the balance of it, but it would do. It was far lighter than the sword I tended to carry. More similar perhaps to the weight of the sword that Silas had made for me, which I rarely ever used.

I settled into a fighting stance. "Do your worst."

"Be careful, when she says that it is never a good sign." I heard Liala say from behind me. I hadn't noticed her coming back outside.

Adriana glanced beyond me at Liala for just a brief moment before she settled her gaze back on me, and then lowered into a stance similar to mine. "Would it be wrong for me to ask you to take it easy on me?"

I smirked. "It wouldn't be wrong, but I've got a gods damned training sword in my hands so I'm not taking it easy on you today." I considered her for a moment. "Though if you'd like me to go get my *real* sword, I would promise at least not to intentionally cut you with it. You're not going to learn anything if I take it easy on you."

She snorted just as Eimear emerged from the manor carrying the throwing knives to work with the others. They all stood watching, ignoring Eimear completely when she walked past them to go get set up at a tree by the edge of the woods.

Adriana took advantage of my distraction, watching Eimear walk away with the knives, and lunged at me. That was a move Zemora would've taken. Adriana appeared to be taking a page from her book today.

I swung my sword up to block her advance, aimed right for my face, and she scowled a little. "If you're going to hit me, you're going to have to try a lot harder than that."

Her expression leveled out with steely determination as she danced around me. For the first few minutes, I remained on the defensive, letting her try her hand at any number of different approaches to land a blow on me. She'd watched me spar with Deiric and several of the others many times. She knew my fighting style by now and she was trying to mimic it or fight *with* it, which wasn't giving her much of an edge on me.

After letting her get her shots in, I finally took up some offensive movements and began dealing blows to her instead. She grew increasingly annoyed with each blow I managed to land on her that she didn't block. Thankfully, we were using training blades or she'd have been bleeding from several wounds to her arms and legs.

"So much for taking it easy on me." She mumbled, blocking a blow I had aimed at her face.

"I told you I wouldn't be." I smiled and immediately sent another blow toward her left side which she spun away from rather than blocking it.

"Yeah, but you could at least move *slower*." She was insinuating that I was using my super human speed. I wasn't, but she wasn't nearly as skilled with a blade as me, so any *normal* speed would seem fast to her, I was sure.

"You need to move faster."

Her eyes narrowed and her brows furrowed, but she kept trying. We went back and forth for nearly an hour before I finally decided she'd had enough. The sun had started to set. I wandered into the manor to get some tea and prepare a bath for myself before I settled into bed for the evening.

Deiric was in the kitchen. He had a steaming mug in his hands as he turned to head for the door and nearly ran into me. He managed not to spill a single drop of it, smiled, and held out the mug to me. "I figured you'd be coming in any minute now."

I took the mug from him and offered him a small smile in return. "Thank you."

He rested his hand on my hip and moved to step around me. "Oh, but there's more." He smirked, and the hand that was on my hip squeezed a little tighter as he spun me around to follow him out of the kitchen, up the stairs, and to our room.

He pulled me along with him into the bathing room, where he had a bath already drawn for me. It was steaming and smelled of lavender, roses, and a hint of citrus. Candles were lit all around the bath, giving the room a soft and flickering glow.

I raised an eyebrow and looked at him suspiciously. "And to what do I owe this pleasure?"

He merely shrugged and gave me a sly smile. "What, is it *that* unusual for me to do something nice for you?"

"Well, no, but…" I let my voice trail off as I glanced around the room. "This is a little unexpected."

"You never really *relax* so I thought I'd find a way to force it on you." He looked me over for a few heartbeats. "Relax, enjoy the bath, and join me in bed when you're done."

I snorted. "You're not going to wash up before you climb in bed?"

He turned to walk toward the door. "I'm sure I could use someone else's bathing room if you *really* insist on me washing up before I get in bed and wait for you."

I sat the mug on the small stool next to the tub, grabbed his collar, and drug him back over to the edge of the tub. "You will do no such thing." I smiled and began to pull his shirt up out of where he had it tucked into his pants. "There's room for two in there, I'm sure."

His hands found my hips again and a sultry smile rose to his lips. His eyes lingered on my lips. "That won't be very relaxing." He muttered, but nothing about his voice suggested he was going to refuse to join me.

"Mm." I brushed my lips against his in the ghost of a kiss before I tugged his shirt up over his head. "That depends on what your definition of *relaxing* is."

He huffed a laugh and kissed along my jaw, then down my neck while he reached around to slowly undo my corset. "I suppose that's true." My corset dropped to the floor and his hands slipped up under my blouse.

I let my hands trace down from his neck to his shoulders, then his bare chest. He sighed and leaned into me, his mouth trailing back up my neck, then my jaw until his lips met mine again. He kissed me slowly, sweetly, like he had an eternity to do so. I suppose technically, he did.

He slowly pulled my blouse over my head, then unhooked my bra, which dropped to the floor just like my corset had. I used the brief moment his lips weren't on mine to point out that the water would get cold.

He chuckled softly. "I'm sure that between the two of us, we could reheat it pretty easily." He kissed me again.

"You know, fire magic and all." He whispered against my lips.

"I suppose that's true." I whispered, throwing his words back at him while I undid the buttons of his pants.

Another huff of a laugh and a brief kiss before he pulled my skirt down off my hips, my underwear with it. The skirt pooled at my feet, leaving me entirely naked except for the boots I hadn't bothered to remove yet. He kissed down my neck again, then my chest, and my stomach before he was kneeling in front of me.

He smiled up at me, and then cupped both my knees with his hands for a moment while he just looked at me. He tapped the back of one knee, shifting his focus to removing my boots one at a time. When he got one off, he tossed it to the side and tapped the back of my other knee, which I bent for him and lifted my other leg so he could remove that boot.

His eyes lazily and slowly traced up my body, before finally meeting mine again filled with so much heat I was surprised he didn't grab me right then and toss me onto the bed.

In the blink of an eye, he stood before me again, pants and boots gone, with a smirk on that ridiculously gorgeous face of his. Then he scooped me up into his arms and stepped into the tub. He lowered me down into the blissfully warm water, and then sat behind me. I tried to turn myself around to face him but he grabbed my shoulders and held me still.

"No." He whispered, his lips grazing my ear. "You're supposed to be relaxing, remember?" I huffed, and he chuckled. He began to gently massage my back after he tossed my braid over my shoulder and into the water in front of me.

I couldn't stop the sigh that escaped my lips as I relaxed back into him, his hands steadily working the numerous knots out of my shoulders. I reached over and grabbed my tea. I took a few sips, and it tasted stronger than I remembered.

"It is."

I glanced back at him.

"Adriana mastered her magic, you've gotten pretty good at flying with Gaisgeach, and the other mages have progressed well in their training." He said softly. "I'm almost certain that Sorcha, Stella, and Zemora are close to mastering their magic, aren't they?" I nodded. "Then you deserve a *real* relaxing evening."

He's right, you know. Gaisgeach grumbled. I scoffed at him. *You don't have to be on high alert all the time with* us *around. Not right now anyway.*

"If you won't listen to me," Deiric started, "you should at least listen to him."

"It doesn't feel right to *not* be on high alert."

"You managed to relax before the battle last year."

He was right. I had. That was before all hell broke loose though. It was when I genuinely saw a life for myself with him, even in hiding. Now, I have a much more complicated life ahead of me.

"A lot was different then." I said simply.

"That doesn't mean you have to be on high alert all the time again. We aren't at war. At least not yet." His hands continued to massage down my shoulders and upper back. "You should take the time to relax now, while we know we're safe here, and we don't have to worry about whatever Ronan is doing."

"It's hard to relax when I know something is brewing."

"That's what the tea is for."

"What exactly *is* in this tea?" I asked, taking another couple of sips. "Neither of you ever told me."

He huffed a laugh. "I didn't even know until this evening."

"And?"

"Cannabis."

I twisted around to look at him before he could stop me. "What?"

He was smirking. "Apparently, it doesn't affect us as much as it would a mortal." He shrugged. "So she put a little extra in there tonight."

"You two are trying to get me *high?*"

He put his hands up defensively. "Listen, I didn't know what it was, and I didn't decide how much to put in there but she warned me it would be stronger. I finally asked and figured a little extra wouldn't get you *that* high."

He studied me for a few moments. I shot him a look that said I absolutely didn't believe him and that this was absurd. "Are you really going to complain? You've slept like a baby ever since you started drinking it before you go to sleep."

I opened my mouth to protest, but he was right. I had slept better the last couple of weeks, and I knew it was the tea but I didn't know why. It made sense that I couldn't identify it by taste. I hadn't ever *drank* that before. Most people smoked it. I turned back around and he went back to working at massaging my back.

We sat for several minutes in silence, before he finally reached over my shoulder and grabbed my braid. He undid the leather strap I had holding it in place, and then slowly, but carefully, unraveled it. By the time he'd finished washing my hair, I had finished my tea, and started to feel a little… fuzzy.

I spun around to face him and straddled him before he could stop me. He opened his mouth to say something, but I stopped him with a single finger on his lips. "I know, I know." I grumbled. "I'm supposed to be relaxing, but I find a *lot* of things relaxing." A sultry smile rose to my lips as I leaned in almost close enough to kiss him. "And I'm tired of waiting." I removed my finger from his lips and kissed him before he could protest.

Chapter 51

Mira

The dress Silas' seamstress made me was absolutely stunning. It was perfect, even better than I could've imagined myself. The top wrapped up around my neck, with a deep plunging neckline that came together between my breasts where a large chunk of blue goldstone rested.

There was a silver chain that wrapped around my ribcage, holding the very small amount of fabric that covered my breasts in place. The skirt hung from the blue goldstone in the front of the dress and draped down around my hips, where it hung just at the base of my spine in the back.

The skirt had a slit up the right side, allowing for easy access to the dagger I sheathed there, even though I didn't need it. I had not told her about the blue goldstone choker Deiric had gifted me, though I suspect that either he or Silas must've mentioned it for her to have added that small detail to the gown.

Deiric wore a vest without sleeves, but as per usual, it was black and the embroidery was silver. The tails of it came to just below his knees, covering most of the black pants he wore and revealing just his tall boots underneath. I was surprised to see him in it. He almost exclusively wore his leathers, or long sleeved shirts, even on the hottest days of the summer.

"What?" He asked as he walked up to me in the bedroom with one brow arched.

"I don't think I've ever seen you wear something *without* sleeves."

"I can change, if you'd rather I wear sleeves."

I chuckled. "No, I like it. It's just unusual." I smiled. "Are you ready?"

He shrugged and hooked his elbow with mine. "Are *you* ready?"

"I suppose so."

He opened our bedroom door and we walked down the stairs to the foyer where almost everyone else had gathered already. The mages would be staying back with Lazarus' men while the rest of us attended the party. Lazarus came down shortly after us, wearing a similar vest to what Deiric had, but it had gold embroidery instead.

"Ready?" I asked. They all nodded or said yes, so I shifted us to the foyer of Aris' manor.

Liala looked around incredulously, like she didn't recognize it. I realized then that she hadn't been back here at all since the attacks. She looked stunning in her turquoise gown. She matched Zane perfectly in his black tunic with turquoise embroidery that I was certain he'd had made *just* to wear with her when she wore that gown. He pulled her a little closer to him. She turned to him and smiled.

"Are you alright?" He said so quietly I almost couldn't hear him. She nodded and smiled, but didn't say anything in return.

The party must have been in the courtyard, because there were very few people *inside* the manor, except us and anyone bustling around with food and drinks. Even so, the foyer was decorated and there were candles lit all over the place in addition to the mage lights floating overhead.

Eimear stuck close to Renwick, and it didn't go without being noticed that they too were matching. She had a beautiful lilac gown, and he wore a lilac tunic with black embroidery. It seemed that Deiric and I were the only couple who *didn't* decide to coordinate. Xander and Leo each wore black long sleeved tunics with gold embroidery.

I motioned for them to follow Deiric and I out to the back of the manor.

"When did you end up with dragon tattoos?" Eimear asked as they filed into a line behind us.

I glanced over my shoulder and smiled. "When I met Gaisgeach."

She raised a brow but didn't ask any further questions. The back doors were open. We walked through and then went down the handful of steps into the courtyard which was a flurry of activity. I could see Silas on the opposite end of the space chatting with Killian. Both of them looked entirely uninterested in being at this party.

"Silas, despite being very good at worming his way up the ladder with politics, is not a fan of parties." Deiric whispered into my ear as we descended the last step.

"Interesting." I said simply. "And Killian?"

Deiric scanned the crowd, as though he was sizing up a threat, and finally said, "Killian is just probably annoyed that Silas decided to go talk to him." He smirked and pulled me with him until he found a spot along the edge of the area they intended to be the dance floor. They were using the sparring area, ironically.

Devlon shifted directly in front of us, which caused me to jolt. He chuckled. "Sorry to startle you. It was easier to shift to you than to wander through the crowd." He smiled. "I'm glad you decided to come." He gestured toward the dance floor. "Cedric and Beitris will be entertaining us this evening. Apparently they're a package deal now."

I arched a brow. "A package deal?"

He shrugged. "I didn't ask questions." He waved his hand dismissively. "Two bards are better than no bards!" He glanced between us for a moment. "Will you actually be drinking with us this time, or bringing your own liquor?"

I smiled. "I'd be glad to have a drink."

He held up his hand and a glass of whiskey appeared in it. "Fantastic!" He handed it to me then looked at Deiric. "And you?"

"Sure." Deiric only gave him a half a smile that didn't meet his eyes, but Devlon's smile remained and summoned him a glass anyway.

"Enjoy." Then he shifted back to wherever he had been before that.

"You still don't trust him do you?" I mumbled after taking a sip of the whiskey.

"You'll find that I don't trust many people." Deiric said softly, but took a sip of his as well. "I'll give him credit that he seems to care about keeping you safe as much as I do, but I still am not going to let my guard down completely."

Lazarus appeared to Deiric's right. "Are you sure that drinking is a good idea?" He said too quietly for anyone but us to hear.

"It's safe. Aris wouldn't be drinking it if it weren't." Deiric said just as quietly and motioned with his chin over to where Aris was sitting with my father at a table across the courtyard. I locked eyes with my father for a heartbeat before continuing to gaze around the party. I had been able to avoid him when I'd come to the last meeting here and I hoped to continue doing that tonight.

"It seems Mika has outdone herself again" Silas said, appearing to my left on near silent feet. "You look stunning."

Deiric tensed slightly beside me, but didn't say a word. I glanced at Silas and looked him over. He had a sinful smile on his lips and his eyes glimmered with mischief.

"What, no mocking today?" I asked with a raised brow.

"I can mock you if you'd like." His smile grew a little more wicked.

I rolled my eyes. "That won't be necessary." I looked over toward the stage, where Cedric and Beitris were setting up. They didn't seem to notice I was here, though I'm sure they knew I would be. Everyone else was milling about, chatting with some of the other party goers or finding a table to sit and eat. Our crew made their way to a table and filled it, leaving three seats open for Deiric, Lazarus, and I. Silas lingered with us.

"I heard there was a wonderful family reunion." Silas finally said after several minutes of people watching and a heavy silence between the four of us.

I snorted. "Oh, it was wonderful indeed." I said sarcastically and I could see his smile out of the corner of my eye.

"Not a fan of daddy dearest?"

I gave him a look that told him exactly how I felt about both my father *and* his attempt at mockery. His smile only got wider.

"It's complicated." I muttered.

"Family is always complicated." He replied, and glanced over to where my father still sat with Aris. "He hasn't stopped glancing over here to keep an eye on you."

"Of course he hasn't." I mumbled. Deiric released my elbow just to slip his arm around my waist instead. "He's going to keep glancing over here until you all leave me alone and he feels like he can approach me."

"Do you *want* us to leave you alone?" Silas asked quietly enough that I was fairly sure my father couldn't hear him from where he sat across the courtyard.

"No." I replied just as quietly.

"Then we won't." Deiric whispered.

*

There were so many mages here that I didn't recognize, and one in particular who seemed to be eyeing up Lazarus at every moment she got. Lazarus, of course, seemed oblivious, though Silas tracked my line of sight and looked just as amused as me to discover her interest.

She was a pretty little thing, probably an inch shorter than me with beautiful copper hair and emerald eyes. I had yet to see her use any form of magic, while the other mages seemed to display theirs at every moment they could. I wondered if either she was completely shy and socially awkward or if she was merely a nightmage. She caught my gaze and quickly looked away before she darted off somewhere I couldn't see her.

"Now you've scared her off." Silas mumbled under his breath. "Pity though, she probably wouldn't have approached him anyway."

I smirked. "Oh I was going to make sure it happened." I said quietly, but not quietly enough for Deiric not to notice.

"What wild plan have you come up with this time?" Deiric mumbled, looking around at the dancefloor slowly filling while Cedric and Beitris began to play. "And should I be concerned that you seem to be making a plan *with* Silas?"

Silas snorted. "I'm not planning anything. I'm just people watching."

"Nothing I'm going to share at the moment." I said with a sly smile as I glanced around the crowd to find her again, to no avail. I finished off my drink and Deiric took the glass before I had a chance to say anything.

"Unless you intend to stand here and awkwardly watch people all evening, I think we should dance." He whispered into my ear as he turned and sat our glasses on the ledge of the raised garden bed behind us.

I gave him a look that suggested I was perfectly fine with people watching all evening, but he took my hand and pulled me out onto the dance floor without waiting for a real answer. He pulled us far enough away from Silas and Lazarus that they couldn't hear us if we whispered among the crowd.

"So what *is* this plan?" He smirked as he began leading me in a dance.

"It seems a pretty lass has taken an interest in Lazarus and I'd like to introduce them." I said quietly.

"The red head?" I looked at him incredulously and he huffed a laugh. "Do you think I don't pay attention? I might look like I'm not, but I don't miss a thing." He went quiet while he spun me away and then back into him so my back was against his chest. "Lazarus seemed to notice her too."

I whipped my head to the side to look at him and he gestured over toward them with a nod of his head. I looked over in time to see Lazarus sizing her up while her back was turned to him.

"Some might say you should be more aware of your surroundings." He whispered into my ear and then spun me around to face him before I could come up with a retort.

"Well maybe if Silas hadn't distracted me I might've noticed."

Deiric just smiled and rolled his eyes. "I can distract Lazarus if you think you can talk her into coming over to meet him."

"And how are you going to do that?" I raised a brow. "The only reason Lazarus is even taking the time to look around and relax a little is because you're with me right now."

Deiric glanced over my shoulder, smirked, and nodded to someone, then looked back at me. "I have my ways." He looked over my other shoulder. "If you are going to try to do it, you'd better do it now." He stopped dancing, took my hand and kissed it, before striding off toward Lazarus and Silas again with a smile.

I didn't waste a moment, and shifted myself in front of her. She jumped and stumbled back a step, then looked at me like I might scold her for being in my way.

I gave her a warm and welcoming smile. "Forgive me for startling you." I made a show of looking her over, and she was indeed nearly *two* inches shorter than me, and very, *very* shy. "My name is Mira."

"It's no trouble at all. I should get back over to my friends." She avoided eye contact and was about to turn and dart off to friends she *didn't* have. It was such an obvious lie, even if her thoughts didn't give it away.

"Nonsense." I stepped with her as she turned slightly and she stopped to finally look at me. "You have been alone for most of the evening if I'm not mistaken. I'm not going to bite you if that's what you're worried about."

"I, uh–"

I snorted. "You don't have to explain. I can hear every one of your thoughts. I came over to say hello and invite you to meet my friend." I gestured toward Lazarus, who was now facing away from us and talking to Deiric and Silas. I could wonder what was so important that it drew his attention away from me later. She followed my gaze and looked over toward them as well.

"Oh, I don't want to be a bother." She mumbled and looked back at me.

"I'm sure he would be delighted to meet you." I smiled again. "What's your name?"

"Rosalind." She said quietly.

"And you're a nightmage?"

She nodded.

"Come on then. I'll introduce you to him." I started to walk around her toward them and gestured for her to follow. She thankfully, albeit slightly reluctantly, fell into step beside me, but I hooked my elbow with hers just to be sure she wouldn't get lost in the crowd. "Deiric, the dark haired one won't bother you at all. Silas, the one with white hair, is a prick," he shot me a glare for a heartbeat and I smirked, "but he won't bother you either." Lazarus noticed Silas glare and heard us approaching now. He turned around just as we were walking up to them.

I caught his glare at me before he schooled his features to be far less threatening when he saw who I was dragging along with me. I smiled triumphantly at him. "And Lazarus looks like he's always in a bad mood, but that's just because he's old and lonely."

She chuckled. Lazarus glared at me again, and Deiric and Silas barely hid their stifled laughs behind him.

"Lazarus, this is Rosalind." I gestured toward her. "She is a nightmage." I turned to face her again. "Don't let his glare scare you. He's actually quite pleasant when you don't insult him."

He held out his hand to her. "It is lovely to meet you." He glanced at me again for a moment with a look that said I'd hear about this later. "Hopefully she hasn't given you a reason to be afraid of me."

She gave him her hand and he bowed slightly before kissing it gently and smiling. "She hasn't told me much of anything about you actually."

He raised a brow. "Good. Can I get you a drink?" He offered.

She glanced at me for just a moment and then nodded. "Sure." She said with a shy smile, and he led her off to where they'd set up a bar.

I turned and smirked at Deiric. "I knew I would like her." He gave me a knowing smile.

"Did I miss something?" Silas asked, stepping closer to us.

"She apparently likes whiskey." Deiric explained.

Silas looked confused for a moment, and then realized we heard her *think* that she wanted whiskey. "It's still a little unnerving at times that you do that."

I shrugged. "You'll have to get used to it."

"Oh I've had plenty of time to get used to it and I still hate it." He rolled his eyes and looked around at the crowd around us again before leaning back into the raised bed.

Shall we dance again? Deiric looked at me with a smile that said he had other activities on his mind, and I didn't miss that his gaze shifted to my lips briefly before raising back up to meet my eyes.

Why not? I gave him a similar smile and let him pull me back out into the crowd of people dancing. I was surprised to see Zane and Liala among them, once we got to dancing and swaying around.

A few moments later, I spotted Devlon and one of our magisters spinning around the crowd. It seemed that the alcohol had certainly started to loosen everyone up and draw them out to the floor. I was so enthralled with our dancing that when the music slowed I didn't notice someone approaching until I heard them clear their throat.

Deiric stiffened and frowned. I turned my head to see my father standing beside us. "I'm sorry to interrupt, but would I be able to have the next dance?" He looked at Deiric first, with his apology, and then his gaze shifted to me when he asked for a dance.

I wasn't able to hide my shock and my mouth gaped open for a moment. I turned to glance at Deiric.

It's your call. He thought.

I glanced back to my father as the music started to flow again in a new soft and slow song. I imagine he chose this moment specifically to allow him the chance to talk to me, uninterrupted. I wasn't sure if I admired him for waiting for the right moment or if I hated him for it. After a few seconds of uncomfortable stillness and silence between all of us I finally reluctantly nodded.

Deiric nodded and stepped back, releasing my hands as he looked at me cautiously and thought, *Just say the word and I'll be right back over here.*

I nodded at him again. He strode toward where Silas still stood leaning against the raised garden bed. My father stepped up to put his hand on my hip and take my other hand in his to lead me in the next dance.

"I'm surprised you agreed." He said quietly as we spun around slowly in time to the music.

"I'm surprised you asked." I replied rather coldly.

He frowned slightly. "I guess I deserved that." He mumbled under his breath. "I wanted to get the chance to apologize for how I acted the day you found me."

I merely arched a brow, but said nothing.

"And I'm also sorry if I ever made you feel like you weren't enough or that I thought any less of you for any decision you made. Or anything you've done for that matter."

"You had your reasons." I spoke without really thinking about what I was saying, but I knew that to be true. He didn't *ask* to be a father, probably never considered it, and certainly by the time *I* was born he hadn't had an example of a fatherly figure for nearly eight hundred years. I couldn't expect him to know how to be a good father. No, he was the equivalent of a captain, someone who trained warriors, not raised children.

"No. None that were good enough to make up for the fact that I failed so miserably at being a good father to you."

He mumbled. "But despite, or maybe rather regardless of my failures, you've become a remarkable woman. I didn't think *anyone* could inspire or affect Lazarus the way you seem to. And I certainly wouldn't have ever guessed that you'd be the turning point in that whole mess." He smiled hesitantly. "Your mother would be very proud."

I couldn't stop the smile that formed on my lips in return. For a moment, I felt bad for simply shutting him down that day, but part of me felt like he needed that rejection to be able to realize everything he just said to me. I was at a loss for words, because I never expected a *real* apology from him. I was just determined to set a solid boundary and protect the little bit of peace I had managed to find.

"I would love to hear what happened while I was imprisoned, from *you*." He spoke again, breaking the silence while I quietly considered his words. "Aris told me most of what had happened, what you've done, but I imagine there was far more to it than that."

"I'm sure there's a lot Aris *doesn't* know." I said quietly. "We didn't give him all of the details. He only knew a very basic timeline until he came to stay with us." I cautiously monitored his face for any sort of reaction, but he remained intently listening.

"I met Deiric after I killed a Chimera." A flicker of surprise flashed across his face. "A vampire he was training tried to compel me in a tavern, which resulted in me getting drugged by a mercenary and playing a damsel in distress." I rolled my eyes at the thought of it.

"And Deiric swooped in to save your ass." My father said with a smirk.

"In a manner of speaking, yes."

"And you just blindly agreed to go with him?"

I shook my head. "No. We made a deal. But even if we hadn't, something told me I could trust him." I smiled, thinking back to those first few days and weeks. "I guess, I was drawn to him just as much as he was drawn to me, even if I didn't know why yet."

To my surprise, my father actually smiled. "I'm not sure I've ever seen you as happy as you seemed to be all night tonight." He paused, and studied me as my smile faded and a look of surprise and confusion took its place. "I'm glad you've found someone who brings out the light in you. Though I will say I'm a little bit frustrated to know that you went off and married him without *any* wedding at all."

I snorted. "I hardly think that a wedding is or was necessary. Neither of us are fans of parties."

"And yet, you're here, and dancing."

I shrugged. "We attend them when we're asked to."

"And Silas. You're… friends with him?"

I raised a brow. "You know Silas?"

"Of course I know Silas. He's hard to miss." He smirked. "But you didn't answer my question."

"I suppose you could call us friends." I shrugged again. "He certainly likes to get under my skin, but he's also proven to be helpful at times."

"Like when he continued to stand next to you after making a comment about me just to make sure I *didn't* approach?"

"You heard that?"

"I heard enough. Do you really want so badly to avoid me that you'd hide behind all of them?"

I gave him a look that suggested that if he didn't act like an ass the last time I saw him, I likely wouldn't feel that way and his shoulders sagged just slightly.

"You set your boundaries clear enough." He mumbled. "But you'll forgive me if I still tried to talk to you anyway. You *are* my daughter, after all. And while we may have an eternity to mend things, I would rather not wait, after everything we've gone through."

"Fair enough." I glanced over his shoulder to see Deiric casually chatting with Silas as they watched us from a distance. Deiric didn't notice my gaze, but Silas did. I looked back toward Deiric just in time to see a woman approaching him.

She was about my height, with dark hair that fell to just above her breasts and bright emerald green eyes. He didn't seem to notice her, with his focus on Silas and me, but her body language and thoughts told me enough.

I scowled. I waved my hand just enough to send a little fire at her to singe her fingertips before they made contact with Deiric's arm.

My father chuckled when he glanced back behind him to see what was going on. "I pity the woman who has to contend with you." He mumbled, releasing me as the song finally drew to a close. "We can catch up another time." He squeezed my shoulder gently and then walked off.

The woman yelped when the fire grazed her fingertips, making Deiric and Silas finally notice her. Deiric seemed amused but shook his head at me, before turning to face her and frown slightly. "Triss." Deiric said flatly. "It's been years."

I was next to him in the blink of an eye, while Silas merely twisted so he was leaning with his hip rather than against his back so he could watch this all unfold. Triss glanced at me, looked me up and down for a half a second, and then turned back to Deiric.

"Fifteen years to be exact." She said with a slight scowl. I didn't hear a single thought from her now, which I assumed was because she didn't want *him* to hear a single thought from her. She glanced at me again. "Aren't you going to introduce me to your new… friend?"

"Mate." I snarled before Deiric could reply.

She raised both brows and stumbled back a step as though I'd dealt her a physical blow.

Deiric casually slipped his arm around his waist. "Triss, this is Mira." He explained, glancing at me with a smile. "My mate and my wife." He looked back and forth between us before settling his gaze on me. I turned enough to lock eyes with him, and he added, "Mira, this is Triss." *An ex-lover, if you could even call it that.* He added in his thoughts.

I arched a brow and looked her up and down once more. I'd gathered as much given the thoughts she had about him when she reached out to grab his arm and get his attention, but to hear him admit it made my blood boil just a little.

And you were worried about me meeting your past lovers.

I shot him a glare.

"You're both mind readers." She breathed, as though she couldn't believe it.

"What was your first clue?" Silas snapped from behind us. "They have silent conversations all the time. It's only mildly infuriating."

That earned him a brief glare from Deiric when he glanced over his shoulder at him before looking back toward Triss. "What are *you* doing here?" Deiric asked her, and didn't even try to make his voice sound pleasant.

She shrugged. "I was passing through, heard there would be a party and that you'd be here, so I stuck around."

I couldn't stop myself from rolling my eyes. Deiric squeezed my hip to remind me to be nice, or at least behave.

"I suppose I should be flattered, but surely you know better than to wait around for me."

"I guess I do now." She muttered and shot an almost imperceptible glare in my direction. "Glad to see you're doing well at least." She said rather dismissively and then turned and walked away.

"Do I want to know the rest of the story there?" I asked quietly, even though she wouldn't have heard me anyway.

"No." He mumbled, and we both turned back to face Silas. He switched one arm for the other, not willing to release me just yet like he thought I'd go after her.

"I'm not going to run after her and kill her." I said, my voice feigning mild annoyance. He looked at me doubtfully. "I only singed her fingers because of what I heard her *thinking* about you."

He cringed. "I'd rather not know that."

The music picked up suddenly into a wild and exciting beat. Cedric started to sing a catchy and fun tune. Before Deiric could think or react, I'd grabbed the hand that was on my hip and pulled him out to the dancefloor behind me. He nearly stumbled into me when I stopped among the crowd.

"I guess that means I'm not getting out of this dance." He said with a smile.

"No, you're not." He immediately matched my pace as we spun and danced to the tune. I spied Lazarus and Rosalind also finding their way to the dancefloor to join in for this number. He spun her around and they both danced gleefully like two lovestruck teenagers. I didn't think I'd ever seen him quite so happy or relaxed.

Chapter 52

Mira

I woke up the next morning with an absolutely mind numbing headache. For some reason, I didn't think that I'd ever feel a hangover like this as a vampire, but I guess we're not totally immune to that either. Deiric was still sound asleep behind me, his arm stretched across my back, and his legs sprawled and intertwined with mine. He was snoring.

I think we both had the same amount of alcohol, and for some reason I suspected that he wouldn't be hungover at all. I moved just slightly to see if I could wiggle out from under his arm, and his snoring stopped abruptly as he moved right along with me.

"We don't have to get up yet." He mumbled.

"Maybe not." I replied. "But I'd like to get some tea before this headache gets any worse."

He huffed a tired laugh and then rolled up onto his side before pulling me all the way back against his chest. "Did you over do it last night?" I could hear the smile on his lips.

"A little."

He nuzzled into my neck and nipped it. "I think I know a much faster cure for a hangover." His breath was hot on my neck, sending a shiver down my spine.

I groaned and lazily tried to pull away from him. "I'm sure the tea will work just fine."

"Maybe it would." He smiled against my neck and this time I felt his fangs graze it. "But you still need to feed."

And so did he.

I spun around and was on top of him before he could react, though he didn't seem to mind. I almost regretted it, when my head throbbed after the abrupt movement, but it was worth it to see that hint of shock dash across his features when I suddenly had him pinned down. The smile that now rose to his lips was anything but innocent. I was straddling him, leaning down so my chest was almost flush with his. I held his arms up over his head with my hands around his wrists.

"Well, this is a surprising turn of events." He breathed.

I huffed. "What, you don't like it when I take control?" I mumbled as I kissed down his neck.

"Actually, I–" His reply stopped short with a gasp and a moan when I bit him. His whole body tensed against me for a few heartbeats before he relaxed, with the exception of his arms. He pulled against my grip, but I held firm. The taste of him would've been enough to cure my headache. He tasted like the finest aged whiskey, smoky but sweet.

"Mira," he breathed. "Let me touch you." He pulled against my grip on his wrists again. "Please."

The moment I released him his arms closed around me and pulled me down onto him. One around my waist and the other slipping up around me and into my hair. Then he lazily traced every inch of me with his hands, while I drank. When I finally had my fill and withdrew my fangs, he flipped us around so he was on top of me.

His blood trickled down my chin, and he licked from where it stopped at my jawline up to my lips before he kissed me with a passion and hunger that was unrelenting.

"My turn." He growled, and began to kiss his way down my neck, then my chest and my stomach. His hand traced a gentle line down my thigh, before he stopped at my knee and his lips traced the same path his hand had gone.

I gasped and my entire body jolted when he bit my thigh. Gods, this was so much better than my neck. I could feel him smile against me just before he slid his hand up my thigh and his fingers brushed over my clit in the ghost of a touch that left me aching for more.

He ran his thumb over me again and I rocked my hips into his touch. A soft whimper left my lips before I could stop it. Each pull he took from me just fueled the building fire within me. I needed more, needed all of him.

He withdrew his fangs and kissed where he'd bit me, then looked up at me. When I met his gaze, he was nothing short of satisfied, drinking in the sight of me. The heat behind that gaze and wicked smile could've been enough to undo me. Blood dropped from his lips just as it had from mine when he crawled up and his lips met mine.

He thrust himself into me and I gasped against his lips. I clawed at his back as he retreated and thrust in again and again. The rhythm was wild, hungry, and I loved every second of it. I rocked my hips with him and it didn't take me long to reach my climax with his name on my lips.

I flipped us so I was on top of him again. My hands traced down his arms until I could interlace my fingers with his. I held his hands above his head, just like I had when I drank from him. He watched me as I rode him, until we were both nearing our climax again. When I was moments from shattering, and I could feel that he was too, I leaned down and bit him again. His hips jerked into me as I slid down onto him and he finished at the same moment that I did, gasping my name.

I rolled off of him, breathless, and collapsed onto the bed. He chuckled. "I didn't realize you'd enjoy me biting your thigh so much."

I huffed a laugh. "I didn't either."

He looked over at me with a smile. "Good to know I can still find new ways to excite you." His breathing was still ragged, as he rolled onto his side and slipped his arm around my waist. "You are…absolutely incredible," he breathed.

"I know." I breathed.

He laughed and kissed my cheek. "So humble."

*

Later that morning when we arrived at Aris' manor for our joint coven meeting Devlon and Garrick were already in the meeting room upstairs. Aris was waiting in the foyer for us. My father, surprisingly, was nowhere to be found.

"They're waiting for you upstairs." Aris said and gestured toward the stairs.

I nodded. Deiric, Lazarus, and I headed up the stairs to our usual meeting room. Whatever conversation they'd been having in our absence stopped abruptly as we came in.

"Good morning." I mumbled as I sat down.

"You seem well rested." Garrick commented with a sly smile.

I arched a brow at him. "Did you expect me to be exhausted or hungover?"

He chuckled. "With as much as you all drank, I would've suspected that yes."

"I sure as hell feel like shit." Devlon grumbled and rubbed his face with his hands as he leaned back in his chair.

"Do we actually have anything to discuss today?" Garrick asked.

Devlon shook his head. "I don't have anything." He glanced between Garrick and I. "We don't have any updates on the other mages we're trying to track down. It has been suspiciously quiet."

"It has been quiet for us too." Garrick commented.

They both looked at me. "Adriana's training is going very well." I smiled. Before I continued, a folded and sealed piece of parchment appeared on the table in front of Devlon. He picked it up and opened it while I spoke. "In fact, I think that she's reached a point where I can say she's mastered her magic."

A flicker of concern crossed over Devlon's features before he looked up at me again.

"That's wonderful!" Garrick said excitedly. "Then we could send her back to the palace, correct?" He seemed far too excited to be rid of her, but I suppose having a royal among us would make everyone anxious.

"We just have one little problem." Devlon said nervously.

I looked at him. "What?"

"The king is dead."

Acknowledgements

I would like to thank my friends who read my first book and were just as excited as I was to continue the story. Your support means the absolute world to me and I wouldn't have been able to create this without you all! Of course, I always have to thank my husband for all of his advice and "lore" expertise. He's helped me through many scenes in the book that would otherwise have been frustrating to write or depict.

Writing out these books has been such a fun journey for me. I never pictured this story moving beyond a single book, but once I got started the characters took over and led me down a much longer path. Many friends of mine have said they saw Mira as me when they read book one, which was an absolute honor, although I don't think I quite live up to her image. I aspire to have her strength, perseverance and courage though.

I hope that all the fans of the first book will enjoy the continuation of Mira and Deiric's story in this book and the final book which I'm already working on. But don't worry… while their main story might end there, that isn't the last time you'll see them.

www.ingramcontent.com/pod-product-compliance
Lightning Source LLC
Chambersburg PA
CBHW030809310726
48980CB00006B/441/J
* 9 7 9 8 9 9 2 9 1 8 2 8 1 *